Out of nowhere . . .

"Congressman, actually, the test has been a grand success," the officer said.

"Please explain that," the congressman demanded. "I see nothing. Your radar shows nothing."

The officer just shrugged. "Despite that, the new aircraft we brought you to see have been overhead all along."

The congressman looked back at him, his expression a mix of incredulity and disdain. "You have lost your mind, sir," he said. "Even at my age, I have twenty/twenty vision. And the sky above us is filled with nothing but stars."

This was exactly what the Air Force man was waiting to hear.

He pulled out a sat phone and said two words into it: "Lights on."

And incredibly, at that moment, three huge C-17 cargo jets suddenly appeared, circling no more than 1,000 feet overhead. They were making no noise, nor were they being picked up on radar.

But they were indeed there.

Congressman Toole began stammering. "How . . . why . . . when . . . *how*?"

Then he fainted dead away.

STRIKE MASTERS

BILL KELLAN

JOVE BOOKS, NEW YORK

THE BERKLEY PUBLISHING GROUP
Published by the Penguin Group
Penguin Group (USA) Inc.
375 Hudson Street, New York, New York 10014, USA

Penguin Group (Canada), 90 Eglinton Avenue East, Suite 700, Toronto, Ontario M4P 2Y3, Canada
(a division of Pearson Penguin Canada Inc.)
Penguin Books Ltd., 80 Strand, London WC2R 0RL, England
Penguin Group Ireland, 25 St. Stephen's Green, Dublin 2, Ireland (a division of Penguin Books Ltd.)
Penguin Group (Australia), 250 Camberwell Road, Camberwell, Victoria 3124, Australia
(a division of Pearson Australia Group Pty. Ltd.)
Penguin Books India Pvt. Ltd., 11 Community Centre, Panchsheel Park, New Delhi—110 017, India
Penguin Group (NZ), 67 Apollo Drive, Rosedale, North Shore 0632, New Zealand
(a division of Pearson New Zealand Ltd.)
Penguin Books (South Africa) (Pty.) Ltd., 24 Sturdee Avenue, Rosebank, Johannesburg 2196,
South Africa

Penguin Books Ltd., Registered Offices: 80 Strand, London WC2R 0RL, England

This is a work of fiction. Names, characters, places, and incidents either are the product of the author's imagination or are used fictitiously, and any resemblance to actual persons, living or dead, business establishments, events, or locales is entirely coincidental. The publisher does not have any control over and does not assume any responsibility for author or third-party websites or their content.

STRIKEMASTERS

A Jove Book / published by arrangement with Kelcorp, Inc.

PRINTING HISTORY
Jove mass-market edition / January 2009

Copyright © 2009 by Kelcorp, Inc.
Cover art by Larry Rostant.
Cover design by Edwin Tse.
Text design by Kristin del Rosario.

ISBN: 978-0-515-14573-1

JOVE®
Jove Books are published by The Berkley Publishing Group,
a division of Penguin Group (USA) Inc.,
375 Hudson Street, New York, New York 10014.
JOVE® is a registered trademark of Penguin Group (USA) Inc.
The "J" design is a trademark of Penguin Group (USA) Inc.

PRINTED IN THE UNITED STATES OF AMERICA

10 9 8 7 6 5 4 3 2 1

In memory of
SGT Jose Miguel Velez
773rd Transportation Company, NY National Guard
Killed in Tikrit, Iraq, on June 8, 2006

PART ONE

CHAPTER 1

Mahoon, Pakistan

Something was wrong.

The battered school bus had clawed its way up the side of Zhob Mountain, as it had just about every day since October 2001, arriving at the USAID-sponsored schoolhouse at 7:00 A.M. Classes at the all-girl school began promptly at 7:15, but it was crucial that the school's protection service be on-site before the students arrived. Yet, today, the security guards were nowhere to be seen.

This had never happened before.

The Islamic radicals who terrorized this part of western Pakistan were bloodthirsty and brutal. Called the Pashkar-e-Daku, or PKD for short, this local branch of al-Qaeda had declared war against Pakistan's women. They threatened any female with death if they didn't wear the traditional head-to-toe burka. They'd chopped off the arms of women seen embracing each other or even shaking hands. The PKD had also murdered dozens of students and teachers in recent years, believing that educating any female was against Islamic law.

The school on Zhob Mountain was the equivalent of a middle school in the U.S. Forty-three girls ranging in age from nine to thirteen attended; most were from nearby villages. Their bright blue uniforms were made by church volunteers in Texas. Five female teachers ran the school; all were American.

The teachers became very uneasy when the bus reached the small wooden schoolhouse located on a flattened-out section about 1,200 feet up the 5,000-foot mountain and found it deserted. The security force *always* arrived before the students. The place looked empty and extremely vulnerable without them.

One of the teachers was driving the bus and this, too, was odd. The vehicle was usually driven by a local man, a native of Bummi, the nearest village. But the normally reliable driver hadn't shown up for work that morning. No driver and no security men to protect the schoolhouse was indeed cause for alarm. But not wanting to frighten their students, the teachers had tried to carry on as if it were business as usual.

The bus pulled up to the front door of the schoolhouse and the students got off. As they filed quietly to their classrooms, one of the teachers used a cell phone to call USAID headquarters in Kohat. When the teacher reported that no guards had appeared at the schoolhouse that morning, and that the bus driver had failed to show up as well, the security chief at the headquarters told the teachers to get the students back on the bus and return to Bummi immediately.

But it was already too late.

The terrorists were hiding in the overgrowth nearby. They showed themselves just after the teacher got off the phone, surrounding the bus and waving their AK-47 assault rifles around wildly. There were two dozen of them; all were wearing black robes, high black boots, white headdresses, and, weirdly, dark blue eye shadow, a trademark of the dreaded PKD.

Their first act was to shoot out the tires on the bus. Then they locked the students inside the schoolhouse, forcing the teachers to stay outside. A can of gasoline was brought up and the exterior walls of the schoolhouse were doused. The terrorists then threw a hand grenade through a broken window. The schoolhouse exploded in flames.

The screams from the girls trapped inside went on for endless minutes; this as the teachers struggled against their captors. Once the schoolhouse had burned to the ground, the terrorists sprayed the ashes with gunfire. But they needn't have bothered. No one survived the conflagration. Forty-three girls died for doing nothing more than learning to read and write.

But an even grislier fate awaited their teachers.

BLINDFOLDED and bound at the wrists, the five teachers were force-marched up and over Zhob Mountain, pushed and prodded by the PKD members all the way. Anyone who fell or stopped to catch her breath was mercilessly beaten. It was spring in Pakistan; the teachers were wearing warm-weather clothes. But just minutes into the march, they were stumbling around in foot-deep snow. The first signs of frostbite soon set in.

Twenty grueling hours followed. Walking through the night and into the next morning, and passing over and around several more mountains, the hostages finally reached the foot of the notorious Bora Kurd. This foreboding 13,000-foot peak towered over the rest of the western Karakoram mountain range. Like the others, it was snow-capped. But unlike the others, a combination of the surrounding shadow play and its murky crust made the mountain look ominously black below the snowline. It was known to have dozens of caves and tunnels honeycombed throughout it, some dating back to the nineteenth century when tribes in this region battled the British colonial armies. Always ringed in a cloak of fog, Bora Kurd was a source of great superstition among the scattered villages inhabiting the remote region. Many of the locals refused to look at it, even on the sunniest of days. They called it by a bastardization of its old Hindi name: *Shaitana Parvata*.

Devil's Mountain.

This was the hiding place of the PKD.

DEVIL'S Mountain was everything the infamous Tora Bora was supposed to be.

Located in southeast Afghanistan, Tora Bora was where

al-Qaeda fled when the U.S. invaded that country shortly after 9/11. Never the postmodern fortress the world's media had made it out to be, Tora Bora was actually nothing more than a few fortified dugouts with weapons stuffed inside. It held just enough firepower to fend off the Northern Alliance until the al-Qaeda leadership could escape—with an assist, unintentional or not, from the politicians in Washington. When U.S. troops finally broke into the place, they found little more than a series of glorified caves connected by rat holes.

Bora Kurd was different. It was a multilevel complex of large, reenforced bunkers, boasting hotel-sized corridors and dozens of individual rooms, large and small. Originally modernized by the CIA in the early 1980s as a staging point for the mujahideen during the Soviet invasion of Afghanistan, when al-Qaeda came into being, connections to Saudi construction interests helped expand the place to twice its size. Illuminated and warmed now by harnessed hydroelectric power from the abundance of mountain streams running around it, the complex could shelter at least several hundred fighters, possibly more.

It was also thick with gun emplacements. Large cannons, rocket launchers, machine guns—dozens of weapons studded its shadowy slopes. Inside, the fortress contained enormous caches of ammunition and even more weapons, of numbers and types known only to the terrorists themselves. Their arsenal was more than enough to fight off any attack by the ineffective Pakistani army, which was why the PKD had operated out of the fortress unimpeded for the past five years.

THE American teachers were half dead from cold and exhaustion by the time they reached Bora Kurd.

Once inside, they were separated and their blindfolds removed. They were each put into a makeshift cell attached to the complex's so-called Great Hall, a large open room that served as the centerpiece of the fortress.

Anne Murphy was one of the abducted teachers. A twenty-six-year-old married native of Baltimore, she'd been working for USAID for three years. She was in a state of shock from the day's events and had suffered cuts, bruises, and frostbite during the long forced march.

Her jail cell was a crude space carved out of the rock. It was cold, damp, and smelled of urine. It held an old metal spring with no mattress, and a clutch of torn electrical wires hanging ominously from the ceiling. There were pools of dried blood on the floor and a battered boxing glove thrown in one corner. She knew right away this was not just a cell, but a torture chamber as well.

Though locked in tight, she was able to see through a slit in the door into the large Great Hall beyond. It looked like something from a sci-fi movie: the elaborate chamber was bristling with communications equipment, weapons, and a bank of TV screens linked to a network of cameras watching all approaches to the mountain from the outside. She was amazed the crude and dirty PKD had such a sophisticated hideout.

She was just getting the feeling back in her fingers and toes when she heard a commotion outside her cell. Returning to the crack in the door, she saw one of her colleagues had been dragged into the Great Hall and was being made to sit on the floor in front of a crude flag of the PKD. A video camera was in place, set up on a tripod. Powerful floodlights had been turned on. Anne was certain the terrorists were going to interrogate the woman and make a video of her confession as part of a ransom demand, a well-known PKD tactic.

Her instincts seemed right as the captors began asking the woman a series of intimidating questions, all while the camera rolled. But just a few minutes into this, everything changed. The interrogator, who was also the leader of the PKD, lined up four of his fighters behind the teacher, taking his place in the middle of them. The female prisoner was forced to sit at his feet, facing the camera.

The PKD leader read a short statement in Arabic, speaking directly into the camera lens. Then suddenly, he produced a huge knife from his belt. Grabbing the teacher by the hair, the terrorist began chopping away at her neck. The screams were absolutely horrible. Blood and tissue sprayed everywhere.

It took nearly a minute before the head finally came off. Then the terrorist leader held it up for the camera to see.

Shocked beyond belief, Anne Murphy had shut her eyes tight and blocked her ears just seconds after the murder began.

But still, somehow, she was able to hear the terrorists shouting, "God is great!"

CHAPTER 2

Dubai, United Arab Emirates

The mosque was empty.

The noon prayers were over; the worshippers had left, not to return until the afternoon devotions.

A stretch limo pulled up to the mosque's side entrance; a man dressed in white robes climbed into the back. He was Amad Amad, owner of Al-Zareesh, a pro-Islamic, Arabic-language TV station that broadcast all over the Middle East and Southwest Asia. Also heir to a huge oil and arms-trading fortune, in a country of rich and powerful men, Amad Amad was one of the richest and most powerful.

He ordered the driver to bring him to the station, just a short ride from the mosque. Al-Zareesh's headquarters was an ornate, tent-shaped building, pearl white, with an antenna designed to look like an ancient lighthouse that soared nearly 200 feet into the sky. The limo roared into Amad's private parking lot, screeching to a stop near a partially hidden rear entrance. An armed security guard opened the limo door and escorted the station owner into the building. Amad took his private elevator up to the top floor and entered his expansive office.

He found two messages waiting for him. One was from

the aircraft manufacturer, Airbus. His personally designed, custom-built A300 airliner was ready for his inspection. On his word, a special crew would fly it in from France. The second message was not so glamorous. It instructed him to dial a special number, one belonging to a throwaway cell phone presently located somewhere in Pakistan.

Amad punched in the number. A raspy voice several hundred miles to the east answered on the second ring.

"We have just created the first roll of footage," the voice told him.

Amad felt his heart skip a beat. "How many involved?" he asked.

"The first of five," was the response.

Amad bit his lip: "And is your asking price still the same?"

The man with the raspy voice replied: "It is. Two million each."

Amad began writing down figures: *5 for $2 million each = $10 million. $10 million = $50 million projected ad revenue.*

"Does the footage 'show all'?" Amad asked.

"It does . . ."

"And if we made a deal, when could I see it?"

The voice said: "This first one, in a few days, just as proof. Then, if you like doing business, we can deliver the rest in the following two weeks or so. If we stretch them out, we both benefit, no?"

Amad scribbled some more: *In three weeks, sweeps!*

"So?" the raspy voice asked. "Are we of the same mind? If not, I have other calls to make. Other people are interested."

Amad asked: "Can you give me a little time to make this work?" He was mildly worried about the reaction of his investors, but not very much.

The voice replied: "Because we are dear friends, yes, you can have some time. But please don't delay too long. This is an opportunity you don't want to miss."

Amad thought another moment, then said: "I realize that. And I'm sure we can do business. Thank you. I'll be in touch . . ."

CHAPTER 3

Nevada

The night wind was howling like an army of ghosts marching across the stark Western desert.

It was midnight. The sky overhead was ablaze with stars, the Milky Way cutting a swath across the intense blue-black sky.

The Humvee bumped its way along a barely recognizable dirt road, headlights on dim, all the windows closed. Even though he was wearing night vision goggles, the driver had to rely on his GPS device to make sure he was heading in the right direction. Beside him was a CIA agent. In the backseat, wearing clothes more appropriate for a sunny golf match was the esteemed congressman Adamis Toole. He'd done nothing but bitch and moan since the Humvee had left the top secret air base at Groom Lake an hour before.

"I don't understand why this trip had to be made in this goddamn jeep," Toole continued to fume. "Don't you people have helicopters? I'm a busy man. I don't have time for this nonsense."

The congressman was a high-ranking member of the U.S. Armed Services committee; his vote was desperately needed to pass a new, highly classified weapons systems that had been testing out here in the desert for the last few months. But the congressman had long been threatening to veto the system for two reasons: He hadn't been paid off by anyone connected with it, plus it held no benefit for the big military contractors in his home state.

"For people who are trying to impress me," the politician whined on, "this is certainly *not* the way to do it. It's the middle of the night, for God's sake!"

The two men riding in front said nothing. They were just couriers. The congressman had been abducted off the Las Vegas strip earlier in the evening. Dragged out of a private room at the Scores gentlemen's club by the CIA employee, he'd been told that a matter of high national security had come up.

A quick trip to Nellis Air Force Base, not a mile away from downtown Vegas, followed, after which the politician was flown to Groom Lake in a C-22 transport plane. The bitching started about halfway through this flight. The congressman demanded information—where was he going and why? But no answers were forthcoming. The C-22 landed at Groom Lake just before 2300 hours. The congressman was transferred to the Humvee and hadn't shut up yet.

Finally the driver saw their destination up ahead. Located at a rare intersection of dirt roads, literally in the middle of nowhere, was what appeared to be an authentic Old West ghost town. It consisted of several dilapidated buildings, a few ancient horse troughs, and the remains of a long wooden sidewalk. Everything in sight was boarded up tight. Situated in an area even more restricted than Groom Lake, this place was known to the intelligence community simply as "Jacks."

The congressman took one look at the old town and exploded.

"This is a joke, right?" he cried. "A prank? To punish me for not giving you guys every little cent you wanted?"

The CIA man was out of the Humvee by this time; another Humvee was parked nearby. He walked over to the waiting vehicle. It contained two members of the Black Berets, the USAF's Special Ops division.

The CIA man just shook his head and said to them: "He's all yours."

THE Black Berets escorted the congressman to a spot about 100 yards north of the ghost town. A third Humvee was stationed here. The congressman was asked to climb up onto the bed of this vehicle; it had an open back. The only other piece of equipment in evidence was a portable radar station mounted on the Humvee's cab roof. Its screen was giving off a faint greenish flow.

There wasn't another light burning within twenty miles of this location—that was the whole point. More military men were standing nearby: Army Airborne, regular Air Force, even a couple National Guard officers. A few civilians were also on hand. Technicians and intelligence people. All of them were looking skyward.

It was now ten past midnight. The desert became eerily quiet as the wind died away. The stars overhead were still on fire, though.

One of the senior Air Force officers finally informed Toole he was on hand to witness a demonstration of the new secret Pentagon weapons system—and that the test was so classified, it would have been impossible to brief him about it beforehand.

Still, Toole was furious.

"All this to show me your latest billion-dollar boondoggle?" he continued complaining to no one in particular. "I'm telling you right now, you will not have my support. Not one ounce of it."

The military men remained undeterred. The senior Air Force officer told Toole that as part of the test, he was about to observe a new type of aircraft that performed like nothing before.

The congressman replied: "Like I haven't heard that a million times? Look at your own radar, man. If that thing is working, there isn't an airplane anywhere near here."

Everyone fell silent at that point. The military men continued looking skyward. And after a while the congressman started looking skyward, too.

The minutes passed. Nothing changed. Just bright unmoving stars above, silence and stillness below. Five minutes came and went, still no aircraft appeared. After ten minutes, the politician was convinced the military had screwed up.

"This will only make it easier to veto anything you men are looking for," Toole declared. "Perhaps next time you will have a little more discretion than bothering me in a gentlemen's club."

Finally the senior Air Force officer climbed up beside the politician.

"Congressman, actually, the test has been a grand success," the officer said.

"Please explain that," the congressman demanded. "I see nothing. Your radar shows nothing."

The officer just shrugged. "Despite that, the new aircraft we brought you to see have been overhead all along."

The congressman looked back at him, his expression a mix of incredulity and disdain.

"You have lost your mind, sir," he said. "Even at my age, I have twenty/twenty vision. And the sky above us is filled with nothing but stars."

This was exactly what the Air Force man was waiting to hear.

He pulled out a sat phone and said two words into it: "Lights on."

And incredibly, at that moment, three huge C-17 cargo jets suddenly appeared, circling no more than 1,000 feet overhead. They were making no noise, nor were they being picked up on radar.

But they were indeed there.

Congressman Toole began stammering. "How . . . why . . . when . . . *how*?"

Then he fainted dead away.

CHAPTER 4

The futuristic jet fighter was designated F-22XL-1H.

It was a variant of the U.S. Air Force's newest combat plane, the F-22 Raptor. At $250 million each, the Raptor was an aircraft of scary capabilities. It could cruise at supersonic speeds without using its afterburner. It could turn on a dime. It could come to a complete stop—almost—in midair. It could fire its weapons from any angle, any altitude, flying upside down, or pointing straight up. It was loaded with stealth and was hooked into an amazing command-and-control network that allowed it to go on missions alone or with a squadron of unmanned combat vehicles. Very simply, the twin-tailed, diamond-shaped Raptor was the most sophisticated airplane ever built.

Except that the XL-1H version was even better.

The XL-1H could fly twice as high, twice as fast, and in theory, deliver death to the enemy twice as swiftly as the standard Raptor. But the XL-1H would not see combat any-time soon, if ever. It was an experimental model, a test bed for technology to be used in future fighter aircraft, all of which would be robot-controlled and move at speeds beyond human endurance.

To this end, the F-22XL-1H variant was powered by a highly classified, intimidating sounding technology called pulse detonation. A sort of "super afterburner," pulse detonation mixed fuel and air like a regular jet engine, but instead of combusting it, the mixture was *ignited*, at supersonic speed, creating massive amounts of thrust. A pulse detonation-equipped Raptor could travel at close to 3,000 knots and cruise at altitudes higher than 90,000 feet.

That's where the XL-1H plane was now: seventeen miles high and rocketing along at 2,950 knots. At the controls was USAF Major Casey "Tommy" Gunn. Hollywood handsome and built like a linebacker, Gunn had a mind like a supercomputer, the instincts of a fighter ace, and the guts of a barnstormer. He was dressed like an astronaut at the moment, which wasn't too ironic, as he was on the short list to begin training to fly NASA's newest spacecraft, the *Orion*, the vehicle that would take America back to the moon and then to Mars beyond.

Gunn was also a combat veteran: Prior to being assigned to Edwards, which was the country's top test-pilot location, he had spent two tours flying F-15s in Iraq, plus one tour as commander of a classified still-activated F-117 Stealth squadron stationed on the island of Diego Garcia in the Indian Ocean. That unit featured a dozen unmarked stealth planes that did everything from carrying out secret air strikes on bases belonging to modern-day sea pirates to blasting mosques used as hiding places by Muslim guerrillas in Indonesia and on Sri Lanka.

Strange then, that at the moment, Gunn's mind was not on the unusual airplane he was flying, or his future at NASA, or his past combat experiences on the other side of the world.

Instead, he was thinking about video games—and a waitress at the saloon located just outside the gates at Edwards.

She was smart, cute, and blonde. His kind of girl. But because his flight status had been extended in the past week, meaning he had to fly even more hours in Edwards aircraft, he'd missed their last two dates, both times being unable to call her as his workouts were always so highly classified.

Tonight would be different. They had a date to play video games at her house. A bottle of tequila was the prize. She was good on the Xbox—and before she'd introduced him to them, Gunn didn't know a thing about video games. He'd had a lot of fun losing Rainbow Six and Warhawk to her since then, though he also suspected that she was circumventing the rules somehow. In any case, he'd also been practicing on his own, and tonight he planned to surprise her with his newly honed skills.

It was getting to be nighttime on the ground. He could see a spectacular sunset in the making over the Pacific about a hundred miles from his location. His flight was coming to an end. His plan was to get back to the ground as quickly as possible—he had the right power plant for that!—put the beast away, debrief, shower, change, and meet her at the Pancho's Astro Bar for some takeout. With any luck, they'd be fed, plugged in, and rocking by 2030 hours.

Gunn finally got the order to return to base; he immediately put the super-fighter into a screaming dive. He passed through 70,000 feet, 60,000, 50,000, thinking with one side of his brain on how well the airframe was holding up to the stress, and on the other to what he would order for his dinner at the Astro.

They had a hell of a nacho plate.

HE was back on the ground fifteen minutes later.

Following the ground crew's instructions, he taxied the secret airplane up to its hangar and pulled it directly into the special air barn. Like parking the Corvette in the garage, he killed the engines and began shutting down the futuristic flight systems. Then Gunn unstrapped and climbed down the access ladder.

That's when he spotted the car with the white roof pulling in behind him. It belonged to the test base's Wing Commander, Colonel Pedro Calandra. He was Gunn's boss.

Calandra met him at the back of the airplane.

"See any dents? Any paint scrapes?" Gunn asked him, running his hand along the fuselage.

But Calandra wasn't smiling. Not a good sign.

The senior officer handed Gunn a yellow envelope. It was a test flight manifest.

"You have to do another run tonight," he said. "It's a short one—to test a new digital altimeter that we need data on before we can put in an acquisition order. The order has to be done by Monday morning and the reps will need two days to work it up. It's a real time crunch, Major. Sorry . . ."

GUNN hurried over to the hangar where his next airplane awaited, reading the flight requirements along the way. It was not as bad as he first thought. It was only an hour's flight and Calandra had told him he could do a double debrief on both his flights the next morning. So, if he was lucky, he could do this mission *and* get to the Astro Bar before 10:00 P.M. It would be tight, but still doable.

He reached the second tier hangar to find a T-38 Talon jet trainer warmed up and ready to go. If the Super Raptor was a Corvette, then the T-38 was a Chevy Nova. Unglamorous and nearing fifty years in age, the only thing a T-38 had in common with the F-22 was that they both had wings. The nose of this particular aircraft was rigged with test modules that would collect data on the new digital altimeter. It wouldn't be for Gunn to determine if the thing actually worked; all he had to do was fly it around a bit and let the manufacturer's reps tap into his data stream. For this flight, he would be just a dog walker.

He climbed into the cockpit and began taxiing while still strapping in. At the same time, he established radio contact with Edwards tower. It was almost 2000 hours, 8:00 P.M. The base was all but closed down by now—everyone in the test section was as anxious as he to begin the weekend, and most of them were already at the Astro Bar getting a head start. Gunn would just be a little late to the party, that's all.

He was out on the runway in two minutes. One last check of his instruments and he was off, going wheels-up just five seconds later.

Little did he know this would be the strangest flight of his life.

NIGHT had fallen and the skies were clear. Gunn climbed toward the dazzling plain of stars overhead, imagining he could feel their warmth. His assignment was to get to 15,000 feet, fly a box pattern over the south side of the base while pumping data down to the altimeter's sales reps. A piece of cake.

He quickly reached 15 Angels and got into the proper alignment. He hit his radio microphone a few times, clearing a channel and indicating it was time for the reps on the ground to start their data recorders running. He followed up by sending a verbal message to them reporting his altitude, flight speed, and weather conditions.

But there was no reply.

Gunn tried again, repeating the message clearly into his helmet mic and waiting for a response.

Nothing.

He checked his FM radio set, and tried a third time. But again, nothing.

He hit the clear/update button on his radio, and sent the message yet again. All he got back was static.

What the hell was going on?

He switched over to his backup radio, an AM setting, and tried three more times. No success.

He was halfway through his first box pattern by this time. Were the guys below asleep at the switch?

He turned back to FM and called Edwards tower directly. When he got no reply there, he knew something was definitely not right.

He spent the next thirty seconds, calling the tower, calling the contractors, and then calling the tower again.

Nothing . . .

This was getting weird. Was the new altimeter interfering with his communication set? He didn't know.

He started his FM set to scan, trying to find an open, working radio channel. Strangely, on the first pass, the scanner found only one. It was located at the far end of the dial, an obscure, little-used frequency.

But before Gunn could send any message, he started receiving one instead. An eerie voice, female, almost robotic, and calling him by name and rank, ordered him to forget the altimeter test and alter his flight path. Instead of flying his box test pattern, he was told to turn due east, toward Nevada, and wait for a new flight plan to be sent directly to his flight computer.

Gunn thought it was a joke—his test section buddies' way of punking him. Transmitting new orders via flight computer was something that was done in B-2 stealth bombers and high-performance jet fighters. Not for lowly little T-38s. But then the voice started ticking off some top-level security codes that, from his experience flying with the secret unit out of Diego Garcia, Gunn knew were legitimate. He also knew whoever was speaking these codes was sure he would recognize them as being highly classified. In fact, they were on a security level akin to a DEFCON 2 alert, the next step to nuclear war.

So, whatever was happening, it was not a prank.

But was it really World War Three? Was he being called to the ultimate battle—in a T-38?

He tried the Edwards tower three more times—but got no reply. He considered turning around and flying back to the base, but that might have been interpreted as disobeying a direct order.

So, he had no choice. Gunn keyed his microphone and answered: "Transmit alternate flight plan."

In the next second, his flight computer began flipping numbers faster than he could follow them. When everything finally settled down, he was able to read his new orders.

Again, they were telling him to fly a route east, over the Sierras and into Nevada. Then he was to turn north, skirt Las Vegas, and keep on going, all while maintaining strict radio silence. He would receive further instructions once he was near his eventual destination; these instructions would come when he came within twenty miles of a certain TACAN, a sort of ground-based electronic navigational aid. One look at the designated TACAN's coordinates told Gunn just about where his next communications would be coming from: 37 by 14 north, 115 by 49 west.

That would put him right above Groom Lake Air Base.

The place better known as Area 51.

GUNN had been flying experimental aircraft off and on for most of his career. The only interruptions were his tours of duty in Iraq and on Diego Garcia. His present home, Edwards AFB, was one of the most top secret bases in the U.S. As such, he had the highest clearances an Air Force pilot could get.

But he'd never been anywhere near Area 51.

Simply put, Edwards was about testing new and different kinds of military aircraft; Groom Lake was about creating way-out stuff that just happened to have wings, and not necessarily for the military. People in Gunn's line of work found little attraction for a place more usually linked with UFOs and dead aliens than true aeronautics. All guys like Gunn wanted to do was fly.

So, again, what the hell was all this about?

IT took him twenty minutes to cross over into Nevada and spot the lights of Las Vegas way off in the distance. As instructed, he changed his heading to due north. Normally on a flight like this, he would have been in touch with any number of air traffic controllers along the way, both civilian and military. This procedure would pass him along as he flew out of one air traffic zone and into another.

But there was none of that this moonless night. It was just he, the hot stars above, and the unbroken desert below. Even the little-used radio frequency from where the strange orders had come was silent except for the slightest bit of static. It gave Gunn the impression that while he couldn't hear anybody, someone might be listening in on him.

The radio finally came alive again ten minutes before he would have acquired visual sighting of Groom Lake and just after he'd bounced signals back and forth from the predetermined TACAN. The faint static suddenly got louder, startling him. He was uncharacteristically jumpy from all this spookiness, an uncomfortable feeling.

At that moment he was sure the mysterious voice was going to give him landing instructions for Area 51—and *that's* what this was all about. Maybe they just needed a hot shit pilot to fly something freaky out there and this wasn't some kind of bargain basement Armageddon after all. If that was the case, then so be it. He just wanted to get it over with and get back to Edwards and try his best to repair relations with his gorgeous barmaid friend.

But he had another surprise coming. The new radio message started with the recitation of the same classified security codes he'd heard previously. But then the odd voice gave him not landing coordinates but further flight instructions.

Instead of setting down at the Groom Lake base, he was told to continue flying in a northeasterly direction for another ten minutes. This time he pushed the numbers into his flight computer himself and waited for it to plot the new course. When the computer stopped churning, he saw it was sending him even deeper into the desert, to someplace hidden beyond the boundaries of the infamous Area 51.

THE next five minutes went by a little eerily. Gunn had been told to fly at 5,000 feet, lower than he would have liked, as this part of the Nevada desert had its share of high mountains, mesas, and buttes. He was constantly checking his instruments to make sure he stayed on the correct heading, all along wondering exactly what was in store for him when he reached the next coordinate. His fuel was getting low; at one point, he began to mix his tanks, transferring gas from one tank to another. That's when the T-38's primitive collision avoidance buzzer suddenly went off.

Gunn looked up to see the strangest thing he'd ever encountered in the air.

It was an aircraft—but certainly nothing about it could be called typical. It was a lot bigger than a B-2 stealth bomber, maybe ten times the size. But as the B-2 was a flying wing, this thing was a flying triangle. It passed directly over his head, not a quarter mile away, going about Mach 3, extremely fast for an aircraft of its size. It looked like a flying battleship, or something from a sci-fi movie.

He only saw it up close for a few moments.

And then, it was gone.

FIVE minutes later, Gunn spotted a low desert plain several miles long by a couple miles wide. It was bordered on three sides by dark hills, high mountains, and a few craggy buttes. In the middle was a large, flattened-out piece of land.

According to his orders, this was his destination.

But there was no air base here, no runway that he could see. So, the orders were a mistake. But then the mysterious voice came on again and told him he had permission to land.

Suddenly two rows of dull blue lights blinked on below. They demarked a substantial airstrip cut out of the hard desert floor. It was not unlike what Gunn had been using back at Edwards; the strange thing was, it was apparent only when the landing lights came on.

He circled once, wondering if there was any air traffic control or whether he was just supposed to touch down. His low fuel situation ended that debate. He made his way down to the low plain and landed, the runway lights abruptly shutting off even before he'd stopped rolling.

Waiting for him in the dark was a portable access ladder, already in place beside the runway. Gunn steered the T-38 up to it and popped his canopy. But he could see no one. No ground crew. No welcoming committee.

He unstrapped and stood up in the cockpit, looking around in every direction. He felt like he was in a dream: Alone, in a jet, on a dark, flat piece of desert, surrounded by stunted brush-covered hills with high mountains beyond. Very strange . . .

But then he took a closer look at the "hills" on one side of him. Odd as it seemed, they appeared to be moving a bit. A slight wind came up and he detected more movement. Mystified, he climbed down the ladder and walked closer to the edge of the runway. That's when he discovered the hill wasn't a hill at all, but a large piece of camouflage netting, perfectly contoured to blend in with the desert surroundings. What's more, beneath the netting was a huge Quonset hut structure the size of an aircraft hangar. Gunn was astonished. It was the perfect optical illusion.

He looked all around him again and now he couldn't believe his eyes. He was surrounded not by hills but by *many* buildings, just as big and just as concealed as this one. He'd never imagined camouflage elements could work so well. Both from ground level and from the air, the place was invisible. A truly hidden base. Out in the middle of nowhere.

Purely by habit he checked the time: it was 2030 hours.

He'd been away from Edwards for less than an hour, yet he felt like he'd flown to another planet. Something was telling him he wouldn't be making the Astro Bar tonight.

He walked toward the far end of the runway, passing many smaller, but no less hidden structures. Finally he came to one dark building that had a sign outside.

It read AREA 153—20IST SPECIAL OPERATIONS WING. Below was an outline of a C-17 cargo plane.

Strange choice of aircraft, Gunn thought.

He walked under the netting and eventually found a door marked FLIGHT OPERATIONS. It was pitch black all around him, the camo cover blotting out the blazing night sky.

"Am I even in the right place?" he wondered out loud.

He tried the door—it was not locked. He opened it and was immediately hit by a wave of sound and light. Inside it was bustling with activity. A couple dozen people, all wearing nondescript desert camouflage uniforms, were moving about or lording over computers. Others were on phones. Still others were working large wall charts. It was a scene typical of any air base's flight operations building.

All at once, they yelled at him: "Close the door!"

Gunn quickly stepped in and shut the door behind him. As his eyes were adjusting to the light, a pretty female soldier appeared, saluting smartly. He mumbled his name and showed her his ID badge. She seemed to know who he was.

"Command is expecting you," she said.

Gunn's ears perked up. That voice. Was it the same one that had been speaking to him? The one who'd hijacked his radio?

He started to say something, but she beat him to it: "Please follow me, sir," she said.

Gunn trailed her through the crowded, busy office. He noticed on one wall a large unit emblem, again showing the silhouette of a C-17 Globemaster and the notation "Area 153."

Gunn asked the soldier, "153?"

She explained, "It means this place is 'three times as secret, three times as isolated and three times as spooky' as Area 51."

"Really?" Gunn asked her.

"Really . . ." she replied.

She left him near a room in a narrow hallway at the rear of the building. The room's door was open just a crack. It was dark inside and all Gunn could see were some folding chairs and a movie screen set up on the far wall.

He stuck his head inside and a voice from nowhere said, "You're here finally? Grab a seat so we can start."

Gunn fell into the first seat he could find and the door slammed shut behind him. He heard the sounds of an old movie projector starting up and a few seconds later a film began flickering on the screen. A title appeared: *Classified— If You Shouldn't Be Watching This, Leave Now.*

FOR the next ten minutes, Gunn watched a series of unusual film clips edited together with no music, no narration. It began with pieces of an old TV show called *The Rat Patrol*. It was the Hollywood version of a four-man U.S. raiding party in World War II, driving around the desert in two machine-gun-equipped jeeps. The heroes were depicted blowing up Nazi installations, laying mines, shooting down Stukas, and picking off German officers—and always getting away in the nick of time. Following this were clips from the more recent movie *Munich*, which depicted Israeli Mossad agents scouring the globe and brutally assassinating Palestinian terrorists. Then came news footage of aerial attacks on terrorist strongholds in Iraq and Afghanistan. The entire presentation was action-packed and violent. But Gunn was baffled why it was being shown to him.

When the film ended, the person running the projector stood up and turned on the lights, revealing himself for the first time. He was a rugged, rock-jawed individual about sixty, with a shiny bald dome and an extreme intensity in his eyes. He was wearing an old Air Force flight suit.

"Welcome to the 201st Special Operations Wing, Major Gunn," he said deeply. "We've been waiting for you."

NOT a half-minute later, Gunn was sitting in this man's office, which was located even farther down the narrow hallway. He was Colonel Doug Newman, U.S. Air Force Special Operations Command and commanding officer of the secret air base.

His office was spare, just a few maps hanging on the wall, and a Mac in the corner. But Newman himself seemed to fill up the room. He was a veteran warrior—scars on both cheeks told that tale. He was also a powerful-looking person, muscular, staid, and sober. "Larger than life" was an apt description of him.

"I have your orders here," he told Gunn in a husky voice, handing him a sheet of bright yellow paper.

But the paper was blank.

Gunn was puzzled.

"It's a small joke," Newman said with a straight face. "But it has a point: We are the blackest program in the U.S. military. No one else is even close. That means nothing ever gets written down here. No paper trails. No trails at all. Understood?"

Gunn nodded. "Understood, sir."

Newman went on: "Point two: What we've been set up to do out here is so sensitive, if word leaked out, we could all wind up in Leavenworth. Or worse . . . That's why we had to use such unorthodox means to get you out here."

Gunn almost laughed. But clearly, Newman wasn't joking.

He went on: "Point three: I'm sure you want to know why you're here and why I showed you those film clips. Well, I think it's best you see us at work first—then we can fill in the blanks."

Newman checked his watch, then said: "So, let's you and me go for a ride."

They left the operations hut by the back door and Newman led Gunn to a small hangar nearby. It was hidden under the same type of exotic camouflage netting.

Gunn ran his finger along the unusual material.

"Impressive, isn't it?" Newman asked. "It's actually a mosaic of electromagnetic images taken of the surrounding terrain and printed on top of each other like photographs. The fabric itself is computer generated and overlays thousands of these images to create a realistic impression of what could be here, on this piece of ground, if we weren't. It also deflects light and heat instead of absorbing it, so it might be the best camo netting ever invented."

They entered the small hangar to find an OH-6 "Flying Egg" helicopter within. About the size of an SUV, the tiny chopper was a favorite of U.S. special operations forces. This one was jet-black with flame decals on its nose and tail, and tinted glass all round. It looked like a sports car with a rotor on top.

Gunn helped Newman roll the copter out from under the camo netting, and then they climbed inside. Newman started the engine, and a minute later, they were aloft.

They flew to the top of a butte located a quarter mile west of the hidden base. It was about 500 feet high, and half that wide. Newman set the little chopper down on the farthest edge of this cliff and they got out.

Even from this height, the desert looked dark for miles around, this while the stars still appeared blazing hot overhead. Newman handed Gunn a helmet containing a pair of futuristic-looking goggles. They vaguely resembled standard-issue night vision goggles, but were obviously more elaborate.

Newman explained: "These things are called RIFs, for 'reverse infrared.' They're the latest in night vision technology. Instead of identifying heat spots and giving you a readout, RIFs key in on cool spots, and then build an image out of everything else around them. Follow me?"

Gunn had to shake his head no.

Newman shrugged. "Okay—for instance, our camo netting down there. It resists penetration by normal IF technology because, while it deflects light, it also disperses in any residual heat. After all, we don't want anyone looking down on us from space. But now, put these on and check it out."

Gunn put on the helmet and activated the power switch. Suddenly the night was lit up in a cool, ghostly blue, allowing him to see the landscape with stunning clarity. He turned back toward the hidden base and was shocked. For the first time he could see just how big it was, at least a square mile or more. The airstrip alone was 5,000 feet long and ran far out into the desert, again, not unlike the runways at Edwards.

Within the base itself, there were more than two-dozen buildings hidden beneath the amazing camo netting. Six of them were the huge, hangar-sized Quonset huts. Three of these giants were in the same vicinity as the operations center. But three more were located about a half mile away from everything else, causing Gunn to wonder why they were so isolated. All the other structures were typical warehouses, barracks, and power facilities. But the ethereal blue RIF tone made everything look like they were on some alien world.

"Amazing," Gunn whispered.

"That's what everyone says," Newman replied, putting on his own pair of RIFs.

He asked Gunn to snap off the goggles for a moment and then instructed him to look toward a flat valley about two miles north of the hidden base. To the unaided eye, this place appeared no different from the rest of the dark desert around them, except for a few clutches of scrub trees here and there.

But once Gunn switched the RIF goggles back on, everything changed again. He realized this valley was anything but empty. In fact, he could see dozens of stone huts, roads, berms—and weapons, such as artillery pieces, rocket launchers, and antiaircraft guns, hidden amongst the trees. And one building alone stuck out: In the middle of this "village" was a mosque.

"What you're looking at is a CSMC," Newman told him, adjusting the RIF's zoom lens for better viewing. "That stands for combat simulation module cluster. They mimic potential battlefields the U.S. military might find around the world in the near future. This particular one is called Unfriendly Compound/Iraqi Out Country."

Gunn couldn't argue with the name. It was as if he were gazing down on a typical desert village hidden in the western part of Iraq. He'd flown over the real Iraq on many occasions—and the resemblance *was* remarkable, right down to the mosque being the most prominent structure in any Iraqi village. As he zoomed in even closer, Gunn could see people moving around the CSMC. They were dressed in clothes native to the Iraqi desert—robes and headdresses. And all of them appeared to be carrying weapons. Again, the similarity to the real thing was amazing.

Gunn had heard rumors about places like this. Back in California at the vast National Training Center, there was a resident brigade of Army Armor called OpFor, as in Opposing Force. Essentially these people played the part of an enemy against which visiting regular Army units would fight as practice for the real thing. That's what this place appeared to be—but on a much grander, much more detailed scale.

Gunn finally said, "How were you able to do this? I mean, a village? A mosque? Way out here? It all looks so real."

"I can't tell you who helped us get the details so exact," Newman replied cryptically. "Let's just say they have a long history of helping the U.S. military in secret ops—and their logo is a mouse with big ears."

Newman turned Gunn's attention back to the secret airfield. Incredibly three huge airplanes had taxied out of their hidden hangars and were now on the long runway, waiting for takeoff. Gunn recognized them as C-17 Globemasters, the aircraft depicted on the unit's logo.

At 175 feet long, and a wingspan of almost the same length, the C-17 resembled an airliner on steroids. With its high T-tail and muscular engines, it also looked like a slightly compact version of the C-5 Galaxy, the largest aircraft in the U.S. military's inventory. Along with the gigantic C-5, C-17s were the main workhorses of the Air Force in its role of moving Army troops around the world and keeping them supplied. C-17s could fly anywhere on Earth in just a matter of hours, due to aerial refueling. As a way of projecting power, they were an awesome component.

But to a fighter pilot like Gunn, they were just plum ugly.

Strangely, he hadn't heard a sound from the C-17s. Again, the three big planes were obviously getting ready to take off, and obviously their engines were turning. But they weren't making any noise.

He turned to Newman, who was anticipating the question. "Another acronym: QSP," he said. "For Quiet Subsonic Platform. Fancy term for noise dampeners. Don't ask me how they work. I have no idea other than it's a highly classified technology and that every moving piece inside the engine is coated with a substance that absorbs noise. Or that's the cover story anyway. All I know is these things fly just about every night, and I *never* hear them."

They watched as the first of the three huge dull-gray airplanes started its takeoff roll. Just 200 feet down the runway, four rockets located beneath the aircraft's wings silently ignited, lifting the big plane off the ground in an incredibly short amount of time.

In seconds, the plane climbed and flew right over the butte, not a hundred feet over their heads. Yet all Gunn could hear was the mildest sound of the wind, rushing by.

"This is crazy," he said.

"You ain't seen nothing yet," Newman replied.

Gunn watched the second and third planes take off, just like the first—smooth, quiet, rocket-assisted. They, too, went right overhead, making absolutely no noise. Like the first plane, they turned north. All three planes were now heading in the direction of the CSMC valley.

"Can you tell me *anything* about what I'm seeing, Colonel?" Gunn finally asked Newman.

"I can give you the short version," the senior officer replied. "We are trying to create a highly mobile quick-reaction force built specifically for desert warfare."

Gunn was still confused. "But you're doing it with—*cargo planes*?"

Newman lit up a cigar and activated a stopwatch. "Watch and learn, Major," he said.

By this time, the first C-17 had begun circling the CSMC to the north. Gunn could see that the OpFor people on the ground, having spotted it, were now running for cover.

The huge plane was orbiting at about 1,000 feet, not very high for a bird of its size. Suddenly it dipped its left wing dramatically, almost as if it was going to flip over. An instant later it began spewing out long streams of red and orange light from openings along its fuselage. These streams of light were so blinding they flared Gunn's RIF goggles to the point where he had to take them off. As it turned out, he didn't need them.

The C-17 was dispensing a fantastic display of pyrotech-

nics. The streams of light were hitting the ground and exploding like hundreds of Fourth of July fireworks. And now the
noise was incredible.

It took a few moments of watching this before Gunn finally
realized what was going on. This was no ordinary C-17.

Again, Newman anticipated his question. "You remember
the Spooky concept?" he asked.

Gunn did. Back in the early days of the Vietnam War, in
order to better fight the communist insurgents, some Air
Force guys got the idea of putting high-powered machine
guns on a C-47 cargo plane. They mounted these guns on the
left-hand side of the fuselage, poking their muzzles through
improvised windows. When in flight, the pilot would tip the
plane in that direction, and the crew would fire the guns, delivering a massive amount of firepower on a highly concentrated area. The concept was a huge success. The Spooky
planes were especially effective in attacking infiltration routes
and protecting insolated U.S. bases about to be overrun by the
vile Vietcong.

This unusual idea was bumped up a few notches later in
the war when even bigger weapons were mounted on the
newer, more robust C-130 Hercules cargo plane. These aircraft, known as AC-130 Spectres, carried Gatling guns, cannons, and even small howitzers. Firing at a combined rate of
3,000 rounds *a second*, a Spectre gunship could perforate
every square inch of an area the size of a football field in just
the blink of an eye. Years later, the Vietnamese communists
admitted that of all the airborne weapons they'd feared from
the U.S., from B-52s down to fighter bombers, the gunships
were the most dreaded. Once they got you in their sights, you
rarely lived to tell about it.

And the AC-130 Spectres were still around; Gunn had seen
them in action in Iraq and they were still a fearsome aerial
weapon.

But—what was this?

"An AC-17?" he asked Newman.

Newman just put his finger to his lips and said, "That's top
secret."

The awesome display went on for two minutes—the strange
thing was, while it looked and sounded like real ammunition

was being fired by the huge gunship, Gunn knew that was impossible, simply because those were real-live OpFor soldiers scrambling around on the ground. "So, what's going on?" he asked.

"In due time," Newman told him.

The gunship finally leveled off and flew away, allowing Gunn to reactivate his RIF goggles. He immediately saw that the second C-17, which had been loitering nearby, was now heading toward the CSMC at a very low altitude and a very low speed. But on arriving overhead, it didn't dispel ordnance. Instead, its side door opened up and paratroopers began jumping out.

They were dropping only a short distance to the ground, their parachutes opening immediately after leaving the plane. As this was happening, the OpFor soldiers were reemerging from their hiding places. Suddenly Gunn saw more of the orange and red streaks of light. But this time they were coming from the OpFor people as well as the paratroopers as soon as they reached the ground.

Again, it looked like a real battle—yet it was not.

Gunn recalled that over at the NTC, the competing soldiers used real weapons that were equipped with laser beams. Like a sophisticated game of laser tag, when a beam hit an opponent, it would turn a yellow card each participant wore to red, thus making him a "casualty."

But again, something more elaborate was happening here.

Gunn watched now as some of the paratroopers formed up and began firing back at the OpFor soldiers. But other paratroopers were running in the opposite direction of the battle. They were carrying lighted flares and putting them at intervals along the flat plain. They quickly laid out two parallel lines about 1,000 feet in length.

That's when the third C-17 reappeared.

Gunn watched as the big plane turned itself up on its wing and made a dive so steep he would have thought it was aerodynamically impossible. It was clear this plane wasn't a gunship, nor was it about to start dropping soldiers. It was coming in for a landing, using the crude airstrip laid out by the paratroopers.

The C-17 slammed down, and again utilizing its wing-mounted rockets, came to a screeching halt in just a couple hundred feet. Its rear door opened immediately, and to Gunn's great surprise, two huge M1 Abrams tanks with U.S. Marine markings came roaring out the back. Now the paratroopers linked up with the tanks and together this small army engaged the OpFor soldiers with incredible verve, obviously intent on getting to the mosque. The only problem was, the OpFor soldiers had practically surrounded the big plane by this time and suddenly the paratroopers and the "enemy" were locked in a fierce firefight that spilled all over the faux village. The noise was ear splitting and could easily be heard even from this height and distance.

Until, suddenly, everything stopped. No more explosions. No more tracer streaks across the sky.

People in white uniforms had appeared inside the CSMC. They began engaging some of the combatants in what looked to be very animated conversations, leaving the rest of the participants just standing around aimlessly. It was as if a time-out had been called in a football game.

"Those are the goddamn refs," Newman groaned, clicking his stopwatch off. "They evaluate every exercise and tell the training force what they did wrong . . ."

He looked at his stopwatch and groaned again. ". . . and apparently there was a lot done wrong this time. Take it from me, everyone out here learns to hate the refs very quickly."

Not thirty seconds later, the battle's participants began to disperse. The tanks and the paratroopers climbed into the third C-17 and the big plane took off with a whoosh of sand and dust. The OpFor guys melted back into the scenery. The refs simply disappeared. In less than a minute, the battlefield was empty again. Except for a few small, smoldering fires, it was hard to tell that anything had happened at all.

"Show's over," Newman drawled, putting the stopwatch away. "And not our best performance, I'm afraid."

Good or bad, though, Gunn's head was still reeling from the fantastic display. But he still didn't understand the weapons.

"They can't be real," he said, finally taking off the RIF goggles. "Although they sure look it."

"I can explain it to you," he heard Newman say over his shoulder. "Or I can just show you."

Gunn turned to see the officer was pointing a strange-looking rifle at him. He froze. What the hell was this?

Newman said, "I'm sorry." Then he pulled the trigger. Gunn felt something hit his shoulder and upper thigh. A hot, searing pain immediately ran throughout his body, reflected by a dull orange light. It seemed like he was about to burst into flames.

But before he could react, the burning sensation suddenly went away.

"What the hell?" he cried as he looked at his shoulder and leg, convinced he would see burn marks there. But there were none.

Whatever Newman shot at him, it stung, it hurt, but it didn't injure him.

Newman put the gun down. "Like I said, it's always best that someone coming here for the first time feels it. It explains it much better than words can."

"But what the hell is that thing?" Gunn asked, pointing at the strange weapon.

"One more for the alphabet soup," Newman replied, showing him the weapon up close. It looked like an M4 assault rifle, but it had a second muzzle, which in turn was attached to a small battery pack and what looked like a small dish antenna. "They are called NLRs–for non-lethal rays. They were first invented for crowd control in Iraq, but someone figured out they might have a use here. As you can tell, they are very effective."

"So, it's a heat ray, like out of *Flash Gordon*?" Gunn asked.

"In a way," Newman replied. "They shoot millimeter waves, as opposed to microwaves or anything higher. Each weapon uses its antenna to direct a beam toward its target; someone at DARPA came up with a way to actually *show* the beams in color, based on their intensity. The waves travel at the speed of light; the energy strikes the subject but only reaches a skin depth of about one-sixty-fourth of an inch. There is minimal risk of injury from the beam because of that shallow penetration, but as you can attest, it produces a heat sensation that becomes intolerable in just a few seconds. The sensation ceases when the individual moves out of the beam or when the operator turns off the system, but again, it sure gets your attention, and when you're down there fighting with these things, they hurt! And when we put a bunch together, they simulate almost perfectly what real guns on an AC-17 could do. Thus, we have the closest thing to using real combat weapons we can get, without anyone getting killed."

Gunn felt his shoulder again.

"Message received on that, sir," he told Newman. "And believe me, you won't have to remind me again."

"So noted," Newman said, flicking the ashes from his cigar and putting the weapon back in the chopper.

Then he said, "Now, how about we grab some chow and I tell you where you fit into all this?"

CHAPTER 5

NEWMAN was flying so low and so fast that conversation was impossible.

They were off the butte and heading west in the little OH-6 copter, following the twists and turns of a winding dirt road, no more than thirty feet off the ground. Gunn just watched the scenery rush by, overwhelmed by his bizarre night in the desert. The last time he'd checked the time, it was still before midnight. But somehow, time wasn't important anymore.

The past couple hours had taken on a surreal quality. One moment, he'd been flying on the edge of the atmosphere, thinking about his barmaid friend. The next he was here, in the weirdest place on earth, a place where fake wars were fought and strange things flew silently in the air. And something told him it was about to get even weirder.

They rounded a bend and Gunn realized his premonition was right. Up ahead he saw a collection of old wooden buildings, a battered, muddy town right out of the Old West. It looked more like an abandoned Hollywood movie set than a real place, yet it was buzzing with activity. There were several dozen Humvees parked on its main street, with a few Stryker

APCs and M1 tanks jammed into the side alleys. There were even a couple helicopters tied up out back.

Newman finally slowed down and put the OH-6 into a tight turn above the place.

"This is Jacks," he yelled over to Gunn. "It's Area 153's unofficial R&R center, open twenty-four/seven—unless we have outside visitors, that is."

They landed on the edge of the main street and climbed out of the copter. Gunn took in a deep sniff of the desert air. The smell that came back was a combination of sweet mesquite and spilled tequila.

The largest building in the strange little town was an exact re-creation of an old Western saloon. Gunn and Newman walked through the requisite swinging doors to find the place packed with patrons—soldiers, Marines, OpFor guys, refs, among others. The authenticity of the saloon was amazing. There was a long, horseshoe-shaped bar at one end, with many wooden tables and chairs surrounding it. The walls were covered with cowboy memorabilia. The windows were made of colored stained glass. There was even a honky-tonk player piano in one corner, belting out a tune.

A huge, well-stocked buffet was set up on the bar. Newman and Gunn got in line and a couple minutes later had filled their plates with eggs, steak, toast, and home fries, the ultimate diner food.

Newman steered Gunn to a far corner table, away from the noise and crowd. A pot of black coffee was waiting for them. Newman poured out two cups and slid one over to Gunn.

Still in a daze, Gunn dug in to his meal—and was pleasantly surprised. The food was outstanding.

"Thank the Navy," Newman told him. "The squids eat better than any other service, and the submarine guys eat better than any other squids. Someone pulled some strings and now all the food for this place is flown in directly from the sub base at San Diego."

Gunn was impressed. "It's great chow," he said, unabashedly stuffing his face. "But now, Colonel—if I may?"

Newman dug into his own meal. "Okay, Major," he said between bites. "I know you've got a million questions. So, ask away."

Gunn's problem was, where to start? He looked around the crowded saloon. Again, dozens of U.S. military types were mixing with people dressed like typical Middle Eastern terrorists, the people he'd just seen in the fake battle. But there were other soldiers in here, too, wearing all different kinds of U.S. uniforms: fighter pilots, tankers, chopper jockeys, SEALs, Space Command. Even weirder, some soldiers were wearing the uniforms of potential enemies of the future, like China and Venezuela. What were all these people doing out here in the middle of the desert?

"First off," he asked Newman. "Can you explain all this? I mean, what is this Area 153 stuff all about?"

Newman meticulously buttered a piece of toast. "Officially, we are in the middle of what used to be called the Nevada Special Weapons Testing Range," he said. "It was a top secret training facility encompassing about five hundred square miles that was started out here back in the mid-1980s after the Iran hostage rescue mission ended in failure. It was meant to be like the NTC, but for training Special Forces troops exclusively. They came here and fought opposition forces with the intent of learning how to win at unconventional warfare, no matter what the environment. If you think this place looks wild now, it was *really* off the hook back then. They'd built dozens of primitive combat simulation modules and they used to battle each other with these holographic weapons called Zoots. Prehistoric NLRs is what they were, and let's just say they didn't always work as advertised. The guys running this place back then also encouraged these insanely cutthroat competitions between the training forces and the OpFors. Combine all that with the way-out stuff being worked on at Area 51 nearby and other places scattered around out here, like S-4? Well, I hear it was really crazy. And it got out of control. So they had to close it down.

"But then, with all the crap that came after 9/11 and then the Iraqi invasion fuckup, they felt the need to open it back up. They started funding it again—and here we are. New name: Area 153."

"But who are 'they,' exactly?" Gunn asked. "Who actually runs this place?"

Newman shrugged. "CIA? NSA? DIA? Pick your poison.

I don't think anyone really knows. I certainly don't. Truth is, it probably goes way deeper than the usual suspects. But whoever is behind it, they turned the switch back on about a year ago, and gave us a little piece of turf to do our thing, just like a lot of the other people you see in here are off somewhere else on the range, doing *their* thing. There are at least a dozen different special ops groups out here undergoing various forms of secret training. The 201st is just one of many."

Gunn glanced around the saloon again; the mixture of uniforms, services, and characters was amazing. It reminded him of a canteen on a movie studio lot. Roman soldiers eating next to ghosts; cowboys eating next to space aliens. That sort of thing. It was almost humorous.

"It's like a Disneyland for soldiers," he said.

"Exactly," Newman replied. But then he nodded to a group of dirty-looking OpFor soldiers nearby. "But don't ever underestimate anyone out here, including those guys playing the mooks for us. Every one of them has done multiple tours in Iraq, and I don't mean shoveling shit in Mosul. Some of them were out in the cold for months, blending in, speaking the language, even fooling the locals. Tough duty. Tough guys. I hear if they weren't in the military they'd be in prison, most of them. It's just their luck that parts of Nevada look and feel exactly like parts of Iraq."

Gunn saw one group of faux terrorists sitting by themselves in a far corner of the saloon. They weren't eating the typical American food. Rather, they were pawing over what Gunn recognized as authentic Middle East fare: yogurt, beans, and rice, all mixed together. They didn't seem to be talking to anyone or one another. There were a few dozen of them, all males except for one striking Asian female. They looked particularly hard-core; each man seemed to have deep, sunken, dark eyes.

Gunn indicated the odd group. "And who are they?"

Newman replied: "No idea. I think they're too classified for us to know about at the moment. Like a lot of other things out here."

Gunn refilled his coffee cup. "You mean like . . . flying saucers, for instance?"

Newman smiled. "Oh, yeah, seen lots of those."

"Is that what's out in those three buildings hanging off the base?" Gunn suddenly asked him.

Newman froze, and then became very serious. "We don't talk about them either, Major. Not yet."

A few moments of silence passed. Gunn decided to cut to the chase.

"Okay, so I understand about this crazy training facility, I guess," he told Newman. "But what are *you* doing out here specifically? You and the 201st?"

Newman pushed his empty plate away from him and lit up a cigar. "Okay," he said. "Time for the real skinny."

He let out a long stream of smoke and let it curl its way up to the saloon's ceiling.

Then he began: "Last year, the CIA did a highly classified study of the worst-case scenarios this country will face both in Iraq and the Persian Gulf over the next decade. Their conclusion: because the whole region is fragmenting so quickly, we will see more radical Muslim groups than ever in the next ten years, specifically terrorist splinter groups run by a new type of religious fanatic called a warlord mullah. If you're familiar with Muqtada al-Sadr of Baghdad, then you know the kind of kook I'm talking about. Bloodthirsty, brutal, unreasonable. And because of all the extended families over there, these warlord mullahs will have access to oil money and therefore everything else that can be bought in the area, including weapons—and I don't mean pop guns. Imagine a bunch of bin Laden wannabes operating unchecked, with all kinds of WMD at their disposal, and you get the picture. For them, 9/11 was just the beginning. They hate Americans and will do anything to cause us pain. The Agency has identified at least a dozen of these up-and-coming warlord mullahs already and it's certain there'll be more to come.

"Now, the majority of these new mullahs have something in common: unlike al-Sadr, they have shunned the big cities and population centers simply because they're so dangerous these days—plus it's hard to keep a low profile with a lot of people around. So, they're going back to their tribal roots and building isolated compounds way out in the desert, under the pretense of starting new religious centers. They're surrounding these 'religious forts' with heavy security, or in some cases with private armies. From the satellite photos, the Agency has learned most of these compounds already have hardened bomb shelters in place, bunkers that can withstand air attacks, cruise missile attacks, you name it. They've found that these shelters are usually hidden in mosques the mullahs have put up on their sites, thinking they'll be untouchable. So, you've got well-financed, well-connected terrorist leaders with access to security and WMD, and pretty much impervious to our best counter-weapons. But here's the real problem: While some of these religious forts have been seen popping up in Iraq, others have been spotted in places like Turkey, Jordan, and Saudi Arabia."

Gunn was surprised. "But aren't those countries considered allies of ours?"

Newman just nodded slowly and tapped his nose twice. It was an old spy signal, meaning: "You got it."

He moved in a little closer. "Now, allies or not, unless we do something about these mullahs, they *will* cause a lot of trouble over the next ten years or so. They might all be just one step up from living in a cave, but they're all technologically astute, too, and soon enough, they'll be able to project power around the globe whenever they want. So, we are trying to build a high-tech strike force to be ready to counter these guys should they start any trouble. Or at least that's what the original specs for the 201st say. In actuality . . ."

He let his voice trail off.

Gunn just stared back at him. "In actuality?" he asked.

Newman gave his cigar another puff. "Well, for want of a better term, what we are *really* doing out here is creating an assassination team. A high-tech hit squad. Mobile. *Quiet*. A way to get these guys before they get us. That's really what the 201st is about. Get in, knock off these assholes, and get out without being spotted."

"You're kidding," Gunn said.

Newman shook his head slowly. "No, I'm afraid not. At least some of the powers-that-be have decided this is something we must do. But it ain't going to be easy."

Another puff and he went on: "Because these mullahs have

set themselves up in these bomb-hardened religious forts, this type of preemptive mission can't be done by airpower alone. Nor by paratroopers, or by just a couple tanks, should they magically appear. However, when all these things are put *together*, in an integrated system, it could work. It would be highly illegal, of course, eliminating people who really haven't done anything to us yet, and well-connected religious icons at that. Plus, to get caught doing this in a 'friendly' country would mean huge embarrassment for the U.S. government at the very least. But successful operations against these mooks will solve a lot of little problems before they become big problems. The CIA figures that it will most likely be one of these warlord mullahs who gets ahold of a rogue nuclear weapon or bio weapon first, before any terrorist state can. I mean, we can jerk around all we want with countries like Iran and Syria getting nukes, but the truth of the matter is these warlord mullahs aren't going to be affected by sanctions or diplomacy. There's even a chance one or two of these guys has some WMD already. So, they've just got to be whacked now, quickly and quietly, without letting the leaders of whatever country they are in even know it happened—at least officially, anyway."

Gunn was speechless. He'd been involved in black ops before, but an aerial assassination squad? He'd never heard of anything even close to approaching this.

"Is this on the level?" he asked Newman finally. "I mean, this isn't some kind of loyalty test or something, is it?"

"If it is," Newman replied, "then I've been wasting the last six months of my life out here. The real trouble is, we've still got a long way to go."

This statement surprised Gunn. What he'd witnessed earlier up on the butte had been frighteningly impressive—until the refs broke it up. He said to Newman: "But judging by what I saw, it looks like you've got it together already."

The senior man almost laughed. "Looks can be deceiving, Major. And that's where the real twist comes in: The truth is, the computer models say that to be done properly, an assassination mission against one of these religious leaders has to be executed in twenty-six minutes—no more. That's when the element of surprise vanishes and the people on the ground start to effectively fight back. And where it's likely we will be outnumbered, as some of these places are protected by several hundred armed men, we won't be able to handle a lot of people who are determined to oppose us, especially if they are intent on destroying the exit plane first. So, twenty-six minutes is our mandated goal. And I hate to say it, but we are nowhere near that time frame. We've got the best people from all four services. We've got the best equipment. We've been training our asses off every night for weeks. But we just can't get the time down. We can't even get past the ten-minute mark."

Gunn was shocked. "Twenty-six minutes?" he said. "That's an eye blink—and it doesn't even address getting in and out, does it? Flying three big planes like that over enemy territory, or at least *inhospitable* territory? I don't care how quiet they are—someone's bound to notice."

Newman relit his cigar and let another mushroom cloud of smoke ascend to the ceiling. He seemed to be choosing his next words very carefully. "For the time being," he said, "let's just say the time frame I'm talking about is arrival over target, softening up, landing the paratroopers and the armor—and *then* getting inside the mosque, doing the deed, and taking off again. All that has to be done in twenty-six minutes. I know it's not much time. But that's what the models say. And if we can do it, no matter where we are, we can escape with no hang-ups. Just like the Mafia."

He poured them both another cup of coffee.

"Now, our capabilities aside, as you can imagine, the idea of developing a high-tech hit team to off guys who, on the face of it, appear to be religious leaders, wasn't popular with everyone back in D.C. That's why we are so hush-hush—and that's why we landed out here, with all these other spooks, in Area 153. And even though this is an important program, getting funding for it was a bitch. Some of those same people who know what we are up to have made it quite clear: If anything goes wrong out here, or if there's a milestone we can't meet, they'll cut us off at the knees. Sad to say, we are close to that point right now . . ."

Gunn drained half his coffee. "Well, it's all very . . . interesting. But now—where do I come in?"

Newman relit his cigar. "That's actually the simple part, Major. We are in dire need of someone like you. Someone who is familiar with high-tech airplanes, but who also has shown leadership qualities and the ability to command people in stressful situations. We ran your personnel sheet. We know about your classified work on Diego Garcia. We also know you've got the tip-top in security clearances. Plus, you're a hell of a pilot. Those are some powerful engines on those airplanes. We need someone who can corral all that power."

Gunn just stared back at him. "Please don't tell me you want me to fly one of those cargo humpers? I'm a test pilot. That's like a bishop being busted down to monk."

"They're *C-17s*," Newman corrected him. "And we don't want you just to fly them. We want you in command. Of the airplane and everything and everyone inside it."

Gunn put down his cup. "But, Colonel, I'm a fighter jock. I feel crowded if I'm flying a plane with a backseater."

Newman shrugged. "And I feel your pain, Major. But we're trying to aspire to a higher calling here—we're trying to prevent something even bigger, even worse than 9/11 *before* it happens. It will take a special kind of warrior to make it all work. We looked at a lot of people, but we decided you're the guy we need."

Gunn shifted uncomfortably in his seat. "But what about the pilot flying the gunship now?"

Newman shook his head. "He's just here on TDY, and frankly, I don't trust him. This thing has to be lid-tight on everything from a national security point of view, but also because, like I said, we're having a hell of a time with certain people in Washington who want to close us down. The present gunship guy just isn't cutting it on the ground; that's why we need his permanent replacement. And not just as a pilot but also as commander of the whole first plane, and by definition, when deployed, you'd be the boss of the entire wing. That would be your job."

Gunn looked around, wondering if any of the bottles behind the huge bar actually contained something to drink. Something strong . . .

"And your first goal," Newman continued, "will be to

straighten out what we're doing wrong. If we don't achieve our time frame soon, we'll be forced to pull the plug on this thing. The specs say we have to be precise, which is hard to do because we have so much equipment moving in space at the same time. It ain't like we're jockeying around a bunch of helicopters. These mullahs have isolated themselves so much, helicopters can't reach a lot of them. That's why we got the big airplanes. And that's why we're counting on you to make this thing work—and to do so quickly."

To emphasize his point, Newman reached into his pocket and came out with a pack of CDs.

"These contain all the personnel files of key people here," he said, handing the CDs to Gunn. "Plus all of our operational specs, tactics, and theory. The specs are a real bitch, as you will soon see. But, once again, it's what these a-holes in D.C. foisted on us to get funding, so we're stuck with them. In any case, you'll need all this if you're going to unscramble the egg. And you'll have to move quick. We have another exercise scheduled for 0515 tomorrow morning."

Gunn stared at the pack of twenty discs. He'd been in the service long enough to know when he was being cornered by the brass. And just the fact that he was here, and had seen all this classified stuff already meant he was stuck. But he just couldn't imagine driving around in the hulking C-17, doing God knows what.

He looked around the saloon again and shook his head. "It's just so strange," he said.

Now Newman actually did laugh. "Believe me, Major," he said. "It hasn't even got to strange yet. In fact, 'getting strange' is our ace in the hole."

"What do you mean?" Gunn asked.

Newman smiled darkly. Once again, he seemed to be choosing his words carefully, but Gunn also detected a glint in his eye. The senior officer cocked his head in the direction of the three mysterious hangars, back on the edge of the hidden base, then said: "Major, when you were a kid, did you ever dream that you could fly? Just flap your arms and fly?"

Gunn shrugged. "Sure—who didn't?"

Newman's intense eyes twinkled a bit more. "Okay, but

did you ever dream that you could fly *while* you were invisible?"

Gunn had to think a moment. "Maybe," he replied.

Newman blew out a huge puff of cigar smoke in triumph, then reached over and shook Gunn's hand.

"In that case, Major Gunn," he said, "welcome to Dreamland . . ."

CHAPTER 6

IT was her laptop beeping that finally woke her up.

Amanda Faith O'Rourke opened her eyes and contemplated her spare surroundings. For a moment she thought she was back in her apartment in LA—it didn't look much different from this place. No furniture to speak of. Nothing hanging on the walls. One tiny window letting in a bare amount of air. She'd always thought of herself as a minimalist. In that regard, this place worked in spades.

She rolled off her mattress, still exhausted, and rubbed her hands all over her lithe body—an old Tzu massage trick her first modeling agent had taught her. Increase circulation in the first minute upon waking; it was like stoking a furnace and the best way for someone in her profession to start the day.

This done, she padded over to her laptop, sitting alone on the small writing desk. Two e-mails had come in since she'd fallen asleep just a few hours before.

One was from her current modeling agency. She was being offered a shoot in San Francisco two weeks from now. A BMW ad—exterior location, near Big Sur. Minimum six hours, maxed at eight with double fees after that. Print ads for everything from *Time* to European *Esquire*. A potentially good gig.

Too bad she had to turn it down.

The second e-mail was from NASA. It was short and sweet: The office of astronaut assignments was moving her name down its active flight list. She sagged to the floor on reading this. It was not unexpected, but still, the words hit her harder than she could have imagined. More than five years of work, schooling, study, training . . . circling the drain.

She pulled herself up, took a deep breath and stumbled into the shower. She let the lukewarm water run over her for what seemed like forever. She had the brains. She had the looks. But neither could help her now.

She stepped out of the shower, studied herself in the mirror—and immediately dropped to the floor and did fifty push-ups. Her way of coping.

Then she toweled off and climbed into her work clothes: a flight suit with the insignia of the 201st Special Operations Wing on the shoulder.

Inside a minute, she was out the door of her tiny quarters and standing in the predawn darkness; it was 0500 hours and already the desert air was getting hot. She straightened one of the Navy lieutenant wings on her collar, whipped her long blonde hair back into a ponytail and then started walking toward the base's flight line.

" 'Dreamland,' my ass," she murmured.

THE walk across the dusty runway took only a half minute. Her destination was the C-17 paratroop plane, or known more simply on the flight line as the Jump Plane. She was its commander.

Her passengers were already loading on when she arrived. They were Special Attachment C, 82nd Airborne Division, U.S. Army. They had yet another jump scheduled for 0515—just fifteen minutes away. But after the disastrous exercise just a few hours ago, it was hard for Amanda to imagine who was dreading it more—her or them.

She'd grown up in a Navy family. Her grandfather had flown Banshees during the Korean War. Her father had flown

F-4s over Vietnam. Her older brother had flown F-14s during the first Gulf War, and more recently, F/A-18s over Iraq. She'd inherited their skills along with her mother's good looks to become this three-headed monster: a Navy pilot in shuttle training, who was also a well-known photo model.

The Navy loved her side job—her layouts were always tasteful, and good PR for Naval Aviation, not to mention NASA. Her modeling agency loved the fact that she was this gorgeous, intelligent, independent woman who aspired to travel to the stars. Just about every photo session used her "cosmic beauty" to its advantage—there were a lot of stars twinkling in the background in her ads. And for a while, she'd been having the time of her life. Until the 201st and Area 153 came calling.

Why did they want her for such a weird, highly classified, even illegal mission? Maybe because her brother was shot down in the first few days of the Iraq misadventure and was still MIA? Or because her father had also been a POW for several years, and hanging tough was in her genes?

Or maybe some appendage-challenged admiral just didn't like the idea of a sexy naval aviator-cum-astronaut appearing in BMW ads.

She didn't know, and would probably never know. Her family was all about service to the country. But she'd never been under the illusion that she could pick and choose exactly how that service would be performed.

Then again, never did she think she'd be flying a humper like the C-17, carrying a bunch of *Army* paratroopers around in the back and looking for Muslim priests to squash. Dear old Dad, and her brother, Jay, wherever he was, would be scratching their heads over all this.

Or at least she liked to think so.

Her copilot was a young Air Force lieutenant named Stanley. He was waiting for her by the Jump Plane. In their few weeks together, he'd been short on conversation but adequate in helping her fly the big cargo lifter. Turning on their flashlights now, they did the preflight walk-around together as the paratroopers continued loading themselves into the back.

As always, the walk-around confirmed her C-17 was in good

shape. The hot, isolated conditions of the Nevada desert had not diminished the ability of the 201st ground crews to keep the big plane in prime operating condition. But at the same time, she could see the fuselage was gathering its share of nicks and dents, the price to pay for taking off and landing on the rough desert airstrip every few hours, night after night, week after week. In fact, the entire airplane was starting to look a little worn around the edges.

The 82nd troopers were fully loaded on by the time she returned to the back of the plane. She met their commander, a hard-edged Army captain named Vogel. He'd been nothing but professional with her since the day they started this arranged marriage, but it went no further than that. The only thing they had in common was wishing they were someplace else. Neither had wanted or requested this duty. Yet here they were.

Vogel's paratroopers had been less hospitable. When she first got this assignment she didn't know what shocked her the most: that she was being transferred to fly the C-17 big boy, or that she was being put in charge of a bunch of Army guys, from the 82nd Airborne yet. The 201st reveled in mixing up the services, a requirement for them to get funding for the deep black project. Still, a Navy broad flying an Air Force plane carrying Army paratroopers? It was odd, yes—but out here, in Area 153, what wasn't?

She felt their disapproval especially this morning, though. As she walked up into the crowded cargo hold, checking the interior power lines, there was more than the usual share of snickering and grumbling. Why today? This would be their thirteenth jump in the last three days as the entire unit continued to struggle to get its timing down. Each jump put stress on the paratroopers' bodies, their equipment, and their psyches. But being male animals, she knew it bugged some of them that not only was a female flying their big taxi, but as airplane commander, she was their overall boss as well. Make that their attractive *Navy* female boss.

This bad vibe became all too obvious when she reached the mid-part of the cargo bay and saw that someone had hung an old Corvette ad of hers next to the jump door. The perpetrator had drawn a Native American feathered headdress over her face and scrawled the words: *Don't forget to yell Geronimo!* A titter went through the paratroopers as soon as she spotted it.

Amanda had minored in military psychology at Annapolis. Her studies had taught her that sometimes a small, peculiar act was needed for an officer to exert authority over the lower ranks. It was a well best visited not too often, but this morning was already going badly and she didn't want it to get any worse. Something needed to be done.

She stopped in front of the paratrooper standing closest to her pinup. As it turned out, he was the largest soldier in the unit and looked like some kind of alien invader in all his modern jump gear and camouflage-painted face.

She asked to see his weapon. The soldier handed her his M4 combat rifle. It was the Airborne's weapon of choice—except this rifle had an extra barrel attached to the top, which sat astride a small black box and a tiny antenna, which in turn was surrounded by multicolored wires and a small battery pack. This was the guts of the non-lethal ray system. When the weapon's trigger was pulled, it fired a harmless plastic bullet and ejected a realistic spent cartridge but also delivered a burst of the yellowish NLR energy that felt so much like a lit match when it touched the skin.

"What shape is your weapon in, Trooper?" she asked the soldier.

"Functional," was the curt reply.

"Have you test-fired it today?"

The soldier stumbled for an answer. There was no rule stating the paratroopers had to test their NLR weapons on a regular basis. They worked all the time. Still, had this been an actual combat drop, with a real weapon, testing it would have been crucial. The paratrooper looked at his CO, Vogel, who could only offer him a noncommittal shrug in reply.

"No, ma'am," the trooper finally replied. "It has not been test-fired today."

"It looks like it needs testing," Amanda told him, examining the NLR gear closely. She glanced around the crowded cargo bay. "Any volunteers?"

The badass paratroopers all shrank back a little. Each of them had been hit by NLRs during the fake battles, painful episodes that none of them wanted to experience again. And certainly not just for kicks. Ten seconds went by, but no one stepped forward. Not even Captain Vogel.

"No takers?" Amanda asked, looking them all up and down. She handed the weapon back to the paratrooper and said: "I guess you'll have to test it on me."

A gasp went through the airplane.

"Excuse me, ma'am?" the trooper stuttered.

All eyes were on her now, watching this little experiment of who was tougher.

"Test it on me," she said, taking a step back and raising her arms.

"Is that an order?" the trooper asked her.

"Just do it," she told him.

The trooper reluctantly raised the weapon, turned it on, and meekly fired off two quick bursts. Both struck her on the right shoulder and they burned like hell. She grimaced—it was impossible not to—but she did not stagger or buckle or move out of the way. She didn't even rub the pain away. She just took a breath, nodded to him and said, "Okay, it works. Turn it off and carry on."

With that, she continued her inspection of the airplane.

She heard no more grumbling after that.

LIEUTENANT Stanley had completed the premission checks by the time Amanda climbed up to the flight deck. It took two more minutes to get all the primaries done and to quick-start the engines. The Jump Plane's four big turbofans came to life with no problem, little smoke and—of course—very little noise. The plane was soon taxiing toward the runway.

This morning would be a master drop—102 paratroopers, with full packs. It was a punishment of sorts. They'd done so badly the night before, and the night before that, and the night before that, that they were essentially going back to square one. Again, as evidenced by the most recent faux battle a few hours ago, the unit's timing was all off. The idea was to hose the bad guys from the air, drop the paratroopers, bring in the tanks, crush the bugs, and then get out—all in a matter of twenty-six minutes. But despite weeks of flash and splash, the 201st hadn't even made it to the bug-crushing stage yet.

The reason for the screwups was a mystery. They didn't seem to be any one person's fault, but rather something hidden and organic was causing a different thing to go wrong each time. The rushed training *had* to be a factor, as was trying to get everybody moving at the same speed—hard to do considering the size of the aircraft. But disparate personnel and equipment aside, each individual plane crew knew what it was supposed to do—and *when* it was supposed to do it. It's just that things hadn't clicked. What was meant to be a ballet, so far had been a drunken hoedown. And with each exercise, it seemed to be getting worse.

Amanda taxied up behind the number one plane—the AC-17 "Fireship"—and received the okay for takeoff. Seconds later, the gunship roared away, and per orders, she followed right up his rump. There was no room for error here as the third aircraft carrying the Marine armor—code name "Heavy Metal"—was right in back of her, riding up her rear end, too.

Despite the violence of the rocket-assists, her plane took off smoothly. She climbed and banked to the left, as the training said she should, leveling off at the belly-scraping altitude of 1,000 feet. To the east, a bare hint of sunrise was starting to show. This meant they had only thirty minutes of darkness left to get the training session in. Flying in a loose line formation, the three planes turned, and once again found themselves approaching the training battlefield known as Unfriendly Compound/Iraqi Out Country.

As always, the Fireship went in first. Tilting on its left wing, it began pouring its weird NLR pyrotechnics all over the ground below. Circling a short distance away, Amanda could see a few OpFor soldiers running about the compound—not many, though, and none in any great panic. Every exercise was supposed to be a surprise attack on the resident enemy of the 201st. Trouble was, they had taken part in so many of these drills, the OpFor guys had become very adept at finding cover as soon as the three big aircraft appeared overhead. *That* was a definite flaw in the planning.

The Fireship went around four times, blasting away like

some great flying monster. It seemed impossible that there could be one square inch on the faux battlefield not touched by the plane's massive NLR streams. In fact, any time Amanda saw the gunship in action, the same thought came to mind: If the NLRs look frightening now, what will it be like when the big airplane was using real weapons?

The gunship finally moved away—and for Amanda, now came the hard part. As Stanley hit the jump-ready light, she pulled down her RIF night vision goggles and pointed the nose of her aircraft toward the center of the target village. Yanking the throttles back to near stalling speed, the big plane began bucking wildly in response. The slow speed was crucial, though; the paratroopers had to land in a very small area and this meant the C-17 had to practically crawl for a few seconds in order for them to hit their marks. But every time Amanda had tried this part of the dance, the big plane just refused to cooperate.

"There's got to be a better way," she whispered, the same words she always used at this point of the exercise. Like all naval aviators, she was trained to go fast, banging and clanging. Trying to go as slow as possible, in such a big airplane, just wasn't in her bones.

But again, she had to try. She could hear the paratroopers getting up into their prejump positions. She eased the big plane down to a scant 500 feet in altitude, extremely dangerous at such a low speed. The plane's controls were shaking mightily now, as was her copilot, Lieutenant Stanley. Suddenly Amanda's crash helmet seemed too big for her head; her palms began to sweat. She checked her air speed and cursed again. Though it seemed like she was standing still, she still wasn't going slow enough. She eased the throttles back even farther and held her breath. She had bad dreams about this part—about the big plane falling right out of the sky.

The seconds-to-jump clock finally ticked down to zero. Amanda gave Stanley a slap on the knee and he hit the Go light. The paratroopers began falling out of the plane. Though she could feel the aircraft getting lighter as each one flew out into space, it seemed to take forever. When the last one was finally gone, she jammed the power sticks forward and held on. The huge plane bucked once, but then began accelerating rapidly. She clawed her way up to 2,000 feet and only then did she allow herself to exhale. Swinging the big plane around to the west, she looked over her shoulder to see her soldiers fluttering to the ground in their low-altitude T13 parachutes. They looked like snow falling on the dark, eerie desert. It was almost beautiful—for a few seconds anyway.

But then, to her dismay, she saw dozens of the paratroopers were overshooting the village completely and were drifting toward the hills to the south. Even worse, others were coming down right in the middle of the OpFor soldiers already out in the open. Some OpFor soldiers were even firing their NLRs up at the descending paratroopers, a nightmare scenario had this been a real attack.

Amanda felt her throat tighten; her stomach went into knots. Her sweaty hands locked into fists so tightly, her nails cut into her skin.

Damn . . . she thought. *Not again . . .*

JUST 500 feet behind and 1,000 feet below the Jump Plane, the Heavy Metal ship was in the middle of an impossibly steep banking maneuver.

Even with the QSP sound dampeners, the big aircraft's engines were whining in protest. Its fuselage began oscillating as it corkscrewed its way down in altitude, a dangerous warning that the C-17 was about to go into a stall. Flying less than 1,000 feet above the ground, a stall now would instantly send the plane nose-first into the hard desert below.

This was foremost in the minds of the people riding in its enormous cargo bay. They were a platoon of the U.S. Marines 4th Heavy Mobile Force. Translation: Marine Armor. These Marines drove M1 Abrams tanks. Not a typical jarhead occupation.

There were two tanks tied down in the rear of the pirouetting C-17. Radically stripped-down versions of the famous M1A1 Abrams, they were unofficially known as JGCTs, for "just the gun, computers, and tracks." They carried no big fuel tanks, because these M1s were meant to operate close to their plane. They carried not a lot of ammo because their stay on the ground was supposed to be short and sweet. They didn't have a lot of communications gear on board either, because they would always be within earshot of anyone they had to talk to. Stripped of just about everything unnecessary and heavy, the Marine tanks could move fast. How fast? If given the opportunity, both could top 70 mph.

But at the moment, the chains and straps keeping these behemoths in place were straining as much as the big plane's engines. The Marines were feeling a bit uncomfortable as well, as they were now at nearly 90 degrees from level and looking down, and not across, at their tanks.

They had reputations to maintain, so the dozen Marines tried their best not to notice their aircraft might be in trouble. They'd been through more than a few rough rides since their Area 153 training began, and as each man was a combat veteran with multiple tours in Iraq, in theory, nothing was supposed to faze them.

But this? This was getting to be too much . . .

Finally someone cried out: "Who *the fuck* is flying this thing?"

IT was a good question.

He was Captain Jake Pulver, Marine Aviation. Angular face, jet-black hair, even a curled lip, he bore a passing resemblance to Elvis Presley. This endeared him to some, made him despised by others. His forte was driving Harrier jump jets. He had a reputation as a cowboy, with good reason: He'd wrecked two Harriers in less than ten months of flying for the Corps. The only reason Pulver wasn't bounced immediately was that Marine Air was always critically short of pilots, a strain made worse by the long Bush fuckup in Iraq. And his recklessness aside, Pulver *was* one of the best Harrier pilots in the business. The Marines simply couldn't afford to lose him.

But they didn't want to deal with him either. So when the highly classified 201st unit came calling, and the Corps was asked to supply one of its top pilots, Pulver was the one they pushed forward.

He never forgave them for it.

At the moment, Pulver was trying get into position to land the C-17 on the fake battlefield. But he faced a problem: the airplane was moving too fast for him to get it where he wanted to go. Even worse, the ground below was not secure in the sense of the game they were playing. Only about half of the flares marking the runway had been ignited and the NLR fight raging between those few paratroopers who'd actually landed near the village and the OpFor guys defending it looked chaotic and disorganized.

Still, Pulver was going in. That his airplane was coming apart at the seams, that every bolt and fastener sounded like it was about to come undone, that the plane's wings were about to snap off due to sheer g-forces, bothered him not a bit. He hated this whole thing, hated everything about the desert, about the C-17s and the 201st. *What the hell am I doing out here playing games?* he'd thought more than once. He wanted to be killing terrorists, for real.

He glanced over at his copilot—the man's face was pale, startling because he was African American. Pulver went left on the controls and straightened out the plane finally, all while keeping an eye on what was happening below. His job was to bring the tanks down as soon as the 82nd cleared a runway. But at the moment, they were working too slowly for him.

"That's how it always is with these fucking Army guys," Pulver was cursing now to his white-knuckled second-seater. "Slower than shit running uphill."

He circled the mock battleground yet again. The fierce gunfight going on between the paratroopers and the OpFors only filled him with more disdain. NLR guns were too mild for him. He'd been shot with them plenty of times and refused to feel anything even approaching discomfort. Toys, he called them.

He went over the battleground a third time and at that point, he'd had enough. He yelled: "Hang on!" And before the second-seater could say anything, Pulver put the big, over-loaded plane into another screaming turn and started descending rapidly.

The noise and confusion in the cargo bay was drowned out by the full roar of the plane's engines. Pulver had managed to completely override the plane's elaborate noise-dampening system by now. He flipped the landing gear switch, and even though his controls were telling him he was approaching at too steep an angle and much too fast, brought the big plane in anyway.

The sight of the approaching C-17 scattered those few 82nd paratroopers setting up the last of the runway lights. The cargo plane hit the ground a few seconds later, bouncing a couple times before slamming down for good. Pulver applied the blown flaps and hit the reverse thruster panels at the same time. The plane's engines began screaming again—one began shooting out flames, the strain was so much. Nevertheless, Pulver pulled back on the throttles, applied the airbrakes, and in one violent motion, skidded the big plane into a spectacular 180-degree turn.

Even before the plane stopped spinning, Pulver dropped the rear door and began shouting orders for the Marines to move out. They did so with great haste. Releasing their vehicles from the quick-snap restraints, the pair of warmed-up M1s barreled out of the smoking airplane, as if the farther they could get away from it the better.

But there was a problem: because of his over-speed, Pulver had not put the big plane down on the improvised runway, but nearly in the middle of the village itself, where the OpFor troops were concentrated. It had been a dramatic landing, but not an accurate one. Dispensing his armor before the other paratroopers were able to consolidate their positions only compounded the error.

This did not stop the tankers though. They immediately began firing their NLR weapons at the OpFor troops who were just as surprised as the paratroopers were to see the tanks so soon. The M1s' guns could deliver a wide swath of NLRs, affecting many individuals at once. And for a moment or two after the tanks began blasting away, it appeared that Pulver's antics were going to pay off. The OpFor guys were confused, to say the least.

But then, a wailing siren erupted and suddenly the area was flooded with men in distinctive white uniforms. All of them had handheld radios and all of them were screaming the words: "Exercise bust three!" into them.

The referees had intervened. Due to numerous infractions, most all of them committed by Pulver and the Heavy Metal ship, the refs were calling a quick halt to the exercise.

WATCHING all this from the circling Fireship was Tommy Gunn.

Though still a bit shell-shocked, he'd taken on this new job as unit commander with vigor, staying up all that night, getting a fast-track course on how to fly the C-17 as well as going over the personnel files of every member of the unit.

To help him on this first mission, he'd meticulously drawn up a dozen or so cheat sheets (an old test-pilot trick), and taped them to the arms and knees of his flight suit. On these sheets were the names of key members of the unit and what they were supposed to be doing and when. Gunn had told himself that whenever he saw someone doing something wrong, all he had to do was refer to the corresponding sheet and make a note of the infraction. Enough notes corrected, and the unit would be rolling smoothly—right?

Wrong. His strategy might have been good in theory, but in practice it was a disaster. In fact, the confusion on the ground perfectly matched the confusion in his cockpit at the moment. He'd conveniently forgotten that, even though he had a perfectly capable young Air Force lieutenant named Bing serving as his copilot, it was up to Gunn to fly the big gunship while playing school marm, driving it low and aggressively, with controls and nuances that were all new to him. The best test pilot in history would have had a problem juggling all these bowling balls at once.

Even with Bing's help, he found his hands were full just getting the big plane airborne, over the target, and then in position to begin painting the training ground with waves of the frightening NLRs. It went smoothly enough at first—but that was because of all of the three planes, his had the relatively easiest assignment. Once he'd peeled off, he'd watched through the zoom function in his RIF goggles as the second C-17, the Jump Plane, struggled mightily to float over the target only to dispense more than half its paratroopers in the scrub bushes way outside the fake village. And those that actually landed near the target? They would have been massacred if it had been the real deal.

This was followed by the dangerous and unglamorous entry of the Marine Armor. Watching the approach and landing of the Heavy Metal plane, Gunn's only conclusion was that the man at the controls was crazy. Even now he could see the Heavy Metal pilot arguing ferociously with the referees while confusion still reigned all over the fake battlefield.

Gunn zoomed in on the center of the chaos just in time to witness something unexpected: one of the 82nd troopers, undeniably fed up with Pulver's antics, walked up to the Marine pilot and leveled him with a massive punch to the jaw. The force of the blow knocked Pulver on his ass, but somehow the Marine pilot was able to bounce back up, right himself, and deliver an equally massive counter-punch, knocking the Army man clear off his feet. Pulver then tackled the offending paratrooper and began pummeling him with his fists. This, in turn, led some of the paratrooper's comrades to start fighting with the Marines in the first tank, while more Army guys began pounding on the drivers and crewmen of the second tank, which by this time, had driven up to the scene. Within moments, a full-scale interservice donnybrook had broken out, to the howling amusement of the OpFor soldiers standing nearby.

The gunship's radio immediately crackled to life; Bing took the call. It was the head referee. Because Gunn was now the 201st operational commander, the ref wanted him to order the troops below to stop fighting.

"What should I tell him, sir?" Bing asked.

Gunn thought a long moment and then ripped all the cheat sheets from his arms and legs. Another exercise ruined. His first as commander . . .

"Tell him to let them fight," he said, wearily turning the plane back to the base. "Maybe they'll get at least one thing right tonight."

CHAPTER 7

Bora Kurd, Pakistan

It was a tiny bit of warmth that woke Anne Murphy from her fitful sleep.

She'd succumbed to pure exhaustion hours before, collapsing to the cold, damp floor of her cell and letting a disquieting sort of unconsciousness come over her. Her last thought was a fervent hope that God would take her before she awoke.

But her prayer had not been answered, for now, as the brief wave of heat washed across her face, she was awake in a flash, thinking she was still in a dream. It took a few horrifying moments for her to remember that she was a captive and that her hands and feet were bloody and frozen from the long march across the mountains and that her colleague had been brutally murdered by these crazy Muslims who she knew were intent on killing her, too.

She did not know what time it was, or even what day it was. Or how long she'd been a prisoner, or how much time had passed since she'd seen her colleague's ghastly beheading. But now, she looked up at her cell door and was surprised to see a beam of light coming through the tiny slit near the lock. It was like a sliver of another world leaking into her little piece of hell. She crawled over to the door and peered out through the slit, for a moment feeling the unexplained warmth on her face and finding it good.

But then reality set in again.

She wiped the icy grit from her eyes and stared out the opening to see that the terrorists had turned on their TV lights again; it was some of that illumination that was bleeding into her cell. And they had taken another of her colleagues from her holding place. This woman, a friend of hers from Cleveland named Sarah, was in hysterics, kicking and screaming as the terrorists dragged her over to the corner of the large hall where the TV studio was set up.

Anne was horrified but could not look away. There was no pretense of an interrogation this time. The terrorists simply forced Sarah to the ground, lined up in back of her, their faces covered by ski masks, and read a brief passage from the Koran, this while one man kept his foot firmly on Sarah's neck to prevent her from scampering away. The words of praise for all things Allah were drowned out by Sarah's cries, so much so the man running the sound for the broadcast was forced to move the boom microphone closer to the man reading the verses. Still, it did no good. The terrorists knew any more adulation of God would be worthless. So the leader simply took out his huge machete and without hesitation began hacking away at Sarah's neck.

Anne vomited; she had to look away now. She fell back to the floor as Sarah's screams turned to bloody gurgles and then to nothing at all. Then the light was extinguished and Anne was left in the dark again, shivering.

She began praying once more, beseeching God to take her and spare her this hideous death. But suddenly, in the midst of her second Hail Mary, she found she couldn't breathe. Her throat began constricting, as if a pair of invisible hands was closing around it. She started gasping, and crawled across the dirty damp floor to the other side of the cell. Cut into the wall here was a hole even smaller than the one in her cell door. This one had a dented metal flap over it—a crude ventilation device. By pushing up the flap, she allowed the brutally cold air to come in. She could also see the world outside the mountain.

She pushed the metal flap outward and sucked in the freezing air. It helped for some reason, filling her lungs and momentarily calming her. She'd started choking because she knew this was how she was going to die—by being hacked in her throat. It was almost too much to take.

She continued breathing deeper, at the same time looking past the cold mist to the landscape outside her cell. She was surprised to see it was early morning. The rising sun was reflecting off a patch of trees on the next mountain over.

And in that bare shaft of sunlight, she saw something else.

Directly across from her location, halfway up the next mountain, perhaps a half mile away, was a dirt road that wound its way down the side of the slope. On that road she saw soldiers.

They were definitely not terrorists. These people were wearing blue helmets and uniforms and carrying rifles. They were moving very slowly, but deliberately down the mountain path, toward the bottom of the peak, to another road that led to the Bora Kurd fortress itself.

Anne's heart began beating rapidly—all thoughts of choking were suddenly gone. She recognized the blue uniforms as belonging to the small UNIFOR army that was stationed as a peacekeeping unit on this wild unmarked border between Pakistan and Afghanistan. These were UN troops—from Bali or some such place, she believed. But at that moment, they could have been from Mars and she would have been happy.

This was a rescue force. They were coming to get her.

Anne didn't know what to do. She was desperate to get a message to the other hostages, to tell them this good news, to tell them to just hold on, that help was on the way.

But she was also wise enough to know any disruption from her would alert the terrorists and that would jeopardize the rescue attempt. So she just pushed herself up against the wall as far as she could and held the metal flap open and watched as the army of blue uniforms drew closer.

But just as the soldiers reached a point about halfway down the mountain, there was a sudden explosion. It was so violent, it shook the dust off the ceiling of Anne's cell. More explosions followed, reports so loud, Anne found herself hugging the wall and tightly shutting her eyes. It was like the mountain itself was shaking. So many weapons were going off, the noise was deafening.

It only lasted for ten seconds or so. When the noise finally stopped, and Anne dared to look out the opening again, her heart dropped to her feet. She could see dozens of the blue uniformed soldiers lying on the mountain road, chewed up and bleeding. The terrorists had seen the blue army coming and had waited for the right moment to fire their huge mountain guns at them. So many weapons had been unleashed on the soldiers, none of them had been able to escape the fusillade. Now more terrorists emerged from the thickets and, adding to the horror, began hacking away at any of the soldiers showing any signs of life.

Inside a minute, not one of them was moving. They were all dead.

Anne slumped back to the floor and began sobbing, Then, she began praying again, begging God to take her.

Before these devils did.

CHAPTER 8

Nevada

Gunn was flying the tiny OH-6 copter way too fast and way too close to the ground. Dangerous behavior for sure, as one wrong move would send him careening to his death.

But he didn't care.

He needed coffee.

It was another dark, moonless night, and Gunn wasn't familiar with the mess of topography between the hidden base of the 201st and his intended destination: the ghost town/chow hall named Jacks. He was tired, more so than he could ever remember. He'd been here in Area 153 for twenty-four hours now and had yet to go to sleep. He was *so* burnt out, he probably shouldn't have been flying at all. But he had a lot of work to do and had run out of coffee and this was the fastest way he knew how to get some more.

Ironically, this was a stand-down day for the 201st. In fact, no exercises were scheduled for the next two days. The respite had nothing to do with giving the weary unit a break—though one seemed in order after their horrendous exercise earlier that morning had ended in a free-for-all. Rather, U.S. Special Operations Command, highest overseer of the 201st, had mandated that the specially adapted C-17s could only fly a certain number of hours a month in the harsh desert environment and all three planes had reached their saturation point earlier that day.

But this was no reason for hallelujahs. Just because they were standing down didn't mean the 201st could take it easy. Just the opposite. The unit's personnel still had to get their physical training in—in this case force-marching with full packs up, over, and around the rugged hills south of their base. Plus they had to do mandatory reviews of their own specs, that is, what each person's job was, and then clean *all* the unit's equipment, including the trio of massive C-17s. In many ways, the next two days would be harder on the 201st than if they were actually running their night exercises. There was no such thing as a vacation day in this corner of Dreamland.

As the unit's new operational CO, Gunn probably had it the worst. Not only was he required to do the physical training, the mandatories, and take his turn with the cleaning crew, he also had to continue going through each person's personnel file, reviewing hundreds of pages of the unit's operational specs—*plus* study the pilot's manual for the still-new-to-him C-17 Globemaster. Newman had warned him it would be rough going for the first week or so, and he was right. But when he dumped all the ops data on him, the senior officer had also told Gunn if he ever needed to get away from this mad-house he'd suddenly found himself in, the keys to the Flying Egg chopper were always in the ignition. Gunn had used up the last of his Maxwell instant packets while spending the past fifteen hours going over the files and specs. Even though buses left the 201st training facility every couple hours to make the ten-mile trek down to Jacks, he didn't have time to wait for a bus. That's why he'd decided to take Newman up on his offer.

Getting the OH-6 airborne had been a bit of an adventure, though. He'd rated in rotary craft when he first started Air Force flight training, this as part of a course to slot selected pilots into flying the Osprey tilt-wing aircraft. Gunn went to fighter jets instead, but it was hard to forget how to fly a chopper. Or so he thought.

He'd managed to get it off the ground with no problem, but the little copter's controls were almost too responsive. A slight twist to the right sent him into a dizzying set of 360-degree turns, not four feet above the runway. Over-correcting sent him spinning in the opposite direction. Luckily the camp was in total darkness at the time, with most people either asleep, schlepping the hills to the south, or lucky enough to be down at Jacks. So, no one saw him. But by the time he got the copter under control, his stomach was going one way and his brain was going the other.

He finally got the copter pointed in the right direction—or what he thought was the right direction—and off he went. He followed a dirt road that he hoped would lead to Jacks, passing the trio of mysterious hidden hangars on the way. But he'd neglected to bring his RIF goggles, so his flight was done the old-fashioned way: by pure eyeballing, twisting and turning his way through the stark and dark desert.

"Should have eaten more carrots as a kid," he thought wearily as he zipped along. "Should have listened more to Mom."

It was with much relief that he finally spotted the clutch of old wooden buildings standing alone in the vast emptiness. One look told him Jacks was especially crowded tonight.

He circled the place a couple times, looking for the best place to set down. Humvees, APCs, and a few tanks were taking up a lot of the parking spaces out front; buses from other training sectors as well as from the 201st had filled most of the alley spaces out back. Gunn was forced to land way behind the saloon and trudge back along the edge of town to get to the main building. He couldn't help but glance up at the stars along the way, though, and marvel at how close they seemed out here. He felt like he could reach up and touch them.

He walked into Jacks and wearily took a plate of food from the hot table. The place was mobbed again; it was filled with soldiers sitting elbow to elbow, Marines, referees, and a host of others. A few of the patrons were from the 201st training site taking their chow break. Many of them were sporting real bandages over real wounds, again the result of the melee that had ensued after that morning's final exercise. Gunn couldn't help but notice the referees had strategically placed themselves between the 201st Marines and the paratroopers, the main combatants in the brawl. A repeat of a fight like the one earlier would probably destroy the old wooden place.

Gunn found a corner seat, away from everyone else, sat

down, and started eating robotically. He was too tired, too worn-out to even know what was on his plate. In his worst day at test pilot school, things hadn't been this grueling for him. But again, beyond food, it was coffee that he craved. When a Navy steward arrived with a full pot, Gunn convinced him to leave it with him.

He started slurping the coffee like a man drinking water in the desert. It took a few cups, along with a few bites of food to get him back to semi-consciousness. Only then did he notice someone had sat down across the table from him.

It was Jake Pulver, the pilot of the Heavy Metal plane. He was sporting a bandage over his right ear and another on his left wrist. This was the first time Gunn had met the Marine aviator face-to-face.

Gunn couldn't help but notice the mountain of food Pulver had piled on his plate. He had at least five helpings of meat loaf, potatoes, and carrots—lots of carrots, interestingly. A gallon of brown gravy was dumped over it all. And as Gunn had one dinner roll on his plate, Pulver had somehow managed to find an entire loaf of bread. And where Gunn was mainlining coffee, Pulver was drinking something else.

"Is that beer?" Gunn asked him, pointing to the large mug with the ocean of white foam falling out of it.

"It ain't chocolate milk," Pulver replied.

Gunn had forgotten his manners—the sight of the cold frothy beer had mesmerized him.

He apologized to Pulver, shook his hand, and introduced himself.

"Good to finally meet you, sir," the Marine pilot replied. "Up until now I was just calling you 'that asshole in the Fireship.'"

Gunn resisted the temptation to tell Pulver what *he'd* been calling *him*.

"How did you find beer here, Captain?" he asked him instead.

Pulver shrugged while shoveling food into his mouth. He was typical-looking for a jarhead—chiseled jaw, cold eyes, and muscular arm tats. But he wasn't a huge individual, certainly nothing like the fat Elvis. Gunn wondered where all the food was going.

"Navy supply guys run this canteen," Pulver explained between bites. "Navy supply guys can get anything. Therefore, we have beer here."

Gunn was surprised. "But is it . . . legal?" he asked. "The beer, I mean?" The moment the words left his mouth he knew they sounded bad.

But Pulver just laughed. "Well, in case you haven't noticed, sir—*nothing* out here is legal. Or didn't Colonel Newman give you 'the talk' yet?"

"Sure, he did," Gunn replied. "About the operation being under the radar, and so on? Is that what you mean?"

"And that we can all go to Leavenworth if we fuck up?"

"He mentioned that, too, yes . . ."

"Did you think he was just using that as an expression?"

Gunn shrugged. "I guess I did."

Pulver stopped eating for a moment and looked over at him. "Well, guess again, sir. He wasn't . . ."

He went to work on his loaf of bread. Gunn couldn't tell if he was pulling his leg or not.

"How did you get your orders to come here?" he asked him.

The Marine pilot shrugged. "Miramar Air Station. I'd just stepped off a transport plane from Iraq. A guy came up to me, a CIA type, and handed me my orders. They looked phony at first, but I recognized the right security codes, and also there was a letter from my old CO. So, they had me."

Four quick bites of food.

"The spook gave me an airline ticket to Las Vegas, a bus ticket to Tonopah, and a phone number to call when I got there. I did as told like a good little Marine, and after a two-hour ass-breaking ride in a Hummer, here I am . . . Flying the Whisper Pigs. How about you?"

"I flew out—from Edwards," Gunn replied.

Pulver stopped eating again. "Test pilot?"

Gunn nodded. Was it even possible to impress this guy?

"What did you fly out in? Something hot shit?"

Gunn shook his head. "Nope—just a T-38 . . ."

"Is it still here?"

"Yes, it's under one of the camo nets near the ops building."

"Does it still fly?"

Gunn hesitated a moment. "I think so. With some gas. Why?"

"Can it fit two people?"

Gunn paused again. "It would be a tight squeeze. Why?"

"Because I'm breaking out," Pulver told him. "Want to go with me?"

Gunn just laughed. "You're nuts . . ."

Pulver just smiled at him. "Yeah, so I hear," he said.

Mercifully the topic changed once Pulver had cleaned his plate and began working on his mug of beer. Pulver was eccentric but also engaging. He was more like a Marine door-breaker or a drill instructor than a pilot. But after spending just five minutes with him, Gunn finally understood why he flew the way he did. He *was* a little nutty.

They talked about the strange aircraft they'd been given to fly—the Whisper Pigs—and how they differed from the fun times Pulver had experienced driving his own personal Harrier jump jet and Gunn his wide array of experimental aircraft.

They also talked about the handful of OpFor guys sitting at a table nearby, eating the same food, drinking the same beer, obviously Americans, but dressed like people who lived half a world away. The garb gave them away as the soldiers who'd been besting the 201st since their first night of operations.

"Those bastards," Pulver said, nodding in their direction. "I'm convinced they're out here not to train us, but just to beat us. They always seem to know when we are coming, right? Even with the no-noise jets and all? I think it's all a fix to make them look good. And make us look bad."

"You mean we're not doing that to ourselves already?" Gunn asked him.

"We ain't helping, I'll give you that," Pulver said. He pulled himself a bit closer to Gunn and lowered his voice. "But, I'll tell you what a guy here told me. If you can handle it."

"Try me," Gunn told him.

"These OpFor guys we're training against?" he said. "I was told they got ahold of one of those crazy laser weapons that was left over from the old days in this place. You know, when things got out of control, before they had to shut it down? This device they have is something that can take out everything out here. Destroy it all. Like an atomic bomb."

Gunn just looked back at him and wondered how many beers he'd consumed before their paths crossed.

"But that doesn't make sense," he told Pulver. "This is all just training. Practice. Make-believe. Those OpFor guys don't really want to hurt us."

Pulver just shook his head and smiled crookedly.

"Oh, don't they?" he asked.

201st Base Command Ops

Colonel Newman lifted his head off his hands and thought: *Where the hell am I?*

He rubbed his eyes and looked around for a few moments. Only then did he realize he was sitting at the desk in his office and that he'd fallen asleep on his computer keyboard.

Again . . .

He wearily checked the time. It was 2230 hours, ten-thirty in the evening. He looked down the long hallway to the mission room and saw it was completely dark. He was the only one left inside the ops building.

He got to his feet, stretched painfully, and turned off the office AC. He had but a half cup of coffee to his name. Rewarming it in the microwave, he made a mental note that he needed to get some more. Returning to the computer, a check of his e-mail found a short hello message from his wife, but nothing from his daughter, for the third day in a row now. He shook away his concern, retrieved the stale coffee, and sat back down.

Yes, the 201st had the next two days off, but it certainly didn't mean Newman could coast through or even catch up on his sleep, at least in a horizontal position. He had a mountain of paperwork to do, reports to write and send back to Washington to be read by the same people who didn't want him out here in the first place. Wasn't that the Army way?

So, like everyone else in the unit, the two down days would be painful—a couple extra meal breaks at Jacks was all any of them could hope for. But, still, on one level Newman was glad they weren't flying. He didn't think his men could take the pace much longer without some kind of catastrophic accident occurring. That was, by far, his number one fear.

He gulped his coffee and searched his ashtray for a stogie with more than a stub of tobacco left to it. Despite his unexpected nap, he was still feeling worn down. The 201st was his baby. While the majority of them had been out here, living with the sand and the snakes for weeks, Newman had been birthing the project for the past year, doing time at the War College, pulling a stint at the NTC, observing Special Forces units under fire in Iraq, Afghanistan, and other places. It had been a long trek and he was getting tired of all the details.

But still, he had to press on. It was *that* important. To him. And to the country.

He was about to return to his paperwork when he heard a soft rapping at his back door. He looked out the window to see a man dressed in a black special ops uniform that resembled a space suit.

"Jesus Christ . . ." Newman whispered. "What can this be?"

He opened the door and immediately let the man in.

Newman knew him. He was Captain Mark Downes, one of the few military people permanently assigned to Area 153. Downes had quite the rep. Not only was he a bigwig in Delta Force, he was also a member of several other deep black op units. There was even a rumor that Downes had worked at the first incarnation of Area 153, the place they called "War Heaven," before it was shut down years before.

He and Newman had become friends since the 201st arrived in the desert. Technically speaking, Downes was training with another top secret unit about fifteen miles over the mountains from the 201st location. But in reality, he had his hands in just about everything going on inside the vast special ops training ground. For some reason, he knew all its secrets. He had previously expressed support and admiration for what Newman was trying to do out here. Still, Newman's heart dropped when he saw him. He knew Downes wouldn't have come here now, at this late hour, unless it was very important.

"No one saw you, I hope," Newman said anxiously as he closed the door behind him.

Downes shook his head. "I took a small PFD/MV—top secret personal flying device. So, I can assure you no one did."

Newman poured him a bit of his leftover coffee and they sat down.

"I know this ain't good news," Newman told him. "I can smell it."

Downes nodded grimly. Even though he was out here in the middle of the Nevada desert, due to his past service, Downes had been able to stay in the loop of what was happening deep inside the U.S. Special Forces command structure. In fact, Downes was one of the most connected people Newman knew.

"I just got a message from friends in D.C.," he told Newman soberly. "Like us, they're working very long hours these days. They somehow got access to transcripts of a secret congressional hearing on various black ops in the making and what they heard about the 201st was not good."

Newman collapsed to the side of his bunk. He'd been worrying about a hammer blow like this. Now, here it was. "Tell me everything," he said.

"The gist of the message is that you're running out of time," Downes said. "Budget pressures are getting more intense by the hour, and the political pressure is, too. Plus, they've been getting negative reports on your progress. People are beginning to wonder exactly what the hell the 201st is doing out here."

This surprised Newman. "Are you saying I have a leak? A spy in my unit?"

Downes shook his head. "No—I doubt that. The stuff is not that specific. But *someone* out here who knows what you're doing—and how you've been performing—has been sending info back to these unfriendlies. And none of it is good."

"But everything we do is supposed to be classified," Newman protested.

"And it still is," Downes said. "But again, someone with

access to your operations—or just someone close by with eyes and ears—has been putting less than complimentary stuff in the pipeline and it's being received badly back in D.C."

"So, what does all this mean exactly?" Newman asked.

Downes bit his lip. "Translation: A congressional fact-finding mission is heading out here, to see you, and to check it out."

Newman's cigar fell out of his mouth, sparkling as it hit the floor. This was the worst possible news.

"Son of a bitch," he said.

"You've struck a nerve back there," Downes told him. "I mean, half the people see the beauty of the project. Half are scared for their asses if we're caught training U.S. troops to whack Muslim holy leaders before they've done anything to us. Anyone who is against this idea, for whatever reason, is looking to knock you off."

Newman held his head in his hands for a moment. He didn't need this, not now. Not ever.

"I'm under no illusions here," he said finally. "This is a gigantic task we're trying to pull off. Tons of technology, inte-gration of disparate units, huge airplanes playing roles they were not designed for, with pilots more used to flying fighters than cargo humps. But, it's not some boondoggle or novelty. I'm convinced what we're doing here is more than training to whack a few mooks. What we're doing is nothing less than showing Washington what the U.S. military should look like in twenty-five years: ultra-fast, ultra-mobile, and adept at the art of the massive hit-and-run."

Downes laughed ominously. "You mean, if there *is* a U.S. military in twenty-five years."

Newman was both furious and dejected. He'd hoped to have the 201st operational inside six months. Now he was learning his time line was shrinking not just by days, but by hours.

"When are these people arriving?" he asked.

Downes finished his coffee. "What I hear is forty-eight hours or so. After a stop in Vegas, we have to assume."

"And who's running this traveling circus?"

Downes just shook his head.

"That's the worst part, Colonel," he said. "It's your old friend, the devil himself: Congressman Adamis Toole . . ."

OpFor Training Sector 4, Nevada Desert

Army Captain Rick Sledge was not a nice guy.

His military record was abysmal. As a young lieutenant assigned to the notorious Baghdad prison, Abu Ghraib, he'd faced charges of assaulting Iraqi prisoners with a cattle prod. When his case was dropped due to lack of evidence, he was transferred to the field, only to be caught up in another controversial case, this one involving the kidnapping and beating of five Iraqi citizens near Fallujah, one of them a pregnant woman. Once again, Sledge's neck was saved by lack of evidence, after which he was transferred yet again . . . this time, inexplicably, to Guantanamo Bay, where yet another prisoner assault charge surfaced.

That Sledge was still in the military at all was a sign of the times. True, he had some influential friends back in Washington and they'd managed to get his Gitmo case quietly dismissed. But, with the overall state of the U.S. military at such a low point these days as far as retaining experienced officers, guys like Sledge could hang on forever. And sometimes, they even got promoted.

His latest assignment was CO of the OpFor unit assigned to the 201st training sector known as OpFor 4. This included the CSMC known as Unfriendly Compound/Iraqi Out Country. It was against Sledge's men that the star-crossed 201st had fought, and lost, almost every night for weeks.

Essentially, Sledge's men were actors. Made up of troops who had seen combat in Iraq, a potpourri of Special Forces types, including a few SEALs and Green Berets, they were wise in the ways of the black ops world. They also looked the part, with scruffy beards and unkempt hair. And as many were dark-skinned to begin with, they could pass for a citizen of any country in the Persian Gulf.

But they were also a lot like their CO; many had run afoul of military law. A few had been at Abu Ghraib at the same time Sledge was there. Others had been named in a host of murder and kidnapping cases in Iraq. But also like their CO, they'd beat the rap and were just too valuable to let go. Plus, when the Nevada testing range opened back up a year before, it was someone's bright idea that the OpFor soldiers shouldn't just *play* mean, brutal types, but they should actually *be* mean, brutal types. This aspect of the program was controversial and a highly classified secret. But truth was, Sledge's OpFor 4 unit in particular was made up of men from the bottom of the military's Special Forces' barrel.

The 150 men of OpFor 4 pretty much lived out in the open. They slept in tents and in a few caves cored out nearby their encampment. They wore the clothes of rugged western Iraqi tribesmen, from the heavy wool headdresses right down to the hard rubber sandals. They got their warmth—or at least some of it—from campfires set up in roughly circular patterns, dug deep and nearly impossible to see from the air.

But they also stayed warm by portable heaters powered by diesel generators expertly hidden in the brush. And their tents had small TV sets with wireless antennas able to grab just about any channel being beamed out on satellite TV. And the line of rocks in a nearby gulley hid a row of Porta-Pottis and portable showers. And hot chow was always at the ready, trucked in directly from Jacks itself.

Not bad duty for a lot of soldiers who, had the wind been blowing in a different direction, would probably be doing hard time in a military prison somewhere.

IT was now 2245 hours, normally the beginning of OpFor 4's workday. But tonight, the mood around the encampment was jovial and relaxed. They knew the 201st was on its mandatory two-day stand-down. This meant for the next forty-eight hours, things would be easy for the OpFors.

Still, they gathered near the village's faux mosque and ate their late-night meal together, as they always did, each man in his *salwar kameez* garb. Dinner consisted of a bowl of cooked lamb parts, rice, and yogurt, all mixed together. There was also Navy beer on hand to be consumed at their leisure. There was none of the pressure felt by the actual training units out here during stand-downs. The only thing deemed important for the OpFor 4 actors was for them to maintain their characters. In other words, the only thing Sledge's guys had to do for the next two days was sleep and work on their suntans.

Once his men were fed, Sledge addressed them briefly, telling them to enjoy the time off and to basically stay out of trouble. Then he dismissed them and returned to his headquarters in the mosque. He was a fireplug of a man, red-faced, with a perpetual scowl. In this charade Sledge played the part of the warlord mullah, the kingpin of this fake religious fort. In fact, his men called him Mullah Sledge. But he, too, had nothing to do for the next forty-eight hours, except eat, sleep, and read the porn magazines that arrived daily with the food from Jacks. His two-day holiday had begun.

Sledge knew there were rumblings higher up about what he and his men had been able to do out here: essentially beat the 201st every time they began their war exercise. But he also knew his men really had little to do with it. The 201st was trying to accomplish something complicated, within a crunched time frame, under a lot of restrictions and mandatories imposed by the congressional oversight committee and Special Forces Command itself. Their specs were ridiculous. The 201st attacked on a timetable. What kind of a surprise was that? And their plan never changed from night one: first the gunship would show up, then the paratroopers, then the tanks. The refs were always anxious to justify their positions out here, so they were very quick to blow the whistle on the training unit, thus compounding the agony. In other words, the deck was stacked against the 201st from the beginning.

But Sledge's hands were not entirely clean in this. Besides being untrustworthy, he was also a snitch. Just as Downes had lines of communication reaching all the way back to D.C., Mullah Sledge did as well—and to all the wrong people. He'd been feeding information to D.C. ever since the training began, reporting every misstep the 201st had taken to his friends inside Special Forces Command. In return, his contacts fed information back to him, telling him the 201st was demoralized—as evidenced by their internecine fight earlier—and coming apart at the seams. This served to make Sledge's group better than it was, and the 201st worst than it was—but again, those were the breaks. If his time in the Army had taught Sledge one thing, it was this: Civilian politics might be bad, but military politics was brutal. The whole idea was to save your own little piece of turf, wherever it may be, even at the expense of everyone else.

To this end, Sledge knew the 201st would never be able to complete a successful training mission, even if by some miracle they made it through his men, through the refs, and into the fake religious fort itself. This was because Sledge indeed had a secret weapon of his own out here. Something left over from the wild days when this place was called War Heaven.

Something that, if activated, would stop the 201st dead in its tracks.

TOMMY Gunn left Jacks soon after his chat with Pulver, the hound dog pilot's paranoid thoughts spinning around his head, like the blades of the OH-6.

He strapped himself back into the copter's minuscule cockpit and started the engines. Now fully recaffeinated, Gunn's plan was to head back to base, get back into the unit's operational specs, and try to figure out why everything seemed to go wrong whenever the 201st did a training session. But then he started looking up at the stars again and something came over him. Though he was rarely given to impulses, when he got airborne, instead of heading north back to base, he went straight up instead, leaving a small cloud of sand and dust behind him.

His new destination was the so-called Alpha Mesa, the tall, flattened-out rock formation that loomed over the western edge of the 201st base. It was probably 1,500 feet high, the mother of all buttes. Up there, Gunn knew the air would be fresh and cool.

He skirted the 201st base on his way, looking down on the camouflaged facilities and marveling how they blended so completely into the landscape. Even the three large hangars set apart from everything else seemed to fade into the terrain the higher he got. *If the base itself was crazy*, he thought, *what the hell was inside those things?*

The trip up to the mesa didn't take more than three minutes. He set down on the edge of the formation and killed the copter's engine. Then he climbed out and just listened. It was a cool night, not cold, and the slight wind served to blow a little normalcy back into him.

And except for that wind, it was totally silent. Just what he needed.

He walked to the edge of the mesa and looked off into the distance. To the east, nothing but desert and stars. To the west, mountains—and more stars. On the southern horizon, just barely discernible, a slight pinkish glow. *Vegas*, he thought. Money, wine, women, and song.

It might as well have been on another planet.

He sat down on the edge of the precipice and let his feet dangle over the side. More lights, to the southwest. That would be Groom Lake, Area 51, he was sure. The most famous "secret" base in the world. He'd heard talk around Edwards that the reason Groom Lake was so well-known was that the government actually encouraged publicizing it, to throw people off the track of the *really* weird stuff hidden even deeper in the desert.

Gunn had always thought it was just that—talk. He knew personally that there were a handful of other secret bases in Florida, California, and Arizona. Just about all of them had to do with aircraft and/or space systems testing—and he'd assumed all along that Groom Lake was the same.

But now, after spending just a day out here, in the deep, deep Nevada desert, he was beginning to think the rumor about Area 51 being some sort of clever deflection might be true.

As if to confirm this, something very weird went flittering over his head, maybe 500 feet up, heading north. It looked like a flying shoehorn, with wings. A kind of greenish tinge to it, making a slight whizzing sound. It turned east, then west, a slow, smooth maneuver before returning to its original heading, its blunted nose pointed to someplace even deeper in the range.

As he watched this thing disappear, Gunn spotted another object moving east, up higher, a deep blue shape. Then off to the west, where he imagined the quasi-secret town of Tonopah would be, another something—a spy balloon perhaps, moving slowly but surely, for all the world looking like a "true" flying saucer.

Gunn just laughed to himself.

What the hell am I doing out here?

That's when he heard the sound. In the absolute still of the desert night, he heard rocks moving, close by.

He froze. What could be way up here? No animals, he was sure. Birds, then? Buzzards?

He hadn't seen any flying around in the time he'd been here.

But who knew?

He turned his head slowly, trying to ascertain the direction of the noise. Rocks were falling, and a soft grunting noise.

What the hell?

Suddenly, not six feet away, he saw first one hand, then two appear on the edge of the precipice.

Before Gunn could react, someone dressed all in black, scrambled up onto the flattened-out peak.

Gunn just sat there open-mouthed. The person looked up at him, pulling off a wool cap.

It was Amanda O'Rourke. Commander of the Jump Plane.

She was just as surprised to see him as he was to see her.

He helped her to her feet. "You *climbed* up here?" he asked her, astonished.

She dusted herself off. She was dressed in tight black pants, a very tight top, and black climbing boots and gloves.

"Yes, I did," she replied, all business. "I find it relieves stress, and it's only a 1,500-foot ascent."

She looked around the summit. "Why? How did you get up here?"

Only then did she spot the Flying Egg, hidden in the shadows.

"I took the easy way," Gunn finally confessed.

She smiled at him, a bit of self-satisfaction. "Don't worry, I won't tell."

He sat back down and she sat beside him, maybe five feet away. This was their first meeting as well; he'd only seen her from afar before this. But if anything, she was even more beautiful up close.

"Nice view," she said. She was barely out of breath, despite the long climb.

"Hard to beat," he replied. "Makes all the nuttiness down there seem far away."

She nodded, as if she was searching for the next thing to say.

"So, how do you like driving the '17?" she asked finally. "Quite an airframe."

"I hate it," Gunn replied quickly.

This made her laugh for real. "Me, too. What did you fly before this? F-15s?"

"And '117s," he said. "And just about everything at Edwards."

"Test pilot? I'm impressed . . ."

He nodded. "Gives me something to do. But of course, my picture isn't in every magazine under the sun." Hers was the first personnel file he'd read.

She waved the comment away.

"That's my pension," she said. "And a way I can help my mom buy a nice house and be comfortable. It's nothing more than that."

Gunn thought the answer sounded a little too rehearsed, but he was sure she heard this stuff all the time.

Just then another weird thing flew over the mesa. This one looked like a small, high-tech version of the old P-38 twin-boom fighter of World War II fame. It was glowing orange.

"Look at that," she said as it swept over their heads, heading north. "I hope that's some kind of UAV they're testing out here. If not, we might be getting invaded by Martians."

"I've been flying since I was twelve years old," he said. "I've never seen anything like that—or what I spotted flying in last night. I mean, I've heard those rumors that the government has UFOs hidden out here and are flying them around. But who knows?"

"That *better not* be true," she said, with some good humor. "I've spent half my life going to school, studying twenty-four hours a day, missing out on what other people experience, just to get into space on the shuttle. If someone at Area 51 can do the same thing just by flicking a switch—then there's going to be trouble."

He laughed at her response and they exchanged an impromptu high five.

"I'm on the short list for *Orion* training," he revealed. "So, I'll go down there and mix it up with you."

"*Orion*? Nice duty," she said. "Will this little adventure put that on the skids?"

"Will it wreck yours?" he asked her back.

She shrugged; he shrugged. There was no way of knowing. He thought he detected her moving a little closer to him.

"We're giving up a lot to do this crazy 201st thing," she said finally.

They both looked up at the star-filled sky. It was brilliant and dazzling, but seemed an eternity away.

There was a long silence, then she said: "I'm supposed to be out there, you know? Not in this mess down here."

Gunn never stopped looking at the heavens.

"So am I," he said.

CHAPTER 9

Pershi-wan training site, Pakistan

The twelve helicopters flew over in a perfect line formation, then landed, one by one, with incredible precision.

No sooner had they touched the ground when their doors flew open and dozens of heavily armed soldiers came streaming out of their holds.

These soldiers hit the ground running, spreading out over the obstacle-laden training field, firing their weapons with the same exactness as the landing of their helicopters.

Two hundred feet from where the copters set down there was an enormous artificial rock-face wall. The soldiers rushed ahead, dodging real explosions and leaping over tangled bales of barbed wire, intent on reaching this rock wall and scaling it.

Within fifty feet of the wall, a dozen soldiers in red armbands pulled ahead of the rest. This advance team stopped exactly fifteen feet short of the wall and deployed a series of small mortars. As they started pulling the triggers on these devices, long streams of bright orange ropes with three-prong hooks on their ends came shooting out of their tubes. The ropes flew high into the air, all of them reaching the top of the artificial rock face and hooking into the soft ground beyond.

Not missing a beat, the main core of soldiers hit these ropes at full speed, scaling the artificial wall with the verve of circus acrobats. The entire force, more than 240 soldiers, was on the top of the wall in less than a minute. Once there, they began setting up heavy weapons, which some had carried piece by piece on their backs. They put together this weaponry with the skill of watchmakers, each man connecting his part to the whole until the weapon was complete: a heavy mortar, a 50-caliber machine gun, a miniature artillery piece. Inside of two minutes the elite force was wielding as much firepower as a small army.

Half the unit stayed with the heavy weapons, the others began running again, now along the flat plain on the other side of the rock face. Before them was a series of stone houses. The soldiers fired their weapons again with incredible accuracy and assaulted these structures without losing a step. They went through them like a wave, some soldiers staying to occupy the "enemy" positions while the rest of the force kept rushing forward.

Watching all this from a wooden tower overlooking the training field was Colonel Zin Zima. He was commanding officer of this elite unit. They were officially known as Attack Section 21. They were the crème de la crème of the Pakistani Army's Special Forces.

Zima's unit was considered to be the best of its type in this part of the world; they were heads above anything fielded by any other country in the Persian Gulf or the subcontinent. Specialists from the British SAS and the Chinese Special Forces had trained Section 21. They used the latest in French and German weaponry. Their helicopters were Hip-8s, the best rotary aircraft ever built by the Russians. Though few in number, Zima's men were both feared and respected throughout the region.

As the unit continued on to attack "enemy" soldiers holed up in a bus on a deserted road, one of Zima's junior officers climbed up the observation tower's wooden ladder. He passed Zima a message. It contained still-secret details of the unsuccessful attempt by the UNIFOR troops to rescue the USAID hostages being held inside Bora Kurd.

Zima was not surprised to read the communiqué.

"So, the UN has failed again," he said. "No big shock there. And our national police want no part of this. And the Americans are too busy to do anything—even if they are aware of the situation yet, which I'm not too sure they are, at least at the highest levels."

He watched as the remainder of his force moved beyond the bus and commenced assaulting an empty jetliner.

"No matter," he went on. "We will do what the Americans can't or just don't want to do."

He looked out at his prized troops again.

"In fact, if we do it first thing in the morning," he said, "we'll have the hostages back by noon."

Bora Kurd

Anne Murphy was awakened by the sound of the bolt being slid back on the outside of her cell door.

She was instantly frozen in fear. They were coming for her this time, she just knew it. A hideous, excruciating death was just moments away.

Crawling into the corner farthest from the door, she began wailing uncontrollably. She thought of her husband, her kids. Her parents. All the things she'd left behind in America. *What a waste my life has been,* she cried inside. *What a waste to have it end like this.*

The door opened. She let out a loud yelp. The shadow of a large man came right across the floor and covered her. She recognized him as the terrorist who always seemed to be the one who dragged the victims out to their slaughter. She screamed again—but the man did not come in. Instead, he dropped a tin plate of food to the dirty floor and slammed the door shut again.

It took Anne a long time before she had the courage to crawl across the cell and inspect the plate of food. It contained a spoonful of soggy rice, a small ball of yogurt, and a few raw beans. It smelled awful, and there were no utensils or anything to drink. Still, Anne gorged herself on the tiny meal, eating it animal-like with her hands.

The food was gone in just a few seconds and she immediately felt sick to her stomach. She prayed that the nausea would pass, her fears that she'd been poisoned almost overwhelming her. It took a while, but finally her insides quieted down. She gathered herself up and sat against the door again, the warmest part of the cell. For the first time since the nightmare began, everything inside her head quieted down.

But not for long.

She heard that familiar sound again—a bolt opening on a cell door. It was not her door, rather it was on the cell next to her, where her colleague and best friend on the USAID education team, Connie Perez, was being kept.

Anne began shaking again at the sound of it. She pulled herself up the door, putting her eyes against the tiny slit. What she saw were her worst fears come true: The terrorists were dragging Connie out. She was battling them mightily, wailing for her husband as they brutally kicked and beat her. She was pulled over under the harsh camera lights and the handful of ski-masked terrorists appeared again, as if on cue.

The boss terrorist took his place in the middle of the line and kept his booted foot on Connie's neck to keep her down while he read his message praising Allah and denouncing the United States.

Connie's wails only increased when the man stopped reading finally. That's when his hand reached inside his shirt and came out with the machete. It was still bloody from the previous execution. The terrorist leader began hacking at Connie's neck, but she was trying to get away and he wound up slicing up her back and shoulders. Finally two of the other terrorists had to pull her back under the lights and hold her as the top man resumed his gruesome work. Connie screamed to the very end—only when her head came off her body did her wails seem to finally die away. The terrorists cheered and praised Allah loudly, then the movie lights were shut off again.

Anne Murphy did not watch the entire execution—she knew by now it was best to close her eyes and block her ears.

But this time it did no good. She vomited up her sparse meal immediately. Even worse, she imagined she could still hear Connie screaming, ever after she was gone.

But then, another noise . . .

Deep, faraway, but definitely mechanical.

She crawled over to the far wall and squeezed herself up against the tiny air vent. She lifted the piece of thin metal and felt the cold air rush in. Putting her eye as close as possible to the tiny hole, she looked out at the world beyond her cell.

It was a cloudy, dank morning, but in the direction she assumed was north, she was just able to make out a dozen tiny specks against the gray, gloomy sky.

Her mind began racing. She began gasping for breath.

She thought: *Are those . . . helicopters?*

COLONEL Zima and the members of Attack Section 21 were too smart to repeat the same mistake made by the UN troops.

The UN soldiers had been brave but amateurish. They knew nothing of the dangers of Bora Kurd—its reputation for sinister doings in the area and its atmosphere of bad luck. The UN had also been foolish to attack the mountain from the ground. The surface roads in the area were all in bad shape, susceptible to the unpredictable weather and mudslides and all within full view of anyone with so much as a pair of binoculars up on the mountain.

Therefore, the fate of the UN troops was sealed before they got within a half mile of the fortress. The terrorists had seen the Blue Hats coming and had silently trained their guns on the would-be rescuers, wiping them out in a few horrifying seconds. Their bodies still littered the muddy road where they fell. Stripped of their weapons and boots, they'd been left for the birds.

Colonel Zima knew all this. He also knew the only way to properly assault the mountain was from the air. To this end his squadron of helicopters was now approaching Bora Kurd, armed and ready for action.

The morning clouds were a perfect cover for the elite assault group. As usual, a dark fog surrounded most of Bora Kurd, especially around its bottom. The wind was blowing to the east, though, meaning that once Attack Section 21 got close enough, the racket their copters usually made would be somewhat muted.

Zima's plan was simple. The Hip-8 copters would swoop in at high speed and drop off their troops just below the summit of the mountain. The copters would then turn into gunships and prepare to suppress any hostile fire coming from the terrorists. The Attack Section 21 soldiers were so well trained, they could dismount from the aircraft within seconds, giving the gunships time to get into the best firing positions—and giving the PKD terrorists almost no time to react.

Once the troops were off the copters they would assault a number of key terrorist gun positions, quickly knocking them out. Zima's intelligence officers had provided him with a list of weapons the terrorists had in place—information they'd boasted had come from the very highest of sources within the Chinese Special Forces. Their largest weapons were believed to be 57-mm artillery pieces. The PKD was known to have hundreds of AK-47s, RPG launchers, and Katyusha rockets. Zima's men knew they could find any of these weapons waiting for them in their assault. But aside from a well-aimed RPG, nothing else could be used very effectively against aircraft, especially helicopters. Zima realized he might take some losses, but he was also confident they would be low.

His drop-and-assault strategy was two-pronged. His men first had to kill the gun positions—but *then* they had to gain entrance to the mountain itself. But again, here Zima was confident. There were twelve copters in the assault force; each contained twenty heavily armed troops. Even if only half the soldiers succeeded in penetrating the terrorist fortress, this meant more than 100 well-trained troops would be assaulting the PKD before the terrorists knew what hit them.

The key was not to sneak up on the mountain flying at low level; this would play into the terrorists' hands. The attack team's helicopters were heavily modified not just in the weapons they carried, but also in the engines they employed. They were fitted with superchargers and their cabins were pressurized. This meant the copters could fly higher than typical rotary aircraft. And this meant instead of approaching the mountain from the ground level up, they could attack it from high altitude on down.

The direction least likely to be suspected by the terrorists.

The dozen copters were approaching now from the altitude of 15,000 feet, again high for rotary craft. The lead Hip-8 was carrying Colonel Zima. His copter would serve as the unit's command aircraft. It was also outfitted with advanced navigation and communications equipment. This copter's navigation operator had pinpointed the exact course to the mountain while the attack force was still forty miles away. The force approached in strict radio silence, but it could still communicate by blinking its navigation lights in Morse code, a trick taught to it by the British SAS.

At four miles out, Colonel Zima gave the signal that the attack force should start descending.

This was an important moment for Zima and his men. Like everything else in the military, his group was subject to constant scrutiny by government officials and by Army higher-ups who were entrenched in the Pakistani national government. Interservice rivalry was their biggest concern, along with infiltration by people who might be religious fanatics and thus sympathetic to the PKD, or might simply be in their employ. But Zima was certain there were no traitors in his group.

Still, this was their biggest mission ever, and it was important that they all perform well today. To do so would not only guarantee their existence, but would also mean that Attack Section 21 would become a permanent fixture in the Pakistani military structure. And there was another reason that taking out this huge PKD faction and their hiding place would be a huge coup for them: It took Zima a long time to convince his government's officials that taking on the PKD and other al-Qaeda groups operating in Pakistan was in the country's best interests. A victory here would prove his point: that Pakistanis could do what the Americans, NATO, and the UN could not. That is, carry out a large operation against the local terrorists and win.

At three miles out the attack squadron broke into two groups. One group headed in a westerly direction, the other maintained a northerly route. They would attack in a pincer movement, further confusing the terrorists.

At two miles out Zima signaled that all troops should check their weapons and be ready to disembark. It was a calculated risk, not going in all guns blazing, but Zima was certain he would catch the terrorists off guard by being quiet, by attacking vertically, and only firing once the majority of his troops had landed.

At one mile out and just about a half-mile above the peak, Zima gave the final order: "Attack and Allah be with you!"

The copters in both groups went into severe spiraling dives, descending rapidly toward the mountain. The fog was clearing slightly, which aided them. The huge mountain loomed especially large in front of Zima's command copter. It was the closest he or anyone on his aircraft had even been to the haunted peak—and it did look intimidating.

But this could not deter them. They pushed on.

At a half mile out, Zima saw what he thought was poetry in motion. His copters were now spread out and diving on the foreboding peak from practically every direction, heading for the gun emplacements just as the plan said they should. He felt pride well up in his chest for his men and especially his pilots. They were elite. This proved it.

Then he saw the first explosion.

Then the second . . .

. . . and the third.

They were just puffs of smoke at first, all the way over near the south end of the mountain. But then Zima saw streaks of fire coming up from the mountain itself—and more aerial explosions. It was all happening so fast, he didn't know what to make of it at first.

But within seconds it became all too clear, The explosions were his helicopters being hit by the terrorists. Not by AK-47s or RPGs—but by antiaircraft missiles.

In fact, so many missiles were streaking up from all sides of the mountain, the air was suddenly full with long white smoky contrails. The missiles were picking off the copters in such a sickeningly routine fashion, Zima didn't have any time to react. His prized choppers were falling from the sky like dead, wingless birds. That's when he realized these were not just lucky shots the terrorists were taking. These missiles were radar-guided. Sophisticated. Entirely unexpected.

As it turned out, Zima's copter was the last one to be hit. Just as he had ordered his pilot to turn away and leave the area quickly, a missile struck the copter square on the rotor mast, blowing it to pieces.

In his dying moments, Zima knew that his intelligence officers had been misled by their so-called Chinese allies. Up to that point, no one who had studied the PKD believed they had anything more than a large arsenal in heavy battlefield weapons and some long-range artillery.

But the sad truth now was that in addition to all that firepower, the PKD terrorists also had SAMs.

ANNE Murphy saw it all.

The copters' near-silent approach. Their almost exquisite attack formation. Their mad dive down toward the mountain. She knew instantly that they were a much bigger, a much more organized force than the UN soldiers who had attempted a rescue earlier.

But she also saw the copters suddenly explode in the sky one by one—and with each one went down her hopes of ever making it out of this hell of captivity alive.

She crumpled to the cold, smelly, hard floor when she saw the last helicopter get hit and crash in flames.

She started crying again, saying over and over: "Who will rescue us now?"

CHAPTER 10

Nevada

It was Amanda who finally convinced Gunn to get some sleep.

They'd spent more than an hour up on the butte, just looking at the stars, talking some, but comfortable, too, when they were silent. Around midnight, Gunn finally flew them back down to the base. Amanda helped him push Newman's copter back into its small hangar and secure its main systems.

That's when she told him, sweetly, that he looked terrible. His eyes were red; his hair was a mess. He needed a shave. He'd been up for nearly two days now and he couldn't possibly do any more work. She suggested it was time to get some zees.

"Get a good five hours," she told him, briefly touching his forehead to make sure he didn't have a fever. "You're really no use to us unless you do."

He bid her a very restrained, polite good night, briefly shaking her hand and promising to take her advice. And then, she was gone, disappearing into the dark, returning to her own quarters.

Gunn staggered back to his billet and collapsed onto his bunk. The coffee he'd drown himself in at Jacks hoping to stay awake had burned him out instead. It was a blessing though. Sleep deprivation could cause hallucinations and abnormal behavior. No shape to be in around one of the most beautiful women he'd ever set eyes on.

So, he had all the right reasons to go into a deep sleep and stay that way until at least 0500 hours the next morning.

Strange then that his slumber didn't last a half hour.

He woke up with a start, smashing his head against the concrete wall next to his bunk, and then falling off the bunk completely, cracking his knee on the hard floor.

He opened up a gash on his head and a bloody slice on his knee. But none of this mattered. Because in those few minutes of unconsciousness, somehow, someway, Gunn had figured out what the 201st was doing wrong.

IT didn't come to him in a dream—that would have been almost too perfect.

Instead it came to him as one of many stray, seemingly unconnected thoughts that were going through his head as he drifted off, this, even though his body was literally shaking from all the caffeine he'd ingested. The weird thing was, this stray thought really had nothing to do with the 201st, or the Nevada desert, or C-17s, UFOs, or his beautiful fellow pilot, Amanda O'Rourke.

Strangely enough, it had to do with his barmaid friend, the waitress at the Astro Bar, and how she used to beat him at computer games. How did she manage to kick his ass *every* time? He wasn't a moron, he flew experimental jet fighters for a living. Just by the law of averages, it would seem he would have won at least a few times. The odd notion that went shooting through his head, something that didn't happen, but that he *imagined* had, was that she confessed to him that she'd gone into the game's software every time just before he arrived at her house, changed a few things around internally, essentially altering the rules of the game in her favor.

That was it. Not even a dream. Just a ghost of a dream.

But it was all he needed.

Gunn sat on the floor of his billet, rubbing the bonk on his head and the gash on his knee and realized, at that moment, he had the answer to their problems.

He started scrambling. Back into his boots, back into his pants and jacket. The next thing he knew he was out of his billet and running down the middle of the dark and gigantic runway, heading at top speed for the Ops Building.

He had to talk to Newman immediately.

HE reached the Ops building, only to find the door locked.

Locked? he thought anxiously. *Why the fuck would it be locked?*

He began pounding on the door, a useless exercise, he was sure.

But then a surprise. Someone opened the door.

It wasn't Newman. Instead it was the same pretty young corporal who had greeted him the first time he'd walked into this building, something that seemed like a million years ago. She greeted him correctly, with a sharp salute, but her face showed much puzzlement. She was the only one in the big ops room, she quickly explained, because everyone else was either out carrying full packs over the hills, washing the C-17s, or asleep. She'd come in just to check if any important e-mails had arrived in the past few hours.

"Where's the colonel then?" Gunn asked her. What was inside his head was still dreamlike—and he had to retain it as long as he could, before it stopped making sense.

"He's not in his office," she replied. "Though he might have been there earlier. I see that he's out of coffee. And his copter is gone."

Christ, could Newman have gone down to Jacks for the same reason Gunn had? To get a caffeine fix? If so, he must have taken the copter out just minutes after Gunn and Amanda had put it to bed.

The pretty corporal made a quick call down to the R&R station. But no one had seen Newman in the last twenty-four hours.

"Is there any other place he could be?" Gunn asked her.

She thought a moment, her face suddenly worried. "If things

have gone wrong, and I mean, *really* wrong, he does have a spot he goes, just to get away from it all."

"Where is it?" Gunn asked her anxiously. "How do I get there?"

She hastily wrote down some coordinates on a piece of scrap paper and handed it to him.

"That's the location," she said.

Gunn stared at the numbers. "But how will I find this?"

"Take any Hummer outside," she told him. "They're all equipped with GPS. Just punch in those numbers and it will take you right to him."

A minute later, Gunn was racing along the hard desert floor, driving a Hummer he'd found parked outside the ops building.

He'd snapped on the GPS and punched in the coordinates as instructed. What came back was a screen showing a spot out in the middle of the high desert about five miles north of the base.

He followed the readout's directions and within ten minutes of hard driving he was approaching the coordinate. The first thing he saw was the silhouette of Newman's little helicopter, backlit by flames leaping from somewhere on the other side of a small bluff. Gunn followed a rough dirt road up to this glow and there's where he found Newman, sitting beside a raging campfire. It was like a scene from a cowboy movie. The spot was on strategically high ground that gave him a commanding view of the vast desert beyond. A dim light behind the next set of hills was a hint that Jacks was over there somewhere. To the south, the even fainter glow of Las Vegas.

"You found me," Newman said watching Gunn drive up. "I thought this place was secret."

"Not from your staff," Gunn told him, climbing out of the Humvee. "Can I have a minute of your time, Colonel?"

Newman half laughed. "Sure, pull up a rock," he said.

Gunn sat down across the fire from him. Newman reached into a nearby bucket and came out with a cold Budweiser. He tossed it over to Gunn.

"God love the Navy," Newman said, indicating the pail of icy beer cans beside him. "Ask and you shall receive."

Gunn popped the beer and practically drained it all in one noisy gulp. Newman promptly threw him another and he drank that one almost as quickly.

Gunn burped, caught his breath, and was finally able to speak. He decided to start off slow. "Sir, I have a few ideas on how we might improve the situation with the unit."

"Really?" Newman asked. "I'd almost given up on anyone finding a solution."

"Well, you might still feel that way after listening to what I have to say," Gunn said. "But hear me out."

Newman contemplated the ragged end of his cigar. "Okay," he said. "But I must warn you, it might be too little too late."

Gunn stopped in mid-gulp. "'Too late'? Why, sir?"

Suddenly, Newman looked like someone had let all the air out of him.

"Sometime within the next forty-eight hours," he began, "a congressional fact-finding committee is going to pay us a surprise visit. These are the people who hold the purse strings for our little enterprise, and for reasons I can't get into right now, we are not their favorite people. Suffice it to say, they'll want a demonstration, and if things go the way they've been going, it will end in a major league fuckup of some sort, and maybe another fistfight, and we'll all be back to dodging road bombs in Mesopotamia or someplace worse."

Gunn was mildly shocked to hear this news. Even stranger was hearing Newman talk about something not in the positive. He was stern, a taskmaster, for sure, but he was also immensely self-confident and likable. To see him so disheartened was a little unnerving.

But Gunn was also a little confused. "If it's a surprise visit," he asked, "how do you know these people are coming?"

Newman tried to relight what was left of his cigar. "A little bird told me—a bird who's plugged more holes in Washington than JFK did. They're coming out for our funeral, is what it is. And that will mean a lot of hard work and effort down the drain—not to mention a big break for the warlord mullahs who we were supposed to be going after. Those Muslim freaks will have a free rein now, and God knows what will happen next. I'm not a conspiracy nut, but I swear some-times, I think that's exactly what those assholes in D.C. want."

Newman finally managed to get his stogie going again. He peered over at Gunn, who must have looked totally shocked.

"But, okay," he said, puffing away like a condemned man who'd accepted his fate. "I brought you here to straighten out this mess. Far be it from me not to let you present your solu-tion. Plus, I'll get hell from Edwards if we dragged you out here for nothing. So, let's have it . . ."

Gunn guzzled another beer even quicker now. Nothing like a little pressure to make the suds go down faster.

He began by saying, "Let me ask a question first, if I may. I realize this is an interservice operation. But why are the ser-vices so mixed up?"

"It was the congressional mandate," Newman replied. "We had to hide our funding to make it look like what we were do-ing out here was some grand interservice bonding mission. Navy interacting with Army jumpers, Air Force interacting with Marine armor. All of us sitting around singing 'Kum-baya.' As the personnel started streaming in, we assigned them airplanes and crews. That's the way the spec was writ-ten, to see if interservice units could be thrown together and still think on their feet."

Gunn nodded slowly. "Well, therein lies one problem," he said. "We've got the right players, they're just playing the wrong game. But, the good news is, it's something we can solve with one move."

Newman almost laughed. "You'll need to translate that for me," he said.

"It's really simple, Colonel," Gunn explained. "You see, I don't think it's the airplanes that are screwing everything up. And it's not even the pilots. It's the airplanes that we've got the pilots flying."

Newman stopped in mid-puff. "I'm still not getting it . . ."

Gunn said, "Okay, let's start with Elvis. Because he's a Harrier pilot, he's used to going slow. I mean, driving a jump jet is half about floating anyway, especially when landing. Going slow. That's what *he's* good at. On the other hand, Amanda is used to banging in. Landing on the deck of a carrier is all about controlled crashes. That's what *she's* good at: going fast—and then coming to a stop, toot sweet."

Newman thought a moment. "So?"

"So, let's switch them around," Gunn said. "Put the beauty queen in the tank plane—the one that has to bang in. And put Elvis in the Jump Plane, the one that has to float."

Newman immediately scoffed. "You're saying all we have to do is switch the pilots?"

Gunn nodded. "No—we've got tons more to do. But, I think that's where we start."

Newman thought about it a moment then puffed his cigar with just a little more verve. "And how about you? What changes do you have for the Fireship?"

"Just one," Gunn replied. "During a mission, there shouldn't be a pilot and copilot. We should take a page from the book of the B-2 Stealth bomber. They have a pilot and an airplane commander. The pilot flies the plane; the commander does everything else. Adopt that with the Fireship. If my copilot just flies the plane, then I can keep an eye on what needs to be done."

Newman flicked the ashes off the end of his cigar. "God, there's no way it can be that easy," he said.

"Well, again it isn't," Gunn cautioned. "That's just the beginning." He thought a moment, then asked, "When is the congressional party coming in?"

Newman looked pained to even hear those words. "What I'm hearing is day after tomorrow," he said. "And even if we were lucky, we couldn't get more than three or four exercises in before then."

Gunn just smiled. The beer was taking effect. "That's okay," he said. "We won't have to."

Newman nearly fell off his rock. "What? You want us to look bad, is that it?"

Gunn shook his head.

"What I want is everyone to read a new playbook," he said. "They already have enough training and skill to do what has to be done. It's just up to us to move it all in a different direction."

"Meaning?"

"Bottom line: We've been playing by the spec ops," Gunn

said. "And spec ops are like the rules they build into a video game. Everything goes in a predetermined way. But if you manipulate the rules, if you get in there and change them around, you can manipulate the outcome of the game."

Newman ran his hands over his tired head. "Once again, can I have that in English, Major?"

Gunn pulled his jacket collar up around his neck.

"I'll tell you what, Colonel," he said. "If I could trouble you for another beer, I'll be glad to start at the beginning . . ."

CHAPTER 11

The next night

It had been a relaxing two days for OpFor 4.

As anticipated, the 150-man unit did little but eat, sleep, watch TV, and drink Navy beer during the enforced stand-down. The weather had been typically hot, but not unpleasant, and the food train from Jacks had rolled on nonstop.

Mullah Sledge had spent most of his waking hours sitting in an old wooden chair just outside the fake mosque, drinking beer and reading Tijuana porn magazines brought in from San Diego by the squids. His only interruptions were a few cell phone conversations he'd had with his connected friends back in Washington. The majority of his men were dispersed throughout the CSMC, either inside their air-conditioned tents, or taking up residence in the couple dozen stone huts—also AC-equipped—that made up the false Iraqi village. The only noise to be heard, besides their diesel generators, was the wind and the occasional cry of a coyote, baying in the distance.

Three of Sledge's men had stayed with him in the mosque. Two had kept an eye on the NLR power packs and monitored e-mails; the third had remained stationed up in the mosque's minaret. The only OpFor 4 guys who were technically on duty, though, were the ten soldiers who'd pulled the short straws and were now dispersed along the edge of the fake village, manning a handful of video-monitoring stations. Called "varmint-cams," they watched for any wild animals—coyotes and foxes, mostly—that might wander into the CSMC village and trip off its closed circuit intruder alarms. Watching the varmint-cams was boring but necessary duty as resetting the closed circuit alarms was a time-consuming and labor-intensive affair.

THE second day turned into night.

Sledge had fallen asleep in his chair in the late afternoon, awakened only when a bit of sand hit his face as it blew by. He yawned mightily now and stretched his lazy bones. The sky above was clear, the stars were just coming out. A perfect evening to drink more beer and maybe grab a porn movie off satellite TV. He knew there'd be no exercise tonight, not just because the 201st was still on flight status stand-down, but because OpFor 4 always monitored communications traffic from the 201st secret base nearby, and it had been quiet over there all day. Sledge was sure the 201st was just as glad as he that they could stay in place again tonight. Why be embarrassed again if you didn't have to be?

Actually, Sledge suspected the whole 201st experiment might already be over and that the unit would never come knocking again. Why? Because one of his D.C. contacts had told him earlier in the day that things were going so badly for the 201st, the unit was about to be dismantled permanently, maybe even sometime in the next twenty-four hours.

"What will we do then?" Sledge mused.

His thoughts were interrupted by two of his men hurrying up to the mosque. They were part of the short-straw patrol watching the village's anti-varmint TVs.

"We got something strange happening, boss," one said.

Sledge checked the time. It was just about 2100 hours; the sun had gone down thirty minutes before.

"Strange how?" he asked them, with another yawn.

"Better that we show you," one man replied.

A few minutes later, Sledge and the two men were walking on the eastern outskirts of the faux battlefield. They stopped at one of the many hidden closed-circuit TV stations that ringed the CSMC. This one was located in a box next to a fence post that looked a couple hundred years old. Night had fallen completely by this time.

"This remote TV picked up something a few minutes ago," one of the men reported, rewinding the TV's DVR system. "And it wasn't no coyote. We caught it on the hard drive."

"Let's see it, then," Sledge said.

The tape began—and it was eerie from the start. The TV screen showed a long expanse of flat, dark desert, green-tinged as the camera's rudimentary night vision capability kicked in. This static scene was suddenly interrupted by two dark figures that seemed to materialize out of nowhere. Distorted by the grainy night vision image, the pair appeared to be dressed head-to-toe in black suits and to possess huge bulging eyes, and maybe even weird clawlike hands.

Sledge was stunned. "What the hell is this? A joke?"

"It's the straight shit, boss," one of his soldiers said. "We got no idea what to make of it."

The two figures moved so oddly, they looked like characters from an alien invasion movie. Or were they maybe the real thing?

In all his time out in the desert, Sledge had never seen anything so weird. He immediately ordered one of his men to call down to Area 51 to see if they had anything classified—flying *or* walking—up in this part of the desert tonight. The answer came back a resounding *no*.

But it only got weirder after the phone call. As Sledge and his men watched, the two figures seemed to dig a shallow hole in the desert floor and bury something in it. Then like ghosts they moved farther down the bare ground and did the same thing. Another shallow hole dug, something else buried, but just barely. They did this six more times. Then both figures looked to the sky—and suddenly, they were gone. Drawn up into the night, again like something from a sci-fi movie.

Sledge was almost speechless. "What's going on here?"

Both men just shrugged anxiously. "We told you it was freaky, boss," one said.

The actual piece of ground where the figures were spotted was about a quarter mile farther out in the desert. Sledge was a war vet, so were his men, but none of them really wanted to do what they had to do next—go out into that dark night and check out exactly what the TV camera had picked up.

"You guys ain't carrying for real, are you?" Sledge asked his soldiers. They both shook their heads. Neither of them was armed with a real gun, just their NLR weapons.

"That's just fucking great," Sledge murmured.

They started out, very carefully, moving as quietly as possible. The night turned very still and windless, only adding to their anxiety. So much so, when a thrush suddenly flew by them, all three were startled enough to hit the deck.

They finally reached the spot where the figures had been picked up by the camera, but they couldn't find even a single footprint. Did the wind blow them away? But how could that be, if there was no wind?

This part of the CSMC's area was hardly ever used, simply because its topography was too flat. Western Iraq was rugged and irregular, wind-blown and rocky. This area mostly resembled a narrow, dry lake bed. Again, it was close to the eastern edge of the combat module, but except for the varmint-cams, it was a place totally ignored by OpFor 4. So why would anyone be out here?

It took them a while, but they finally located one of the filled-in holes where they'd seen the two figures bury something. They started digging, again, carefully.

After a few seconds of scratching, they found what they were looking for. It was about the size of a D-cell battery, wrapped tightly in what looked to be dozens of pieces of aluminum foil. It was cold to the touch, but it seemed so innocuous Sledge really didn't believe this was what they saw the figures burying.

But then they found another one. Same thing—about the size of a D-battery, wrapped tightly in foil, cold to the touch. Then another, and another.

Finally Sledge stood over the spot where the first object was discovered, and instructed his men to stand where the last two were found. It was hard to get a good view in the dark, but when they were in place, they realized they were standing in a perfectly straight line.

That's when they heard a muffled scream.

They immediately hit the ground again, their NLR weapons up. Then Sledge saw something moving in a ditch nearby. He looked closer and realized it was two of the training range's referees, sitting back to back, in the sand, in the dark.

"Am I seeing things?" he wondered aloud.

He and his men moved toward them carefully. Only when they got close did they realize the refs were bound hands and feet with rope and had duct tape over their mouths.

Sledge's men quickly untied them.

"What the fuck is going on?" Sledge barked at the two men.

But the refs didn't answer. They couldn't. All they could do was point to a spot in the sky over Sledge's left shoulder. Sledge and his men turned in that direction—and were shocked to see what the referees saw.

A C-17 was coming right at them.

All three had to duck as the huge airplane went over them, its wheels down, landing not 100 feet away.

Again Sledge screamed: *"What the fuck?"*

Even as the C-17 was touching down, he could see its huge rear-end ramp opening. The plane screeched to a stop in just another 100 feet and a moment after that, two tanks came charging out of its cargo hold, hitting the desert floor in an explosion of dust and exhaust.

Sledge tried to say something, but nothing would come out. He was speechless. This didn't make any sense. This was nowhere near the place where the 201st airplane was designated to set down during the exercises. And besides, the 201st wasn't even supposed to be flying! One of his men screamed at the referees, "Those assholes are on stand-down!"

"Why bitch to us?" one ref bellowed back, as he and his colleague finished untying themselves. "Those assholes accosted us and tied us up out here!"

But then, more trouble. One of Sledge's men spun him

around and pointed to the faux village about a quarter mile away.

"Jesus—boss, look!"

To Sledge's astonishment, a second C-17 was passing over the fake village, going very, very slowly. As he watched, the door on the side of the big cargo plane opened up and suddenly the sky was full of paratroopers. They were coming down fast, and all in one spot.

"Bastards . . ." Sledge breathed. *"Cheating bastards!"*

Sledge grabbed his two men and began running, leaving the referees to fend for themselves. They ran as fast as they could along the ditch and across the thorn-covered flat land, giving wide berth to the landed C-17 and the pair of tanks, which were now blasting everything in sight as the airplane kept crawling along, right behind them.

Sledge had to get back to the mosque, and running through this open area was his only chance. But halfway across the shortcut, he felt a strange sensation on his arm. It was burning, like he'd been shot with an NLR. Rubbing his arm fitfully, his first thought was that his own weapon had gone off.

But then he looked straight up and saw a single stream of red NLR beams coming down at him. He hit the ground and rolled up to a nearby stone wall, his men crashing into him a second later. The beam went over them, and kept on going, only to hit some of the OpFor 4 guys who had been sleeping in the fake village's cool stone huts nearby and had been awakened by the sudden arrival of the first C-17. Other single beams were coming down deeper inside the village as well, like so many fingers of intensely bright light, moving around, probing everywhere. Many of the soldiers caught in the painful glows began to panic. The NLR beams were so powerful, they seemed to be knocking some of these men right off their feet.

It took a moment for Sledge to realize what was happening—but then it became all too clear: The huge Fireship was right above them. Flying very low, very quietly and very deliberately, its gunners seemed to be targeting OpFor 4 soldiers individually, instead of using their typical blunderbuss approach. Incredibly, many of Sledge's men were being picked off one at a time with high-powered precision bursts.

The 201st paratroopers were landing everywhere now; many were firing their NLRs at Sledge's men who'd been sleeping in their air-conditioned tents at the opposite end of the faux village. None of these men had anything to return fire with. Most of OpFor 4's NLRs were back in the mosque on their rechargers. Trouble was, the tanks and the taxiing C-17 airplane were moving to cut off the building from the rest of the CSMC. The tanks were being especially aggressive, spraying their NLR beams back and forth like a scene from *War of the Worlds*.

This was madness. The rules said anyone hit in the head or chest with a direct NLR had to drop out of the battle as KIA. Anyone hit on their extremities could take up to three hits, then they had to become a casualty, no longer able to fight. In all the exercises combined, Sledge's men had not suffered more than a few KIA and only about a dozen casualties—mostly because the 201st never got very far, and if they did, few of Sledge's guys paid much attention to the three-hits-you're-out rule anyway. The truth was the NLRs, though painful, rarely penetrated the OpFor 4's thick Iraqi-style *salwar kameez* robes, especially from long range.

But now, the paratroopers were among the OpFor 4 soldiers and firing at them up close. And they were laying on the NLRs so thick, that their beams *were* penetrating the heavy clothing. They were causing so much pain, Sledge's guys were doing anything they could just to get the hell out of the way, including lying down, with their hands over their heads, and just plain giving up. In less than a minute, half of Sledge's force was out of the fight.

And still, there was not a referee in sight.

Meanwhile, Sledge remained trapped near the stone wall, trying his best not to be seen by the sharpshooters in the orbiting gunship. The situation was insane. It was also backward. The 201st landed their tanks first, setting them down in the most unexpected, yet, as it turned out, the most advantageous position possible, a kind of back door to the village. The suddenness of their arrival was enough of a distraction to allow the paratroopers to land—and Sledge was still astonished at how the Jump Plane had moved so slowly across the sky. Once the paratroopers came down, they immediately started pushing his men back toward the village—and in doing so, forced them out into the open. That's when the Fireship appeared and started hosing them one or two at a time. And those few OpFor soldiers making it through this gauntlet found their route back to the village blocked by the tanks and the taxiing C-17.

"Bastards," Sledge whispered bitterly. "They're not playing fair at all . . ."

It was strange because at that moment, Sledge reached into his pocket and came out holding one of the items he and his men had dug up at the beginning of this nightmare. It had become smaller and colder and wetter. He finally unwrapped the tinfoil to find inside the remnants of a simple ice cube.

Ice cubes? Sledge thought. "They marked the runway not with hot flares, but with ice cubes? Why?"

Then it hit him: The 201st used RIFs—reverse infrared. Instead of telegraphing where their tank plane was going to land with dozens of blazing flares, the 201st instead used their RIFs to greatest advantage, seeing cold instead of hot to demark the runway—and did so far away from where they had been landing every night for nearly two months.

"Bastards . . ." Sledge whispered again.

He couldn't stay where he was. He and his men had no other choice but to run through the cascades of NLRs raining down all around them and try to make it to the mosque. It would be painful—but it had to be done.

On his count, they jumped up and started running. Almost immediately it was like the wrath of God fell on them. All three got hit more than enough times to make them casualties, if not KIAs and out of the fight for good. But they kept on running.

They scrambled around the tanks, through another ditch, skirting the edge of the village and then up through a grove of scrub trees. This way they made it back to the mosque somehow, even though a tidal wave of paratroopers was on their heels. Sledge passed many of his men along the way and just about all of them were playing by the three-hits rule and cowering under anything to prevent them from getting blasted by more NLRs. Some of them yelled at Sledge as he rushed by, telling him the game was up and that he should come and hide with them. But Sledge couldn't. For many reasons he *had* to get back to the mosque.

Though he lost his two companions along the way, Sledge finally made it to the front door of the fake holy building. He screamed up to the man stationed in the minaret and told him to blow like crazy on his whistle; this was the retreat order for the rest of the OpFors. But it was the last thing that man was able to do. As soon as he started whistling, he was hit from all sides by NLRs being fired by the paratroopers. The man took so many hits he lost consciousness.

To Sledge's eyes, only those few OpFor 4 stragglers closest to the mosque were able to run back to it. He could see nothing but total confusion in their ranks. Apparently none of them could fathom what was going on. As they rushed past Sledge and stumbled through the mosque's front door, just about each one was mumbling the same thing: "This is fucking crazy!"

Sledge stood at the door, pushing them inside. Nothing like this had ever happened before. His immediate plan was to get inside the building and fire on the attackers, hoping they would never attack the mosque directly. At least, that was the thinking. But judging by the speed with which the 201st was advancing on them, Sledge doubted they were going to stop at the mosque's front door.

His so-called drop-dead strategy was to climb down into a space dug below the mosque—the mullah's hardened bomb shelter. There really was no other battle plan after that other than to stay hidden and hope for the best.

But it was also here that Sledge kept his secret weapon—though in a million years he never thought he'd actually have to use the thing. It was called a Zoot bomb, a holographic nuclear device. Technically it was a powerful electromagnetic generator, which when activated, dispensed a pulse so massive it could zap every electronic component, big and small, for miles around, causing anything electrical to cease functioning.

Or at least that's how Sledge thought it worked.

The question now was: Should he really trip this thing? It was here only because in the real warlord mullah scenario, there was always a chance that a Muslim leader might have a nuclear weapon or two hidden in his religious fort. And as these mullahs were supposed to be crazy, they would probably detonate the damn thing if they were cornered.

So, should he?

Would it prevent him from being blamed for this catastrophe? From getting embarrassed by a training unit that was twenty-four hours away from being dismantled? He didn't know. But if this all fell in on him, his friends in D.C. might not be able to save his ass this time. And that might mean the end of his checkered military career. Then what the hell would he do?

As he was musing on all this, the last of the stragglers went streaming by him with great speed, fleeing the NLRs that were still coming down from all directions.

Sledge counted just thirty-seven soldiers inside the building—less than a third of OpFor 4's original number. Actually, he was surprised so many had been able to make it. Many had their robes up and blocking all but their eyes, the aftereffects he supposed of being hit by so many NLRs at once. Finally he closed the mosque's big door and locked it. Anyone unlucky enough to be left outside was on his own at that point. Even now Sledge could hear people banging on the door, begging to be let in. But this only made him double up the door's locks.

There was a lot of confusion among those who had made it into the mosque as well. Pushing and shoving, some of them. He ordered them to quiet down, then sprinted up the steps to the minaret. He looked out from its tiny balcony and saw a very demoralizing sight: The landed C-17 had moved into position to block all further access to the village from the desert around them. Meanwhile, the two M1 tanks were heading in his direction at impossibly high speed.

That's when Sledge turned to his right to see that a gang of 201st paratroopers below was taking aim at him. He fell backward through the minaret's hatch door just a second before the combined energy of at least a dozen NLRs came at him.

He saw the wooden timbers of the hatch turn bright red as he dropped to the stairwell. It had been such a powerful NLR blast, the wood above him appeared to smolder.

"Have they turned up the power on those things?" Sledge wondered.

He flew down the tower's stairs and ran to the rear of the mosque. Even as he was doing this he could hear the pair of speedy tanks clanking their way up to the mosque's front door.

Sledge found the hidden door that led to the underground hardened shelter and pulled it open, this as the first tank came crashing through the front of the mosque. So much for not attacking a holy place . . .

Sledge was screaming to the stragglers to dive through the hatch—and they needed no further prodding. The robed soldiers were literally jumping into the hole in the floor.

Sledge watched in horror now as the second tank broke through the mosque's door, both its big gun and its machine guns firing full blast. Paratroopers began flooding in as well. Sledge was sure the entire building would come crashing down on all of them at any second.

He screamed, "Where the fuck are the referees?"

Then he dove into the bunker himself, slamming the hatch shut behind him.

He and the thirty-seven stragglers huddled together as all hell broke loose above them. It sounded as if the 201st was literally tearing the mosque apart.

Finally, the noise calmed down and Sledge could hear himself think for a moment. He happened to look at his watch—and realized for the first time it was broken, smashed when he hit the ground to avoid getting clipped by the crash-landing C-17. Time had stood still in a weird way. To him, it seemed the entire attack exercise—from the landing of the C-17 to the sudden appearance of the paratroopers and the even more amazing appearance of the gunship—had happened in slow motion, playing out like some kind of fever-dream movie. In his head, it had taken less than a minute.

Once again, he took a head count of those inside the hardened bunker. There were only a few lights installed down here—a mistake, Sledge realized—and the place was crowded. But counting everyone here with him was the only thing he could think to do, this as the 201st troopers above began their rampage again.

As the noise overhead grew even louder and more disturbing, Sledge knew he had a big decision to make. He made his way over to the bunker's far corner and pulled at the canvas tarp that was covering something there.

Immediately the bunker was filled with a very weird green glow—the light coming from the holographic Zoot bomb.

Sledge really had to think about this now. The weapon was self-contained, powered by an internal battery that came to life at first touch. A huge red button was the only other attachment on the device. It would be simple enough to use: Push the button and everything electronic for miles around would stop working. The tanks above, the NLR weapons, all communications equipment—everything, just like that.

But what about the planes circling overhead?

Sledge really didn't care about them now, sweating in his own sudden fever. There were miles of desert around, flat desert, they could land on. They'd be okay. Wouldn't they?

Again, he was not a nice guy, because nice guys were chumps. And he did not want to take responsibility, or the bum rap, for what had just happened here.

So he reached for the device's button, intent on pushing it—when suddenly a hand came out of nowhere and grabbed his wrist.

Sledge spun around to see an unbelievable sight: The room was filled with soldiers—but they weren't his men. Rather they were all wearing the unmistakable sand-colored camos of the 201st.

The people who had come in with him, they hadn't been his people at all. It had been these 201st soldiers—wearing woolen Iraqi clothes. They'd flown in aboard the taxiing C-17 and stolen into the village amidst all the confusion. Sledge was stunned.

He looked into the eyes of the person holding his wrist, and was astonished once again. It was not some rough-and-tumble dirty soldier in front of him—but an extremely attractive woman. And she looked very pissed off at him.

They stared at each other for a long moment. Then this woman reached into her pocket and came out with a kid's squirt gun. She put it up to Sledge's temple and pulled the trigger, spraying the warm water all over his face.

Then she smiled and said, "Bang, bang—you're dead."

COLONEL Newman almost did a jig.

Right there, on top of the mesa, he almost broke out into a little victory dance, even though he'd never danced a sober step in his life.

He couldn't help it. What he'd just witnessed had been perfection in motion. The 201st had not only changed the rules, they'd thrown the rule book away. And the results were stunning. OpFor 4 had been thoroughly routed and their base of operations thoroughly destroyed. It was all because the energies of the hardworking 201st had been pointed in a slightly different direction. That's all it took. Everything Newman had been trying to accomplish for so long finally came to fruition.

"Now, that's how it's done!" he bellowed jubilantly.

The trouble was . . . the man behind him did not share his happiness.

It was Congressman Toole.

He was standing atop a rock farther back from the edge of the butte, surrounded by an entourage of aides, each with a stopwatch in hand.

The congressional fact-finding committee had decided to put off hitting Las Vegas for a day and get the visit to Area 153 out of the way first. Thus, they had arrived earlier than anticipated, just minutes before the latest exercise began. But again, to Newman's good luck, the exercise had gone brilliantly, thanks to Gunn's innovative tactics and his "no rules" strategy.

Now, as Newman watched a series of silver flares rise up from the CSMC battlefield, he knew all of the objectives had been officially secured. The paratroopers were hurrying back onto the C-17 heavy metal plane, along with the tanks, and even a few OpFor 4 "POWs." The plane quickly took off, met up with the Fireship and the Jump Plane circling above, and headed back for the 201st base.

And that was it. The practice raid had been a stunning success, and with the congressional fact-finding committee on hand, it couldn't have come at a better time.

Or so Newman thought.

He turned slowly to see Toole smiling at him.

"Very impressive, Colonel," Toole said. "But we have a problem . . ."

Newman walked over to him as his toadies helped the diminutive congressman down from his rocky pedestal.

" 'Problem?' " he asked Toole, authentically puzzled. "How could you possibly find a problem with that?"

Toole pointed to his gold stopwatch.

"It took too long," he replied.

Newman looked at his own, much less elaborate stopwatch. He couldn't believe it: The exercise had taken twenty-six minutes . . . and thirty-three seconds.

"Thirty-three seconds over?" he said, trying mightily to control his temper. "That's a matter of a few heartbeats . . ."

"But the specs clearly say you had to pull this off in twenty-six minutes and no more," Toole told him officiously. "I mean, on a battlefield, anything could happen in thirty-three seconds, right?"

Newman knew quite a bit about Congressman Toole, but his pure evil nature was coming through now. He was a bitter man. A grade-A prick. And at that moment, as ridiculous as it sounded, he knew those thirty-three seconds would be enough to doom the project.

Toole's entourage climbed into their helicopter; its pilot was beginning to start its engines.

But Newman couldn't give up without a fight. He caught Toole just as he was stepping onto the aircraft.

He had to yell over the copter noise to him. "So, you're killing all this hard work, for a mission this country desperately needs, just because we went over the spec by thirty-three seconds?"

Toole laughed, then yelled into Newman's ear, "That's what I'm telling my committee, yes," he said. "But the real reason is you guys made a fool of me the other night out in the desert. I don't care if your unit can conquer the world. I don't care if your airplanes can fly to the moon. You make an ass of me, and you pay. That's how it works."

With that, Toole climbed aboard his helicopter and flew away.

CHAPTER 12

THE assembly was called for 1200 hours, high noon; the hottest part of the Nevada desert day.

The 162 people of the 201st—air crews, support people, and staff—lined up in two neat rows in front of the base's ops building. By this time, rumors were swirling among them that even though their last exercise had been a great success, the program had been cancelled. The reason: Disagreements between Colonel Newman and the Washington politicians who held the purse strings. The news came as a blow to everyone involved. They'd put up with the heat, the sand, the snakes, and the scorpions to build the atypical raiding unit from the ground up, and it was a challenge they'd all met well.

But it had also been for naught. By the time they began to line up to hear Newman's address, it was clear the 201st would soon cease to exist.

Gunn, Amanda, and Pulver were standing front and center. Atop the hills on the southern and eastern end of the base, they could see a number of Humvees in evidence, their occupants looking down on the assembly. These were soldiers from other secret Area 153 training units, here to pay their respects to the 201st on their dark day. It was always sad to see one of the black missions fraternity be dissolved, because a little piece of the entire special ops community went with it. Carrying this tribute further, there was a flyby of a secret aircraft that moved so swiftly over the base, those assembled saw it for no more than a second. Again, this was apropos. This was how the occupants of Area 153 said good-bye.

At the stroke of noon, Newman walked out of the ops building. He was wearing his dress uniform, a SOF beret and sunglasses. It was an odd, formal look for him.

Newman saluted the assembled personnel and had them stand at ease. He began reading from a prepared statement, but from the start, the words sounded difficult coming off his tongue. He had to stop more than once to compose himself. His usual booming voice was long gone, as was his swagger. He seemed like a broken man.

The moment was so filled with drama, Gunn barely heard what Newman was saying. Few people did. While he mentioned things about budget-cutting in Washington, and how the 201st really *did* accomplish their mission by proving the "big raid" concept could work, it was clear the words were as hollow coming out as they were going in, especially when Newman read the official order stating the 201st was no more.

The brief ceremony ended when Newman had his XO lower the unit's banner from the flagpole next to the ops building and replace it with a plain white pennant. This was another tradition inside the secret training ground: Whenever a unit was dispersed or moved on, a white flag was left on their flagpole, a symbol that whatever had happened here was happening here no more. To Gunn, it looked a little bit too much like a flag of surrender.

Newman then folded his speech, gazed out at those assembled, and started to say something else—but stopped. Whether he thought better of it or whether he got choked up again, it was hard to tell.

In any case, he simply straightened up, saluted his people

crisply, then turned on his heel and disappeared back into the ops building, alone.

GUNN returned to his quarters immediately after the gloomy assembly broke up.

A few people lingered after Newman's speech, but what was there left to say? They'd been screwed by the hacks in Washington; not the first secret ops unit to suffer that fate, and certainly not the last.

Gunn's plan now was to pack, write one final report—as requested by Newman's XO of all senior officers—and then scare up some fuel for his T-38. If he could find enough JP-8 to fill his tanks, he could fly back to Edwards and join the real world again. Naturally, this brought back thoughts of his waitress friend. Would she even talk to him again? And who could he ever tell about his foray into this crazy world of black ops, ghost towns, and strange things that fly in the night?

No one, he guessed. No one would believe him.

It didn't take him long to pack. He'd come to Area 153 with just the clothes on his back, and had accumulated very little in his time here. So, he spent most of the afternoon writing the final report, striving to emphasize what a rewarding experience it had been working with the 201st and especially Colonel Newman. In his short time with the secret unit, Gunn had gained tons of respect for the senior officer. He'd had many COs in his career, but none as dedicated, yet humane as Newman. This made it even more shameful that the government was pulling the plug on the 201st. Operators like the colonel just didn't come along very often.

The report took three hours and three drafts to get right—Gunn's longest ever. Once done, he spent a half hour getting his billet in shape. He was mostly concerned that his lav was clean before he left. He didn't want to leave the crap duty to someone else.

Because nothing heavy could go on at the base in the daytime—at least, not on the outside—he knew he would have to wait until at least 1900 hours before he could get the fuel he needed and then get prepped for takeoff. It was now just past 1800—which was odd because for the first time since coming to Area 153, Gunn had nothing to do, nowhere to be.

In other words, he had some spare time. A whole hour of it. It was like a gift from above. This meant he could finally lie down and get some rest.

He stretched out on his bunk trying hard not to wrinkle the sheet. But no sooner had he closed his eyes . . . when there was a knock at his door. He thought for sure it was someone on the ground crew arriving early to take him to his T-38. So it was with great surprise that he opened the door to find Amanda O'Rourke waiting on the other side.

The sun was setting by this time and her blonde hair, uncharacteristically ruffled and wild, was surrounded by a halo of emerging stars. She was still in her flight suit, but it was open at the top. She looked slightly confused, slightly anxious—and absolutely gorgeous.

Why was she here? Gunn thought quickly. To say good-bye? Or for something more?

No . . .

"Newman wants to see us," she told him urgently. "And I mean, right now. It's an emergency."

THEY hurried over to the ops building. Bursting through the front door, they found the staff office was already dark and empty. The walls were bare, the computers had all been removed, and much of the other gear was waiting in boxes to be taken away.

They walked down the long corridor leading to Newman's office. It, too, was dark. But it was even darker inside the office itself.

They found Newman sitting behind his desk, still in his dress uniform, still wearing his sunglasses. The only illumination was coming from a weak desk lamp. The senior officer was staring at a piece of red message paper. Red usually meant bad news in the secret ops community.

He didn't greet them. He just started speaking.

"There's a situation in Pakistan," he started slowly. "American hostages have been taken by an al-Qaeda splinter group called the PKD. Really bad actors. Vicious and fanatical. They snatched five USAID workers and they are beheading them one at a time—for money. The NSA has intercepted phone calls between this group and an Arab TV station in the Persian Gulf. There's no doubt they are executing these hostages on camera and selling the videotapes for cash to this Arab news network."

Newman paused, took in a long, deep breath, then continued: "Now, this thing hasn't even hit the media yet. But we do know the terrorists are holding these hostages inside a mountain in the worst part of Pakistan. It's right near the Afghan border, which is probably the most lawless place on earth. This mountain is like Tora Bora, except our intelligence people say that unlike that place, this one is heavily fortified and the fanatics inside are up to their asses in weapons, and I'm not just talking about AKs and RPGs. They have sophisticated stuff and apparently they know how to use it, because two rescue attempts by non-U.S. forces have already failed."

Newman paused for another uncomfortably long moment, just staring at his hands folded nervously on his desk.

"That means someone else has to rescue these people," he said. "Or at least try to. And they have to do it soon . . ."

Another pause.

"The problem is no U.S. special ops force is available to take this on. Or at least not in time . . ."

A very long pause.

"So," Newman said, measuring each word to come carefully, "I'm sending in the 201st . . ."

Gunn and Amanda were stunned. They collapsed into the chairs on the other side of Newman's desk.

"Did I just hear you right, sir?" Amanda asked him.

"Yes, you did, Lieutenant . . ." Newman mumbled in reply.

"But—we've been deactivated, sir," Gunn said, concerned that Newman would even consider such a bizarre action. "The unit is packed up. The buses are coming from Tonopah in the morning. By noon tomorrow, everyone will be blown to the four winds."

Newman held up his hand to gently interrupt him.

"I know all this, Major," Newman said. "And I even know the 201st is the wrong unit with the wrong equipment for this mission." He paused, then said, "But I'm sending you in anyway. Anyone who is willing to go, that is."

Gunn and Amanda looked at each other, practically speechless. Had Newman gone off the deep end?

"Sir—wasn't the unit *officially* deactivated by the Pentagon?" Amanda finally asked him.

Newman nodded slowly. "It was, and that was by request of the congressional oversight committee, which passed it on to the National Security Council, which I'm sure passed it on to the White House itself. But I can't let that affect my decision—no matter what it means to me careerwise or legally. Or criminally. No one else can do it."

"But are you sure, sir?" Amanda pressed him gently. "I mean, you're right: There's got to be other SOF units who are better suited for this. Even if we were still a unit, we have paratroopers and tanks, flat-ground stuff, desert stuff. It sounds like you're talking about a mountain fortress. That's more a job for the 10th Mountain or Marine Recon."

"Once again, I checked," Newman insisted quietly. "And all elements of those two units are engaged elsewhere. The quickest any of them could be turned around is a week—but we don't have a week. We've only got a day, if that, at the rate they are killing these hostages. The 201st might not have the right equipment, but you were built to move quickly and to do so undetected. That's what you have going for you."

"But, Colonel," Amanda tried again. "This is . . . *highly* unusual to say the least. There's got to be some underlying reason for it. Is it just some way to prove to the people in Washington that they were plain wrong about shutting us down?"

About thirty seconds went by with no reply. But then Newman took off his sunglasses—and that's when Amanda and Gunn realized for the first time that he'd been crying.

Newman began to speak again, but now his voice was barely audible.

"The reason is," he said, "one of the hostages those bastards have . . . is my daughter."

Dead silence. For a long minute.

"My only child," he eventually managed to struggle on. "Her name is Anne. She's over there, teaching their kids—and those animals snatched her, and now they want to *kill her*."

Newman wiped his eyes. "And again, I know it will be my career," he said. "And that it will mean a court-martial, and prison time for me. Plus, I'll have on my conscience the lives of anyone who gets killed doing this. But I ask you: How could I live with myself knowing I had the means to rescue my own daughter plus those other people, and didn't use it?"

The two pilots had no reply. Never in his life had Gunn witnessed such an emotional moment.

"But how, sir?" Amanda finally asked Newman. "*How* can we get there? Our planes might be quiet, but people will see us. The U.S. military will see us. Other *countries* will see us, at least on radar. How can we possibly do it?"

Newman wiped his eyes again, stood up, took another deep breath, and then said, "Come with me. I'll show you how."

NEWMAN led them out to his OH-6 chopper. In theory, the tiny aircraft could fit more than two inside, but it would be a tight squeeze. Nevertheless, Newman climbed into the pilot's seat and Amanda and Gunn jammed themselves into the remaining space. As a result, Gunn found himself pressed up tight against the beauty queen pilot. Despite the very strange goings-on, he was almost overwhelmed by how good it felt to be so close to her.

They took off and headed deep into the desert. The night was dark and once again moonless, so it was hard for Gunn to see where they were going exactly. But at one point, he looked down and spotted the three isolated hangars on the edge of the base. It appeared one of their doors was open.

They flew for another ten minutes, going down off the high plain, and finally landing on the hard desert floor below. They quickly piled out of the copter.

They were in the middle of another grand Nevada valley; it ran flat and unbroken in every direction, stretching off into the darkness. It was completely void of any light. Only the stars blazing overhead.

Newman scanned the skies around them, then pulled out a sat phone and punched in a number.

He had a hushed conversation with someone, then turned back to Gunn and Amanda and said, "Watch this . . ."

He snapped his fingers—and suddenly there was an airplane directly above them.

It was a C-17. Flying east to west, very fast, and very low, not more than 1,000 feet up. It was making no sound.

They saw it for about three seconds, then Newman snapped his fingers again—and the plane suddenly disappeared.

Gunn and Amanda were both astonished. Gunn said, "Is this sleep deprivation? Or have I finally gone nuts?"

Amanda cried, "What's going on here, Colonel?"

But Newman didn't reply. Instead he spoke another order into the phone and the plane materialized again. It was now about a half mile south of them but heading back in their direction. It climbed up to a more respectable 5,000 feet and started doing incredible maneuvers all over the night sky, appearing here, then disappearing, only to appear farther up or over.

"How is this possible?" Gunn was saying. He thought maybe it was a holographic projection they were looking at, but knowing at the same time this was impossible, because he could *see* this thing was there, and that it was *real*. But it just kept disappearing.

Newman spoke into the phone again and the plane reappeared overhead, up around 7,500 feet and this time stayed visible. But it was also turning so sharply, it looked like it was going to fall out of the sky.

Amanda exclaimed, "Who's flying that thing?"

Newman almost laughed. "Take a guess . . ." he deadpanned.

The plane came in for a landing on the hard desert floor and rolled up to where the three of them were standing. The front cockpit window popped open and the pilot stuck his head out.

It was Pulver, of course. No one else flew like him.

"Anyone want to go to Disney World?" he yelled down to them.

Only when they were standing next to the aircraft did Gunn

realize it was just like one of the three they'd been flying non-stop the past week, except this plane was painted in dull, nonreflective black. Newman encouraged them to touch the fuselage and indeed they did, as if to prove to them that it was real.

Again, Gunn thought he was going nuts. "Please, Colonel," he beseeched Newman. "You've got to tell us what the hell is going on."

At this point, Newman produced two sheets of paper from his pocket.

"I will," he said. "But first, you must sign these forms. By doing so you are agreeing to the highest security clearance in the U.S. government. Basically what that means is you'll be jailed for life if you breach this trust."

"Aren't we going to jail anyway?" Gunn said under his breath.

Newman passed them a pen and he and Amanda quickly signed the forms. The curiosity of the fantastic display had them hooked.

"Okay, Colonel, that's done," Amanda pleaded with him. "Now, please—is this some sort of 'alien technology?' Are all those Area 51 stories true?"

Newman smiled weakly. "The explanation might be out of this world, Lieutenant," he said. "But it's much better than alien technology."

The big plane didn't really disappear, he explained. It just seemed that way due to a technology he called "Star Skin."

"Take a close look at the fuselage," Newman told them.

Gunn got really close up. He could see the plane's skin had what appeared to be a matrix of twinkling sensors imbedded in it. There had to be millions of them.

Newman explained: "Those sensors can detect stars, star formations, clouds, atmospherics, or any mix thereof appearing above the aircraft and recreate them exactly onto its bottom. Get it? The aircraft can pass right overhead and not be seen by anyone on the ground because what they think they are looking up at is the night sky. Watch . . ."

Newman gave Pulver another signal and the Star Skin was turned on again. Sure enough, the underside of the plane suddenly lit up with hundreds of tiny white and bluish lights, perfectly mimicking the night sky above. Pulver inched the plane forward a little, but most of the "stars" underneath seemed to stay stationary, with a few new ones appearing under the nose and a few "old" ones disappearing off the tail.

It took a few tries, but then it was clear to Gunn and Amanda how the technology worked.

"Fantastic, no?" Newman asked them.

"Fantastic, yes!" Amanda exclaimed.

It was all becoming clear to Gunn now. Along with heavily dampened, silent engines and a thick coat of Stealth paint, with this almost magical chameleon effect, at night, this plane, and he assumed two others like it locked away in the other secret isolated hangers, really *could* become invisible.

And had they stayed together, these would have been the *real* aircraft of the 201st, which was why Newman was never concerned about the time or methods it would have taken to reach one of their religious fort targets. He knew getting in and out would be the easy part.

"We had to train you in the backup planes because we couldn't even let people *out here* see this technology," Newman explained. "It was just too secret."

"It's freaking amazing," Gunn finally breathed.

"I second that," Amanda said. She was still bowled over by what she'd just seen.

"Well, hang on to the accolades," Newman said. "Because there's more."

The senior officer signaled up to Pulver again. The rear door of the huge plane opened on command.

Newman, Gunn, and Amanda walked up into the C-17's hold. Newman flipped a switch somewhere, the lights came on—and the two pilots were again stunned. The interior of the airplane looked like something from a sci-fi movie: all tubes and wires, blinking microprocessors—and guns. Many, *many* guns, each one sticking out of its own porthole on the left-hand side of the plane. Gunn had once seen the inside of an AC-130 Spectre, a platform that carried four large weapons. He recalled thinking at the time what an ungodly amount of firepower that was for one airplane.

Now he was looking at that same idea—taken to the extreme. This airplane was carrying four times as many weapons and four times the amount of ammunition as a Spectre gunship, along with four times as much technology to make it all work. It just didn't look real somehow.

"Want the quick tour?" Newman asked them.

They walked deeper into the enormous cargo bay. It looked like a Rube Goldberg nightmare, between all the ammo belts and power lines, running in every direction imaginable. But slowly, a method to the madness emerged, a symmetry to the seeming chaos.

Newman said, "What we've done here is stick with the AC-130 concept but just increased it in force, with a few improvisations."

The first weapons they came to were a pair of M102 105mm howitzers, a field gun that had been deployed to support U.S. Army infantry units in the past. Newman explained the M102 could fire as many as ten shells a minute and throw them up to seven miles away. "Devastating for enemy strong points and personnel alike," he said.

Next came a trio of 20mm M61Vulcan cannons. Not unlike those used on fighter jets such as the F-15 and F-16, these weapons had rotary barrels, similar to the old-style Gatling guns except they could fire at a rate of 3,000 rounds per minute. "I've seen the results of these being used on someone on the ground," Newman said. "They can shred a human being in an instant."

Following the Vulcans came four Mk-44 Bushmaster 30mm cannons—long, scary-looking weapons. "These fire air burst rounds," Newman explained. "They'll explode in a precise space at a precise time, either above or near a target, depending on how you set them. If someone is hunkered down behind a fortified area, you use these."

Installed next to the Bushmasters were four 7.62mm GAU-2 miniguns. "These are similar to the Vulcans," Newman said. "But with two differences: They can fire *4,000* rounds a minute. And, they are usually loaded with HE-1 rounds. You know, as in heat incendiary? Want to start a big fire or scare the crap out of somebody? Use these . . ."

Next to the quartet of miniguns came a pair of 40mm Bofors cannons. These extremely high-powered weapons were actually antiaircraft guns adapted for airborne use. "A shot from these guns can penetrate 50mm of armor plate at more than a quarter mile away. Anything in the way closer than that is toast."

The last weapon in this murderer's row was the fiercest weapon of all: a Phoenix CIWS gun. Gunn couldn't believe it when he saw it. This was a monstrous Gatling gun used to protect capital naval ships like aircraft carriers and cruisers. "Radar-directed, 6-barrel, 20mm shell," Newman explained. "It can also fire 4,000 rounds per minute but over a very large area. It throws up so much lead, so quickly, nothing in its path can escape. Simple as that."

Again, Gunn tried to take it all in, but it was hard to do. Amanda felt the same way. It was a mind-boggling array of weaponry—real-world stuff that suddenly made all the NLR simulators seem like kids' toys.

They climbed up into the flight deck. Pulver was still strapped into the pilot's seat, looking like a kid with a new, multimillion-dollar toy. For some reason, he'd been in on the secret before Gunn and Amanda.

Newman reached across the pilot's seat and pointed to an LCD screen installed just above the flight computer.

"This displays the icons for the weapons system," he said, tapping the display box and revealing a row of individual symbols running across the screen. "As you can see, each weapon is represented. Once you're ready to unload on something, you'll do the sighting automatically, then depending on the target, you will have your weapon of choice. All you have to do is touch the weapon's icon. The fire control computer will do the rest."

Newman pointed over his shoulder in the direction back toward the base.

"In those other two hangars up there we have two more planes equipped with the Star Skin," he told them. "One is outfitted for paratroopers, the other already has two tanks in its cargo bay. They are ready to go, just like this one."

It was at that moment that Gunn realized Newman was truly serious about deploying the 201st.

"So you really want us to fly these things and go do your rescue mission?" Gunn asked him.

"Yes, I do," Newman replied soberly.

"And we'll be invisible getting there," Amanda said. "And invisible when we're coming back?"

Newman just nodded gravely. "That's right."

Gunn looked over the huge gunship. He'd never been in a position like this before—being sent on an unauthorized, probably illegal mission. It *was* for a worthy cause, no doubt about that. And obviously time was looming as a big factor if the terrorists were as crazy and bloodthirsty as Newman suggested.

But he still had one big question.

"Are you sure about this, Colonel?" he asked. "Not just about the legality of it, but about these new airplanes, the technology, the weaponry, and where we have to go? Will it all work? *Can* it all work?"

Newman just shrugged. "I don't know, Major," he whispered. "But I do know that the way our military is stretched so thin these days, and the fact that no special ops force can be turned around so quickly and that these hostages are in the wilds of Pakistan, the most likely response, even before this hits the media, will be to do a missile strike on that fortress. Especially if they think all the hostages are dead, or will be dead soon. These days it's just easier to send in some bunker-busting cruise missiles than it is to dispatch a real live unit and attempt a real life rescue. So you can see where I'm at here?"

Gunn could only nod in agreement. "Yes I do, sir."

Newman put his hand on Gunn's shoulder. "So if it all works, or if it doesn't," he said, "I don't know. But all I can ask is that you give it a try . . ."

PART TWO

PART TWO

CHAPTER 13

Somewhere over the Pacific

"What exactly are we looking for, Major?" Lieutenant Bing asked. "A hole in the ocean?"

Tommy Gunn wished he had a good answer. But he didn't.

It was now 2200 hours, local time. The trio of C-17s—new call signs Ghosts 1, 2, and 3—had left Nevada a little more than four hours before and had been heading west ever since, trying to beat the sun. Gunn's aircraft was in the lead. Pulver was about a mile behind him, and Amanda, driving Ghost 3, was a mile behind Pulver. They were flying under strict radio silence and far off the normal air lanes. The 201st Special Operations Wing's first real mission.

But already, it seemed headed for disaster.

Reconstituting the unit proved to be no problem. No one had left the base yet and, as it turned out, every person connected with the combat side of things—the paratroopers, the Marines, the aircrews—jumped at the chance to go on the rescue operation, along with a handful of airplane techs and ground personnel. It was hectic, but they were all packed and ready to go not two hours after Newman first showed the Star Skin C-17 to Gunn and Amanda in the desert.

Just before their hurried departure, though, Newman had given Gunn three manila envelopes. One contained a CD that, when pushed into his airplane's flight computer, showed exactly where they had to go in Pakistan as well as the first leg of their course to get there. The second envelope contained photographs of all five of the USAID hostages, including Newman's daughter, Anne. The third envelope Newman had labeled: "Landing for Fuel and More." But he'd also written instructions on the outside that warned, because of security concerns, the contents should not be viewed until the Ghost planes were at least four hours out of Nevada. When Newman handed this envelope to Gunn, all he said was "Trust me."

So, exactly four hours into the flight, Gunn tore the top off this third envelope and reached inside. All he found was a single piece of plain white paper with a simple message scratched onto it: 183° longitude by 33° latitude. It was a coordinate in the middle of the Pacific Ocean.

The coordinate looked pretty typical at first. They had to assume it was an island—what else could it be, out in the middle of the vast Pacific? But when Gunn and his copilot, Lieutenant Bing, punched the coordinate into their GPS-linked navigational suite, the computer said there was nothing at that point except open water. Bing tried again and again, but got the same result each time. Open ocean, no land anywhere nearby. Their only conclusion: In the haste to leave Nevada, Newman had written down the wrong coordinates.

In other words, they were flying to a place that didn't exist.

This was not good. They didn't really have a plan for the hostage rescue. All they knew was if they had *any* hope of saving Newman's daughter and the other surviving USAID workers, they had to first make it halfway around the world to Pakistan before the sun came up again and their cover was blown. This meant their planes had to travel at nearly 550 mph, the C-17's top speed, throttles kicked to the max. This was extremely fast for such a big airplane and it meant using gas at a very high rate. As a result, their fuel reserves had dwindled away very quickly. And even with 2,000 miles already under their belts, they still weren't halfway to their destination.

The problem was no aerial refueling planes were standing by to gas them up, as might normally have been the case. The 201st was on a completely unauthorized, wholly illegal mission. The only thing that awaited them was court-martials and probably prison time if any of them made it back alive. So, the U.S. Air Force and its tanker fleet would not be providing them with fuel. They were under no illusions about that.

Yet Gunn knew breaking radio silence and calling back to the 201st hidden base to get the right coordinate was useless because the minute the unit was shut down, U.S. Special Forces Command changed all its frequencies—routine whenever such a highly classified project was dissolved. He'd even considered calling Newman's cell phone, but at 15,000 feet above the Pacific he knew there was no service anywhere near them.

The only other alternative, turning around and going back to Nevada, was not an option either. They were already way past the point of no return, fuel-wise, possibly the very reason Newman had insisted the third envelope not be opened until four hours into the flight—just to make sure they *didn't* get spooked early on and decide to turn back. Yet there was nothing at the place he wanted them to go.

The result of all this? If something didn't change in the next ten minutes, they were all going into the drink.

IT would have been almost comic, if it weren't so potentially tragic, especially when it came to the airplanes themselves. Fuel issues aside, the new C-17s flew infinitely better than the battered and bruised ones the 201st used to train in the desert. Like new cars just coming off the line, the trio of top secret planes had less than 100 air miles between them when they left Area 153, barely enough to break in their new, powerful, sound-dampened engines. Their cockpits were beyond anything currently considered state of the art: everything was advanced LCD, touch sensitive or voice activated, with nary a lever, button, or switch panel to be found. The planes' autopilots were brimming with artificial intelligence, able to follow the most precise flight instructions laid down by

GPS coordinates, and capable of making thousands of adjustments every second to maintain course or avoid detection. Even the flight decks were better, with bigger seats, a galley, a lav, and yellowish low-level lighting. Plus each plane had its own personal armory, stocked with dozens of M4Gs special ops weapons, M68 sights, an aiming device that projected a red dot on the intended target, and M203A1 grenade launchers, capable of firing a 40mm projectile.

As for the planes' ability to become invisible? It was hardly noticeable by anyone on board, yet they all knew it was working. There was a TV screen installed in each cockpit that showed what the fantastic Star Skin was doing at any given moment. As they were presently flying in clear skies, the entire underside of their fuselages and wings were covered with twinkling stars, perfectly mimicking the heavens above. And as the airplanes moved through the air, so did the star patterns on their skins. But, even more remarkable, the Star Skin actually worked both ways, as the top of the planes and their wings were showing a sensor re-creation of the ocean waves below, meaning they were invisible to anyone looking down on them as well.

It was astonishing technology, especially when combined with the planes' radar-avoiding stealth characteristics. But again, none of it would do them any good unless they got some fuel—and got it quickly.

They were finally within ten miles of the mysterious coordinate, but still, the GPS was warning them nothing was there but ocean. Gunn was contemplating telling his crew to break out the life rafts, if they had any, when suddenly Bing tapped him on the arm and pointed out the right side window. Gunn couldn't believe what he saw: There *was* an island down there. It was hard to make out, tiny, and nearly hidden beneath a huge cloud of fog, but there nevertheless.

"Can this get any weirder?" Bing breathed, indicating that the GPS navigation suite still didn't see the speck of land.

"Don't ask," Gunn replied.

But he was supremely puzzled, too. An island that didn't show up on GPS? How was that possible?

He asked Bing to turn on the radio and try to contact someone below. The copilot punched in some standard radio frequencies and started calling. After a few tries, a mechanical, prerecorded voice came on the speakers. It reminded Gunn of the voice he'd heard the night he first arrived over Area 153.

The voice gave them brief landing instructions and nothing more. No sign-off, no "over and out." Gunn and Bing just looked at each other and shrugged.

"The beat goes on, I guess, "Gunn said. With that, he pulled back on the throttles and started descending toward the fog-covered island.

The other two C-17s were flying off Gunn's wing by this time. Their crews, too, were thankful to spot the mist-shrouded scrap of land. As one, the three planes went into a low orbit above the island. Gunn pulled down his RIF night vision goggles and took a good long look. As viewed through the cool blue of the reverse infrared, the island couldn't have looked creepier if it had been designed by Hollywood itself. It had rocky cliffs, craggy beaches, and ultra-thick jungles. It even had a tiny volcano sticking up out of the fog.

"Isn't this where King Kong lives?" Bing asked.

Gunn lowered the big plane even more, getting below the mist and looking for a good landing approach. Now he could see the island was about a mile long, maybe half that wide, and covered with the dense overgrowth, except for a long runway on the eastern side. A dozen hangars ran along this airstrip; several more structures could be seen at its far end. Just like the 201st desert base, all these buildings were covered with the exotic electromagnetic camouflaged netting. Add in the real jungle and the fog, and they could hardly be seen at all.

Gunn banked hard, straightened out, and set his aircraft down with a bump. The two other Ghost planes came in right behind him. Rolling up to the edge of the taxiway, they stopped and just waited. There were no lights, no sounds, no signs of life at all. Just darkness and the fog. A lot of it . . .

Gunn's eye was drawn to the handful of structures at the opposite end of the runway. They weren't hangars. Rather, they were made of steel and concrete and shaped like overgrown igloos. And again, each one was covered with the electromagnetic camouflage netting.

But even stranger, the largest igloo of the five had a sign painted on it that read: "S-4 West." S-4 was the place within Area 51 where the U.S. government kept all its secret UFO technology—or at least that's what the conspiracy nuts said. So why was this building, way out here, on an island that didn't exist, called S-4 West? Was it a joke? Or was it something else?

"This place reminds me of Area 153," Bing said, taking it all in. "Without the frills, I mean . . ."

At that moment, a Humvee emerged from the gloom and made its way across the runway. It stopped at Gunn's airplane and a man in a nondistinct camo uniform climbed out. He was short-statured, maybe early forties, with a slightly ratlike look to him. He was wearing sunglasses even though it was the middle of the night.

He came aboard Ghost 1, made his way up to the flight deck, and introduced himself to Gunn simply as "Lieutenant Moon." Then he said, "You have landed at a classified facility. Your presence here is completely unauthorized."

Gunn just stared back at him. "Are you saying we've landed at the wrong place, Lieutenant?"

The undersized officer just held his hands up, indicating he had more to say. "No, that was all just for the record, Major. *Off* the record, I am a friend of Colonel Newman. He's briefed me on you and the situation and I'm here to help. But nevertheless, we can't discuss anything about what goes on here at this base. Do we understand each other?"

This was deflating, because Gunn already had a million questions, like how can an island not appear on any map or be recognized by GPS? And why was a building at the end of the runway named S-4? And where did all this fog come from?

But he knew such things would have to wait.

So, he just replied: "Yes, Lieutenant, we do."

With that, Moon took a walkie-talkie from his pocket and barked one word into it: "Go!"

That's when everything changed. It was as if someone threw a switch. Lights came on all over the base. The doors to the hangars nearby suddenly swung open and three convoys of aircraft maintenance trucks burst out into the night. They screeched up to the Ghost planes even before their engines had stopped turning, disgorging a small army of ground crew personnel along the way. These people immediately went to work, chocking off the airplanes, unlatching access panels, hooking up power hoses.

"Wow, these guys are like pit crews at a NASCAR race," Bing said, watching it all from the flight deck window.

"Maybe even faster," Gunn replied.

IT took only twenty-two minutes for all three Ghost planes to be refueled.

This would have been an astonishingly quick turnaround under the best of conditions; Moon's crew had done it at night, in thick fog, with planes they weren't familiar with. More remarkable, in that time, they also stocked the three C-17s with extra provisions, medical supplies, and cold weather gear. To help the aircrews stay awake, each unit member was issued a packet of amphetamine tablets, typical for special ops missions. Moon's guys even installed inflatable fuel bladders inside each plane's cargo bay. Each one carried hundreds of gallons of gas, ensuring that the 201st would have enough fuel to make it to Pakistan and possibly back again, without any more stops.

Once everything was loaded on, the C-17 aircrews began making their last-minute preflight checks. After downing two amphetamine tablets, Gunn did his own walk-around of Ghost 1, checking the ailerons, the tail, the landing gear. The pills were designed to put the amphetamine into the bloodstream very quickly, and for him they worked just as advertised. From that point on, everything seemed to move in fast motion.

He was almost finished with his inspection when he saw Amanda frantically waving to him; she wanted him to join her at the rear of her plane. Gunn hurried over and by the time he arrived, a heavy forklift was in the process of loading a large pale blue module into the back of Ghost 3. The module was about the size of a typical cargo container, and bore a slight resemblance to a shrunken Winnebago motor home, without the windows or the wheels. Gunn had no idea what it was; neither did Amanda.

Moon was supervising the module's on-loading, directing the forklift's driver as he squeezed it in alongside the pair of M1A1 Abrams tanks.

Gunn and Amanda walked over to him. "What's this, Lieutenant?" Gunn asked him, pointing to the module.

"It's a place to keep intelligence gear," Moon replied cryptically. "Things we can use on the mission."

Gunn stared back at him. "Did you just say 'we'?"

Moon nodded. "Yes, sir, I did . . ."

Amanda asked him, "You mean, you're coming with us?"

"Yes, I think I should," Moon told them. "I believe Colonel Newman told you that landing here was for 'Fuel and More?' Well, I guess you can say I'm the 'more.' He had a feeling you might need all the help you can get. Asymmetrical help. He left it to me whether I wanted to go or not—"

"'Asymmetrical'?" Gunn asked him. "You mean, psy-ops?"

Moon nodded again. "My job will be simple: I'll try to drive the terrorists crazy—or better put, drive them even crazier than they are now. With the task you have before you, it can't hurt."

As he was saying this, Gunn spotted Pulver hurrying over to him.

"What's going on with my plane?" he asked Gunn.

He pointed to some of Moon's men as they were pushing a tiny black helicopter into the back of his aircraft. Gunn recognized the copter as an OH-33, an extremely rare bird, probably the smallest military helicopter ever built. With its rotors and tail section folded up, it was barely larger than a mid-sized sedan.

Gunn indicated the small copter and said, "And that, Lieutenant?"

Moon just shrugged. "I might need my ride when we get there, sir."

Before the three 201st pilots could react to this, a soldier appeared out of the mist and handed Moon a message. It was printed on red paper. The color of trouble.

Moon read the message—and his face dropped a mile.

"It's from Colonel Newman," he said. "He's received an NSA intelligence burst. They just intercepted a phone call from the PKD's hideout indicating the terrorists have murdered another hostage. By the NSA's count, that's four executions already. That means there's only one hostage left . . ."

"Damn," Gunn whispered. His voice was shaking slightly.

"There's more," Moon said, taking in the rest of the message. "The NSA overheard the mooks referring to that last hostage as 'a young white female.' I believe Newman's daughter is the only hostage who fits that description."

"So she's still alive," Amanda said.

"She might be," Moon replied. "But here's the real problem: They're doing the final execution tomorrow, no later than daybreak. The NSA heard the PKD leader haggling over the price with the person they're selling the execution tapes to."

This was extremely bad news. Again, their first order of business was just getting to Pakistan in one piece. Newman had found them a place to set down: an old CIA airstrip built during the days of the Afghan-Soviet war. It was located practically right next to the mountain where the hostages were being held, which was very advantageous. They'd hoped to land at that spot undetected and then figure out what to do from there. But if the PKD was executing Newman's daughter at daybreak the next day, that meant they would have to get to Pakistan, land, *and* do the rescue—all before the sun even came up.

Gunn checked his watch. "That means we don't even have a half day to get there. Now it's more like just five or six hours."

"Meaning this mission is over before we can even start it," Pulver said, angrily. "Even with the fuel bladders and full tanks, we still have a *mutha* of a flight ahead of us. We'll never get there in time."

"Maybe," Moon said, deep in thought. "But maybe not . . ."

He snapped open his BlackBerry and he hit a few buttons. A map of Asia popped onto the screen. It showed the second half of their predetermined flight plan. This was a course that would bring them due south, past Taiwan to the Philippines, followed by a turn west, then a sharp turn to the northwest, and eventually, to the badlands of Pakistan. From there, the original plan called for them to land, attempt the rescue, and if it worked, take off for a short ride to a friendlier part of Pakistan, where they would set down again—and face the consequences. Total flight time to the trouble zone from here: ten hours minimum. And that's if everything went smoothly, including the weather.

Moon rechecked the red message, then said: "Maybe the solution presented to us is not one of speed or extra fuel. Maybe it's one of taking an alternate route."

He hit more keys on his BlackBerry, and then pushed Enter, causing the screen to blink once. When it cleared, it showed the same display of Asia as before, but now the unit's flight path, indicated in red against the green of the map, had changed radically.

Moon showed the revised screen to Gunn—and Gunn almost laughed in his face.

"You're kidding, I hope?" he said.

Moon shook his head. "Not at all."

"But do you realize where you're asking us to go?" Gunn said. "It's not possible. Not without getting ourselves killed."

"It's not *im*possible," Moon replied. "Not if all your technology works."

"But, what if it doesn't?" Gunn insisted, feeling like his head was about to explode from the fast-acting speed pills. "I mean, just about all of it is new and untested."

Moon just shrugged again.

"Well, if it doesn't work, Major," he said, "then what difference will it make?"

THE trio of planes took off five minutes later. They found their way through the fog and into the night sky, quickly reaching an altitude of 5,000 feet.

Gunn slotted into the lead spot, then took out a newly burned mini-CD Moon had just given him. They were still racing the night as it moved across the globe, and constant maximum speed remained crucial. And they still had a long way to go. But what they were about to do now was scary.

Gunn looked over at Bing, who was looking back at him very soberly. He pushed the new mission CD into the plane's flight computer. There was a few seconds of churning, the screen displaying waves of alphanumeric symbols. But finally, the program began.

The first thing it showed was their destination: the wilds of Pakistan and the isolated airstrip right next to the terrorist's fortress mountain.

Then the program displayed the unit's original flight path: again, the one that would have taken them south, around the rim of Asia, and then west again, to their goal of Pakistan.

But then the mini-CD really started churning—the result of Moon's latest alterations. When it stopped, the flight control screen went blank, and then blinked twice. Only then did their new flight plan appear. It showed them maintaining a westerly heading, turning south only after they had completed more than three-fourths of their journey. This "shortcut" would shave many hours off their trip time, not to mention allowing them to keep up with the night.

But there was one huge drawback. By taking this route, they were going to fly directly over China. Not exactly a friendly country.

"Damn, Major," Bing exclaimed, studying the new mission images. "All this crap *better* work. Stealth, Star Skin, everything. It all better be flawless, or we're screwed."

Gunn studied the computer screen again and popped another amphetamine pill.

"Amen to that," he said.

CHAPTER 14

Near Keifeng, China

Xiang Xia had lost his horse.

It happened earlier that evening, just before the stars came out. Ten-year-old Xia, one of two sons from a poor village family that lived about twenty miles west of Keifeng, had been ordered by the village's political boss to feed the village livestock with hay and leftover rice stalks. Only when this was done could Xia feed his horse, a Mongolian pony that lived with the communal pigs, goats, and chickens.

But Xia had disobeyed. Grabbing not hay or rice stalks but a bag of oats first, he opened the livestock corral, intent on feeding his horse before getting to his other chores. But as soon as the gate swung open, the horse bolted by him and galloped away.

This part of north central China was rife with danger after dark. Though it was only a couple hundred miles south of Beijing, the landscape was harsh, stark, and rural. It was not uncommon to see large cats that had descended from the highlands to the north roaming the outskirts of Xia's village, looking for food. Snakes, scorpions, and ghosts were other things that needed to be avoided at night.

Still, because young Xia had disobeyed the village elder,

his father had sent him out to retrieve the horse alone. And if it took all night, trudging around by himself in the freezing temperatures, then so be it.

Xia had spent four hours doing just that, and by midnight, his hands and feet were purple from the cold. He'd walked three miles in that time—endlessly calling the horse's name, trying to find his tracks, or his droppings. But so far, the search had been fruitless.

Scared, tired, and out of ideas, Xia climbed the top of the tallest hill within 100 miles, intent on performing a superstitious ritual that had been in his village for centuries. At that point, he believed it was his last chance of finding the horse.

Out of breath by the time he reached the crest of this high hill, Xia sought out the largest, most pointed rock he could find. Whispering a prayer to the sky gods, he closed his eyes, wound up his arms, and prepared to hurl the rock high into the air. The idea was that wherever the point of the rock came down, he should follow in that direction to look for his lost pet.

Xia threw the rock as high as he could—but then a strange thing happened. No sooner had the rock left his hand than it bounced back and hit him on his forehead. He fell to the ground, startled by the impact. An instant later, a great rush of wind went by him, carrying a storm of dirt, sand, and dust with it. Then everything was quiet again.

What happened? Xia had no idea. There was nothing above him but the clear, star-filled sky. Nothing around him but desert. So, maybe the gods were playing with him?

He picked up the same rock and again closed his eyes and threw it high into the air. This time, he heard a loud *clunk!* and was nearly blown over by a second great gush of wind. And the rock returned yet again—this time striking him on the shoulder.

Xia was so startled he fell back to the seat of his pants. This was not making any sense, even to a cold, frightened ten-year-old boy. He grabbed the rock a third time and sent it aloft once more. But this time he kept his eyes open—and this time he saw the stone "bounce" off the starry sky, just an instant before the wind came up a third time and was suddenly gone.

Xia sat there mystified, rubbing the lump on his head and wondering what had happened. Then he realized that if these were not the gods toying with him, then it had to be the village's ghosts.

Suddenly, he was very frightened. He jumped up and turned to run, only to find his horse standing nearby, looking as startled as he.

But Xia didn't care. He ran right past the animal, down the hill, and back to his village, crying and scared.

He had to tell someone what had just happened.

Zhua Gong village, 350 miles west of Beijing

Wu Ching was almost finished packing up his family's meager belongings. Carrying one box at a time, he'd carefully taken them from his small, dilapidated house and loaded them onto his broken-down truck, all the while hoping its rusty, fragile undercarriage would support the extra weight.

It was the middle of the night. His wife and three children were sitting in the bed of the truck, crying uncontrollably amidst the boxes and old patched-up suitcases. They'd been forced to shoot their dogs and cats a few minutes earlier; there was no way the government would let the pets go where they were going. In fact, Ching was lucky the authorities were allowing him to keep all three of his children. Some of his neighbors had had their children taken away from them and deposited into state orphanages. Population control here in Zhua Gong was a high priority, as it was throughout all of China.

This place, a long river valley where Ching's family had lived for hundreds of years, was the site of a new hydroelectric dam, a project even larger than the gargantuan Three Gorges Dam, hundreds of miles to the south. The new dam would provide power not for the citizenry of this area, but for sale—to Korea, Manchuria, Russia—and for high prices. The thousands of people who lived here were being kicked out for no other reason than to help feed the greed of the central government in Beijing.

Two policemen were standing by, watching Ching work,

but doing nothing to help. Because Ching had resisted this forced relocation to the very end, the police were sent to make sure he was really leaving this time. The policemen had spent the time smoking cigarettes, drinking rice wine, and whacking Ching on his ankles with their wooden batons whenever they felt he wasn't moving fast enough. But for the most part, they just stood off to the side and laughed at him.

Ching had been forced to do this work by the light of two torches. Electricity in the village had been cut off two weeks ago, just one of a series of moves by the authorities to make sure everyone in the area was gone before the construction brigades moved in. This made leaving here even sadder. Their house, hanging off the edge of a cliff, looking down into the valley, was the last in the village to be emptied of its life, its warmth. It wasn't right—and everyone knew it. But it was happening just the same.

His last box loaded, Ching hitched his horse to the front of his broken-down truck. His engine had blown out long ago; he would have to rely on real horsepower to leave his ancestors' family land. Ching fed the reins through the broken windshield and then climbed in. He looked back at his humble house. It had been a place of happy memories before all this began. Now those memories would be ruined forever.

The policemen lit their cigarettes from the torches, then moved toward the house, intent on burning it down. As the policeman held the burning straw, Ching found himself wishing that somehow, someway, the gluttony of the central government would come to an end and that the Chinese people would be saved from indignities like this.

As he was thinking this, his eyes were lifted upward and that's when he saw a very strange thing off in the distance. Out on the eastern horizon, the stars seemed to be rippling a bit, moving back and forth in a wave—and that wave was coming right toward him. To Ching it was as if the sky itself was tearing itself open slightly and then repairing itself, like a zipper opening and closing again.

Then a great wind came up and this caused the policemen to take notice, too. They turned and saw the strange effect coming at them—it seemed to break into three as it went very low, right over their heads. It startled them so much they dropped their flaming torches and began jabbering at each other.

One cried, "We have drunk too much!"

The other policeman retrieved his flashlight and with shaking hands, pointed it skyward. The beam found something. It was there for them all to see . . . but it was not easy to explain exactly what it was.

The other policeman yelled: "The sky is not true in form tonight!"

Watching all this from the front of his broken-down truck, Ching thought some kind of invisible spacecraft was going over them, something that was there, yet couldn't be seen. Something that mixed with the stars. His family was frightened beyond words, and commenced wailing even louder. The drunk policemen were scared as well. Whatever happened lasted only a few moments and then it was gone, followed by three great bursts of wind. When they were able to compose themselves, the two policemen turned on their radios and began chattering to their central control station, saying the little village of Zhua Gong was being invaded from space.

Oddly, this caused Ching to smile. This weird incident, happening in the middle of this depressing, disconcerting time, actually gave him a glimmer of hope

At least Beijing doesn't know everything about heaven and Earth, he thought.

THE two Chinese J-7 jet fighters had been having their troubles all night.

The pair of aircraft, knockoffs of the elderly Russian MiG-21, made up one-tenth of the Quing Jang squadron, a far-flung training unit located at the edge of the Lanzhou military district in western China. Quing Jang was as remote as one could get in the Chinese military. It was so isolated, it practically straddled the Chinese-Pakistani border.

The base's commanders had been trying to conduct a night-time exercise with a new class of trainee pilots. Having received their first instructions in antique MiG-21s, the student pilots were attempting to transition to the Chinese version of the airplane—but it was not as easy as it sounded. The training squadron had been conducting uneven day exercises for the past few weeks, but the weather had been bad, with lots of early spring snow, and two planes had crashed. Now, in their first night exercise, there had been many delays getting the training squadron's six remaining airplanes ready for flight, due to myriad communication and engine problems.

It wasn't until midnight local time that most things were fixed—but even then, only the two of the six J-7s were deemed airworthy. And because they had spent a good part of the night idling on the runway, their fuel tanks were already half empty on takeoff, further complicating their flight. This had the base commanders shortening the exercise to just a fifteen-minute, low-level orbit around the base. Then everyone involved could finally call it a day.

The first five minutes of this flight went smoothly. After takeoff, the two student pilots climbed to their assigned altitudes and began their long slow turn around the base. Their radios were working fine and there were none of the engine problems that had plagued the rest of the squadron. All this raised the hopes of the senior training commanders that their long day wouldn't be totally lost.

But then the pilot in the lead plane made a desperate call to the base's control tower. He was on the verge of complete panic, yelling more than talking and breathing very rapidly. The control tower officers ordered the recruit to calm down and tell them what was happening. But the young pilot could barely speak.

Once he caught his breath he told them that he'd just collided with another aircraft, that something had actually grazed his starboard wing, shearing off its tip, and sending a long string of sparks into the night. The startled control tower officers quickly ran a radar sweep of the area—but it came back clean. The only other aircraft within 100 miles of the lonely base was the second J-7 training jet, flying about two miles behind the first. Still, the young pilot was terrified.

One of the squadron's senior officers got on the radio and told the lead pilot to take a deep breath, get his bearings, and bring himself back to reality. The senior officer assured the young pilot that there was nothing up there with him but the sky and the stars. But the student pilot wasn't buying it. He continued to insist that something was riding right alongside him, that it had hit his wing once already and that it was huge but practically invisible. He began taking evasive maneuvers, saying whatever it was, it was sparkling and "covered with stars."

The control tower officers immediately contacted the second J-7 flying behind the first. But that pilot reported seeing nothing but clear night skies.

The senior officer was disheartened now. He knew from experience that Air Force trainees had a tendency toward the fantastic, especially when they were flying alone at night for the first time. Their depth perception became skewed, their vision played tricks on them. They began to see things, imagine things.

The control tower called the lead plane again—its young pilot was swerving all over the sky by this time. The tower finally convinced him to bring his plane back to level again and to lower his speed. Once he did this, the senior officer ordered both pilots back to base.

Only then did everyone involved finally admit that this particular night exercise had probably been doomed from the start.

*"**JESUZZ**—what the hell happened back there?"*

That was the question bouncing around Gunn's aircraft as it headed toward the border of Pakistan.

The collision with the Chinese jet was the climax of what had been a nerve-wracking flight across the northern tier of China. It had taken them just four hours, they were still in darkness, and somehow, still in one piece. But it had been a very tense affair. They had seen more than a dozen Chinese military planes along the way; thankfully most of them at a distance. They'd also flown right over two Chinese military installations, one at Jiang Ji and the other at Gwang Fi, coming up on them so fast, they had no alternative but to keep flying straight over them, balls to the walls, and hope that all their masking technology worked. In the end it did, just enough to save them from disaster several times. But this did not mean they hadn't been detected. Many people saw them pass over; they knew this because the Ghost planes were flying so low, they could clearly see these witnesses looking up at them as they streaked by.

Flying low was part of the overall stealth system; getting in below radar was just as important as the stealth paint covering the airplanes from stem to stern. But this meant dozens of farmers, isolated villagers, and people who lived in the western steppes of China had spotted *something* going overhead. When this happened the Ghost crews just crossed their fingers and hoped that whoever was seeing them would not pass the information on to the authorities, or at least not too quickly.

Again, all this made for some anxious moments during the flight. But that was nothing compared to the encounter with the J-7 fighter. That was thirty seconds of sheer terror.

Gunn's C-17 was in the lead during this dash across the Middle Kingdom. Pulver was right on his ass, and Amanda right behind him. They flew more than 2,000 miles at less than 500 feet altitude, some of it as low as fifty feet, where just the whisper of a mistake would send the guilty party crashing into the ground below. It had taken the combined concentration of the flight crews for all three planes to maintain such a high speed at such a belly-scraping altitude. At some points they were so low, a well-placed BB gun could have taken them down.

By using the zoom function on his RIF night vision goggles, Gunn had spotted the pair of J-7s about a minute before they entered the same airspace. The J-7s were flying east to west, at about 500 feet, just as the three Ghost planes were. But the fighters were traveling at less than half the speed of the hulking C-17s, meaning they were quickly approaching a collision course with them.

The three U.S. aircraft had stayed in touch during the flight not by radio but by blinking their navigation lights in Morse code, another old spy plane trick. Once the J-7s had been spotted, Gunn had Bing blink a message back to Pulver and Amanda telling them to be prepared to do a coordinated avoidance maneuver. The idea was to move as one, gain altitude, and get out of the way of the two Chinese fighter jets. The trouble was the lead J-7 was flying so erratically, with no rhyme or reason to its movements, it was going to be hard not to plow right into it. This nearly brought disaster to them all.

Gunn guessed correctly it was probably a trainee at the controls of the lead J-7. It was just bad luck that the old Chinese jet was flying at the exact same altitude and heading as the three Ghost planes. Gunn knew from experience that at times like this, aeronautics became more complex than usual. Not knowing which way another aircraft was going, leads to guessing, and guessing is usually fatal in the air.

As it turned out, the dance lasted just a half minute—but it was a scary half minute. Using his RIF night vision goggles, Gunn kept a bead on the lead J-7 visually, at the same time certain its pilot couldn't see him. When they were but 1,000 feet away from each other, Gunn pulled back on the throttles and pushed his big C-17 up, hoping the J-7 would keep going straight. But no such luck. The Chinese fighter climbed in the same direction as he. So Gunn dove—but the J-7s pilot, overcorrecting himself, dove, too. Gunn hastily pushed his plane to the left—and for some reason, the J-7 pilot did, too. At this point, they were less than 100 feet from one another, with Gunn coming up quickly on the jet fighter's tail.

It was insanity because the J-7 was agile, yet moving sluggishly, and the C-17 was enormous, and filled to the rafters with extra fuel, but Gunn was moving it around like a jet fighter. Finally, he had no choice but to go back to full military power and let the C-17 overtake the J-7, Pulver and Amanda following his lead. The maneuver saved Gunn from colliding full force with the jet fighter. But the big C-17's tail section did clip the J-7's wing, just barely, as it rushed by, causing a long stream of sparks that weirdly seemed to do no more than add more stars to the night sky overhead.

Then just like that, it was over. No doubt freaked out by feeling all three Ghost planes whoosh by him, the Chinese pilot recklessly dove as Gunn and the others climbed in altitude. They lost sight of the Chinese fighter and his trailing companion an instant later.

But the nail-biting wasn't quite at an end. Gunn had to know if his plane's Star Skin integrity had held during the encounter. According to his flight controls diagnostic suite, it had. He then ordered the airplane's air defense radars to do a quick sweep in every direction, including up, looking for any more Chinese fighters. But the sweep came back empty. The sky belonged to them once again.

An orgy of nav light blinking went on between the three C-17s as they plunged through the thickening, colder air. It took a minute, but then it was clear that all was okay on planes two and three as well.

At that point, Gunn finally was able to take his eyes off what he was doing and turn around to check on the man riding in the C-17's extra jump seat behind him. It was Lieutenant Moon. Cool and calm beyond words up to this point, Moon was now shaking visibly, with what could be seen of his face around his sunglasses appearing very pale.

"Don't worry, Lieutenant," Gunn said to him. "Next time, we'll take the train."

NOT ten minutes later, the trio of C-17s streaked across the border into Pakistan.

They had to climb up to 15,000 feet to pass over and in some cases fly between the towering mountains that separated the far western reaches of China from the northeastern edge of the so-called Land of the Pure. They were all glad to get some air under them after flying so low for so long, even though they had to go up on their wings a few times to fit between the closely stacked peaks.

Five minutes in, they spotted the Wunar River and turned southwest. If anything, the terrain below became even more rugged. Even through the cool blue image of their RIF goggles, the landscape looked cold and forbidding, like a faraway moon revolving around a faraway planet. To be lost down there meant to be lost forever.

As soon as they'd turned southwest, they were only 150 miles from their destination: the Kunga Mountains, the range that held the haunted fortress of Bora Kurd. If they maintained their current high rate of speed, they'd be there in twenty minutes.

Everything was working well aboard the three airplanes. Their fuel was holding up and the Star Skin was performing perfectly. Not that they had to worry much about the Pakistani Air Force. They rarely flew up here, in this isolated part of their wild and wooly country. Best of all, Gunn and Company still had almost three hours of darkness left. Three hours to save Newman's daughter's life.

But there was some bad news. Throughout the dash across Asia, Bing had been monitoring an NSA spy satellite that Moon had been able to tap in to. Utilizing the intelligence agent's laptop to pull down real-time images of what was in front of them had helped greatly in getting across China unscathed. But when Bing requested a shot of their eventual destination, he made a disturbing discovery.

"The LZ looks socked in with something," he said, simply.

He showed the spy-sat image to Gunn. It depicted a huge white swirl over the Kunga Mountains. It looked larger than a category 5 hurricane.

Gunn asked: "What the hell is that? Fog?"

Bing shook his head. "I think it's snow, sir. Lots of it . . ."

Gunn took a closer look at the image. "Jesuzz, Bada, that's *got* to be wrong," he said. "There isn't that much snow in the world."

Bing adjusted the knobs on the spy-sat screen, but nothing changed for the better. If anything, the disturbing image grew larger.

Moon stuck his head between them and tried adjusting the spy-sat screen himself, hoping it was just interference they were dealing with. But again, nothing changed. "If it's snow," he said, his voice ice-cold, "then it could be a *wuda*—that's the local Pashtoon dialect for 'big winter storm.' High winds, as much ice as there is snow, lots of blowing and drifts. Those things are so powerful they've been known to take off the tops of mountains."

"Well, that's fucking perfect," Gunn spit out. "We have smooth weather the whole way . . . and now this?"

They were approaching their LZ at nearly ten miles a minute, yet with every second they got closer to the Kunga Mountains, the larger the satellite image of the disturbance became. It was so bad, the old CIA airstrip where they were supposed to land was impossible to see on the display screen.

They tried screwing around with the laptop for another couple minutes, but it was no use. There was only one conclusion: It wasn't the laptop. It wasn't the satellite. This really *was* a snowstorm over their landing site—a monstrous one. Even now, looking out the cockpit window with his RIF night vision goggles on zoom, Gunn could see colossal clouds swirling way out on the horizon.

He glanced over at Bing. He could tell the copilot was thinking the same thing as he: The Star Skin worked great when the stars were out. It also worked in cloudy skies and overcast or if they were flying over the ocean, or any kind of water. But how the hell would it work in a snowstorm? The Ghost planes were dull black when the Star Skin wasn't doing its thing. Would they suddenly turn all white? If they didn't, wouldn't that mean they'd stick out like three enormous sore thumbs?

"The question of whether the Star Skin will work in these conditions is academic," Moon told them, still trying to adjust the spy-sat display's buttons. "It shouldn't have to work, because there's no way we should be flying into a storm like that one. *No one* should be flying into it."

Gunn asked Bing to blink out an abbreviated Morse code message to Amanda and Pulver; both were riding off his wings. Basically he asked them if they saw what he saw, weather-wise. Both blinked back in the affirmative.

"What's the plan?" Pulver's plane added.

Gunn didn't know. This change in atmospherics was completely unexpected. If this had been a typical mission—like an air strike, or an interdiction—it would have been called off and the strike craft ordered home. But this was hardly a typical mission. And judging what was at stake, there was no option of turning around and heading home. And where was home anyway? Fly all the way back across China, to the secret island in the Pacific?

So, his return message was: "Proceeding—but with caution."

Pulver's reply was typical. "Rock 'n' roll . . ."

Amanda's was more sober. "You lead, we follow . . ."

FIVE minutes later, they crashed headfirst into the *wuda*.

The controls on Gunn's plane started to shake immediately, not a good sign for an aircraft that was fly-by-wire, all electronics and microprocessors, as opposed to old-fashioned pulleys and hydraulics. The stick's vibrating told him the gunship's multiprocessor arrays were having a hard time figuring out just how to fly the plane, how to keep it level and within the flight envelope.

Gunn told Bing to keep his eyes glued to the weather screen and to warn him whenever the wind speed buffeting them increased more than five knots.

The copilot began sounding off right away. "Off the nose, coming from the northwest, thirty-five knots . . . forty . . . forty-five . . ."

The first of the snow was already impacting the front of their airplane, hitting their windscreen with the force of bullets. Gunn called back to the weapons crew, telling them to double check everything that could be tied down was, and not just once, but doubled.

Meanwhile, Bing never stopped calling out the wind speed: "Sixty-five knots—off the nose. Close to seventy . . ."

The big gunship was bucking wildly now; Gunn had the throttles pushed to the max, but it was as if they were standing still. It was all he could do to maintain his forward motion and not fall out of the sky. They were basically flying blind, the wet and heavy snow was sticking to the nose even though the C-17 was plowing through the gale at almost 500 knots. The windscreen wipers were working overtime just to clear it away. All this and the fact that the control panel lights were unexplainably growing dim and then coming back brighter than before, only to fade back to dim again became very troubling. Suddenly Gunn realized that this was the most difficult aerial situation he'd ever been in, that after more than 3,000 hours in the air, and flying some of the wildest experimental aircraft ever to come off a drawing board.

Between calling out the wind speed, Gunn had Bing keep the Morse channel open to Amanda and Pulver, constantly reporting his altitude and speed, and just barely seeing their replies blinking back through the storm. Amanda's responses indicated she was going about her business as calmly as possible. But Pulver was uncharacteristically quiet. Not a good sign. Gunn caught himself glancing at the C-17's futuristic situational awareness screen every few seconds. He saw the three blips that represented the three big airplanes flying as tight as possible through the maelstrom. Looking at the screen was just his way of checking that Pulver was still with them.

They were now less than five minutes away from their landing zone and the three planes, flying now at just 3,500 feet, were still being tossed all over the sky. Gunn wasn't paying attention to the weather anymore. He was more concerned with finding the smooth, flat valley they'd been promised as a landing site, the place where the CIA had built its secret airstrip many years ago. He'd been searching his flight computer's readout screen for this magical place, but so far, he was having trouble identifying anything even closely resembling it. He was even clicking his GPS screen on top of the preshot computer images, but nothing was matching up.

"Maybe it doesn't exist," he caught himself thinking. "Like King Kong island."

But just then two images on the head-up display screen suddenly came together—and he found himself looking at the promised flattened-out area. He kicked in his ground-imaging radar and there it was, through the snow and through the ice. Incredibly, it *did* look like an ancient runway or something. Now all they had to do was to somehow make it down there in one piece.

The next two minutes passed with agonized slowness. The big plane was still bouncing all over the sky, flying into a headwind that seemed to be holding them back like some giant invisible hand, this as the ghostly image of the hidden landing strip started blinking on and off.

It only got worse when Moon informed them: "In this part of the world, *wudas* are considered bad luck, especially by the local Pashtoons. They believe they're caused by the devil and other bad spirits, and with the snow they spread, they also spread much misfortune."

A little too much information, Gunn thought.

Finally they were just a minute or so away from the hidden valley. Even though it was very close, between the darkness and the snow no one on board could even see the peak of the mountain where the terrorists were hiding. But no one was even thinking about them—at the moment all they wanted to do was prevent the three big planes from running into one of the many other mountains surrounding the hidden valley.

And Gunn made sure Bing continued his running Morse code dialogue with the other planes, as it was also important that all three pilots knew where each one was at all times. The chance of midair collision was great as well, now that they were entering a very confined airspace, in the dark, in the midst of a blizzard yet. It would have been difficult flying even under the best weather conditions.

Finally the last minute passed and Gunn believed they'd arrived over the hidden valley airstrip. He wasn't sure because the image he'd acquired had blinked off again and never came back on. No matter. On his call, all three airplanes fell into a ragged orbit above where he thought the designated LZ should be. Now came the really hard part. Their bare essential of a plan called for a squad of paratroopers to jump at this point, get down to the valley, make sure it was the right place, then lay out some flare-type hot sticks—to demark the landing strip, just like their training days back in Area 153.

But there was no way Gunn was going to order anyone to jump from a plane under these conditions—even though he was sure that Pulver had more than a few volunteers among the 82nd who wanted to go in.

The problem was not only didn't they have a Plan B, they didn't even have a Plan A. But Gunn didn't need a playbook to tell him what had to be done. If the primary landing point could not be secured by the paratroopers due to bad weather, then the landing point would have to be handled by the command plane. That meant him. It was a stark choice, but the correct one. His plane had the least amount of personnel on it. Counting himself, Bada, Moon, and the gun crew, they were an unlucky thirteen. Pulver's plane was packed with 102 paratroopers and crew, and Amanda's plane was carrying an even two dozen.

So, Gunn's plane would go in first, somewhat blind and hoping to wind up on the runway. If they landed safely, then they would mark the landing strip, and the others would follow.

If they crashed, then the others would be on their own.

And so would the person they'd come to rescue.

AS Amanda struggled to keep her aircraft steady in its long, ragged 360 around the LZ, her copilot, the young Air Force lieutenant named Stanley, read out the Morse code messages coming from Gunn's lead ship. Essentially they repeated Gunn's cold decision: that he was going in and if he made it, the other two planes should look for the lighted runway and then come in as well. Amanda and her crew of twenty-three first, then Pulven's packed plane after her. And if they didn't spot anything below? The message didn't go on from there. It didn't have to.

Amanda watched as Gunn's plane started spiraling down into the whirlpool of snow and blowing ice. She couldn't believe this was happening. Doing anything in this brutal weather seemed suicidal. But there was no other choice. And there was nothing she could do now . . . but watch.

Ghost 1 continued falling, slow and steep; Amanda could tell Gunn was employing the variable slats on his aircraft's wings to give him the ability to drain off as much air speed as possible. He had also lowered his landing gear, slowing him down further. Everything looked as good as possible. But then the big gunship was swallowed up by the storm and suddenly disappeared. And Amanda couldn't help but think that it was gone forever.

A minute went by. She kept circling, Pulver one mile behind her, their radios silenced, eyes peeled for any sign of anything below, but seeing nothing. Even her aircraft's ground-imaging radar was being blotted out by the increasingly heavy snow, its screen was just showing blank images, colored in dull gray. She caught herself thinking the worst:

What if Gunn's plane had crashed and the weather was so thick that she and Pulver would be unable to see the smoke, the flames? Even though Ghost 1 was full of extra fuel, as they all were, the storm was so violent it might hide even the most spectacular explosion.

She tried to get her head back into the situation, but couldn't. She kept remembering the first time she and Gunn had actually had a conversation, up on the mesa, that brilliant night that seemed so long ago. They had looked up at the stars, each with their own sense of yearning, never knowing how linked they would be with those same stars, while still staying down here on Earth.

This was no way to end this adventure, she thought.

She kept flying in circles, checking all her monitoring devices, and using her own RIF goggles, dialing up their enhanced vision mode, but unable to see anything but tons of snow blowing around. Some of it was so thick, so intense, it could have easily hidden a cloud of smoke, raging in the gale.

How long do we do this? she thought. *How long do we circle out here like fools, above the most remote place in the world, before we have to get around the fact that Gunn's plane didn't make it and he's dead and gone and we have to admit defeat, abandon the mission, and find the safest and least embarrassing place to land?*

Ten minutes, she decided.

They would circle for ten minutes more. Then, they would have to leave.

Round and round they went, battling the snow, burning fuel, fearing the worst.

Amanda could almost hear Pulver screaming at her, even though he was a full mile behind: *Let's get on with it!* she was sure he was saying. *Either land or let's get the hell out of here!*

Five minutes ticked away . . . but she saw nothing below that indicated Gunn had made it down safely.

Six minutes. Seven. Eight. Still nothing.

Nine minutes. Nine and thirty seconds . . .

Amanda was tempted to break the radio silence, just for a

moment. But she knew that might endanger everyone else left alive.

Nine and forty-five . . .

She tipped the big plane even more, straining her eyes to look through the blowing snow. But she saw nothing but the wind . . .

She looked at her watch . . . ten minutes . . .

Time was up.

She felt the lump in her throat get bigger. At the same time she became furious with the Islamic terrorists—all Muslims everywhere. What a waste of time. What a waste of life!

She righted the big plane and started blinking her navigation lights so Pulver would know what was coming next. She started a long turn to the south. Maybe they could make Diego Garcia without getting shot down.

That's when her copilot, Stanley, cried out: "Wait—wait a moment! What's that?"

Amanda looked down to her left—but again she saw nothing but the fiercely blowing snow.

"I don't see anything," she told him.

"Not down there," he replied. "Down *there* . . . one o'clock, off our nose."

Amanda had to raise herself in her seat to see where he was talking about. But there it was. Faintly, but unmistakably, a greenish speck of light, flaring through the snow.

She couldn't believe it—she'd been looking in the wrong spot all the time!

She turned the big plane back to the north and reduced speed drastically. Now the green speck was on her left. As she was doing this, she saw another speck appear, then another, and another . . .

By the end of one more orbit, the green specks had perfectly lined a landing strip. She immediately began blinking a message to Pulver. Some of the Marine tankers in the rear reported Pulver was blinking back.

"That was a little too dramatic," she said to Stanley, pushing the controls in preparation for a landing.

"Sure was—unless . . ." he replied almost nonchalantly.

"Unless, what?" she asked him.

He said: "Unless those are actually terrorists down there—and they're sucking us in."

AMANDA brought her plane down to 1,500 feet, lowered her gear, and began slotting into her landing profile.

She would not have more than one chance to land at the old CIA airstrip. The line of mountains to the south would prevent any more than one attempt. She would either have to touch down, or impact on one of those southern peaks—there was no other choice.

Down to 1,300 feet now, airspeed draining off to 150 knots, she leveled out, her eyes locked onto the twin row of green lights quickly coming at her. She'd landed F-18s onto Navy carriers at night, and in bad weather, but rarely in this kind of bad weather, or this kind of night, and never in this kind of plane. It would be a challenge to say the least.

Down to 1,200 feet in altitude, airspeed at 135 knots. She wouldn't be able to get her speed much lower than that without falling out of the sky completely. The twin lines of green lights were just a quarter-mile in front of her now, and coming at her extremely fast. Stanley was reading off their altitude. They were dropping rapidly. Still she couldn't see the ground, just the lights and the snow.

1,000 feet . . .

800 . . .

650 . . .

At 500 feet, Amanda applied the air brakes, lowering the variable flaps on the wing. It was like stomping on the brake pedal in a car going 130 mph. The whole plane shook from one end to the other. She heard a collective gasp from the Marine tankers in back, but she couldn't worry about them now.

500 feet out . . .

400 . . .

The plane seemed to stand still for a moment. The wind was blowing so fiercely, Amanda felt like she was approaching the landing strip sideways. It was all she could do to pull the plane's nose back to straight ahead.

200 feet . . .

100 . . .

She still couldn't see the landing strip, even though her instruments were all telling her it was there, somewhere.

Down to 50 feet, 45 . . . .

"Jesuzz!" Stanley suddenly cried out. At the same instant, her flight computer began blaring out a warning: "Pull up! Pull up!"

Suddenly filling her field of view was Gunn's airplane, sitting cock-eyed at the end of the airstrip. It was only then she realized she'd come in for a landing at the *opposite* end of the runway than Gunn had. Worse, the huge gunship had obviously skidded sideways on the snow-covered runway and was now blocking it. They would slam into it in approximately three seconds . . .

Amanda let her instincts take over. She simply pulled up on the controls slightly—and her plane leapfrogged over Gunn's aircraft, just barely missing its tail. Then she pushed back down on the stick—and the next thing she felt was a jarring *bump!*

And just like that, she was down.

Now she literally stood on the brakes, applied reverse thrusters, reverse engines—all at the same time. The computers were overcompensating for the slippery runway, but her shuttle training taught her how to counteract this. It took a deft touch when it seemed like the rest of the world was going mad all around you, but that was her thing.

The combined braking action finally took effect and she could feel the big plane finally start to slow down. The ground itself was now more visible; the green beacons seemed very bright in the wash of blue inside her night vision goggles. They began slowing down rapidly, and even though it seemed like the C-17 was going to go up on its nose at any moment, it was a good feeling. Amanda let out a breath of relief. She couldn't remember a time when she was so happy to be back on the ground.

But suddenly, the Marines in the back began screaming.

She twisted in her seat to look out her window—and was shocked to see Pulver's plane was practically right behind her!

"Jesuzz!" she cried out.

She hit the controls—the left brake and left rudder instantaneously. This caused her plane to fall off violently to the left. Pulver went streaking by two seconds later, touching down, and skidding his way down the runway.

Two seconds after that, Amanda's plane finally came to rest. Yet both she and Stanley were still standing on the brakes, as if frozen in place.

It took a few more seconds for her to realize that she could relax. She collapsed back into her seat—then reached up and gently tugged Stanley back down, too.

She held his hand for a moment and he held hers. They both took a deep breath. Then she said, "Remind me to kill Captain Pulver when this is over."

Stanley laughed nervously. "Not if I get to him first."

But in the midst of regaining their composure, they saw something very strange: A dark figure was running along the runway, fighting the precipitation and the two-foot-deep snow. They followed this person with their RIFs as he reached the back of Pulver's just-stopped Ghost 2 and started banging on the side access door. The door was finally pushed open by a gang of paratroopers just recovering from their own heart-stopping landing. They exchanged words, and in seconds the rear ramp of the C-17 troop ship opened into the blowing snow. Seconds after that, another gang of paratroopers pushed the tiny OH-33 helicopter out of the back of the airplane.

At this point Amanda and Stanley realized the dark figure was Lieutenant Moon. They could see him instructing the snow-covered paratroopers how to unfold his tiny aircraft. It took just a few seconds. Then Moon climbed in and started the copter's engine, further whipping up the blizzard blowing all around them.

He let the aircraft warm up for no more than ten seconds and then he could be seen talking to two of the paratroopers. After a rushed conversation with the 82nd CO, Captain Vogel, the two paratroopers climbed onto the tiny copter and held on for dear life. Moon pulled up on the copter's controls and the small aircraft went straight up into the storm, the two hulking paratroopers practically hanging off of it. Amanda checked her watch—it was 0343 hours local time. They'd been on the ground less than two minutes, but already Moon was onto the next step.

"He doesn't screw around," Stanley said, watching the copter vanish into the maelstrom above. "Is he attacking the mountain by himself, just him and those two jumpers?"

Amanda just shook her head.

"He'll save us a lot of trouble if he does," she said.

CHAPTER 15

Bora Kurd, 0345 hours

A man named Amil the Syrian was in charge of protecting the fortress of Bora Kurd.

He was a veteran of the dreaded Shu'bat al-Mukhabarat, the shadowy Syrian intelligence service whose agents were experts at kidnapping and murdering political opponents. He'd also spent time in the Syrian Army's Special Forces unit Al-Sa'iqa, a barely disguised assassination squad that specialized in car bombings and blowing up airplanes in flight. In between, he'd served as a weapons broker for Hezbollah, the Iranian-backed terrorist organization that was currently the bane of Israel's existence.

Mid-forties, with a huge mustache and a shaved but woefully uneven head, Amil was as close to a true military leader as the PKD terrorists had. As a younger man, he had taken on the identity of a Pakistani national and had spent time in the British Army where he learned, among other things, the art of fortification protection. Deserting on the eve of the 1991 Gulf War, he returned to the Middle East to use his newfound knowledge to make money fighting the Great Satan.

His boss these days was the top man inside Bora Kurd, the

head of the PKD, the one known to all as the Mountain Sheik. A protégé of Osama bin Laden himself, and blessed with a vast array of wealthy contacts in the Persian Gulf, the Sheik had been convinced by Amil's arguments that while the PKD's guerrilla-style tactics had served them well over the years— just as the tactics of the mujahideen worked well against the Soviets during the 1980's Afghanistan war—because Bora Kurd was such an important place, for many reasons, it should be vigorously defended in a logical style if it was ever attacked. This meant the PKD had to start thinking more like a military unit and come up with a strategy to protect their most precious asset.

To this end, Amil got the Sheik to construct dozens of permanent weapons emplacements all over the mountain. This turned out to be a wise decision, both when the UN Blue Hats arrived in their foolish attempt to rescue the USAID "visitors," as well as was when the more dangerous Pakistani Attack Section 21 helicopter force attempted just as futilely to do the same thing.

Amil's ring of weapon emplacements had halted both attempts, and he had no doubt they would prevent further ones from happening in the future. Having a reputation and the ability to back it up was very important in the Islamic world these days. The myth that Bora Kurd was both haunted *and* impregnable was fast becoming a well-deserved one—thanks to Amil.

His emplacements were simple, three-sided concrete pillboxes, hidden deep in the snowy, scraggly overgrowth that covered most of the ghostly mountain. The emplacements held a mixed bag of military hardware Amil had bought secretly from the Chinese. His premier weapons were the high-powered ZU-23J multibarrel cannons. Known for their outstanding accuracy at very long range, these guns could hit a target nearly two miles away in any direction including straight up. This meant they could be used against aircraft and ground forces alike. Amil had no less than four dozen of them, set in rings, all around the mountain. They were positioned in such a way that their radar-controlled fire would be supporting and interlocking in the event of enemy attack. It was these weapons that shredded the rescue force of UN Blue Hats.

Amil had also installed two rings of SAMs, specifically Russian-made SA-8s surface-to-air missiles. These weapons were extremely versatile; when the Russians used them, some were mounted on tanks, others were put on naval ships. Amil's SAMs were set up in fixed positions, their six-foot-long missiles capable of hitting a target nearly ten miles away. It was a barrage of SA-8s that had so quickly brought down the Pakistani Special Forces copter unit.

Supplementing these large weapons emplacements were dozens of smaller ones: pillboxes containing 50-caliber machine guns, Katyusha rocket launchers, and heavy mortars. All of the gun posts were manned by up to a half dozen PKD fighters each, armed with AK-47s and grenade launchers. These men were the closest thing any terrorist organization in the area had to regular infantry. Amil had even instituted a system of subcommanders and combat fighters, the extremist version of officers and enlistees, to ensure discipline when it was needed.

To keep these men occupied during their guard duty, Amil allowed them to use their AK-47s to shoot randomly into the half dozen small villages located around the base of the mountain, a means of terrorizing the haunted peak's neighbors, as well as giving the combat fighters needed target practice.

Another secret to keeping these men in some kind of military form was changing them out frequently. Most of the combat fighters spent four hours out in the cold, on duty, followed by two hours inside, before doing another four hours back outside. Then came a rest period and the schedule started all over again. Amil had more than 200 fighters at his disposal; moving them in and out of their gun positions on a regular basis kept them happy and warm while also keeping the mountain secure.

It also freed up the rest of the PKD fighters to do missions like the one that had brought the abducted Americans to Bora Kurd. Occasionally, the PKDs would go on forays into Afghanistan, to steal weapons, money, food, and gasoline, and to terrorize the locals with kidnappings, rape, and outright murder. For these reasons, it was no surprise the Mountain Sheik's fighters were considered the rule of law in this otherwise lawless part of Pakistan.

And it didn't stop there. The PKD's long-term goal was to become the most feared terrorist organization in the world. To accomplish this, they'd set out to acquire a nuclear bomb, developed plans to smuggle it into the United States, and when the time was right, detonate it. That's why there was a part of the fortress, known curiously as the "White Rooms," where no one but the Mountain Sheik and Amil could go without permission. For anyone else to do so meant instant execution, no matter where you were in the PKD's hierarchy.

The secrets hidden inside the White Rooms, Amil hoped, would crack the world open someday . . . which made what happened shortly after he retired this particular snowy evening even more unsettling.

Because before the next day was over, Amil would come to realize the world might have to be cracked open much sooner than he would have ever thought.

IT was his bodyguard who woke Amil with the disturbing news: The subcommander of one of the large ZU-23J gun sites on the mountain's western side had vanished. There one moment, he was gone the next.

Amil had a mouthful of questions as he hastily climbed back into his dirty robes and boots. What could have happened to this missing man? Had he fallen off the mountain? Unlikely, the bodyguard told him. His assigned area was not that steep. Could he have deserted? Amil asked. Again, not likely, replied the bodyguard. The man was not only a well-paid mercenary-type, he was also a distant cousin of one of Amil's wives. Family meant everything in this part of the world. If this man had run away, the bodyguard said, he would have done it with the knowledge that Amil would have his entire family killed, relatives or not. Besides, the bodyguard said, there was massive *wuda* happening outside, with high winds and heavy snow, and there were no signs it was letting up anytime soon. Where, then, would this man run to? Amil could only agree. Whatever happened to him, the man probably didn't go AWOL.

With this, Amil and the bodyguard started the long walk up through the fortress tunnels, heading toward the western end of the mountain.

Even though it was the middle of the night, Amil had to find out for himself what was going on.

THE center of the Mountain Sheik's fortress was the Great Hall, with dozens of smaller compartments and tunnels running off of it. The Sheik's relatives, who owned a huge construction company in Saudi Arabia, had built the hall as well as everything else inside the fortress. Again, its original purpose was as a secret staging point against the Soviets during the Afghan War in the '80s, but it had been vastly updated and modernized since then. It was lit by sodium lights. It had a workable heating and ventilating system. It had fresh water, cooking facilities, space for sleeping and praying, and even a small hospital. And while the maze of tunnels that ran off the Great Hall and throughout the mountain resembled an ant farm, there was order to the seeming chaos. Those tunnels that ran up and down led to the gun emplacements. Those that ran sideways were for moving to and from the living areas. And most important was the narrow tunnel built just below the Sheik's living quarters. That was designed to serve as the mountain's escape route, should it ever be needed.

As a child, Amil had watched a grainy, scratchy copy of the first *Star Wars* movie. It was the only Western-style film he'd seen to that point and it had fascinated him. Even now, any time he found himself walking through the Great Hall, two words would pop into his head: *Star Wars*. To him, the Great Hall looked like a grand re-creation of the set used at the end of the movie. Except . . . for the area that had been devoted to the PKD's TV studio/execution point. Amil always tried to avoid looking there, only because the thought of hacking off someone's head in front of a video camera ruined the illusion that he was somehow living inside his favorite movie.

Amil moved quickly through the huge man-made cavern now, glancing only briefly at the guards stationed near the rooms that had served as prison cells for the captured American aid workers. While ten men were assigned this duty, eight of them were presently asleep on the floor near their posts, the doors to the cells they were supposed to be guarding swung wide open. It was a stark reminder that only one American hostage was still alive—and only one more videotape had to be made. And that was going to be made not much later than daybreak, if not sooner. In fact, Amil could hear wailing coming from behind the only cell door that was still locked. The hostage within knew a horrible death was close at hand and she was pleading with God to save her.

Savage business, Amil thought as he hurried along, trying to block out the prisoner's cries.

And nothing like *Star Wars*.

IT took Amil ten minutes to reach the gun emplacement known as Site 16, carefully avoiding the restricted area around the White Rooms as he did so. Site 16 was where the missing officer had vanished.

Leaving his bodyguard behind, he stepped out a hatchway and into the freezing, blowing snow. The *wuda* was still raging full-tilt. Pulling his robe tighter around him, he spotted the four remaining Site 16 fighters inside the three-sided concrete emplacement nearby, huddled next to their giant ZU-23J gun. Their personal weapons discarded, their hands and feet were shaking from the cold—or was it from fright? Each man's eye shadow was leaking down his face and they all seemed to be looking very far away. Amil took all these things as very bad signs.

He wedged himself into the bunker with them and managed to flick on his cigarette lighter.

"Tell me, brothers, what happened here?" Amil asked them, holding up the flame so he could see their faces. "Where has your officer gone?"

The men could barely speak. One man just snapped his fingers and said: "Poof!"

A second man said, "Our subcommander was here, and then he wasn't. I turned my head and he disappeared."

"I believe Satan got him," a third man said. "I believe the devil flew in here himself just a few minutes ago and that he is nearby and that we may all be cursed."

"We *did* hear strange noises a while ago," the fourth man confessed. "Noises like the wind, yet not the wind."

This man then spit to his left, an act the others quickly followed. It was a small ritual to ward off the devil, but seeing it greatly disturbed Amil. These four men were Pashtoons, part of a large local tribe, many of whom were PKD fighters. They were a highly superstitious lot and prone to panic if they thought satanic spirits were after them. If they truly believed something supernatural had befallen their missing officer, that could only mean trouble.

Amil stepped out of the bunker and walked a few feet down the nearby path. The storm was raging all around him. The wind was incredibly fierce, and the snow was coming down at a tremendous rate. He looked off the mountain, and scanned the miles of rugged, almost silvery country below.

It was hard to see, and even harder to breathe, the wind was blowing at such high speed, but still, Amil thought he noticed something peculiar down in the valley next to the mountain. What he recalled as being a nearly flat piece of land a couple miles in length now seemed to feature several shallow hills, topography that looked oddly unfamiliar to him. Was this just an illusion caused by the snow piling up? he thought. Were those just snowdrifts building as a result of the great *wuda*? He couldn't tell. But it looked very peculiar.

Thinking this, he took a deep sniff of the air blowing around him and was startled by what his substantial nose picked up. Along with the usual damp, musty odor that pervaded the mountain inside and out, there was something else on the wind. An oily smell. Smoky. The stink of exhaust, maybe? Of jet fuel? Or maybe both?

Amil had been around airplanes enough to recognize that odor—and now he felt an uncomfortable sensation rising in his chest. Why would the smell of aircraft fuel be out here, in one of the most inhospitable places in the world? Who would be foolish enough to be flying in this kind of weather? It made no sense, yet Amil was sure what his nose was telling him was true.

He scanned the sky and then the valley below him again. Something was wrong here, he could feel it just as he could feel the blowing snow stinging his face.

And instinct told him it was connected somehow to the missing man. His wife's distant cousin.

He looked all around him again and then wondered out loud, "Brother? Where the hell did you go?"

SUBCOMMANDER Muhammad Sahir had never flown before.

That was just one of the reasons Site 16's missing officer was shaking so badly now. In fact, Sahir was so frightened he couldn't stop wetting himself.

The last twenty minutes had been a terrifying blur for him. One moment, he was up on the mountain, near his post, trying to relieve himself in the storm—the next, two monsters came out of the blowing snow, knocked him to the ground, and began beating him viciously. He was handcuffed, gagged, and his legs were tied with rubber bungee cords. Then he was trundled down the path for fifty yards or so, until he looked up and saw the tiny helicopter hovering silently above the snow, like some kind of giant insect fighting the great wind. That's when he wet his pants for the first time.

His captors strapped him to the side of the helicopter—not inside the compartment where people would normally fly, but to the skid on the outside! A nightmarish descent down the side of the mountain followed; Sahir screamed through his gag for mercy the entire way. But of course it did him no good.

On landing, he was taken off the small helicopter, and carried into the belly of a much larger aircraft, a huge jet airplane hidden in the middle of the snow-covered valley. He had no idea how it got there, or how long it had been lying in wait a stone's throw from Bora Kurd—but its size was tremendous. It was something he imagined the size of a whale to be, not that he'd ever seen a whale or even the ocean for that matter. The strange thing was, from the outside this huge airplane looked invisible, its color blending in perfectly with the snowy surroundings. Sahir didn't know that an airplane was even there, until he was put inside it.

He was now inside a compartment that was itself inside the huge airplane. The compartment was made entirely of pale blue plastic and was immensely clean, even though, like everything else inside the plane, it smelled of kerosene. There were things hanging on the walls and from the ceiling. Electronic things, weird things. Needles, blinking lights, strange weapons, and such. It was totally alien from the caves and stone huts Sahir had lived in all his life. To him, he was in the belly of a beast.

He was tied to a chair with the same bungee cords that had held him onto the helicopter. A small man in a military uniform had helped his captors bring him here; this man had been sitting in a chair in the corner, just staring at him ever since. He was wearing sunglasses even though there was only one, very dull light inside the compartment, and he seemed insanely calm. Sahir was sure this man was an American. And that scared him very much.

After staying like this for what seemed a very long time, during which Sahir urinated on himself several more times, the man in the sunglasses finally stood up and pushed a button on the wall. A large TV screen suddenly began lowering from the ceiling, stopping just a few feet in front of Sahir's chair.

Then the man drew out a razor-sharp knife and very deliberately put it against Sahir's throat.

"Before you die," he whispered in Sahir's ear, "we will talk."

Hearing this, Sahir peed himself for the last time.

Then the man pushed the knife even deeper into the skin of Sahir's throat and asked him a very queer question, "How can a fly get inside your mountain?"

TOMMY Gunn couldn't think straight.

He, Amanda, and Pulver—along with the captain of the 82nd, Vogel, and the Marine tankers' senior man, Captain Steve Cardillo—were inside Ghost 3, trying to come up with a workable rescue plan. They had chosen Amanda's aircraft because it was covered with the most snow and had the most open space inside, squeezed between the two tanks and the extra fuel bladders.

The storm that had nearly killed them was now their protector. The Star Skin worked better than advertised; its chameleonlike properties had turned the plane's fuselage and wings into a fair approximation of the color of snow and kept it that way. Plus so much real snow continued to fall, the three planes were nearly buried in it anyway. They could have all been colored fire-engine red and still not be seen from more than a few feet away.

So, they were here, they had beaten the sun, and now they had to plan for what lay ahead. But again, Gunn couldn't concentrate, because of the screaming.

As Newman himself had suggested back in Nevada, the 201st was the wrong unit for this mission. Bringing tanks to attack a 13,000-foot high mountain fortress was almost as foolish as bringing paratroopers to do the same thing. Moreover, there was no way they'd be able to fight their way up the mountain, inside or out. They had no idea how many PKD fighters were inside the fortress, but they were sure it was at least double the 140 people who'd come on the rescue mission—probably a lot more. Fighting an uphill battle against such unknown numbers was the last thing they wanted to do. Everyone agreed on that.

So they would have to attempt something from the top down, which meant only one option: Have the gunship soften up the mountain's defenses, then somehow drop the 82nd onto the peak and fight downward.

This idea had many, many drawbacks—and if the ride over wasn't long enough for them to think about what they were facing here, then it was now, in this meeting, that it was finally beginning to sink in. The theorem "you go to war with the army you have" was pure foolishness, but that's exactly the situation here. It would have to be top-down or nothing.

What they needed, though, before they could do anything else, was intelligence—even just a few morsels to let them know what to expect inside the fortress. Trouble was they didn't have very much time to get it and even less to figure out how to use it.

But that's what all the screaming was about.

Amanda's plane was also where Moon's mysterious module lay. And that's where Moon was at the moment—inside the strange blue square box with the terrorist he'd so quickly snatched off the mountain. That's where all the screaming was coming from. The man was pleading for his life.

Moon was obviously interrogating him—but therein lay the problem. Trying to concentrate while listening to the mountain fighter beg for mercy was almost impossible. Even Vogel, the hardened 82nd CO, was blanching at the chorus of blood-curdling shrieks coming from the module. It sounded like the soundtrack from a slasher move.

What the hell kind of person was Moon? Gunn wondered. *Genius? Psychopath? Something in between?*

The screams stopped eventually, but that made the vibe inside the airplane even worse. After about a minute of silence, the door on the module opened and Moon stepped out. He didn't seem ruffled or distracted. He was in a hurry though.

He quickly made his way past the tanks and over to where the officers were gathered, putting on a cold weather parka as he did so.

"I need about thirty minutes," he told them, checking his watch. "It's now about 0400. I'll be back before 0430 hours. If everything goes well, we can strike sometime after 0500. But we'll still have to hurry."

He revealed a small black box he was carrying with him. It had a single red bulb on its cover. The bulb was blinking softly.

He opened up the box for all to see. Inside was a fly. A common, ordinary housefly.

It was sitting completely still on a piece of white silk. But other than that, it looked not the least bit unusual.

"Just in case I don't come back," Moon told them. "I want you all to see that this piece of technology is intact before I leave."

They were all stumped, though. No one had any idea what he was talking about.

"It's a bug," Pulver finally said, the master of understatement.

"Wrong," Moon corrected him. "It's a fifteen-million-dollar bug . . ."

With that, he pulled up his parka, adjusted his sunglasses, opened the plane's side hatch, and stepped out into the howling blizzard.

As soon as he was gone, the five officers walked over to the module. Moon had left the door open, possibly on purpose.

They peered inside to see the PKD fighter, still in his chair, tied to it with bungee cords, body upright.

But he was quite dead.

On the TV screen in front of him, a video was playing continuous loops of the same, bloody, quick-cut images: People being beheaded by Islamic terrorists in Iraq. People jumping to their deaths rather than be burned alive in the Twin Towers on 9/11. Car bomb victims dying in the streets of Islamabad and Karachi. Children being mutilated while still alive by Muslim soldiers in Somalia.

The terrorist's eyes were wide open and locked on the video screen. He looked like he was in mid-scream, yet his face was absolutely white. Even his lips had no color. It was as if he'd been drained of blood, yet there was no blood leaking anywhere. Not on the chair or the floor or the walls. No place. There was a handful of hypodermic needles hanging nearby, but there was no evidence any of them had been used.

Still . . .

"This is freaky-deaky," Pulver said.

Gunn couldn't disagree. He'd come upon corpses in the past, enemy fighters killed in battle. But nothing quite as disturbing as this.

"I've seen this before," Amanda said. "In one of my psywar courses at the Academy. Pale complexion, throat swollen, extreme distress of facial features . . ."

"You mean, you know how he died?" Vogel asked her.

She nodded gravely.

"If I had to guess," she said, "I'd say he's been frightened to death."

CHAPTER 16

EXACTLY twenty-nine minutes after he left, Moon returned to Ghost 3.

He half stumbled back through the access door, covered head-to-toe with snow and ice. Even his sunglasses were coated with a layer of slush.

In that time, the 201st officers had continued sketching out a vague rescue plan, but again, were sorely lacking in knowledge of what lay inside the mountain waiting for them.

So all eyes were on Moon as he pulled off his parka and shook the precipitation from his hands and face. He indicated that the officers should join him in the module. They climbed up into the square blue box and Moon closed the door behind them. With a flick of a switch, he stopped the horrific image loop still playing on the video screen.

"The body?" Moon asked simply.

"Out back," Gunn told him. "Under the snow."

The intelligence officer just said: "Thanks for that."

But strangely, Gunn wasn't listening to him. He was looking around the interior of the blue box module instead, the first time he'd really had a chance to. It seemed much larger inside than it looked from the outside. It resembled a good-

sized cabin on a cruise ship, but there was a definite mad scientist edge to it. There were more than a dozen video screens
mounted on its walls, with just as many computer terminals
and communications sets hanging everywhere. One wall held
a display of weird-looking weapons, futuristic battle helmets,
and what appeared to be all-metal combat suits. A box nearby
contained several dozen hypodermic needles.

Moon started banging on a nearby keyboard, and in a few
seconds the large video screen came to life again, this time
with the image of a snowy plain as if seen through a night
vision scope. In the background, beyond a few scrub trees,
was the foot of the mountain they'd come here to attack: Bora
Kurd.

"Is this happening live?" Cardillo asked, astounded at the
clarity of the image.

"It is," Moon replied, fine-tuning the screen. "From a place
about a half mile down the valley from here."

He banged a few more keys and the image became even
sharper and cleaner. The night vision aspect seemed to slowly
fade away. Then Moon checked his watch and said: "Any moment now . . ."

A small figure entered the frame from the right. It was a
boy, maybe in his young teens, wearing rags and barefoot,
carrying two huge buckets through the deep snow.

"This kid lives in a village not far from where this was
taken," Moon explained. "His family owns the only cow
within twenty miles of this place. And so here he is, right on
time."

The boy moved across the screen

"This is what the dead mook told you?" Amanda asked.
"The bovine situation out here?"

Moon just said, "Please watch."

The boy made his way across the snowy field, struggling
with the two big buckets of what they could now tell was
milk. To the left, right up against the base of the mountain, a
small stone hut could be seen partially hidden beneath the
heavy brush. It looked about a thousand years old.

When the boy with the pails was about three-quarters of
the way across the field, the door to the hut opened and a man
cautiously stepped out. He was holding an AK-47 rifle and

wearing a black ski mask. Another man was behind him, waiting at the door; he, too, was carrying an assault rifle and wearing a mask. They were obviously PKD terrorists.

The first man walked about ten feet into the field and took the pails from the boy. When it appeared the boy was asking the man for some kind of payment, the man brutally slapped him across the face. The blow was so hard, the young boy was knocked off his feet. Then the armed man picked up the pails and passed them to his colleague waiting back at the hut.

At that point, Moon started manipulating the computer's joystick—and incredibly the camera started to move. It was obvious he was controlling it. But how?

"Remember that fly?" Moon asked them. "That fifteen-million-dollar bug? Its official name is SCRAM—small camera, remote airborne, modified."

"It's a robot?" Gunn asked, astonished. "That bug?"

"It's a *flying* robot with a camera attached," Moon mildly corrected him. "Courtesy of the Sandia Labs."

He called up a three-way diagram of the SCRAM on one half of the video screen; the five officers studied it with no little amazement. It looked like a real, living fly in all respects, except a tiny camera lens was visible on top of its head—though one would need a microscope to really see it.

"That lens is the size of the head of a pin," Moon explained. "But it has a resolution better than the best cell phone camera on the market. And the audio is coming from a microphone even smaller than the camera lens. But it all works somehow, and it is surprisingly robust. At the moment it is hovering just above a tree limb about twenty feet away from where the kid and the terrorists are."

Moon returned full screen to the scene in the field. They watched as the man who took the milk began kicking the young boy, this as the kid was desperately trying to get away from him.

As this was happening, Moon started steering the SCRAM again with the computer's joystick. Suddenly it was moving very fast, flying toward the terrorist who'd first taken the pails of milk. As he and his companion went back into the hut, the fly-cam followed them in.

"This is . . . unbelievable," Vogel gasped.

They all watched as the two men opened a door at the back of the hut, revealing an entrance to a tunnel beyond. This was a passageway that led right into the mountain itself.

"Welcome to the Bat Cave," Moon said, almost to himself. "Right where our departed friend said it would be."

The fly-cam followed the men as they walked up the gradually climbing passageway. Soon enough, carrying the pails of milk became a chore.

"I'm guessing the milk is for the head poo-bah," Moon said. "The rest of them must pour plain old water on their Rice Krispies."

The passageway became so steep, the two terrorists needed handrails to pull themselves up.

"I was told this tunnel is actually their only escape route," Moon reported. "Should the shit ever hit the fan inside the fortress, this is how they'd all get out. A very valuable thing to know, don't you think?"

Finally the terrorists reached a trapdoor with a ladder leading up to it. The fly-cam landed for a few moments as the men opened the hatch and climbed the ladder. The fly-cam then followed them right up to the next level.

Suddenly the 201st officers were looking at the inside of a large hall.

"Bingo," Moon said excitedly. "Welcome to the center of the PKD's universe."

The officers were astounded at how elaborate the huge hall was. They could see dozens of armed men scattered throughout it, some lounging around, some just passing through. They were all dressed in the same dirty black robes and white headdresses that the PKD wore. All were wearing the PKD's trademark eye shadow, too.

The fly-cam left the two men carrying the pails as they entered what was the food area, and flew up to the ceiling in order to better look down at the big room.

"Any chance of our getting caught doing this?" Amanda asked Moon.

Moon almost laughed at her. "Seriously, Lieutenant," he replied. "Do you think anyone is going to notice a fly in this place?"

From the top of the Great Hall, they could now see hundreds of PKD fighters moving not unlike bees in a hive. Some appeared to be reading from holy books as they walked. Others were sitting in small groups, eating and drinking tea or cleaning weapons. Many more didn't seem be doing anything at all except ambling about. Keying in on one man carrying several AK-47s, Moon expertly manipulated the fly-cam to zoom down from the ceiling and follow him into a side compartment. Once inside, they realized this compartment was huge in size and that it held weapons. Lots of them.

"There's their armory," Moon said. "Or at least one of them."

Panning the room with the SCRAM's lens, they were able to count at least several hundred AK-47 assault rifles, neatly lined up on racks built right into the rock wall.

"Look at all those AKs," Moon breathed. "Lots more than I'd have thought."

"What's this? Each guy has three or four rifles?" Gunn questioned. "Seems wrong somehow."

"Unless it means there's about four times as many guys inside this place than I would have estimated," Vogel said.

Cardillo groaned. "I don't want to hear that," he said.

"I don't either," Moon said. "But if it's the case, then we have to find their weak spot—and find it soon."

Moon deftly returned the fly-cam to the large hall and started zooming around again. They were able to see entrances and exits, power supplies, fuel storage places. He passed one room that featured a closed-circuit TV system—a dozen screens showing images from cameras set up at various points on the mountain side.

Another room held two frightening items: scores of typical canvas vests, items that could have been ordered from any American clothing catalog—and boxes of explosives.

"Suicide bombs," Amanda gasped.

Then, finally, the fly-cam found the jail cells.

"I'm not sure I want to see this," Gunn said.

Moon maneuvered the fly-cam down to the five doors with guards near them. Only two of the guards were awake, though, and only one of the doors was still locked.

"That confirms the NSA report," Moon said, grimly panning over to the makeshift TV studio close by the cells where the executions had taken place. "They've already killed four of the hostages—and there's only one more to go."

"God, could it really be Newman's daughter?" Amanda asked.

"We won't know until we get inside," Moon replied, checking his watch. It was now 0435 hours, about 85 minutes before dawn. "And we can't get inside until we look around some more."

Over the next five minutes, Moon maneuvered the fly-cam up and down a number of passageways, all the while downloading the images to the computer's hard drive. He was specifically looking for places where weapons were kept, where ammunition was stored, and where tunnels or passageways ended abruptly; dead ends, so to speak. Once the attack began, the 201st troopers would have this intelligence on hand, so at least they wouldn't be entering the fortress blind.

The big trouble, though, was the number of fighters inside the mountain redoubt. The five officers took a count of how many individual terrorists they could see, and in just those five minutes, they'd spotted at least 500 of them—and this didn't count all those fighters manning the gun positions on the outside of the mountain, nor the ones they saw inside the Great Hall.

The rule of thumb was that when attacking a well-entrenched enemy, it took at least four people on offense for every one person on defense, if the attacking side had any hope of victory.

Yet the entire 201st combat contingent only numbered about 140 people—whereas there might have been as many as 1,000 fighters holed up inside Bora Kurd.

Gunn just stared at the video screen, almost dizzy from watching the fly-cam darting back and forth. His spirits were plunging, and it wasn't just because his amphetamine tablets were wearing off.

One thousand fighters? A huge arsenal? Hundreds of weapons on the outside and who knew what exactly awaited them inside?

He just shook his head.

"How the *hell* are we going to do this?" he said.

AFTER leaving Site 16, Amil the Syrian climbed back down to the Great Hall, and then hurried over one passageway to where the Mountain Sheik's living quarters were located. He had to talk to the boss.

Two bodyguards were standing outside the door leading to the Sheik's residence. Even though Amil was second in command of the fortress, the guards practically ignored him when he told them he needed an audience with the Sheik right away.

The Sheik was busy, they replied harshly. He's on the phone, negotiating. He can't be disturbed.

Amil began pacing nervously up and down the damp passageway. Every once in a while he heard snippets of the conversation going on behind the Sheik's closed door. At times it sounded as if the Sheik was talking very angrily. Other times, it sounded like he was laughing. After a while, Amil couldn't tell the difference.

Finally, word came out that the Sheik was almost off the phone. A rough and invasive frisking followed, then Amil was let into the Sheik's inner sanctum.

He'd been in here before, of course, but he was always awed by how luxurious it was. The place was a large, hollowed-out shaft, trimmed down to an oval size. Three of the walls, the floor, and the ceiling were covered with heavy matted rugs. There were several divans and beds used for sitting. Electric lights illuminated the place, giving it an odd bluish glow. Several candles were also flickering away. A fire was crackling in the large fireplace that dominated the fourth wall. On its mantel, still damp with blood, was the machete the Sheik had recently used to execute the four Americans.

The Sheik himself was sitting awkwardly on the largest divan, still talking on a cell phone. In front of him was a valise full of other cell phones. All different makes and sizes, they were the Sheik's pipeline to the outside world. He had a special antenna hooked up at the top of the mountain; it was connected to a wire that wound its way down through the fortress, thus providing him with cell phone coverage.

The phones were all satellite compatible. The Sheik employed a random selection process to determine which phone he should use at any given time. Once used, the phone would be discarded immediately. This way the Sheik was able to keep one step ahead of the American intelligence services who were always on the lookout for him, always trying to listen in on his phone calls.

The Sheik was lanky, dark-skinned, with a scraggly beard. He wore the same clothes day in, day out, a series of robes and blankets pulled this way and that. He had piercing eyes that reminded Amil of another character from American movies: the Mafia godfather. The Sheik had a stare that could go right through you. And with a blink, he could have you tortured and killed. He was someone who needed to be shown respect at all times. He was also someone who had to be told bad news gently—or else. As if to underline this, an enormous bodyguard stood in their shadows.

Amil knelt on a pillow in front of the Sheik and waited until his conversation was over. It was obvious the PKD leader was upset with whomever he was talking. Amil pretended not to listen in—but he knew what was going on here. The negotiation for the last execution tape was indeed still ongoing.

Finally the Sheik simply ended the conversation by throwing the cell phone across the room. The bodyguard immediately retrieved it, and crushed it with his bare hands. Then he threw the pieces into the flames raging in the vast fireplace.

The Sheik fixed his gaze on Amil. "Speak . . ." he said, as though he was bored. "And make it quick."

Amil began softly, in Arabic, and reminded himself to keep it simple. He explained that while everything was working well as far as the outside defenses were concerned, one of their gun crew subcommanders was, at the moment, missing.

"Missing?" the Sheik asked.

"He cannot be found, sire," Amil explained. "And it's troubling only because it has never happened before."

The Sheik digested the news and then asked Amil: "Well, what do you think happened to him?"

The Syrian was prepared for the question. "My theory is

the cold got to him," he replied. "The weather, the snow—a lot of snow has fallen through the night and there's a lot of ice as well. I think he slipped and fell and hit his head and went unconscious and was buried by the snow. I also think we'll find his frozen body when the storm quiets down."

"And what about the fighters he'd been commanding?" the Sheik asked. "What theories do they have?"

Amil had to choose his words carefully here. He waved away a fly that was suddenly buzzing nearby. "Those men deluded themselves into thinking their officer's disappearance was caused by evil spirits," he told the Sheik. "The devil, and such."

" 'Evil spirits?' 'The Devil?' " the Sheik asked, his left eyebrow arching up a notch. The Sheik knew the ramifications of such things among his Pashtoon warriors; even his bodyguard made an audible grunt on hearing the words.

"How do you know that?" the Sheik asked Amil.

"Because they told me as much," Amil replied. "Plus I saw them spitting over their left shoulders, repeatedly, I might add. But they've been removed from their post. They are in the hospital room. And I will deal with them."

"Immediately?" the Sheik asked ominously.

"I assure you, yes," Amil told him quickly.

The Sheik leaned back on his divan. He repeated the words: "Evil spirits." Then he asked, "How much of a problem could this be? These Pashtoons can be a strange lot, as you know. Loose tongues could wag—and rumors are hard to stop."

Amil reminded himself not to shrug or use any hand movements or gestures. To do so would show indecision.

"I will prevent it from becoming a problem," he replied forcefully. "You have my word."

Suddenly the Sheik switched from Arabic to English by way of French. He did not want the bodyguard to hear what he had to say next.

"Should you inform our Bien Cache Guerriers as well?" the Sheik asked Amil, quietly, referring to the occupants of the off-limit White Rooms, "Will this affect them in any-way?"

Amil wondered if this was a trick question. The fortress's

secret soldiers were rarely mentioned, even in this secure setting.

"I don't think that will be necessary," he finally replied. "Unless you do, sire?"

The Sheik didn't reply. He just waved his hand casually, indicating that he was done talking with Amil.

AMIL'S bodyguard was waiting for him outside. The Syrian was twice as anxious now than when he'd first gone into the Sheik's chamber.

"Those four fools from the gun emplacement—are they still in the hospital room?" Amil asked the bodyguard.

The bodyguard replied, "Yes."

"I hope they have not talked to any of the other fighters," Amil said, waving away the pesky fly again.

"I made sure they didn't breathe a word," the bodyguard replied.

Amil let out a small sigh of relief. Then his eyes turned dark. He told the bodyguard: "Follow me."

They hurried back down the passageway heading for the fortress's tiny hospital. Amil still had a bad feeling in the pit of his stomach. Something was wrong somewhere—his instincts were telling him so. And while one person missing did not mean a whole lot to a place that held hundreds of fighters, he knew that sometimes things could have a cascading effect, especially when it involved the superstitious Pashtoons. Now that the Sheik was involved, he had to be careful with every move he made.

The "hospital" was basically a stunted tunnel, cored into the rock, with two cots and a sink. The staff consisted of a male nurse from Iran. The four fighters from Site 16 were huddled inside this crude space when Amil and his bodyguard came in. The gun crew was drinking weak tea and warming themselves under dirty blankets.

If there was one thing in short supply inside the fortress these days, it was blankets. That's why Amil asked the men to stand and pass their blankets to him. After each man complied, the Syrian asked him to face the wall. Then Amil nodded to his bodyguard, who revealed a razor-sharp knife he'd been holding behind his back. Three of the men had their throats slashed before they knew what hit them.

The fourth fighter turned around terrified and looked Amil straight in the eye—betrayal and tears coming at the same time.

Amil stuck his own knife into the man's stomach. He collapsed to the floor.

"Clean this up," Amil ordered the stunned male nurse, wiping his blade on the not-quite-dead man's clothes. "And then dispose of them. And this will be the end of any devil's talk here."

CHAPTER 17

IT was now 0510 hours. There were about fifty minutes of darkness left.

Up until now the night had been the 201st's friend, along with the bad weather. But the storm was losing steam and the sky was beginning to brighten ever so slightly overhead, signs that time was running out for the rescue force.

Wheels were turning however. The paratroopers were climbing into their jump gear, the Marines were booting up the computers on their tanks. With the push of a button, Moon had translated the fly-cam images into a three-dimensional map of the interior of the fortress. This would be invaluable to the 201st once the rescue attempt was finally launched.

But again, the SCRAM had uncovered some disturbing evidence of what really hid within the mountain. First, there were at least four to five times as many PKD fighters within Bora Kurd than the 201st had previously guessed. But there were also indications that a separate armed group was inside the fort as well, one that was highly secret. The fly-cam had heard the Sheik call them Bien Cache Guerriers, roughly French for "well-hidden warriors." What was that about? And why would these fighters be separate from the rest of the PKD? Moon and the others had no idea.

The only thing they knew for sure was that the attack on the fortress was going to be more difficult than they'd ever imagined—and they'd been imagining the worst since leaving Nevada.

Moon had an idea, though—something that came to him after listening in on that conversation between the Sheik and one of his henchman, especially the part about the terrorist commander they'd snatched off the mountain just an hour earlier. If anything, it reinforced Moon's notion that the local Pashtoons who made up the bulk of the fighters inside the fortress were a superstitious lot—and that was something that could be used against them. If Moon's new plan worked, it just might throw off at least some of the PKD fighters before the real combat began.

But it would also be extremely risky.

THAT'S why Gunn and Amanda were now in the cockpit of Amanda's Ghost Plane 3. They were getting ready to see if taking off from the snow-covered landing strip was going to be as hairy as landing on it had been.

The two tanks were still tied down in the back of the plane, but Moon's module had been repositioned. It was now hanging off the edge of the airplane's open cargo ramp.

The intelligence officer had been holed up inside the compartment since ending the fly-cam's first voyage through the PKD's fortress. The fifteen-million-dollar bug was now resting on a ledge overlooking the Great Hall, its lens pointing at the one remaining jail cell whose door was still closed. As long as it stayed shut, then the 201st still had time to do what they'd come here to do.

Moon told them all he needed was to get airborne in one of the big planes and circle the mountain for about ten minutes, no longer. In that time, he was hoping to drop some psy-ops bombs on the terrorist fighters, or at least those on duty at the dozens of gun positions outside. But he had to get fairly close to the Bora Kurd's peak to accomplish this. This meant the big C-17 had to fly around, slowly, quietly, well within range of the mountain's hundreds of weapons, while Moon did his thing. The Star Skin, the noise-dampened engines, the stealth—it all had to work perfectly, again. Or they'd be blown out of the sky.

That is, if they could even get the big plane off the ground.

Which was why both Gunn and Amanda were going.

Again, it was Amanda's plane, but even she agreed it might take two experienced pilots to get it out of the snow and into the air. Which was good, because there was no way Gunn would have let her go alone. And if things went wrong? Then it would be up to Pulver and the copilots to get the unit out of harm's way in the remaining pair of C-17s.

Sitting side by side, Gunn and Amanda had started the engines with no problem. They had some excess exhaust but no noise. The Star Skin was still activated and the snow was nearly up to the plane's wings, making them look like little more than a large drift on the field of white. But even though time was extremely important now, it was still necessary for them to wait for a good gust of wind before starting their takeoff roll; their thinking was a substantial blow might cover their takeoff. The problem was the storm was almost over. Plus, the stiffer the wind from the rear, the harder it would be to get the plane into the air. But like so many other things on this mission, they had no alternatives. No options. No Plan Bs. This was it.

Finally Pulver signaled them from his aircraft to say a mighty wind was sweeping down the valley, heading in their direction. Gunn looked behind him and, sure enough, a tsunami of snow was blowing their way. Both he and Amanda knew it was now or never. They popped the brakes and with both hands on the same set of throttles—common procedure for big plane takeoffs—they started the huge C-17 rolling down the snow-covered runway.

It was a strange moment for Gunn, hungry, sleep-deprived, but artificially rejuvenated by two more speed pills. The plane was vibrating tremendously as it plowed through the deep snow, being carried by the great gush of wind. It felt like the wings would snap off as they urged the engines to their minimum takeoff speed—without using the rocket-assists, of course. The airstrip was only so long and if they went beyond it, and were suddenly rolling along on dirt and not cracked asphalt, there was a real chance the plane would flip over nose-first—and kill them both. And even if they did get airborne, once again, everything on board *had* to work perfectly or a couple hundred big guns and almost as many SAM missiles would be fired at them and reduce them to cinders in an instant.

Yet none of this was foremost in Gunn's mind at the moment. What was making the biggest impression on him was that Amanda's hand was on top of his as they pushed the throttles forward, that he could feel the warmth of her skin through her glove, through his, through the cold. Through everything.

Is it possible for someone to be too beautiful?

That's what he was thinking as the huge airplane somehow lifted off and clawed its way into the sky.

THEY went straight up to 13,000 feet, just about the height of Bora Kurd. Then they leveled out and started a long, slow orbit around the mountain's peak.

Once in position, Gunn left the flying to Amanda and made his way back through to the plane's cargo bay, over the fuel bladders, and around the tanks to Moon's module. The diminutive intelligence agent had set up two enormous loudspeakers on the plane's open cargo ramp. The noise from the wind made it hard to talk, but through shouting and hand signals, Gunn was able to get the gist of what Moon was up to.

He'd prepared an MP3 WAV file that contained many voices, all talking at once, in many different dialects, blaspheming Allah and the Muslim religion. Moon played a bit of it for Gunn. The sound file was full of obscenities and phrases that Moon assured him Muslims would consider sacrilegious.

"So the idea is to make them blush?" Gunn yelled to Moon.

Moon shook his head. "The idea is to make them feel unwashed and unlucky," he yelled back. "Things that are precursors to bad spirits being in the area."

"But will this sort of thing really work, though?" Gunn

asked him, watching the top of the peak as they silently completed their first orbit around the mountain's top.

"It did in Afghanistan in 2001," Moon told him. "When we were fighting the Taliban? They were holding a town called Khrash. Real die-hard fanatics. They were dug in deep and we couldn't get them out no matter what we dropped on them. Finally we had a psy-ops plane circle the city one night, broadcasting the worst things possible about Islam. It freaked them out to even hear the words uttered. It also confused them, and even better convinced them the devil was talking to them. They panicked, and pretty soon, our SigInt guys were telling us the Taliban fighters were leaving the city and heading back for the hills. Twenty minutes later, we called in B-52s and carpet-bombed them. That's all highly classified by the way."

"So it *does* work then?"

Moon said, "Well, it worked that day. But we tried it again in Tora Bora and other places—and the Taliban just figured out it was a psy-ops plane flying around and managed to ignore it. So, it's not a perfect science. That's why I think I have to throw a little extra something at them, too."

"Like what?" he asked.

Moon hit a button on his laptop and suddenly he was looking at the readout screen that showed the integrity of what the plane's Star Skin was doing at any given moment. Because the stars were still out overhead, the entire bottom of the plane was covered with them, while the top was still colored in a kind of dirty snow color.

"If I could just manipulate this somehow," Moon said, studying the star readouts. "Think of something that would *really* freak them out. Without exposing our position, of course."

Gunn got a sinking feeling in his stomach. "Yeah—of course," he said, thinking of all the guns and SAMs that would key in on them should their chameleonlike ability suddenly fail them. "Let's not let them know we're here. Because if you do . . ."

Moon finished the sentence for him: ". . . then, we're screwed."

Gunn left him as the intelligence agent was still trying to

think of a way to manipulate the airplane's Star Skin in order to freak out the PKD fighters. But while he was there at least, no great ideas seemed forthcoming.

"Oh yeah," Gunn thought grimly as he walked back to the cockpit. "*This* is going to work."

IT took a while, but Amil the Syrian finally got back to bed.

Counting the earlier interruption, he figured he'd gone without any substantial sleep for almost four days now, ever since the American hostages had been brought to the fortress. In that time he'd taken care of many things, big and small, all dedicated to keeping his fighters sharp.

And he knew it was important that they be cautious. But he was almost certain the Americans would not attempt a rescue operation. It had been their policy ever since the Iraqi invasion to let their hostages die, to abandon them, just like they'd abandoned Daniel Perle, Nick Berg, and others. The Americans just didn't have the guts anymore.

Or at least that's how he felt before the incident at Site 16. But even now, after the four gun crew members had been disposed of and all talk of the bad spirits surrounding the mountain had dissipated—even now, he could still detect the stink of jet fuel in his nostrils and he was still puzzled at why that particular smell would just pop up, in the middle of a huge snowstorm.

Maybe it was just the atmospherics of *wudas,* he tried to tell himself. Or maybe he'd simply imagined it. The tension was thick within the fortress, and stress could do weird things to a person's body. The good news was that tension would be over once the final hostage was beheaded and the videotape sent on to the Persian Gulf. Then the Sheik would have even more money to spend and some of that would no doubt trickle down to Amil's pockets.

So when he finally returned to his quarters, and put his head back down on his sleeping mat, Amil was feeling a bit calmer, a bit more secure.

That's when he heard a knock on his door.

He wearily told the person to come in, thinking it was his

bodyguard. Instead it was a man named Abyeh, one of the gun position subcommanders assigned to the southern side of the mountain. Abyeh was covered with snow and out of breath—obviously he'd just come from the outside.

"My honored high commander," he gasped to Amil. "I've just been informed of some disturbing news . . ."

Amil rubbed his tired eyes. "What is it this time? Someone has run out of ammunition? Or food? Or someone is too cold?"

"No, sir," Abyeh said. "I've just heard that thirteen men on the south side of the mountain are claiming the devil just spoke to them . . ."

Amil stared back at him, feeling uncomfortable in his bedclothes. He made him repeat the message.

"Had they talked earlier to the men at Site 16?" Amil then asked.

Abyeh vigorously shook his head no.

"They talked to no one, sir," Abyeh said. "Except who they claim are bad spirits."

This was not good. Amil had thought he'd nipped the superstition thing in the bud, but apparently he was mistaken. He hurriedly got dressed and rushed up the tunnel, following Abyeh with great haste. They reached an intersection that led up to the southern edge of the fortress. Here Abyeh stopped dead in his tracks. He didn't want to go any further.

"You do not want to continue serving Allah?" Amil asked him harshly. "Just because a few of your delusional brothers are hearing voices in their heads?"

Abyeh thought a moment, then said, "That is correct, Imam. Because I'm afraid I'll hear them, too."

With that Abyeh turned on his heel and fled back down the tunnel.

Amil was tempted to chase after him and execute him on the spot—but something more important had to be done first. It was dawning on him that they were protected from just about anything inside Bora Kurd, except their worst enemy: superstition. Devils? Bad spirits? Mysterious voices in the night?

It was all nonsense. But still, Amil knew he had to prevent

a panic from sweeping through the fortress before it was too late.

HE reached the top of the tunnel and went up the ladder leading to the outside. He opened the hatch and found himself in a snowy swirl near a weapons emplacement containing a large Zuni all-purpose gun.

He found its five-man crew inside, with at least a dozen other men, huddled together, wearing the same faraway look in their blackened eyes as those fighters who'd manned Site 16. They all looked up when he came in, but none showed the deference that Amil usually commanded. They looked too scared for such things.

Amil ordered them to return to their gun positions—but none of them moved. They remained seated, pressed together, gaunt and shivering against the cold. A second order and then a third had the same response. They just weren't listening to him.

Amil looked down the hill to the next weapons station. It was empty, as was the one beyond. He looked farther up the mountain, near the peak, and saw another group of fighters huddled together—at least twenty of them, meaning nearly ten gun stations were empty at the moment. It was clear that the same thing had frightened all of them and that it was spreading.

Amil turned back to the nearest group of fighters, furious that they were ignoring him. He gave them the order again, but still to no avail.

Finally he screamed: "Why aren't you listening to me?"

To which, one man replied: "Because we are listening to the devil instead . . ."

Amil almost laughed, but then, suddenly, frighteningly, he heard a voice too . . .

It was there, on the wind, speaking in many languages, but mostly Pashtooni. The words were vile, anti-Muslim, and highly blasphemous against Allah.

Amil felt a sudden tightening in his throat. His feet seemed encased in the ice of the mountain. He looked down at the frightened fighters, holding one another now, their eye shadow running. They were just peasants, of course. If they were not here they would have been tending a poppy field somewhere. He knew he really couldn't expect much from them other than to fire their weapons when he told them to.

But now he was hearing what they were hearing. Many voices, over and over. Even for a less than fanatical believer as Amil, it was almost paralyzing because it was just so weird.

Still, he knew there must be an explanation for it.

He started scanning the skies around the mountain. He'd heard of the psychological warfare employed by the Americans during the rout of the Taliban years before. Maybe that's what was happening here.

The only trouble was, back then the people on the ground could actually see the psy-ops plane flying overhead. But now, as Amil scanned the early morning sky, he could see nothing but stars.

Still he had to believe this was an American psy-ops trick, possibly a prelude to some kind of rescue attempt. But there was no quick way he could convince the Pashtoons of that—so what could he do? Round up all the fighters assigned to the gun emplacements and slit their throats, too? What about those superstitious fighters inside the fortress? He was sure Abyeh was now running free, quickly spreading the word about the devil outside. Amil knew not all of the fighters within would be affected by it, but a lot of them would be. And suddenly his fighting force wasn't as strong, as capable, as invulnerable as he thought.

That is, assuming this *wasn't* the voice of the devil, speaking in many tongues to them from on high.

Amil stood in the frozen wind, starting to shiver, looking everywhere trying to spot the psy-ops plane, but still finding nothing.

His only option now was to execute these fighters gathered close to him, and frighten the others into returning to their posts to get ready for whatever was to come. It made sense. Where killing these fifteen or so men would be a loss, it would be better than losing the two hundred fighters manning weapons all over the mountain.

He was just about to order the fifteen men to go below, back inside the mountain, when he heard a collective gasp and saw them all shrink back even deeper into the gun emplacement. Where they were just frightened before, now all of them seemed absolutely terrified. Even worse, Amil could see fighters from other gun emplacements nearby reacting in the same way. In seconds he could hear men all over this side of the mountain start to bellow and weep and cry out as if in pain.

What happened? Why were all these fighters suddenly acting like this? Then he realized many of them were pointing skyward and collapsing as if the worst possible vision was suddenly floating above them.

So Amil returned his gaze to the sky overhead and suddenly he saw what they saw and he knew why they were reacting this way. And he started to react that way, too.

A group of stars right overhead had started moving, forming something, a definite shape.

Amil nearly soiled himself. Psy-ops voices he could almost understand, but this?

He watched openmouthed as the stars went spinning this way and that until they settled into a pattern. And that's when Amil really felt his heart turn to ice.

"Who could do this besides the devil?" he heard himself cry to the unexpected agreement of all those men within earshot.

For directly over the mountain's peak, the stars had formed what in many ways was the most frightening, most hated image any Muslim could see.

Right above the peak, the cosmos had formed a perfect Star of David.

Amil could not move. It was like he was dreaming. He was not as superstitious as the Pashtoon warriors—he was a Syrian, given more to dour expectations of his soul's ultimate fate. But this was just *so strange*.

He stood there for the longest time, but then suddenly, he started running. Back to the hatchway, down the ladder, back down the tunnel.

This mountain *was* haunted.

By the worst kinds of ghosts . . .

And he had to get out of here, quick . . .

CHAPTER 18

PULVER was sitting in the Ghost 2 cockpit, staring up at the slowly brightening sky.

"We'd better get going soon," he said to himself. "This long night is fading away."

He and his copilot, Lieutenant Jackson, were doing their preflight preps, getting ready to finally start the rescue operation. They had the plan, not in hand, but in their heads. It was so simple nothing even had to be written down. But in this case, simple almost meant futile.

Their job was to put as many 82nd paratroopers as possible atop the sharpened peak of Bora Kurd. It would be a grim mission, as it was widely assumed that not all of the 102 paratroopers jumping were going to make it, that many would probably be blown off course before they even came close to landing, doomed to drift to places where any kind of rescue would be impossible. Even now, Pulver was waiting for Captain Vogel, the commander of the 82nd to come forward with some ideas on how best to approach the perilous drop, which was good, because it was certainly something that Pulver had never tried before.

Normally as loose as a combat pilot could get, Pulver was

feeling very uptight at the moment. He'd watched the Star of David formation float directly overhead earlier and wondered just how crazy it might be driving the PKDs inside the fortress—if at all, that is. These were not positive thoughts, but he couldn't help it. The words *heroic failure* just kept bouncing around his head. And deep down? He was beginning to wonder if any of them would make it out alive.

"Ready for me, Captain?"

It was Vogel who broke into his dark thoughts. Pulver invited the Army officer up to the C-17's flight deck. They only had a few minutes to talk before the rescue mission was to begin, so Pulver continued doing his preflight checks.

Vogel sat in the jump seat behind Pulver's station. He had Moon's 3-D map with him. It was very detailed, showing the terrorists' armories, where they kept their explosives, where a lot of their fighters seemed to be concentrated. But both Pulver and Vogel knew the map might not be worth much in the end if the PKD fighters proved as fanatical about protecting their mountain fortress as they were about burning young girls alive and cutting off the heads of innocent women.

Still, they had to press on. Pulver asked Vogel: "So, can you tell me how best to fly this drop?"

But Vogel seemed particularly dispirited, even worse than Pulver.

"That's the problem," he told the pilot. "I don't think we can make this jump."

Pulver stopped what he was doing and turned back toward the Army officer.

"Can't make it?" he asked. "Why not? We all know it won't be a clean jump. But it can't be. This is war."

Vogel's weary face fell a bit. "I know that," he said. "What I'm talking about is an operational problem. You know our jump procedures. We need a five-minute ground reference point, another one at sixty seconds, a third at thirty seconds. The problem is the way today's plan is we won't even be in the air for two minutes before the doors open. No reference points makes for a *very* scattered jump. And any more scattering out here we really don't need. This thing is going to be extremely fucked up as it is. But I can't go up there knowing *none* of my men have a chance of making it."

Pulver held up his hand, and then tapped Jackson on the shoulder. "Hey, Mike," he said. "Can you go check the tires again?"

Jackson got the hint. He climbed down off the flight deck, leaving the two senior officers alone.

"Okay, what's the problem exactly?" Pulver asked Vogel once Jackson was gone.

"It's the plan itself," Vogel replied. "We're going up with 102 people. Now, with the ramp down and our self-activating parachutes, we can all go out the back of the plane, almost like a HALO jump, and we won't have to mess around doing it in two lines at the doors. But even with the back ramp open, we can't *all* go out at once. It will still take some time. Yet the footprint we're being asked to land on is barely the size of a football field—not to mention it's on top of a mountain, and rugged, with high winds and all. Landing paratroopers on such a high-altitude target? We're not supposed to do these sorts of things."

Pulver looked the man straight in the eye. He agreed with him completely, but that was not the point.

"Well, like everyone's been saying, we're not supposed to have tanks out here either," he told him pointedly. "But we do, and we have you and your men. And we have this mission—and we're going to take off in just a few minutes. So just tell me, what do I have to do to make it work?"

Vogel laughed grimly. "Can you stop the plane in midair for about ten seconds until we all get out?" he asked with a weak smile. "That's how impossible it is."

Pulver just shrugged. "Is the only alternative climbing up the side of this fucking mountain?"

The man nodded once. "It is."

"And you said ten seconds?"

Vogel looked back at him queerly. "Yes, but . . ."

Pulver just held up his hand again, cutting him off. "Then get your men and ready. We're lifting off in under five minutes."

Vogel started to protest, "Yes—but, I was only . . ."

"Four minutes and thirty seconds," Pulver interrupted him, turning back to his flight controls. "You'd better get going."

Vogel started to say something else, but Pulver just gave him a quick salute. The meeting was over. Vogel hesitated another moment, but then returned the salute.

"Good luck, Captain," he said.

Then he was gone.

THE next few minutes crawled by.

Pulver finished his preflight checks. Jackson returned and climbed back into his seat, reporting the aircraft's tires were ready for flight.

Ghost Plane 3 had come in for a blustery landing earlier, skidding its way down the slippery runway, its air brakes squealing as they struggled to slow down. It finally ground to a stop, just long enough for Gunn to jump out the front door and for Moon's module to be pushed off the back. Then per the plan, the Ghost 3 started a very slow roll, off the runway and onto the hard ice-packed valley floor itself. It started moving slowly away from the airstrip and down the valley. Meanwhile Gunn had run back to his own airplane, Ghost 1. That huge jet was now moving in front of Pulver's plane.

Pulver checked the time. It was 0544 hours. He looked up through the windshield again. The stars were still burning bright. In front of him, Gunn's airplane was ready to go, waiting at the edge of the frozen airstrip, blowing away the snow as it moved.

"God help us all," Pulver whispered.

Finally the last few seconds ticked away. At exactly 0545, Pulver watched as Gunn's big C-17 began rumbling down the ancient runway. It immediately kicked up a spray of snow and ice, along with no small amount of frozen dust below. It made for an eerie sight—cold, wind blowing, lots of snow and dirt going everywhere—yet, there was practically no noise coming from Gunn's snow-white ship.

Somehow, the big plane became airborne. It didn't climb into the air as much as Gunn had lifted his landing gear and flew it by default. It was still heading straight for the end of the valley where another huge mountain tore into the sky. At the last possible moment, the big plane banked hard right and slowly climbed, going up almost sideways. In an instant, it disappeared into the night.

Just then, Jackson tapped Pulver urgently on the shoulder. He didn't say anything; he just pointed to the ridge nearby, about 100 feet off their right wing. A couple dozen people were standing there. Not Americans. They were locals. They weren't carrying guns, nor did they look hostile. They were dressed more like peasants than terrorists.

"Damn, we've got an audience," Jackson said. "What are we going to do now?"

Pulver thought a moment then went back to what he was doing. "It's too late to shoot them now," he said. "I guess they're just here for the show."

He got the plane moving, rechecking with Vogel in the back. His men were ready for the very dangerous jump, or as ready as they could ever be.

Pulver taxied the plane to the edge of the airstrip; it was buffeted slightly by turbulence still left over from Gunn's departure. That's when Jackson tapped him again. He pointed toward the people watching them again and saw one of them, a young boy, was waving a very tattered, yet unmistakable American flag. He looked like the same kid who'd had his milk stolen by the terrorists.

"Oh, no worries there then," Pulver said, pulling the throttles back to idle. "They must have just heard Amanda was in town."

GHOST Plane 3 had started out slowly on its strange journey along the valley floor. But it had gradually picked up speed and was now moving along at about 50 mph.

Amanda tried her best to steer the huge airplane, being careful to keep it straight and true as it rumbled along. To an uninformed observer, the plane would have probably looked like it was in trouble. It certainly wasn't going fast enough to take off. But then again, it didn't have to be. It wasn't going airborne. Her job at this moment was to be a very earthbound delivery truck driver. The purpose: to get her cargo, the two M1 tanks, into position so the assault on the mountain could begin.

The valley was about a half-mile long and the edge of the mountain fortress was located at the far end of it. It was thought that some of the PKD fighters, maybe some particularly high-value ones, might try to flee the fortress once the shooting started inside. As it was known that the tunnel behind the stone hut was the fortress's escape route, it was best that the tanks be waiting nearby, just in case.

Again, it was particularly ironic that for this part of the mission Amanda wasn't being called on to do any flying. The simple fact was it would probably take the tanks too long to drive down the valley on their own. Besides, they were still sporting their sand camo paint scheme, which would have made them easy to spot, clanking across the valley floor. So the unusual job of moving them was given to Ghost Plane 3.

The trip took just a few minutes. Reaching the end of the valley, Amanda brought the big plane to a stop, deftly turned it 180-degrees, and backed it up as close to the stone hut as she dared. True, the plane was masked and the snow was still blowing in gusts, and it was still dark. But she also knew there were hundreds of enemy fighters embedded close by in the fortress's mountainside and all it would take is one with really good eyesight to glance downward and suspect something odd was happening.

So, she brought the plane's rear ramp within 100 feet of where the fly-cam had started its journey and then stopped. This was as far as she could go.

She called back to the Marines to dismount their tanks. They did this in less than a half minute, squeezing out between the fuel bladders, and immediately seeking the partial cover of the nearby hedgerow.

Then Amanda wished them good luck and started back to the far end of the valley, her job done, almost too well.

At that moment, she thought; "What the hell am I supposed to do now?"

PULVER was anxious to get going. All his on-board systems were coming back green. Jackson reported no problems with their engines. The weather was windy, with lots of blowing snow, but above them, the early morning sky was clear, with many stars left. Perfect conditions for them and what they had to do.

Pulver radioed back to Vogel. "Green?" he asked the man.

"Green . . ." came the reply.

Pulver hesitated a moment, then added, "Don't worry, Army—we'll make this work."

He sensed Vogel was going to reply, and he did: "Thanks, Marines . . ."

Pulver checked his watch. It was now 0548 hours. Gunn would kick things off in just two minutes.

He went over what he had to do in his mind. The takeoff would be hairy, but judging from the others before him, manageable. The drop itself would come less than two minutes later. The paratroopers would have to be in their "ready" mode the moment the plane's wheels left the ground. Then it would be up to him to get them all on the peak of the mountain in one piece. Again, that would be the hard part.

But Pulver couldn't help but think what was in store for the paratroopers once they'd landed. Moon's plan—to scare a lot of the enemy fighters inside the fortress—seemed like a good one. But even if fifty percent took the bait, then the paratroopers would still have about 500 fighters to deal with.

Not the best odds . . .

Pulver checked his watch again. One minute to go before Gunn lit this candle. He checked his instruments again—everything was still looking good. For a mission where everything had to move quickly, time had suddenly slowed down dramatically. Typical, Pulver thought, for what lay ahead.

He was about to check his watch yet again, when Jackson turned to say something to him. Pulver saw the copilot's mouth open, but no words ever came out, because at the exact moment, an enormously intense flash of light filled the cockpit. It was as bright as the sun and blinded them both. An instant later, the ground beneath their plane started shaking violently; the noise was deafening.

All Pulver could hear was someone in the back yelling, *"What the fuck was that?"*

Islamabad, 120 miles away

Captain Shabaz Perviz was commander of Islamabad Airport's military air traffic control tower.

It was Perviz's job to make sure any military planes landing at the big international airport were directed to the proper runways, the proper facilities, and the properly secured zones. Keeping the Pakistani Air Force separate from the civilian airliners at the frequently confused and chaotic facility was a 24/7 operation.

Perviz was on duty early this morning because an important arms shipment was coming in from a supplier in France. The aircraft, a leased 747, was filled with assault rifles and ammunition destined for beleaguered Pakistani forces, especially those stationed near the disputed border of Kashmir. Perviz was usually on the job by 0800 hours. But today, as the arms shipment was due at 0600, he'd been here since 0500, just to make sure all was moving smoothly.

It was a calm day, forecast to be hot, with rain arriving around noon. Perviz knew this because the tower also contained a weather station, complete with a seismograph, an installation made after the horrific earthquake of 2005. This station was set up right next to Perviz's desk.

Perviz's assistant, Sergeant Bahool, arrived shortly after he did and, as always, made him a pot of weak green tea. They were alone in the ATC tower, a forty-five-foot high structure located at the northern edge of the airport, about a quarter mile from the airport's civilian control tower.

Sergeant Bahool had just set the tea down in front of Perviz when the young man froze in place, looking out the tower's window, directly north.

"Allah, forgive me—but what is that?"

Perviz turned around and saw it, too: an intensely bright white light was erupting from somewhere over the northern horizon.

Perviz's first thought, "Allah—one of our nuclear weapons have gone off!"

What it looked like was sunrise—but Perviz knew this couldn't be. The sun wasn't due to rise for another twenty-five minutes, and besides, this glow was most definitely coming from the north, not the east.

The two men stood transfixed at the window, watching the glow turn from white to red to orange back to white again in a matter of seconds.

"What could it be?" Bahool asked again. "Allah be praised— why is this being shown to us?"

A thought came to Perviz. He looked at the seismograph and felt his eyes go wide. The graph needle was moving crazily.

Whatever was causing the strange, violent glow was shaking the earth as well.

But where was it happening?

Perviz checked the graph's mapping function and found the ground disturbance was occurring about 120 miles to the north, up near the Kunga Mountains, in Wabistan, the most notorious part of Pakistan. It was registering 2.5 on the meter.

Everything changed at that point for Perviz.

"Wabistan," he whispered to Bahool. "Where the killers live."

He shut off the seismograph and ordered Bahool to pour him a warmer cup of tea.

"Those people up there?" he told the assistant. "We leave them alone . . ."

Bora Kurd

Gunn's eyes were on fire.

His eyelashes felt singed. His pupils red hot.

But his face felt the worst. It was like he had been severely sunburned, oddly, the same sensation he'd felt from the NLR blasts back in Nevada. But what had just come out of his airplane was anything but nonlethal. It had been pure Hell—from the heavens, from his wings, inflicted on the earth below.

But how did it happen?

As soon as his eyesight returned, he focused on the plane's weapons control panel. Again, the way it was set up was as a line of icons, each one representing one of the sixteen massive weapons on board the AC-17. All he had to do was select an icon on the screen, push the engage panel, and that weapon would fire. Select two icons, push the engage panel, and two weapons would fire. The computer would even suggest which weapons to use. It was supposed to make for devastating yet pinpoint targeting.

But one look at the screen told him it *hadn't* worked as advertised. There had been a glitch in the system somewhere—maybe in the software, or on the firing panel itself. It didn't make any difference now. What was done was done.

But his eyes still felt like they were on fire.

IT all started shortly after they got airborne. Everything on board had checked out green. Gunn's weapons crew was ready; the weapons themselves were all online. They still had twenty minutes of darkness left, enough for him to use the Star Skin cloaking to do what he'd come a half a world away to do.

He remembered taking two more speed pills just after takeoff and feeling the amphetamines enter his bloodstream immediately. Everything sped up *and* slowed down after that. He felt revived, alert. Speeding . . .

He did one circle around the mountain, he and his crew anxiously looking out the windows at the enemy's gun emplacements, so close they could reach out and touch them. But no one on the mountainside saw them, no one heard them. No one fired a shot. Were the PKD guns even still manned? Had Moon's psy-ops trick worked at all? There was no way they could tell. The weapons were certainly there—their muzzles could be seen sticking out of the snowy brush that covered most of the mountainside. They had to assume the gunners were still there, too, or at least some of them were. And after all, it would take just one shot from a ZU-23J, or one SAM missile launched, and the big, fuel-laden AC-17 would be blown out of the sky.

The plan was for Gunn to hit those gun emplacements nearer to the top of the mountain first, and then work his way down, the thinking being that those weapons closest to the summit posed the greatest danger to the paratroopers in the

Jump Plane, which, after all, was the purpose of all this. To get as many of the 82nd soldiers on to the top of the mountain safely. If they were lucky, and if all the AC-17's weapons worked, and they were able to target a lot of different gun emplacements quickly—and if the enemy gunners really couldn't see what they were shooting back at—if *all* that worked, there was a chance the big gunship might actually survive the first five minutes of the battle.

So, all was going well up to that point. They began their second circuit of the peak, flying about 500 feet out, at very low speed, left wing tipped, the Star Skin on. Using his RIF goggles, Gunn spotted three Zuni gun emplacements, lined up in an almost perfect row not twenty-five feet from the top of the mountain. They seemed to be the best place to start.

Gunn called up the targeting ball on his fire control computer. Using the sidesaddle HUD sighting glass, he lined up the trio of gun emplacements and locked them in the computer. The computer calculated the distance and was supposed to suggest which weapon was the best one to fire.

But that's when the problem started.

As soon as he was ready to engage, Gunn looked at the weapons control panel, expecting to see maybe two of the Bushmasters icons lit up, or perhaps a couple of the Vulcan rotary guns. Or one of the M102 howitzers.

But what he saw was completely unexpected: *All* the icons were lit up.

This didn't make sense. Surely the software didn't want him to fire all the weapons at once. He hit the clear button and quickly went through the procedure again, somehow keeping those same three gun emplacements in his sights. But again when he asked the computer for a weapons selection, all sixteen icons popped on again.

At that same moment, two warning lights began flashing on his flight control panel. He heard Bing say: "Shit, this isn't good."

The warning lights were coming from the gunship's defensive systems suite. Someone on the mountainside was painting them with a targeting radar. Whether it was one of the Zuni guns or a SAM site or whether someone down there had just turned on a radar set to warm it up and recalibrate it—there was no way of knowing.

But it also left Gunn no choice. The weapons control screen was still lit up with all sixteen icons and a panel that was blinking the words "Engage fire."

So he pushed it . . .

And the flash was so bright, both he and Bing were blinded instantly.

The first thing Gunn remembered doing was tearing off his RIFs—the flaring was incredible. But it did no good. It was still so bright in the cockpit, it was like they were flying directly into the sun. The plane itself began shaking mightily, worse than when they were flying low over China or when they'd smashed head-on into the *wuda*. The closet thing Gunn could compare it to was a session he'd done in the space shuttle simulator when it shook so much it felt like the marrow in his bones was turning to jelly. It was that sensation— times ten. It felt like the plane was coming apart at the seams and that he was coming apart with it.

He tried punching the weapons control panel over and over again, trying to get it to disengage, but the computer was having none of it. Every weapon was opened up and firing full bore—and there was nothing Gunn could do about it.

The strange thing was the plane kept flying while the weapons kept firing. Somehow, he and Bing dreamily steered the huge aircraft around the top of the mountain—once, twice, three times—unable to stop the streams of fire and shells streaking to Earth, pounding the mountain first into sand, then dust, then glass. Unable to even see beyond the glow.

What they would figure out later was that when all the weapons fired and stayed on, the glare was so bright the Star Skin picked it up and only intensified it, over and over again, until the plane itself looked like a small piece of a star—which made everything even more frightening.

This was nothing like the laser beams stuff back in Nevada.

This was breathing fire.

What was most amazing to Gunn, though, just seconds into this, was the feeling it gave him. Maybe it was all the speed he'd taken, or the excitement of the moment, or both—

but from his head to his boots, he felt for a moment that he was some sort of god, like he'd been transformed into a deity. This was how gods felt, he thought in this instant of madness. Effortlessly dispensing all this power and death literally at the flick of a switch. After a while, Gunn stopped hitting the disengage panel and just let it happen.

Though he couldn't see much of it, he knew the devastation they were inflicting would be beyond description. Which weapon was doing the most damage? The CIWS gun, spraying its shells everywhere? The Bushmaster antiaircraft guns? All the rotary weapons, firing nonstop? The howitzers . . . ? It really *was* like making a rain of fire.

And the men in the back, his weapons crew—what was it like for them?

Gunn had a closed-circuit camera screen on his flight control panel that allowed him to look in the back from six different angles. In a quick glance, he saw his gun crew in the midst of a frenzy, lording over the computers, running the weapons, replenishing the ammunition loads, going about their business with workmanlike speed and precision, as if *this* was the way it was supposed to be. A strange, *strange* thing.

Maybe they knew, too, that the destruction they were causing was beyond belief. With all weapons firing at once, it was almost like a broom, sweeping around the peak, leaving nothing unaffected in its wake. Gunn recalled news films of napalm being dropped in Vietnam and wondering how anyone below could have survived the ten seconds of horror the jellied gasoline caused. Well, what was coming out of his plane was like a nonstop spray of napalm, sweeping up and down, back and forth. And then there were the colors. These they *could* see. Red, yellow, purple, orange—beautiful in the most perverse way. And occasionally, they would see secondary explosions among the colors—a bright flash in a sea of bright flashes. Fire upon fire.

Gunn could not imagine, not in his high state, or in his human state, what all this was like on the receiving end. He had a notion that whoever he was killing, those terrorists who had probably killed many Americans or wanted to, that they were not feeling any pain, that it was just heat and then nothing. If so, maybe they were getting off too easily. Maybe they should be made to suffer more. But then again, maybe that's what the mercy of God was about.

It only lasted for about thirty-five seconds, a short lifetime for a divinity. That equaled five complete orbits around the mountain's peak, even though he could have gone on for ten, fifteen, twenty circuits even. But it was not necessary.

Finally he hit the disengage panel and it actually disengaged. In effect, it was like lifting his finger off a stuck trigger. Once the engage light went out, everything just stopped.

It was only when all the flames broiled away and the wind grabbed some of the smoke and blew it away, too, that he and Bing could finally see exactly what they had done.

But what they saw, they couldn't believe.

The top of the mountain was gone.

NOT two seconds after the intense glow went away, Pulver kicked off the brake on his C-17 and the big plane went streaking down the snowy airstrip.

He had his helmet sunshield down, even though it was still fifteen minutes before dawn and he'd told Jackson to do the same. The gunship had stopped firing, but the mountain was ablaze, so much so that it was almost too bright to look at. But it was clear that Gunn had done his job, maybe a bit too aggressively. Now it was time for Pulver to do his.

It was only once he was airborne and away from the glow that he pushed the sunshade back up and clicked down his night vision goggles.

"Here comes the hard part," he thought.

He rose to 12,500 feet, nearly straight up, and then twisted back 180 degrees to the north. He had worked out his flight path on the flight computer. Now it was burning a hole in the HUD screen in front of him.

Despite his reassurance to Vogel, this was going to take not just tricky, but outright dangerous flying.

His original plan to drop the paratroopers in such a tight area was to put the aircraft in an incredibly tight turn, and keep it there . . . until every man was out the door. To veer off course even slightly in mid-drop would mean killing at least half of the soldiers he was charged with delivering.

Added to the problem, while it seemed that Gunn had done his job, and had eliminated the huge antiaircraft threat that had blanketed the mountain—indeed approaching it now, the vertical landscape looked more akin to something on the moon—Pulver had to recognize the fact that there still might be some PKD fighters inside the fortress who'd survived the apocalyptic lambasting the outside had taken and that these people might provide opposition for the paratroopers once they started floating down.

To Pulver, this meant moving quickly.

And that was it—enough thinking. He knew what he had to do. Treat the C-17 like it was a Harrier, or better yet, some kind of stunt plane. He called back to Vogel and gave him the sixty-seconds-to-go signal. Vogel yelled back that his men were already standing up. Pulver turned the big plane back toward the south and then jinked to the east. He would reach the mountain heading east and then go into his violent maneuver.

Thirty seconds, he could see the mountaintop clearly now—or what was left of it. Incredibly, at least two hundred feet of the peak was gone, blown right off by the gunship. Now the summit was no longer full of deadly peaks, but was flat and rocky. Pulver lightened up a little on seeing this. Gunn had actually given the paratroopers a larger area to land on, though judging by all the smoke and scattered flames, it might be like landing on an active volcano.

Twenty-five seconds, approaching on course, Pulver lowered his speed. He yelled for the flight crew to hold on, it was about to get bumpy.

Twenty seconds. He opened the huge rear cargo ramp; suddenly the interior of the Jump Plane was very cold.

Fifteen seconds, Vogel reported his troopers were in position.

Ten seconds, one final call back to Vogel. All was ready to go,

Pulver thought, *It's now or never.*

Five seconds—Jackson reached over and tapped Pulver's hand twice for good luck.

Three . . . two . . . one . . .

Pulver put the big plane into a violent climb, pushed the

throttles full max, and hit the jump button, all at the same time.

An instant later, the paratroopers started falling out the back . . .

CAPTAIN Steve Cardillo, the Marine tank commander, saw the whole thing.

The bright, blinding flash. The endless explosion. The waves of fire and smoke, and the very real vision that Bora Kurd had been turned into a volcano that had just blown its stack.

He was sitting in the turret of one of the two M1 tanks idling in the hedgerow about 100 yards away from the stone hut that hid the mountain's escape tunnel. The stone hut looked like something from the Middle Ages—a few branches and a bent tree doing a bad job of hiding it from view. But again, if any terrorists were trying to escape what was going on inside the mountain, this was probably where they would come out.

So being here had given Cardillo and the other Marines a perfect view of Gunn's aerial assault on the mountain. They were all combat veterans, but they had never seen anything like this. One moment the mountain's snowy peak was there, looking ominous as always; the next, the Star Skin–cloaked plane opened up with every weapon on board, and the top of the mountain simply disappeared. It was incredible to watch, more like a scene from a movie than real life.

But the most immediate result of the massive air strike was probably the most unexpected. About a minute after the Marines saw the huge chunk of the summit literally blown away, a great rush of water came streaming down the sides of the mountain. The instantly melted snow caused by Gunn's assault had created a tidal wave of mud and debris—and it was now falling like waterfalls everywhere. It was an incredible sight to behold.

The combination of the mind-blowing gunship barrage and the flood that followed had practically denuded the mountainside. All that remained were small, scattered fires, charred trees, and hundreds of waterfalls of mud and crap splashing down. Even if any of the PKD fighters manning the gun emplacements had escaped Gunn's onslaught, it would have been hard for them to survive the crush of water and debris that came in its wake. The Marines could see more than a few bodies rolling down the mountainside with the newly-created falls.

Then they saw something even stranger.

The Jump Plane suddenly appeared over the mountaintop, making its way through the columns of flames and smoke. The rear ramp was open, and through his RIF binoculars, Cardillo could even see the faces of the paratroopers standing in the open cargo bay.

Then they heard the plane's engines let out an unholy scream, unexpected because they were supposed to be noise-dampened. Then they saw the big plane's nose go up dramatically and a burst of flame from its rocket assists. And then, just like that, the plane simply froze in midair.

It just didn't look right. The huge C-17 was . . . hovering. At least in a sense. What it was really doing was fighting against gravity, trying to climb at the same time it was trying to fall, it's wings twisting back and forth and turning slightly, too. But in those few seconds that the paratroopers were pouring out of it, there was no other way to describe what the airplane was doing except to say it was staying still.

It didn't take long for all 102 of the paratroopers to get out of the plane: They jumped en masse and started pulling their rip cords immediately. Not until they were all out did the plane's engines scream again as it started moving away.

But it was clearly in trouble, too. Its rocket-assists burned out. It had stayed in the stalled state too long. Falling off to the left, it clipped its wing on the edge of the newly flattened-out summit, and started plunging downward.

Before Cardillo and the others could even react, though, they heard the plane's engines scream again, and incredibly the big aircraft got some air under its wings—and amazingly, *miraculously* managed to level off.

It came down in a cloud of smoke and dust, its entire fuselage vibrating, engines now louder than ever. But again, the nose of the airplane came up, the wings dipped this way and that, and then it bounced in for an approximation of a fairly good landing right back where it had started on the old CIA airstrip.

Cardillo just shook his head. It had all happened so quickly. From dropping the paratroopers, to nearly crashing, to recovering, to landing—all of it had taken no more than thirty seconds.

"I always knew that guy was nuts," Cardillo said.

WATER . . .

Everywhere. Coming down the passageways. Cascading out of the tunnels. Pouring out of the ventilation systems and even the lighting fixtures.

Hot, steaming, black water. It was flooding the insides of Bora Kurd.

Amil the Syrian was in the middle of stuffing his travel bags when he thought the world had ended. He was in his quarters, putting as much money and valuables as he could grab into a sack, intent on fleeing the fortress through the escape tunnel, when the entire mountain began shaking.

He didn't know what it was. An earthquake? An explosion in the armory? Or was the mountain indeed a volcano and had picked this moment to blow its top?

Amil was thrown to the floor by the massive tremor; all his belongings landed on his head. It felt like the entire planet had moved. Or that someone had just dropped a nuclear bomb on them.

Whatever it was, it just reinforced his desire to get out of the mountain and leave it to the devils and the ghosts.

He grabbed whatever valuables he could and stuffed them in his pockets. Then he ran out of his living quarters only to find the passageways all around him were running thick with the hot black water. Some of his fighters were clinging to the walls, desperately trying not to get caught up by it. Others had failed and were being swept away, scalded and drowning at the same time. Now Amil felt like he was living inside a different kind of movie. Not *Star Wars*, but a disaster film. It just didn't seem real somehow.

Amil had never been this frightened, this unnerved. He'd assassinated people, set off car bombs, blown up airplanes in flight. Until now, he thought he had balls of steel. But after what had happened earlier out on the mountainside—after he saw the stars themselves twist and turn and make the mark of the ultimate devil—he wasn't sure what was real anymore. When dozens of his gunners saw the same vision as he, there was no way he could prevent them from fleeing back into the fortress, abandoning the gun emplacements Amil had been so proud of just hours before. And now this? A flood *inside* a mountain? This *had* to be the work of the devil.

When he'd decided to flee, Amil had considered going to the Sheik and offering to get him out, too. This had nothing to do with his feelings for the leader of the PKD—he had no feelings for him. Amil looked at this as purely a monetary matter. If he saved the Sheik, then the Sheik would have to reward him.

But now that this unexplained deluge was rushing through the fortress, Amil decided he'd be lucky if he were able to save himself.

But then there was the matter of the Bien Cache Guerriers. The fortress's secret soldiers. What about them? How would they get out? Helping them might not be that bad of an idea.

Amil made it to the Great Hall somehow. It, too, was awash with the black steamy water, but the water was not as high and was not flowing as rapidly as just minutes before—signs that the worst of the flood might be over.

The Great Hall was in ruins, though. The rugs, the divans— all swept away. Equipment, smashed and broken everywhere. Many of the lights had gone out, and in the semi-darkness, it was hard not to step on a body or trip over glass and debris. Shorn wires were crackling with sparks, the moans of the not quite dead filled the large expanse. The flood was gone, but it had turned the large cavern into yet another kind of movie: a horror film.

Amil made his way over to that part of the hall used for making the execution videos. The cameras, the lights, and the boom mics had all been swept away or destroyed, but the closed-circuit TV board, with its links to cameras out on the mountainside, was still working, though just barely. Eleven of the dozen screens on the control board were showing nothing but static. But one camera was still working and it was showing an incredible scene. Located halfway down the mountain on the western side, it was now pointing up toward the summit and it clearly showed that the top of Bora Kurd was gone—blown away by some unknown force. The fire from this blast had melted tons of snow and the resulting heated water had raced into the fortress, causing the great flood. Amil couldn't believe it. Torrents of this same water were now cascading down the side of the mountain as well, washing away many of the gun emplacements and any of the PKD fighters who had stayed on to man them.

But the camera also showed something else, something even more frightening, if that was possible. Amidst the fire and smoke still pouring off the summit, Amil caught a glimpse of shadow overhead, a set of wings seen against the slowly brightening sky. It was an American military aircraft—he was sure of it—and paratroopers were falling out of it. It was only in view for a second or two, hanging in the air much longer than seemed possible, and then it weirdly disappeared. But Amil saw it long enough to know it must be connected to what had happened on top of the mountain. And that could only mean one thing: The Americans *were* coming.

That sealed it. Amil had to get out of the mountain, quick . . .

Many of the fighters who'd survived the flood were now stumbling into the Great Hall, dazed and confused and looking for someone to tell them what to do. A few subcommanders were also in hand. Amil gathered them all near the main armory, self-preservation his sole concern now. If the Americans were going to enter the fortress, Amil had to delay them somehow until he could save himself—and maybe the secret warriors.

So he ordered his subcommanders to start issuing what might have been the fortress's most lethal weapon; this is how the PKD would fight the Americans if indeed they were coming. The effort to militarize the terrorist group had failed, Amil knew that now. So they would resort to their old tactics, go back to doing something they did very well.

The deadliest weapon was not a bigger or better gun—but dozens of vests lined with explosives. An army of suicide bombers would be waiting when the Americans arrived inside Bora Kurd. The resulting confrontation would surely give Amil enough time to escape. If he was lucky.

He turned to go, but then spotted the jail cells at the end of the hall. He thought a moment, then took out his knife.

There was one more thing he had to do.

THE first thing Gunn did after landing back at the old CIA runway was pop two more amphetamine tablets.

He sat in the pilot's seat of the gunship for a long time, not moving, not doing anything but allowing the pills to take effect. Out of the corner of his eye, he saw Lieutenant Bing doing the same thing—or was he praying? Gunn couldn't tell.

They finally unstrapped and climbed out of the airplane. The gun crew emerged via the cargo ramp; each one looked stunned and amazed, like they'd just gotten off the ultimate ride at the ultimate amusement park. They all stared at the smoking mountain; in their wildest dreams, none of them had ever thought they would cause so much destruction. They seemed mesmerized by it.

All except Gunn. He was looking in the other direction. He'd fantasized that Amanda might be waiting for him when he landed. That she was going to hug him when he climbed out of the plane, and be happy and relieved that he'd come back in one piece.

Her plane was here, as was Pulver's wounded bird. But she was nowhere to be seen.

Gunn joined Bada and the others looking up at the mountain as it continued to smolder away. The 82nd was on the top, and by all indications it had been a highly successful drop. There certainly hadn't been any return fire from any of the weapons on the mountainside. Between Moon's psy-ops campaign and the massive airstrike by the AC-17, the fortress's vaunted defense had been neutralized. Now it was up to the Army.

Eventually Gunn and Bing just looked at each other and shrugged, as if to say: *What do we do now?*

Moon answered that question a moment later. He burst from his blue module, which was now sitting on the runway itself, and ran over to them. He was carrying one of the futuristic-looking helmets Gunn had seen previously hanging up inside his mad scientist's laboratory.

"I've worked out an improvement on the three-D map," he told them, holding up the helmet. "And I programmed it into this. If someone is wearing this helmet up there, they'll be able to follow the map through a HUD—and do a lot of other things as well."

Gunn looked at the strange helmet, wondering if something so Flash Gordon could actually work.

"Put it on," Moon urged him.

Gunn pulled the helmet over his head. It was as uncomfortable as it looked. It was more like an oversized football helmet than the Fritz hat most U.S. forces wore in combat.

Moon tapped him on both sides near the ears, and the small speakers on each side of the helmet came to life. Suddenly Gunn's range of hearing increased by a factor of ten. He could clearly hear the crackling of the flames way on top of the mountain just as well as the conversation of his gun crew fifty feet away. Nothing was overwhelming; everything was just a lot clearer.

"Flip down the visor," Moon told him.

Gunn pulled the tinted piece of plastic down over his eyes—and was stunned. It was like he was suddenly seeing the world in high-definition. Everything was brighter, clearer, crisper. And extremely vivid, color-wise.

Gunn breathed: "This is freaking amazing."

Moon almost laughed. "You ain't seen nothing yet," he said.

He hit another touch panel on the helmet's visor and a grid came up level with Gunn's vision. And, yes, the closest thing he could compare it to was a head-up display in a jet fighter. There were numbers and graphs and symbols, which measured the distance between him and whatever he seemed to be looking at. Another tap, and the image in front of him went into zoom-mode. He looked at the top of the mountain, touched the panel, and was instantly zoomed in on what was happening at the peak. In fact, he could clearly see the faces of several 82nd Airborne troopers looking off the mountain and down at them in the valley. He could almost hear one saying, "What the fuck are they doing down there?"

Gunn couldn't believe it.

"So, it works, right?" Moon asked him anxiously.

"It sure does," Gunn replied.

Moon then banged a few things into his laptop—and suddenly Gunn could see another image forming on the eye visor. It was the 3-D map of the interior of Bora Kurd, but this one Moon had pieced together from the actual fly-cam intelligence-gathering footage. Gunn was stunned once again. On one level it seemed like he was already inside the mountain. Everything looked so real—or as real as a realistic video game.

"Here's the deal," Moon told him. "You get up there with this hat on. Go in with the troops. I'll have the SCRAM up and flying again—I'll keep it one step ahead of you. You'll be able to see what I see and I'll be able to see what you see. Just follow where I tell you to go, and we can maybe roll up a lot of these assholes in short order."

Gunn was still fascinated by the technology of the futuristic helmet—but again, like a lot of things on this mission, he found himself wondering, Would it really work? Then he thought of what Moon had told him earlier when he'd asked a similar question. The reply was: If it didn't work, what difference would it make?

Gunn popped another amphetamine pill and then said: "Okay—let's do it."

Moon handed him an M-4 rifle and started him walking toward his mini-chopper.

But Gunn had another surprise coming, because at that moment, Amanda and Pulver stepped out of Moon's module—and they were wearing the Flash Gordon helmets, too.

Gunn immediately protested. "You can't let her go up there," he said adamantly to Moon. "She's never been in a combat situation before!"

Moon was busy getting his helicopter started. "Major, she's in a combat situation *right now*," he said with some exasperation. "We all are. I need *three* pairs of eyes connected to me down here. Good eyes belonging to people who can make snap decisions. One thing you and her and Elvis there have in common is that you're all fighter pilots. I need those kinds of reflexes if this thing is going to work. Besides . . ."

"Besides what?" Gunn asked him.

"Besides, she wants to go because she knew you'd be going," Moon told him.

Gunn looked back at the intelligence officer, surprise obviously registering on his face. "She told you that?" he asked him. "Really?"

Moon was losing his patience. "Yes," he answered Gunn. "And you can pass her a note in gym class later on, okay? But for now—can we get this show on the road, please?"

The next thing Gunn knew he was in the tiny OH-33 copter, squeezed in next to Pulver who had managed to squeeze in next to Amanda.

Pulver looked none the worse for wear after his heart-stopping flight to the top of Bora Kurd. Gunn wondered what his secret was, this while he managed to gulp down yet another amphetamine tablet.

Moon lifted off and started flying very fast to the top of the mountain. Gunn looked out the side window and saw his copilot Bada Bing standing next to the AC-17, its work done. The young pilot was saluting Gunn as the copter left the ground. It was only at that moment that Gunn wondered what lay ahead exactly, and whether he'd ever see Bing or the AC-17 again.

Moon drove the copter close to the side of the mountain, which gave Gunn and the others an opportunity to see up close the destruction he'd wrought.

To say the mountain looked as if it were a volcano and the top had blown off was actually an understatement. *All* the trees and overgrowth on it were gone. Just about all of the PKD's gun positions and pillboxes lay bare—ammo and fuel were still exploding all around the huge mountain. The snow melted by the holocaust was still streaming down the sides, creating long muddy rivers of soot and ash. Smoke and flames—and bodies—were everywhere.

They reached the mountain's peak, or what was left of it. Again the summit looked like a moonscape. The 82nd troopers could be seen moving about the newly flattened summit, walking among the steam fissures and crackling fires, gathering their weapons and sorting their ammo. Someone had even raised an American flag above it.

Moon landed and the three pilots jumped out.

"Just keep in touch at all times," Moon told them. "Follow my lead—I'll tell you where to go and where not to. Good luck."

With that he lifted off again and returned to the valley below.

Captain Vogel was soon right beside them. In a spontaneous moment, he hugged Pulver.

"All of my men made it," the CO told the pilot. "Thanks to you. And that means, as long as you hang around with the Army, you'll never have to pay for another drink again."

"I can handle that, I think," the Elvis look-alike replied.

Vogel quickly snapped back into character and studied the Flash Gordon helmets.

"We're anxious to get this under way," he said. "We haven't had any contact with the mooks yet—I'm sure they're still recovering from the shock inside. But it's already been fifteen minutes and they obviously know we're here. So let's go."

Vogel divided his men up into three groups as they had found three separate entrances on top of the blasted-off mountaintop. The 82nd had been busy clearing large amounts of debris away from the three entrances.

"Just a few words before we go in," Vogel told them now. "We've got two priorities here if I read it right: Rescue any hostages that are still alive and try to secure the videotapes of any executions. Am I right?"

Gunn and the others nodded in agreement.

"Okay, now I'm not about to tell any of you to hang back and stay safe, because obviously that isn't what today is about," Vogel went on. "But I will tell you this: Clearing a cave is the most difficult military operation there is. They can run on for hundreds of feet—and there could be an enemy around every corner. And we have to assume these guys know the layout of the place, so they have the advantage. Now, making it all even worse, bullets tend to bounce off cave walls. So, if you fire your weapon inside one of those passageways, you not only risk your bullet hitting a friend, you also risk that bullet coming back and hitting your own ass. So be careful. We're going in there in force, and I'm sure those gizmos you're wearing will be of great help. But it's going to be methodical. Understand?"

There was no complaint from the three pilots.

At that point Vogel gave his men the signal and just like that the paratroopers began pouring through the holes in the top of the mountain. Gunn checked his Flash Gordon helmet and saw everything was working: the head-up display and graphs all perfect. All he needed was for Moon to get back to his module and get the SCRAM flying again.

It was time to go. Pulver was the first one into his rabbit hole, going in even before the Airborne's squad leader. Typical Marine behavior, Gunn thought.

He and Amanda eyed each other briefly. Gunn was hoping she'd say something personal, but all she said was, "See you at the objective, Major."

He just nodded and said, "Okay—see you in the Great Hall." Then she was gone, following Vogel into the second rabbit hole.

Gunn was assigned to Charlie squad, the third unit going into the mountain. Their means of ingress was a gaping hole in the fortress's ventilation system. The gunship's barrage had blown the top off it and it was now just a plain metal shaft that plunged nearly straight down.

The officer in charge of Charlie squad was a young African American, Captain Lewis. He looked like he could have played pro football; he was built like a running back.

He told Gunn to stick with him for two reasons—for protection, but also so he could get Moon's instructions as quickly as possible.

"If everything works out," Lewis told Gunn, "we might be able to actually do something constructive here."

With that, the thirty-four paratroopers in Charlie squad went into the shaftway.

They didn't have to go very far to find themselves in one of the mountain passageways. Fifty feet into the shaft they came upon another hole that had been blown inward and this gave them access to the fort itself. Gunn was relieved, as he did not want to crawl through a vent shaft all the way down the mountain. He was a little too claustrophobic for that.

It took just a minute or so for all of Charlie squad to make it into the passageway. It was long and full of shadows, illuminated by the weakest lightbulbs imaginable. The fortress obviously had some kind of emergency power on, but Gunn was surprised they still had electricity at all.

The passageway curved downward from them and they could hear a lot of commotion happening ahead. Just as the unit was ready to move out, Moon's voice came into Gunn's ears. The intelligence agent was back in his module and operating again. The 3-D map of the fortress quickly popped up on Gunn's HUD display. He could see Charlie squad's position on it and saw that a major intersection of passageways was located about fifty feet down from their current position.

"I just flew through there," Moon told Gunn of the intersection. "It was clear then. Move forward, but be careful. There are definitely PKD guys in your area. They're confused, but they're still armed and dangerous."

Gunn passed the info on to Lewis who gave the silent orders for his men to start moving. They quietly stole down the passageway, staying very close to either side of the cave wall.

To Gunn's eye the paratroopers were very professional—and highly trained. The only problem was, they were all wearing snow-white Alpine uniforms, and now they were in the darkest of combat environments possible. Still, he began thinking that if the other two squads were moving as easily as this, then perhaps they would make it to the Great Hall sooner than they all thought.

They reached the intersection of the passageways and it was clear just as Moon said it would be. The light was a little brighter here and what they saw ahead of them was a convergence of three more tunnels, one larger than the other two, all three heading downward.

Once again, they moved slowly, carefully checking out every angle and cutout of the main tunnel.

That's when Moon's voice was back in Gunn's ear again.

"You've got about forty guys about twenty feet from your position," Moon told him. But the intelligence agent had said it so matter-of-factly Gunn hesitated for a moment.

"Bad guys?" he asked foolishly.

"Of course they're fucking bad guys!" Moon hissed back at him.

Two seconds later, the bullets started smashing into the cave wall over Gunn's head.

"Jesuzz! Get down!" Gunn yelled. But the paratroopers were already hugging the tunnel floor. The spray of PKD bullets had them deciding that real quick.

A full-scale firefight erupted in the span of a half second. The chattering of the AKs filled the tunnel, as the paratroopers lay exposed and unprotected. Meanwhile the terrorists were well positioned behind corners and rocky outgrowths.

It was the perfect ambush spot and the 201st had walked right into it.

"There's forty-four of them," Moon was telling Gunn—in other words, ten more than Charlie squad. "All with AKs—lots of ammo."

Gunn could hardly hear Moon at this point, though—the sound of the PKD's weapons was just too loud.

"Jesuzz—can't you do something?" Gunn whispered to him desperately. "They're going to roll over us!"

"What do you want me to do to them?" Moon hissed back. "Bite them? I'm a fly for Christ's sake . . ."

But again it was hard to hear Moon as now the paratroopers were at least firing back at the terrorists. The situation was still critical, though.

Gunn could feel the bullets whizzing right over his head. He didn't mind admitting it: It was frightening. He was a fighter pilot—what the hell was he doing in this situation? He realized at that moment he was probably the *worst* person on the squad to be wearing the futuristic helmet, not the best.

"Are there any friendlies near us?" he asked Moon through quick, nervous breaths. "Anyone close by who can help?"

"No . . ." Moon replied emphatically. "But hang on a moment—maybe we have a solution here."

More bullets cracked off the wall right behind Gunn. His ears were ringing, they were so loud.

"Shit—hurry, Lieutenant!" he said.

Moon was back on ten seconds later. "Okay—" he started. "Take five guys and back out of there."

Gunn thought he'd gone crazy. "Are you kidding?" he yelled back at Moon. "They'll fill us full of holes if we move."

Moon came right back: "I'm right above you and they don't

have a clear shot at you or the five guys behind you. So just do it. Trust me."

Gunn shook his head and started crawling backward. He ran into a paratrooper, and whispered Moon's orders. Then the both of them began crawling in reverse. This went on for a minute until he and the five paratroopers were completely out of the line of fire.

Gunn took three deep breaths. "Okay, now what?" he asked Moon.

Moon said: "Back up to the last intersection. Go now, the way is clear."

Gunn relayed the directions to his five compatriots and they double-timed it back to the last intersection they'd come to.

"And now?" Gunn asked Moon.

"Take the right side tunnel," was the reply. "The narrow one."

Gunn studied this tunnel. It curved downward and was without any kind of light.

"Are you sure?"

"I'm sure," was Moon's curt reply.

The six of them proceeded down the dark tunnel. Soon enough they came to a vent shaft that had been torn apart by the air strike and the massive flood that followed.

"Go into it," Moon told Gunn. This time he didn't question the intelligence agent. He and the paratroopers climbed into the metal shaft—it was the same one they'd used when they first came into the mountain.

"Go about twenty yards down," Moon told them, adding, "and be quiet about it."

They did as told. And twenty yards down they came to yet another hole blasted out in the vent.

"We go out here?" Gunn asked Moon.

"Yes," he replied. "But be careful—and look to your left."

Gunn was the first to slide out. He looked to his left and saw the forty-four PKD fighters firing at the rest of the squad. Through Moon's help, he and the five paratroopers had come up right in back of them.

"Jesuzz," Gunn breathed. He couldn't believe they had wound up in this position. "Now what?"

"Kill them, for God's sake!" Moon yelled at him.

Again, the paratroopers needed no further prompting. They started firing immediately.

Gunn could see their bullets impacting on the backs of the nearest PKD fighters. Eight of them went down without the rest of the terrorists even knowing it. The paratroopers opened up again, now getting head shots on the PKDs—Gunn saw at least two skulls explode almost instantaneously.

By this time the terrorists knew something was wrong. Many of them turned to look behind them, but Gunn's men never stopped firing. Woefully exposed with no one covering the rear, the paratroopers killed them all in one long, loud barrage.

Then, just like that, it was over. Gunn was stunned. His heart was racing: The half-dozen speed pills he'd casually gulped down in the past thirty minutes were just now kicking in. The paratroopers who been trapped farther up the shaft now crowded around Gunn.

"That fucking helmet is the balls!" one of them yelled. "We're supermen with that thing!"

They all slapped him on the back and then started running down the tunnel.

"Let's go get some more!" another trooper yelled.

Meanwhile Gunn just looked at his rifle.

He hadn't fired a shot.

THEY quickly moved down the next passageway, checking out living spaces along the way but finding nothing except lots of personal items—clothes, blankets, holy books—damaged by the flood.

They reached the next intersection of tunnels and passageways, the passageways twice as wide and better lit than the tunnels. Moon was in Gunn's ear the whole way.

Gunn turned the next corner when Moon told him to stop. Gunn signaled the paratroopers to stop with him.

"Around the next corner there are, let me see, six . . . no, seven mooks," Moon was whispering in Gunn's ear.

Gunn looked in the direction of the next corner, and by boosting his virtual vision, he could see the shadows of the terrorists on the wall opposite where they were hiding. He tapped the side of his helmet. He could hear jabbering in what he knew now was Pashtooni.

"What are they carrying?" Gunn whispered back to Moon.

"Hang on," Moon replied.

Gunn turned up his hearing a little more and could actually hear Moon's fly-cam buzzing around.

"They're carrying AKs," Moon said. "And they're loading. If you're going to take them, do it *right now*!"

That's all Gunn needed to hear. He gave the signal to the paratroopers and then started running. Suddenly he felt invulnerable knowing the terrorists around the corner were totally unprepared, and didn't even have ammunition in their weapons.

The seven PKD fighters were astonished when Gunn came around the corner. He hesitated just a moment—he could see the absolute surprise on their faces, and puzzlement, too, no doubt looking at his crazy helmet. It was the last thought any of them had. Gunn sprayed them with his M4, killing them all.

He stood frozen for a moment, looking at the smoke rising from the seven dead bodies. He'd killed enemy soldiers before, but nothing so up close and personal.

The paratroopers arrived a moment later, but didn't even have to fire their weapons. Gunn had done it all.

Lewis looked at Gunn's smoking M-4, then at the dead terrorists.

"You're getting good at this," he said.

They moved on.

THEY were running again, even though Moon was screaming in Gunn's ear not to run, or at least not to run so fast. It was disrupting the signals to the Flash Gordon helmet, weakened, anyway, by the fact that they were inside a mountain.

But there was no way Gunn could slow down now. The paratroopers were running full-out—even Lewis, who'd previously urged them to be methodical—and Gunn was leading the charge.

They reached the next intersection, when Moon screamed in his ear: "Stop! Bad guys next corner."

Gunn skidded to a halt, grabbing two paratroopers as he did so. Several more tripped over them, until finally the whole squad tumbled to a halt.

"Situation . . ." Gunn hissed with whipped-up bravado to Moon.

"Ten more bad guys," Moon hissed back. "But only four are carrying AKs. The rest are unarmed. The AKs are loaded."

Gunn passed this information along to the paratroopers, by way of hand signals.

"They're waiting for you," Moon went on. "But they don't know you're so close by. Move in, but for God's sake, be careful."

But Gunn didn't hear this last sentence. The proper thing to do would have been to carefully set up firing positions, reconnoiter the bad guys a little more, and then—using established military principles—try to overwhelm them. Instead, Gunn brashly moved up to the wall around the corner from where the PKD's ambush lay, pushed a M80 grenade into his M4's launcher, and casually fired it around the corner.

The explosion shook dust from the roof of the tunnel. Before the smoke even cleared, the paratroopers followed Gunn around the corner, firing wildly. There were indeed ten PKD fighters around the bend, but only half had weapons and three of them had been splattered by Gunn's grenade. The other two armed men got off a total of three shots—all of them harmless—before the paratroopers shot him over and over again. When they finally stopped firing, the other five terrorists shrank back against the wall. They were unarmed and the paratroopers knew it.

"Don't waste bullets on them!" someone yelled.

So using the butts of their rifles and their heavy combat boots, the paratroopers stomped the five men to death. It was one of the most disturbing things Gunn had ever seen; but he was caught up in it, too. Even Lewis was urging his men on, until it was clear that the terrorists were dead.

"That's how you fight in a cave, muthafucker!" one of the paratroopers yelled.

The rest of the paratroopers howled in loud agreement—
even Lewis. Then they all started running again, including
Gunn.

HE was out of his mind on speed and adrenaline now. His
heart was pumping so fast, he felt like it was going to explode.
This was all unreal to him, especially because he was wearing
the Flash Gordon helmet. He could hear better than anyone
in the game and he could see better. He had a bug-sized eye flying recon. He wasn't quite Superman—but he *did* feel like he
was inside a video game, like the one he'd played with his
barmaid friend, and this made him laugh. Something that was
so foreign to him two weeks ago—now he was *living* it.

They reached another intersection and Moon was hissing
in his ear again. He reported that they were coming up on a
large group of PKD fighters hiding amongst some rubble that
had fallen in during the massive air strike. It was a very dangerous situation in a confined area. But this didn't affect the
paratroopers.

Gunn could hear the PKDs clearly, and he could see their
shadows moving around. Within a few seconds, he knew where
every fighter was hiding—either behind a rock or mounds of
rubble—via the helmet's zoom lens. Gunn relayed this information to Lewis, who had ordered his best grenade men to
come up front. With guidance from Gunn, these troopers
tossed grenades above or close to each hidden terrorist, blasting every one of them. This way it took just a half minute to
subdue the enemy fighters. The paratroopers overran their
position, pulling their knifes and stabbing to death any terrorists who'd survived the barrage of explosions.

It was very bloody, and certainly *not* by the book. But the
squad prevailed unscathed and moved on again, this time
even quicker than before.

Still Moon was in Gunn's ear—again urging him to slow
down, that there was danger everywhere. But even though
Gunn was relaying all this to Lieutenant Lewis, and Lewis was
yelling it out to his men, it didn't change anything. They weren't
a military unit anymore—they were a mob, with guns . . . and
people to kill.

They came to another long passageway that sloped downward. It contained many rooms and this meant many doorways for PKD fighters to hide in. Indeed, Moon reported at least a dozen enemy fighters concealed somewhere along the way. But because they were so scattered, and because he couldn't get an exact count, Moon suggested the squad engage them carefully, rooting them out one at a time. But the paratroopers didn't have time or patience for this. They simply charged down the long tunnel, firing their weapons in all directions and daring any of the PKD fighters to take a shot at them. When one did, he exposed his position for Gunn's enhanced vision to see. Gunn then directed the paratroopers' counterfire and the terrorist was shot repeatedly, until there was nothing left of him. Those terrorists too frightened to fire were hunted down and stabbed or kicked to death. Gunn joined in on these killing frenzies. Sometimes he found himself just shooting his M4 wildly.

They cleared the passageway in less than two minutes this way. Then, they began running again.

THEY came to yet another intersection and Moon was back in his ear.

"Stay where you are," he was telling Gunn.

"But why?" Gunn asked him. "We can see all the way down to the next tunnel. It's clear."

"Stay in place," Moon repeated. "I'm over on the eastern edge helping Alpha Team get out of a jam. So just cool your heels and I'll be right back to you."

"How's Bravo Team?" Gunn asked him. But Moon was on to other things.

Gunn passed Moon's order on to the paratroopers—who did not take it well. They were even more pumped than before. Stopping cold just wasn't on their agenda.

Lewis calmed them down, and they did take a breather for a few seconds. But the sound of gunfire from several different places in the fortress served to whip them up again.

"Hey, that helmet works even though the fly isn't looking over your shoulder, right?" one of the troopers asked Gunn.

Gunn nodded.

"Then let's dance," the trooper said. "You be our eyes and ears. We don't want those slobs in Alpha or Bravo to make it to the big prize first. Let's go!"

In the end, the paratroopers didn't give him a choice. They all started running again, Lewis along with them. Gunn jumped to his feet and started running as well. He couldn't help it. He was laughing, it was so damn exciting.

They made it to the end of the next tunnel, allowing Gunn to move up to the intersection alone. He scanned the convergence of passageways, tapping his ears to get his super-hearing, and adjusting his eye shield to get super-vision.

"Down there!" he yelled. He'd picked up a shadow walking up the tunnel right toward them. "One person, coming closer. Probably unarmed."

A moment later, a man in white robes suddenly appeared. He seemed to be old for a terrorist—white beard and slightly stooped. He seemed so out of place, the paratroopers didn't shoot him right away.

And that was a mistake.

Because the man approached them, smiling, laughing even, as if he was giving up. But then he opened his robes to reveal that he was strapped with sticks of TNT.

Suddenly he leaped forward and pulled Gunn down with him. One moment, Gunn was standing there, the next he was wrestling with this crazy old man with a white beard and a hundred pounds of dynamite strapped to him!

"Jesuzz," Gunn started yelling. *"Jesuzz Christ!"*

The man was strong for his size and age and Gunn was so absolutely stunned by it all, the guy had the advantage on him. Gunn tried to get himself away from him, but the old man was digging into him with his fingernails. He was laughing, all the while trying to pull the detonation cord with his teeth.

Gunn could hear the paratroopers yelling at him, encouraging him like this was some kind of schoolyard fight. But Gunn was scared for his life, certain the vest bomb was going to go off at any moment.

Finally he was able to get the man to unclench his hands from him and suddenly he was free. Gunn started kicking like mad to get away from the man.

He managed to roll away about five feet. The paratroopers took cover. The man pulled the detonator cord.

The blast was tremendous; it reverberated up and down the entire mountain. Gunn was knocked back ten feet, landing in a crumple against a handful of similarly thrown paratroopers. When everything cleared, the bomber was gone in a puff of smoke. Nothing remained of him but bits of bloody dust.

Gunn felt like someone had hit him on the head with a baseball bat. And for a moment, he thought the explosion had perforated him, too.

But then he pulled the Flash Gordon helmet off and saw that it looked like a sieve. It was full of holes, caused by sharp pieces of rock sent in every direction by the blast.

Gunn had gotten his bell rung, but the futuristic helmet had taken the brunt of it, stopping all the deadly rock shards, some just a half inch before they would have penetrated his skull.

All contact with Moon was lost, of course—and for him, the video game was over.

But somehow, Gunn was still alive.

He threw the helmet away, turned, and found himself facing a large wooden door, closed tight with a padlock the size of a small car.

He fired his M4 directly on the large padlock, blowing it to pieces.

Then he kicked in what was left of the door; the thing turned to splinters and fell off its hinges.

Then he took one large step forward—and found himself standing in the entrance to the Great Hall, the inner chamber of the PKD's hideout.

"I don't believe it," he gasped. "We're the first ones here . . ."

As crazed and rampageous as they were, the paratroopers had to stop in the entranceway for a moment and take it all in. Even though it was severely trashed now, and the lighting was very low, it was apparent the images the fly-cam had taken of this place hadn't done it justice. They were amazed at how big and elaborate it was. The notion that the terrorists had been hiding in one big cave was a false one, at least when it came to this space. It was like a grand banquet hall in some ornate temple.

Most surprising was the hall's TV studio. The image on the fly-cam had made it seem somewhat crude. But the actual place looked not unlike a studio in a big-city TV newsroom. The first thing Gunn noticed, though, was the blood on the floor. Even though the great flood had passed through here not too long ago, it had been unable to wash it all away.

All this gawking took a matter of nanoseconds—like everything stood still for just a moment. But then the rescue force got moving again.

Gunn was the first to enter the Great Hall, weapon up, ready to drill anything that moved. The paratroopers were close behind, moving carefully in the gloom. Many noises were echoing around the hall—gunfire, explosions, screaming, shouting. It felt like the mountain itself was shaking with all this noise, the result of all the fighting going on in the labyrinth of tunnels leading into this place.

Through the murk and shadows, Gunn spotted a clutch of terrorists at the far end of the Great Hall. They weren't firing their weapons at him—rather they seemed too scared to run or even move. Strange . . .

The paratroopers opened up on them immediately—but as soon as the first bullets hit home, there were five explosions, right in a row. This had Gunn and the troopers hugging the muddy floor once again as fire seemed to scorch every corner of the large space. At first it was like someone had taken out the terrorists with a high-powered cannon. But another explanation made more sense: Like the old guy Gunn had just grappled with, these terrorists had also been wired up with explosives.

They could hear more explosions going off all around the huge cavern and in the passageways and rooms connected to it. In fact, the mountain seemed to be shaking even more now than it had been just seconds before. Gunn surmised that the other two paratrooper squads were close by and they were running into the suicide bombers as well—and in closer quarters. It was best then that Moon was off helping them. Still, Lewis warned his men to shoot anything that moved—but make sure they did it at a distance.

Despite all this, Gunn had never felt such excitement: The adrenaline was still drowning him. He spotted another group of terrorists directly across the Great Hall from them. Their robes seemed overly bulky, a clue they were also wearing bomb vests. Suicide bombers were only effective if they got in a crowd, and that wasn't happening here. Still, like the first group, these fighters seemed reluctant to move, whether to advance or retreat. It was clear someone had planted the bombers here in case the Americans made it to the Great Hall, but apparently they'd failed to tell them what to do beyond that.

Lewis saw them, too—and came up with a plan. His men took cover and once again he called up the best grenadiers in the squad. He had these men lob a string of grenades into the middle of the wired-up fighters. The grenades went off—and their combined shrapnel caused a chain reaction, detonating the TNT belts on all five terrorists simultaneously.

The paratroopers cheered, and then started cursing the blown-apart terrorists. Soon enough, fresh blood was soaking the floor of the Great Hall.

That's when Gunn looked to his right and saw the row of crude jail cells at the far end of the hall.

His breath immediately caught in his throat. His heart began beating even faster. Finally—*this* was what they had come so far for.

Gunn used hand signals to communicate to Lewis what he'd spotted. The squad leader left half his men near the Great Hall's entranceway, and then he and Gunn led the rest of the soldiers toward the cells.

There was more gunfire within the hall, and Gunn thought he felt bullets whizzing by him, but he didn't care. He had his weapon up and was firing back in the general direction of where he thought the gunfire was coming from, but he wasn't aiming at anything. He was too excited, too pumped.

He was the first one to reach the jail cells, sliding to a stop on the highly polished, slippery floor. The guards were long gone by this time and just as depicted on the fly-cam, only one of the cell doors was locked. The rest had been abandoned long ago.

Gunn looked inside the first open cell door. What he saw

in the shadows was a headless torso, thrown on a bunk, a bloody towel covering that portion of the neck that remained after the beheading. He had to repress an attack of nausea. Falling back out of the room, he staggered to the next cell door and looked in. All he wanted to see was some poor wretch waiting for him, eyes wide with the hope of rescue. But again, this cell was as the first. A lifeless, headless body, thrown like garbage in the corner. The next two cells were the same: headless bodies dumped like so much trash. Just the fact that the terrorists never disposed of the bodies added a ghoulish edge to what was happening.

Gunn was in a state of absolute rage by the time he came to the fifth and final cell. The padlock was still on the door and this filled him with hope. Again, they'd come all this way to do this. All the training, all the BS they put in during their time in Nevada. Their long, fast trip out here, half a world away—it had to mean something. It *had* to be worth it.

With much anticipation, Gunn blew the padlock off the door with a single shot. He wanted his heart to soar—he wanted so much to whip open that door and have Newman's daughter fall into his arms.

But it did not happen.

Gunn kicked in the door—and the first thing he saw was a name tag that someone had adhered to the wall. It read "Anne Murphy." He frantically scanned the smoky, dark room. He spotted a bunk and hurried over to it. A figure was lying on the cold metal spring, covered by a blanket. Gunn picked up the blanket, took a deep breath, and then pulled it back—only to find the fifth dead body. It was Anne Murphy, the colonel's daughter. She'd been tied to the bed and stabbed to death.

Gunn collapsed to his knees. He felt the whole world crash in on him. More paratroopers burst into the cell and saw what he'd discovered. They all collapsed as well. Judging by the amount of fresh blood, she'd been killed not long before they'd arrived.

"We're too late," Gunn was saying over and over. "Just by a few minutes—just a few goddamn minutes."

They all stayed like this, in a shared state of shock, as the battle raged on just outside.

The video game excitement was gone now. Gunn felt a

crude, burning anger rising up inside him instead. What was the point of all this? Who could kill people like this in the name of God?

Nothing made any sense to him anymore. This wasn't a holy war, or politics. This was just madness, on a grand scale. At that point, his whole demeanor changed.

He heard himself spitting out six words: "Someone's got to pay for this . . ."

THE paratrooper squad Amanda had followed burst into the Great Hall about two minutes after Gunn.

They'd fought their way down the eastern side of the mountain, using Moon's direction and the ventilation system to bypass areas where suicide bombers were lurking or ambushes had been set up. In each case they'd doubled back, caught the PKD fanatics from behind, and wiped them out. It had been violent and bloody, but they'd all made it.

Amanda had surprised herself during all this. She'd rarely been any closer to a combat zone than 5,000 feet above it. From the seat of an F/A-18 Hornet jet fighter, everything was antiseptic. Drop a bomb, watch it on your targeting scope, see the puff of smoke—target destroyed. Simple, and as detached as that.

That all changed when she saw the destruction meted out by Gunn's AC-17 on Bora Kurd. Despite the long, wild journey it had taken them to get here, during the dash across China and through the worst of the snowstorm, it really hadn't hit home until the moment she literally saw a two-mile high mountain taken down a couple notches. It was as if the 201st had changed nature itself.

Now she was in this underworld and the people who lived down here—after what they'd done, and what they'd planned to do—simply didn't deserve to live. She'd fired her M4 during the firefights in the tunnels. She'd even lobbed a couple of grenades during the nastier gunfights. If she'd hit anyone, she didn't know—but she hoped she had. Her bombs had killed terrorists from one mile up, if her weapon had killed them from a few feet away, what difference did it make? It wasn't like arresting them, holding them, rehabilitating them would do anyone any good. The only way to make sure they never hurt anyone again was to kill them first. Simple as that.

These were her thoughts as her squad broke into the eastern side of the Great Hall. They, too, were astonished how big and elaborate it was. The fly-cam images of the place were akin to taking a picture on a camera phone of the Taj Mahal. The dirty, unwashed PKD fighters were living in the most amazing underground structure imaginable.

But at the moment the Great Hall didn't look so great. There were many terrorists' bodies lying about, pools of blood everywhere, plus the residue from the great flood had left mud and debris everywhere.

The 82nd CO, Captain Vogel, was right beside her. "Like Rome," he said, taking it all in. "After the fall . . ."

She and her squad dodged their way through some bullets, wiping out pockets of PKD fighters still hiding in the shadows, some wearing bomb vests, some not. At one point, they made contact with paratroopers from Charlie squad and learned that all the hostages were dead. Amanda transmitted this information to Moon via her Flash Gordon helmet. The intelligence agent was quiet for a long time—like with everyone else, the sad news took a while to sink in. Then, he told Amanda the most important thing now was to secure the videos made of the hostage beheadings. As of the last NSA intelligence burst, the videos had not yet been sent out to the Persian Gulf buyer.

To this end, Amanda and Bravo squad made their way through the chaos and reached the PKD's TV studio, which took up a good portion of the Great Hall's eastern side.

The set was professionally designed and the broken equipment lying everywhere looked to be of the highest quality. Most disturbing were all the bloodstains on the studio floor.

Amanda was more interested in what was behind the studio though. Every facility like this had a control room, and this place was no different. She and Vogel found a glass door nearby and kicked it in. Behind it was a control room similar to that in any typical TV studio. And this one was filled with videotapes.

Hundreds of them . . .

"The mother lode," she said to Vogel.

But immediately they realized they had a big problem. Again, if they couldn't rescue the USAID hostages, then the least they could do was seize the videos made by the terrorists as they were executing them. The worst-case scenario would be four or five videos. But how were they going to find that handful among the hundreds held on the dozens of shelves on hand here?

"We can just destroy the whole place," Vogel suggested, realizing their dilemma.

Amanda said, "But what if they are not here—we'll never know if they're out there somewhere. Plus, who knows what kind of intelligence might be on these videos?"

So destroying all the videotapes was out. But still, it would take some doing to package everything up. But they had an even bigger problem. The videotapes were the DX kind, mini-cassettes used by TV stations, but not the general public. They had no DX players on any of the three airplanes; they had no way to play them because all the equipment in the Great Hall had been destroyed. So again, there was no way of knowing whether they had the right tapes or not.

"We have to somehow look for them," Amanda told Vogel, immediately pulling down a rack of tapes and trying to read their labels. But now it was Problem #3: They were all labeled in Pashtoon. She wasn't able to read or understand the language.

Luckily a few of the troopers could.

"Look for the word 'futah,'" one said. "It means 'devils.'"

Thus started a mad search through the hundreds of tapes lining the walls. Amanda was conscious of the time remaining. She knew they couldn't stay inside the mountain forever.

More paratroopers crowded into the control room and took up the search. Amanda told Moon what she was doing, then took the Flash Gordon helmet off in order to better read the labels on the cassettes.

Five minutes of searching proved fruitless, though. That's when she spotted another doorway in the hall nearby marked with a crude sign that read TV STORAGE. Leaving the search to the troopers, and paying attention to the sounds of gunfire still echoing through the Great Hall, she tried the door on this room and found it unlocked.

This place she would search by herself.

BEHIND the door were two PKD subcommanders—Hammad Sajad, and his cousin, Jameel. They'd both sought refuge in the darkened storage closet when they first realized the fortress was under attack. This was like a nightmare for them. Like the rest of the PKD, they'd felt impervious here, in the haunted mountain, with the people of the countryside nearby deathly afraid of them and even the Americans having no courage to come here and take them on.

But now, these mysterious soldiers who moved like ghosts were running through their tunnels, were blasting away at their peak, were cutting down their comrades like they were so much firewood. Both Hammad and Jameel had done their share of killing, rape, and torture in the name of Allah. They'd sent suicide bombers to their deaths; they'd both helped behead the USAID hostages. But both were now scared to death. Neither man wanted to die, for Allah or anyone else.

They were armed with AK-47s as well as long, razor-sharp knives known as *kufus.* They were desperately hoping that none of the invaders would bother to look in here, a storage room for the TV studio's equipment. But both men were whimpering now as they heard the American solders ransacking the control room nearby. They had no idea what had happened to many of their colleagues; they could only assume most were dead. They had no idea where the Mountain Sheik was. If he was dead, then they would be marked men no matter what happened. They had committed so many acts of treachery in their leader's name, if he was gone, then they would have many people after them. This only added to their fright.

They heard a sound. Someone was on the other side of the door. Even though there was still chaos going on in the Great Hall, they could tell someone was trying to get into the storage room.

Both men drew out their razor-sharp knives; they would have to kill this person silently.

The doorknob moved again, and the door started to open. Both men stepped back into the shadows.

They lifted their knives over their heads. And waited . . .

Amanda took one step into the dark room.

She flicked on the penlight attached to the end of her M4, and scanned the storage area. The strong, thin light illuminated another shelf full of DX videotapes and other TV studio paraphernalia. She groaned—more stuff to search.

She turned up the power on her light and walked over to the shelf.

As before, most of the stuff was marked in Pashtoon, but a few smaller boxes were marked in Arabic.

Five of them were numbered with recent dates. And they weren't DX tapes. They were DVDs. She thought for a moment. The execution footage was heading to the Persian Gulf. Maybe then their labels might be written in Arabic.

She started to open one box when she saw the shadow behind her. In one of those moments that seemed to take forever, the shadow turned to a glint, and the glint to a flash of light, and then the cold sting of razor steel against her neck.

Her last thought: *How was I so foolish?*

The knife began to move across her throat . . .

That's when two shots rang out . . . and suddenly the knife wasn't there anymore.

Amanda stayed frozen. At first she thought the bullets had hit her, too. But then she heard two thumps—and saw two dead mooks hit the floor hard, one on either side of her.

She turned slowly to see a figure at the door, a smoking M4 in his hand. The person who'd saved her life.

It was Pulver.

CHAPTER 19

Outside Bora Kurd

Moon had watched so many firefights he'd lost count.

He'd seen the paratroopers from all three squads rampaging through the passageways, mowing down anything in their path. He'd witnessed explosions in such confined areas that when the smoke cleared there was nothing left of the people who just seconds before had been standing just below his fly-cam's lens. He'd seen horrible things; he'd seen heroic things. The 82nd troopers, saving each other, covering each other, fighting for each other. Moon had been in the black ops business for more than two decades. But he'd never seen anything like the battle inside Bora Kurd.

He'd watched as the 201st finally made it into the Great Hall, shared their confusion in discovering the center of the PKD's universe all but empty. He'd felt the tug on his heart when they found Newman's daughter finally, and the rage that came from Amanda nearly getting killed, too. At that point, he wished he'd had an M4 and was up there with the 82nd and the others, drawing blood from those who had caused so much misery.

But he knew his place was down here, off the mountain and in his module, flying the SCRAM. And now that the mystery of the fifth hostage had been solved, he no longer had to linger inside the Great Hall. He began flying around again, heading lower as the paratroopers continued cleaning out every stunted tunnel and alcove on the middle levels, intent on killing every PKD fighter they came to, suicide bomber or not.

One thing was for certain: Moon knew they would not be taking any prisoners.

THEY'D previously determined that there were three easily accessible ways to get into the mountain, all from the top. But as far as Moon could tell, there really was only one way out: through the escape hatch down at the stone hut.

Yet, while the 201st had killed hundreds of the PKD fighters already, and were killing them still up around the Great Hall, hundreds still remained unaccounted for. Between the psy-ops venture, the massive pounding courtesy of the AC-17, and now the gun battles within the fortress itself, Moon hoped the terrorist army was in a panic and on the run. But then again, they could also be regrouping and planning a counterattack.

So, *where* were they?

That's what he was trying to find out.

He maneuvered the fly-cam deeper and deeper into the fortress—wielding around tunnels, air shafts and passageways. He saw blood on some of the tunnel floors, and terrorist bodies that had dropped along the way. Other passages were blocked, though, from explosions and the floods, and that proved to be a problem. Even with the 3-D map of the place, Moon felt like he was caught in a labyrinth, a maze, which kept coming back on itself. What he came to realize was while there might only be one escape tunnel, there were many ways to get to it.

So he finally brought the fly-cam in for a landing at the convergence of several passageways, turned up the audio, and just listened.

Eventually he heard a cacophony of sounds: not just voices, but the noises of a crowd. Shouting, wailing. Anger. Praying, beseeching a higher power. He started the fly-cam again and just followed these sounds.

That's when he finally found what he was looking for.

In one of the lowest passageways in the fortress, more toward the northern edge than he would have thought, he came upon a huge crowd of PKD fighters jammed into a small, shrinking space. It was absolute bedlam inside this passageway. There had to be several hundred fighters here—the missing mooks he'd been looking for. They were all pushing and shoving one another. Many were wounded. Many were crying. He saw brutal fights, people being stabbed, clubbed, shot. All clear signs of panic.

Right away Moon knew what was going on. This passageway led to the escape tunnel and terrorists were trying to get out. But the escape tunnel was too small to accommodate them all at the same time. So, the PKD *was* on the run.

But this presented a problem. The combination of the psy-ops and the paratroopers attacking from the top down, might have worked too well. Again, at least several hundred of the brutal terrorists were here, practically trapped at the bottom of the mountain. It was a golden opportunity to wipe them out for good. Yet, the 201st was still up in the Great Hall, fighting the last of the suicide bombers, nowhere near the retreating terrorists. Moon cursed himself and the cosmos. Their timing was just a bit off.

As he was contemplating this, something else caught his eye. In one passageway up and over, there was a compartment. And unlike every other compartment in the entire mountain fortress, this one had a white door.

He deftly flew down this passageway and hovered outside this white door. His microphone was picking up sounds coming from the other side; there was a group of people inside the room, maybe as many as a dozen or so. But he could not hear any sounds of distress or panic. Moon wondered if whoever was behind the white door knew what was happening just one passageway over.

Then a break: The door opened a bit and someone inside stuck their head out. They were checking if the way was clear, before ducking back inside. The door was only open for a few seconds, not enough for Moon to get a good look at the person's face, especially in the dim lighting. But in that short time, he *was* able to fly into the room.

He'd been right. There were about twelve people in this chamber, but the light was very, very low. These people seemed different right away. There were no divans or sleeping mats in here. He saw folding chairs, a table, and mattresses and bunks scattered about instead. This place had its own kitchen and he saw dirty bowls with forks and knives in the sink. He saw a pot for making coffee, but no kettle for boiling water. The people in here didn't eat with their hands, and they didn't get their food directly from the cooking pots like the fighters in the Great Hall. They drank coffee, not weak tea.

The dozen people were dressed in Afghan-type clothing, but except for one—a familiar-looking bald man with a large mustache—they didn't seem as ragged or dirty as the PKD fighters. And they were wearing combat boots, and not high black boots. And he doubted any of them were wearing blue eye shadow.

There was only one conclusion: These people had to be the Bien Cache Guerriers, the secret warriors the Sheik had talked about in the conversation he'd listened in on. But *who* were they really? And what were they doing here?

Moon flew to the far corner of the room and tried to get a wider view. These people were packed up and ready to escape the mountain—there was no doubt about that. But it was obvious they weren't panicking. They were staying very calm, just sort of hanging around, despite the fact that the Bora Kurd fortress was falling down all around them.

They were waiting—for something. But what?

Moon began flying around the room again, checking out exactly what these people had packed to take with them. Most of it looked like typical field gear, backpacks and duffel bags. Other containers obviously carried guns and ammunition. Others held what looked like Alpine-style combat uniforms.

But then he saw one box that stuck out from the rest.

At first he thought it was a very elaborate beer cooler. It was an odd greenish color, the size of a large suitcase, and it looked like something from the 1950s. Moon maneuvered around a bit more, trying to get a look at it head-on, from the back, from the top, but its contents remained a mystery. The only thing the old container reminded him of was something that medical waste might be carried in.

He tried to maneuver the fly into a position where the lighting would allow him to see the faces of these people—that was all-important now. But just as he was able to attach the fly to a wall near the group, a shadow came into the frame. The next thing Moon saw was the close-up of a face—a person was looking right at the fly, and therefore right into the camera itself.

Moon only saw this face for an instant, but in that time, he knew this person was not Arabic, and not even a native of the area.

He clearly had blond hair and blue eyes. Caucasian.

A white terrorist . . .

This person contemplated the fly for a few more seconds.

Then with a powerful slap, he swatted it off the wall, terminating the transmission.

CAPTAIN Steve Cardillo was leaning so far back in the turret of his M1 tank, he thought his spine was going to crack.

He couldn't help it—he was trying to keep an eye on what was happening on top of Bora Kurd, more than two miles straight up. But it was proving almost impossible.

The mountain's western side was sheer enough that with the right angle and a strong pair of binoculars, you could almost see all the way to the summit. But at the moment, there was so much smoke and fire billowing out of the top of the mountain fortress, there was no way of telling what was going on up there. So, finally Cardillo just gave up.

His two tanks were still in position, behind the hedgerow in the field near the stone hut, which they knew held a secret passageway into the mountain itself. Nothing much had happened since their arrival here about thirty minutes before.

As there was no radio communication between the disparate sections of the 201st, Cardillo and his tank crews couldn't even speculate what was going on with the rescue attempt. The only thing they knew for sure was so much smoke and fire was sprouting out of the top of Bora Kurd, it looked like the entire mountain was burning from within.

Cardillo asked his crew to double-check their ammunition supply. They had twenty shells for the big gun, plus 100 percent rounds for the two turret machine guns. Plus, each man was carrying his own M4 and a sidearm. But judging by what was happening so far away from them, Cardillo was sure they wouldn't see any action here—no matter which way the rescue attempt went. He felt like he was on the side-lines, out of the battle completely.

That's what happens when you bring tanks to a fight for a mountain . . .

No sooner had this thought crossed his mind than he saw something else come sprouting out of the top of the erupting fortress. Somehow making itself visible amongst all the smoke and flames, a bright red object shot straight up and out of the maelstrom. As soon as Cardillo spotted the first one, another one appeared. Then another. And another.

They really did look like something that would be blown out of an erupting volcano—but Cardillo thought maybe they were something else.

Flares maybe?

He didn't recall anything in the all-too-short precombat briefing about anyone shooting off flares or what it was supposed to mean, or whether it would mean anything at all.

So, was someone trying to tell him something?

He thought about this for a few seconds and then, just on a hunch, he told his crew to get ready, something might be up. He yelled the same thing over to the number two tank, positioned about fifty feet away. Using hand signals, he pointed to the bright flames coming off the peak and gave an exaggerated shrug. The man sitting in the number two turret just returned the pantomime. He had no idea what they were either.

The explosion went off two seconds later.

It was so powerful it knocked Cardillo back into the tank and slammed the hatch on top of him. He recovered quickly, shot back up through the hatch, and began shouting orders to his crew to prepare for action.

What he saw next was a cloud of smoke coming from what was left of the old stone hut. The blast had blown a hole in the structure—and, now, bizarrely, three people were being pushed through that hole.

Black robes, white headdresses, black boots . . . eye shadow.

These were PKD fighters. Someone had blasted away the stone hut as a way of getting out of the fortress. *Maybe that's what the flares meant?* Cardillo thought. He didn't know and at the moment he didn't care. The enemy was just 100 yards away from him. Without even thinking about it, he simply yelled: *"Fire!"*

What happened next happened in sort of a blur. On Cardillo's command, his crew opened up on the PKD fighters with the tank's big 122mm gun, scoring a direct hit on three terrorists. But the resulting explosion was far greater than anything one of their tank shells would have caused. It was as if they had hit a cache of TNT or something.

This explosion was far more violent than the first. Cardillo managed to hang on this time, and when the smoke cleared again, he saw an amazing if gruesome sight. The three people they hit must have been wired with explosives because the resulting blast had all but destroyed the rest of the stone hut, along with a good piece of the mountain. The three men had been forced outside knowing their TNT packs would be detonated once they were fired upon. The combined explosion had resulted in a gaping hole, which led directly into the fortress's escape tunnel.

And now, suddenly, a flood of terrorists was rushing out of that hole.

Again, Cardillo didn't even think about it. He yelled for his crew to fire—and they did, vaporizing at least a dozen more terrorists. The second tank did the same thing, throwing a shot right on the newly opened hole, and taking another dozen or so PKDs with it. But another two dozen terrorists were right behind them.

Both machine guns opened up, too, as Cardillo raked the opening with his 50-caliber, stopping only when his tank's big gun went off. It was madness. The enemy fighters were falling through the opening they'd made only to be cut down by the combined fire coming from the two M1 tanks. But it made no difference. Another wave of PKD fighters came pouring out of the hole, and another wave after that, and another after that.

This was not just a few fighters stumbling into their deaths this time. This was a horde of terrorists, fighting one another to get out of the hole in the mountain because there were so many behind them doing the same thing.

Cardillo didn't even have to yell *Fire!* this time. His crew and the guys in the other tank immediately opened up on the cascade of PKD fighters and never stopped shooting. Cardillo continued to add his machine-gun fire to the confusion, his tracer rounds passing through the smoke and aerated blood. He could see bodies being hit, bodies going down, bodies being blown apart. Many terrorists were on the ground screaming in agony and pain, but yet they still kept coming, dozens stepping on the bodies of their brethren in an effort to get away from the mountain.

Cardillo called down to his gunner to put a round right on the opening itself. This was done not more than three seconds later—but *again* it made no difference. It blew apart the half-dozen terrorists who happened to be fighting their way out of the hole at that moment, but it didn't stop the flow of PKDs trying to get out of the mountain.

"Fire at will!" Cardillo yelled, back to working the turret machine gun. But again he needn't have given the order; the two tank crews never stopped firing in the first place.

This went on and on *and on*—the tanks killing three dozen, four dozen, *five dozen* PKD fighters. Then a hundred. Then a hundred and fifty . . .

Yet they still kept coming.

After five chaotic minutes Cardillo heard his loader yell up to him, "Last three!" This meant the tank had just three rounds left for its big gun. They were almost out of machine-gun ammunition, too. And the PKD fighters were still pouring out of the escape hole unabated. And now some of them were firing back at the tanks.

"Son of a bitch . . ."

Cardillo knew there was only one thing he could do.

He yelled over to the other tank, "Withdraw!"

With that both tanks began backing up at high speed, out of their hiding spots and onto the open field beyond. As soon as they stopped firing, out of the corner of his eye Cardillo saw a small group of armed men come out of the hole. They did not head down the valley like the rest of the PKD fighters. Instead these dozen or so men crossed the bloody snowfield on his right and disappeared through the hedgerow 100 feet away, as if they were heading toward the village where the kid with the milk pails had come from. These people were not dressed like the PKD fighters, either. They were wearing robes, but underneath, Cardillo could clearly see they were also wearing military-issue Alpine uniforms and Fritz-style battle helmets. Again he only saw them for a second as the tank's backward withdrawal picked up speed. He wouldn't think about them again until much later.

Still backing up at high speed, about 500 feet from the hole in the mountain, both tank drivers did amazingly quick 180-degree turns. In seconds the tanks were now going forward, but their turrets were still facing backward and still firing their weapons. Cardillo was intent on getting back to the landing strip at full speed. Trouble was, the hundreds of PKD fighters, some firing their weapons, some simply running for their lives, were all heading in the same direction—right for where the three C-17s lay parked and undefended.

LIEUTENANT Bada Bing was also trying to make out what was going on atop Bora Kurd.

He was sitting inside the cockpit of Ghost 1, his RIFs plugged in and turned on, gazing toward the summit of the mountain, hoping the reverse infrared effect would give him some kind of clue how the fight was going.

But it was just about impossible to make out. There was so much smoke and fire surrounding the summit only guesswork could answer the question as to whether the 82nd had even entered the fortress yet—or whether some two-mile-high battle was still going on at the mountain's blasted-off peak. Or if any of the rescue force was even still alive at all.

He was an Air Force pilot and had done a tour in Iraq, flying F-16s. But this was his first real taste of combat, and he had spent most of it sitting here, doing nothing, feeling tense, but frustrated, too. In the deepest part of his heart, he wished he'd been able to go into the mountain with the paratroopers. At least he would have done some good in there.

He was the only person aboard Ghost 1. His gun crew and

the handful of ground personnel who'd come on the rescue mission were holed up inside Ghost 2, the Jump Plane, as it was the one most hidden from the enemy's line of sight. It was presently sitting at the far northern end of the snow-covered runway, left where it nearly crash-landed after returning from dropping off its 102 paratroopers. A few people were also inside Ghost 3: The plane's copilot, Lieutenant Stanley, was sitting in the cockpit, basically waiting just like Bing was. It was parked about 100 feet from the other end of the runway, again in the same place it had stopped after delivering the two tanks to the far end of the valley.

Ghost Plane 1 was sitting perpendicular to the middle of the runway. Upon returning from its bombastic strike on the mountain, Gunn had deliberately slid it off the airstrip to make room for the other two planes, should they have to leave in a hurry for any reason. As a result, its nose was pointing straight at the mountain, its right side facing the snow-covered valley.

That's why Bing was the first to see the commotion at the far end of the vale.

What he saw first were twin tails of dirt and snow being tossed into the air. *What the hell was this?* he thought.

He activated the zoom function on his RIFs and a moment later these twin tails of snow and dirt became focused and Bing realized that they were being caused by the two 201st tanks heading back to the landing zone at very high speed.

But why? Bing put his RIFs up to maximum zoom—and he had this answer quickly as well. The tanks were going as fast as their super-engines could carry them because they were being chased by a throng of armed men. And they were heading right for the old runway.

The tanks arrived just twenty seconds later. Cardillo's tank pulled right up to the C-17 and he yelled up to Bing, "There are about five hundred of them!"

"Who the hell are they?" Bing yelled back.

"PKDs!" Cardillo screamed back to him. "They broke out of the mountain and now they're heading this way!"

Bing immediately turned his goggles back down the valley and now he could clearly see what Cardillo was talking about. At least five hundred armed men were coming toward him. Some were running, some walking, some just stumbling along. Many looked like they were in shock, but many were also carrying weapons, like AK-47s.

Bing couldn't believe it. What was going on here? While many of these people looked dazed, they sure didn't look like they were coming his way to surrender. Then it hit him. He knew the tunnel where the two tanks had been sent to guard was the PKD's escape tunnel. Were these people escaping the chaos inside the fortress? If so, then what would happen when they reached the runway?

"What are we going to do?" Bing yelled back to Cardillo.

The Marine captain just shook his head, looking back at the approaching mob. They were now just a quarter mile away.

"We're just about out of ammo," he yelled back to Bing. "And I don't think we'll hold them off for too long with our sidearms!"

Bing couldn't disagree.

"We're going to warn the others," Cardillo yelled to him, and then he was gone.

Bing couldn't believe this was happening. What should he do? Abandon the airplane? Go hide somewhere? What about the others here at the runway? These people would tear them all limb from limb.

And they'd be here in about two minutes.

Even if they all managed to hide, at the very least the horde would destroy the three C-17 planes and no matter what happened inside the mountain, the 201st would be stranded here—if any of them lived.

What the hell was he going to do?

Then it hit him. Bing quickly turned around in his seat, and jump-started the plane's four big engines.

Then he began to steer it toward the runway.

MOON was inside his module, which was still sitting on the runway, eyes glued to the video screen, trying like mad to get the fly-cam back online.

But it was no use. The "bug" had been squashed just as he was about to get a good look at the people behind the white door at the bottom of the PKD fortress. That had happened about five minutes ago. What had happened inside the mountain since?

This was the question Moon was pondering when he saw the tank pull up outside his module. One of the Marine crewmen started screaming for Moon to "get his ass out here, ASAP!"

Moon was so startled he jumped out of the module. Cardillo was in the turret of the tank and all he had to do was point to the field next to the airstrip. That's when Moon saw the hundreds of PKD fighters moving en masse up the field, heading for the old snow-covered runway.

Right away, he knew what had happened.

"The escape tunnel?" he yelled back to Cardillo.

"They blew a big hole in it and they came pouring out like high tide," the Marine officer yelled back.

"How are we going to get out of this?" Moon asked Cardillo as the gravity of the situation was dawning on him.

"I don't know," Cardillo admitted. "We killed a shitload of them back at the tunnel's entrance, but we had no idea so many of them would be coming out. We just about ran out of ammunition mowing them down. And now here they are."

Moon had no idea what to do. It wasn't like the horde of armed men was going to just pass through. The few Americans here with the airplanes were trapped, with few weapons, hardly any ammunition, and absolutely no place to run. There was no way anyone could have foreseen this. But again, in a way, this was Moon's fault: His psy-ops plan had worked too well and in the end all the Pashtoon warriors wanted was to get out of the haunted mountain.

As this, too, was sinking in, and the vanguard of the terrorists were only now just a couple football fields away, Moon and Cardillo smelled something unusual in the air.

Jet exhaust . . .

They looked left and saw that Ghost Plane 1 was moving. Its engines could not be heard and it was still a bit hard to see, even though the sunrise was just minutes away. But it was definitely taxiing onto the runway, turning itself around.

"Is that Bing?" Moon asked. "What's he doing?"

One of the Marines inside Cardillo's tank yelled out: "He's taking off! He's saving his own ass!"

That appeared to be the case. As Moon and Cardillo watched, the big plane rumbled its way down the center of the runway—from all appearances it looked like it was preparing to leave.

But then it turned sharply and went off the runway again, rolling back to where it had been before. The only difference was, it was now facing the other way. Its left-hand side was now parallel to the approaching army of PKD fighters.

Moon started to say something, but the words never did get out of his mouth. The flash that came an instant before he spoke blinded them all. It was like the most intense lightning bolt imaginable—times a hundred. It lit up everything and everyone—the snow, the surrounding mountains, the tanks, the Americans, and the PKD fighters—catching them all in a kind of freeze-frame.

The noise was just as frightening. Not an explosion really—more like a gigantic wave crashing down on one's head, over and over again, never ending. Moon found himself blocking his ears as he was trying his best to keep his eyes shut and turned away. Cardillo was doing the same thing. It was like the sun itself had exploded.

The noise lasted for about ten seconds. Then it just as suddenly stopped. Moon opened his eyes and the bright light was gone, too. He turned back to the field and saw only streams of smoke and steam rising from the left side of Ghost Plane 1.

On the field in front of it—and for quite a distance down the valley—there were bodies and parts of bodies. The field of snow was now covered in blood. The PKD fighters had been literally vaporized by the combined fusillade of the sixteen massive weapons on the gunship, once again all firing at once. The same force that had sheared off the top of a mountain had just been leveled at the mob of terrorist fighters. Those Americans who'd been inside Ghost Planes 2 and 3 now crept out to see what had happened. It was shocking, bloody, and gross. But it was also redemption.

Through his quick thinking, Lieutenant Bing had saved them all.

PART THREE

CHAPTER 20

THE long night was over and a heavy snow had fallen, covering the bodies of the PKD fighters shot down in the field near the old runway.

Bora Kurd was still burning. The 201st were all out by now, having retrieved all the videos and DVDs from the fortress's TV studio, as well as the bodies of the hostages and their own dead. Eight paratroopers had been killed in the assault; several more had been wounded but none severely. Nearly a thousand PKD fighters were dead, but as far as anyone could tell, the Mountain Sheik was not among them.

It was time for the 201st to go. The crews were loading the last of their remaining equipment into the airplanes. The recovered bodies of their comrades were amongst the cargo, wrapped tightly in plastic sheeting that would serve as body bags. Also stored on board were a dozen or so satellite phones they'd found in the Mountain Sheik's empty quarters.

At the moment, Moon couldn't wait to get out of this place. The plan was to try to make it to Diego Garcia, the U.S. base in the middle of the Indian Ocean and face the consequences from there. They'd failed in rescuing the USAID hostages, but they'd been very successful in eliminating a major terrorist force in the area. Whether that would be taken under consideration when the unit was put under lock and key remained to be seen.

Moon's module had been put on the gunship, his tiny chopper squeezed into Ghost 2. He checked his watch now. It was almost 0800 hours. With any luck, they would be airborne and on the way out within fifteen minutes, before anyone who was anyone realized a major battle had been fought here.

The 82nd guys were tightening the last of their gear and stowing away their extra stuff. He could see Gunn and Amanda doing last-minute walk-arounds of their aircraft.

Pulver passed by, gave him an enthusiastic thumbs-up, and handed him the remains of the fly-cam he'd somehow recovered from the mysterious white room. Of them all, it was obvious Pulver had enjoyed himself the most during this adventure. He was reckless and almost impossible to manage, but he'd also followed orders, did what had to be done, and proved incredibly brave, especially when dropping the paratroopers on top of Bora Kurd, all while never losing his dopey bravado. Moon had never seen anyone fly a plane like him.

Still holding what was left of the fly-cam, Moon was about to walk back to the gunship when he became aware of a commotion over his right shoulder. He turned to see that someone had climbed to the top of the shallow, snowy ridge next to the airstrip.

Moon recognized this person right away. It was the kid who had delivered the pails of milk to the terrorists earlier that day, the reason Moon had been able to get the fly-cam into the mountain fortress in the first place.

The kid and his fellow villagers had watched the strike force takeoff on their final assault of the mountain and had waved makeshift U.S. flags as they cheered them on.

We did them a favor, too, Moon thought.

The kid was waving again. He wanted to say something to them. Pulver was still nearby. The pilot took out a small U.S. flag he always carried with him and motioned to the kid to come over.

"We can leave him a real one," Pulver said to Moon. "Maybe that will stick with him after we're gone."

The kid walked toward the airplanes cautiously. It was

apparent he'd never seen anything quite so grand as the three C-17s.

Pulver met him halfway across the snowy runway. He said to him, "Next time, we'll give you a ride, I promise."

Everyone in the strike force was watching now. It was like they were all thinking the same thing: "If only this kid can grow up not to hate us."

Pulver held out his hand to give the kid the flag. The kid looked at the flag, and then opened his coat, as if he had a present to give Pulver.

But underneath he was wearing twenty sticks of TNT.

He said, "I'm sorry . . ." then pulled a cord.

The bomb blew up—killing both the boy and Pulver instantly.

THE nearby village was called Quodsom.

Less than 100 people lived there in a scattering of stone houses surrounding a dilapidated animal corral.

The villagers were neither Sunni nor Shiite; they were a small sect of Cheshtiya, Muslims known for their passive nature. They and their ancestors had been scratching out a living here for more than a thousand years, and in that time, they'd found themselves in the middle of many conflicts, both religious and not.

Now they were in the middle again.

They'd been terrorized by the PKD fighters living in the fortress ever since they'd arrived in Bora Kurd. The fighters had stolen their milk every day, precious nutrition needed by the youngest people in the village but denied them by the PKD gunmen. The terrorists had also stolen their food on a regular basis, and had raped the village's young girls on several occasions.

Now, the villagers were paralyzed with fear as they saw a different army of gunmen vaulting over the snowy ridges which separated the village from Bora Kurd's mountain valley.

These people were dressed in smart uniforms, not rags, and wore helmets, not towels on their heads. These were Americans, but different enough to look like people from the stars. And they were furious, and the people of the village knew why.

The Americans began kicking in every door, and pulling out anyone they found inside. The man who was the de facto leader of the village tried to stop them, but he knew it was hopeless. They had waved these same men on to victory earlier in the day. Now he was convinced they were going to kill everyone in the village, him included, and for the first time in a thousand years only the dead would occupy the land here.

Gunn and Amanda had been the last ones over the ridge and down the path to the small village.

They were astonished how fast the Marines had reacted after the suicide bomb killed Pulver. Even before the smoke had cleared, the Marines had grabbed their weapons and were running at breakneck speed toward the village to exact their revenge. The trouble was the 82nd troopers were right behind them, as were the rest of the aircrews.

This left only Gunn and Amanda to actually check Pulver's body—what was left of it. Gunn retrieved a ring the pilot wore on his right hand, and that was it. The powerful bomb had vaporized the young boy. There was a stain of blood on the snowy ground where he had last stood.

Gunn was in a state of shock; Amanda was, too. It didn't seem real. One moment, Pulver was there, joking as usual, and bragging about his exploits inside the mountain during the battle—and then, he was simply gone.

Now they were racing down the path to the village not sure what was about to happen, not sure what *should* happen. In shock—and looking for answers.

The soldiers and Marines had roused everyone by the time Gunn and Amanda arrived. They were separating the men from the women and children, but at that moment it didn't seem to mean much. The air was thick with retribution and after what they'd just gone through inside the mountain, especially seeing the decapitated remains of the American hostages, killing another 100 or so Muslims wouldn't be a problem for the 201st. Some still had blood on their uniforms from the battle that had ended not an hour before.

Moon was in the middle of it, shoving the villagers away from him, even though they were begging him to listen. He was making all the males crouch down and put their hands on their heads. The 82nd troopers laid their rifle barrels on the back of the necks of several men, much to the wailing of the nearby women. The Marines, meanwhile, ransacked the small stone houses.

Finally, a very elderly man reached up and grabbed Amanda's arm.

He knew only one word in English, "Blood . . ."

He was pointing to the back of the last stone hut in the village.

"Blood . . . blood . . ."

At that moment, it seemed that within the next instant the villagers would be massacred.

That's when Amanda just yelled, "Stop!"

Everyone froze.

She ran around the back of the building; Gunn was right behind her.

What they found startled them. There was a wounded man lying there, trying to cover himself with snow. But the snow was turning red because he was bleeding so much.

Gunn called for Moon, at the same time yelling to the Marines to hold their fire.

They kicked the snow away from the man to find he was wearing a black ski mask and heavy robes. Gunn reached down and pulled the ski mask away to find a bald man with a misshapen head and huge mustache.

He did not look like a typical Islamic terrorist.

Moon studied him up and down and then realized why he looked familiar.

"This is the guy we saw talking to the Sheik on the flycam," he said. "He was also in the room with the white door with those Bien Cache Guerriers just a little while ago."

There was an empty weapons bag nearby and now things were beginning to make more sense. The Bien Cache Guerriers had obviously escaped the mountain in the confusion and had come through here, the nearest village to the fortress. They'd wired up the young boy with explosives and sent him toward the U.S. aircraft, and probably on threat of killing his family, hoping to slow down any pursuit. Then they left behind this wounded man.

"But where are they now?" Gunn wondered. "And what are they up to?"

Moon stood the wounded terrorist up and dragged him into the nearest stone hut.

"Give me five minutes," he said ominously. "I'll find out . . ."

THE screaming actually lasted for more than ten minutes.

Those outside heard the wounded man begging for mercy in French and English. Most disturbing, Moon could be clearly heard saying, in both languages, that mercy was not on the agenda, that the only choice he was giving the man in exchange for cooperation was the least painful way to die.

It seemed to go on forever as the frightened villagers remained under the guns of the 82nd and the Marines.

Finally, there came a single shot from inside the hut—and it was over. Moon walked out, wiping some grease from his pistol.

He looked at Vogel and said: "Please give these people all of our extra MREs, and any blankets we can spare. We're going to need a couple favors from them."

Then he turned to Gunn and Amanda and said, "We've got a big problem on our hands."

THEY walked a short distance away from the village, joined by Vogel and Captain Cardillo.

Once they were out of earshot, Moon lowered his voice and said, "Here's the situation: This guy was from Syria, a hired hand. He's the guy who set up all the weapons for the PKD. He also helped the Bien Cache Guerriers escape from the mountain. He got wounded so they left him behind; this after they wired the kid.

"These Bien Cache Guerriers are all Caucasian and they have a small nuclear bomb. I saw its container before one of them crushed the fly-cam. It's one of the old Soviet Union suitcase bombs that have been bouncing around for decades. The PKD got it directly from bin Laden—and it was by his orders that they recruited the Bien Cache Guerriers to carry it into America. That's what this whole thing was about. And that's what they're on their way to do right now."

The other officers were shocked. "Jesuzz—a nuke?" Cardillo asked. "Are you sure?"

Moon pulled something from his pocket; it was a small booklet that looked like it had been printed in the 1950s. It was written in Cyrillic Russian, but the symbol at the top of the page told them everything they needed to know. It was a large yellow triangle with a black trefoil inside it. The international symbol for a hazardous radioactive device.

"He had this on him," Moon said of the recently departed terrorist. "This was his proof that what he was telling me was the truth. He said the Bien Cache Guerriers were just waiting here in the mountain, biding their time, until the Fourth of July or something. Then we came along. And we forced them to accelerate their timetable."

The other officers let out another collective gasp.

"Again, I saw these guys in that white room," Moon continued. "They're Germans, I'm guessing, but believe me, they can all pass for Americans, no problem. Upscale, educated, white, Yuppie scum Americans. They plan to bring this bomb into the U.S. and detonate it somewhere in the country next week. And no one will be able to stop them because they'll fit in so well. Plus there's a chance they're getting help from the inside."

"God damn," Vogel breathed. "We've got to tell somebody about this. It's a catastrophe in the making."

But Moon just shook his head. "That's just it: Who the hell will listen to us?" he said. "We're almost as illegal as these guys are."

Amanda nodded in grim agreement. "He's right," she said. "By the time they're through interrogating us, these guys will be walking into Macy's with their 'package.'"

"It's up to us," Moon told them. "We're the only ones who can go after them."

Vogel was puzzled. "Go after them? But how? How the hell do we know where they are, or where they're going exactly? They've got a good head start—and after what we've done here, I don't think it's like we can go flying around looking for them—at least not in the daytime."

"That's just it," Moon said, wiping the rest of the grime from his sidearm. "I know where they're going. I know what their plans are. And I know who was behind all this—because that guy just told me before he went on to meet Allah and the seventy-two whores.

"Now, the way I see it, there are three things we have to do before we end this book. Three things to make sure this sort of crap never happens again—and to make sure the people who really killed Newman's daughter, and Pulver, and those other people don't get away with it. The real question is, of the people we have left, how many do you think will be interested in a sequel?"

Vogel looked at Cardillo who just looked at Gunn and Amanda.

"I'd say, only all of them," Vogel finally replied.

THEY freed the Cheshtiya and asked them to bury their dead. In exchange for MRES and blankets, they agreed with the villagers that the burial site was temporary and would be kept a secret. At some point they told them, more Americans would come here, with more blankets and food, and claim their departed colleagues.

The villagers vowed to see the agreement through.

Then the 201st returned to their airplanes, knowing they had to stay hidden for another day. To their great luck, another storm blew in, hiding them and finally dousing the flames atop Bora Kurd. This gave them time to work out a plan—a precise one this time.

They had three objectives, each one different, each one dangerous. If the flight from Nevada to Pakistan and what transpired here would be considered hazardous, then what they were about to do would be considered suicidal. But no one wanted to back out, no one didn't want to see it through. The prevailing attitude was the U.S. had to stand up to the terrorists no matter how, no matter when—and not by spending billions of dollars that claimed to protect everything, but didn't really protect anything at all.

Just as Newman couldn't have lived with himself if he hadn't sent the 201st to try to rescue his daughter, now, collectively, the 201st couldn't go on if they didn't personally go after the people who planned to light off a nuclear device inside the U.S. If past experience were any indication, to turn it over to someone else now—like Homeland Security or the FBI—would mean dropping the ball, even if they *could* get anyone to listen to them.

No, the team was in agreement. Even though they were exhausted, depleted, wounded, and bloodied, they had to take care of this themselves. For the murdered hostages. For Pulver. For their country.

They waited on the old airstrip for the entire day, always looking to see if anyone from the Pakistani government would brave the snowstorm to come up and look at what became of Bora Kurd. But no one did. Even the Cheshtiya stayed in their homes. The Kunga Mountain range was so off the beaten track, it might take until the snow melted before any one from Islamabad dared to come up and take a look.

This worked to the 201st's advantage.

Between all the planning, Moon had spent a lot of time inside his blue module. He was looking ahead, trying to conjure up ways he could help the 201st for what they had to do. By nightfall, he'd come up with three devices that would have made any real mad scientist proud.

One was called "Program 99," another "HAE-1" as in High Altitude Eavesdrop, and the third simply "NOAB."

As it turned out, all three would come in handy.

FINALLY, night fell.

By this time, each plane's crew knew what they had to do. They would be going in three different directions and they all knew the chances of them seeing one another again were extremely remote. The mood was sober then, but not grim. They were Americans, and their country was in danger and they were the only ones with any hope of saving it. Plus, they'd lost unit members, and that was like losing someone in the family.

This is what they *had* to do. Simple as that.

Once again, Gunn was doing a preflight check of his aircraft. It was dark and the snow was blowing, but these things seemed almost normal to him now. They were just a few minutes from takeoff and what the night held for them, he had no idea. Moon's information and intelligence had been right on the money in the past. They could only hope it stayed that way.

As he was checking his aircraft, he kept an eye out for Amanda, hoping she'd be checking hers. They'd sat near each other during the long day of planning sessions, but had not exchanged any words, or even any random glances. Still, Gunn was amazed that while everyone else in the unit, having been to hell and back, looked as gritty as GIs who'd just fought a days-long battle, she looked as beautiful as the moment they'd left Nevada. It killed him to think he'd probably never see her again.

He was checking his wheel wells when he heard someone come up in back of him. He was sure it was Lieutenant Bing—he'd be assigned to fly Pulver's plane and Gunn had told him to touch base before he left. Gunn wanted to make sure the young pilot was okay after all the blood he'd spilled, for good reason, the day before.

So it was with great surprise when Gunn turned around to find it was not Bada, but Amanda.

His face must have looked shocked, because she smiled and said: "Sorry for sneaking up on you."

"Anytime," was the only word that fell out of his mouth.

She hesitated a moment and then said: "I just wanted to wish you good luck, happy flying. You know, all that . . ."

"Same to you," he replied, getting nervous. He was more jittery talking to her than thinking about what lay ahead.

She looked down at the snowy ground for a moment. "It's hard to believe he's gone," she said. "I thought I heard his voice a few times today."

Gunn knew who she was talking about. And he, too, swore he'd heard Pulver today, his distinctive twang, yapping somewhere in the background.

"I'm not a great believer in these things," Gunn finally said, "but I think he's really still here with us. He'll be watching us. It's hard to get rid of a guy like that so easily."

She laughed at that, but there were also tears in her eyes.

Gunn knew if there was ever a time for him to embrace

her, to kiss her, this was it. But he just couldn't. She was just too damn beautiful.

"Can I give you something?" she asked him suddenly. "Something I've been carrying around, but I'd like you to have it now. You know. Just in case? It would make me feel better . . ."

Gunn was very surprised to hear her say this. "Sure," he finally managed to reply. "Anything . . ."

She reached into her pocket, took something out, and pressed it in his hand. Then she reached up and touched his cheek with her fingers.

Then she turned and walked back into the snow and was gone.

Gunn opened his hand to see what she had given him—and laughed.

It was her squirt gun.

CHAPTER 21

GHOST Plane 2 was the first aircraft to take off. Its wheels left the old broken-down runway at exactly 0400 hours.

Bing was behind the controls; his hands were shaking. He was nervous, and not just because he'd killed more people yesterday than the rest of the 201st combined. It was because he was sitting in the seat formerly occupied by Captain Pulver, not a comfortable place to be. It was as if Pulver's ghost was hovering over him, watching every move he made. Luckily Pulver's regular copilot, Lieutenant Jackson, was flying with him.

Once airborne, he turned the big plane to the west and climbed as fast as he could.

Again, their mission this day was actually split into three parts. Bing's had been given the code name First Base. As Gunn had told him just before he took off, his task was probably the most important of all.

What Moon had learned about the Bien Cache Guerriers was a fable of twenty-first-century terrorism and how money could be made from killing and maiming innocent people. Not only were the Caucasian terrorists planning to pull off a spectacular attack in the U.S., they planned to extensively videotape this attack, before, during, and after—and then sell the footage to an Arab pro-al-Qaeda TV station, which would then have the exclusive airing rights, and thus would garner hundreds of millions of viewers around the world. It would prove to be a bonanza of money, prestige, and ratings. No surprise, this was the same TV station that had made the deal with the PKD to air the decapitation executions of the hapless USAID workers. The TV station was called Al-Zareesh. Its studio was located in the filthy rich emirate of Dubai.

It came down to simple math really. If the TV studio was suddenly out of the equation, it might not prevent the Bien Cache Guerriers from carrying out their acts, but it would prevent them from cashing in on them, as well as relieving U.S. families of knowing their loved ones being shot, mutilated, and blown apart wouldn't be shown on TV, at least not by Al-Zareesh.

So this was Bing's mission: to eliminate the TV studio. His means to do this was sitting in the back of the big C-17, being watched over by the members of the 82nd Airborne. It was one of Lieutenant Moon's concoctions: a barrel full of TNT taken from the PKD's storage bunker inside Bora Kurd. Nearly one hundred sticks in all fitted with a crude impact timer, it was doused with jet fuel for good measure. Moon had jokingly nicknamed it the NOAB. As in "The Nephew of All Bombs."

Finding their target would not be difficult. It was located right on the Persian Gulf coast, on a piece of very expensive waterfront property, very close to downtown Dubai. It boasted a 200-foot antenna, which was dressed up like an ancient lighthouse and had a spinning strobe light on top. With the C-17's forward-looking infrared imaging capability, its satellite ground tracking radar link, and the crew's plain old 20/20 combined eyesight, spotting their target would not be a problem.

Getting there might be though . . .

BING had to fly the big plane several hundred miles, keeping as hidden and as quiet as possible. Flying over Pakistan in the dark with the Star Skin on would prove to be a breeze. The complication would be flying across a wide swath of the Persian Gulf, which was one of the most heavily traveled, and heavily patrolled waterways in the world.

He knew what he had to do. Once he was out over the water, he brought the big plane down to nearly wave-top level and hit the throttles. At top speed, it would take them just about an hour to reach their target.

Everything went well for the first part of the flight. They were flying low, the Star Skin was working on both sides, top and bottom, and their engines were barely purring. The waters below them, in the early morning darkness, were crowded with vessels from fishing *dhows* to supertankers, but there was no indication that anyone had spotted them.

It was going so smoothly that just as Bing was thinking that maybe they were going to make it no muss, no fuss, his air threat warning computer exploded to life.

Lieutenant Jackson pushed the array of activation buttons as an alarm went off throughout the C-17. Air-to-air missile radars seemed to be honing in on the big aircraft. Translation: two jet fighters might be pursuing them.

U.S. Navy fighters . . .

The radarscope told the tale. An extension of their radar sweep showed a U.S. aircraft carrier about thirty-eight miles north of their position. The vessel was heading toward the upper Persian Gulf, but it was just Bing's luck that he'd skirted the edge of the carrier's forty-mile exclusion zone. Navy procedures dictated that anything flying within this zone was technically considered a threat to the carrier itself.

Just how the fighters had seen the stealth plane, Bing didn't know. Maybe it had been a visual sighting. Maybe not. He put the C-17 down even farther and then got a slice of luck when just moments after the hot air-to-airs were detected, the missiles went cold. What happened? Maybe the fighters had been testing their weapons or perhaps the Navy jets had been chasing someone else. But it was clear now, they were not aware the C-17 was in the area.

That is, until Bing flew right over a Navy destroyer.

They were so low that it was impossible for them not to be

seen. Bing had no idea what they looked like as they nearly shaved the mast off the destroyer, but it was enough to set off every bell and whistle on the warship.

Suddenly the pair of fighters was turning back and heading in their direction again.

"Sheeeet," Bing said. "This is not good . . ."

Now came a point where Bing started flying the big plane in a way he wasn't so sure it should be flown.

He had to go on the assumption that while they could see the fighters on their masked radar screen, the fighters could not see them, at least not yet.

So first he climbed, nearly straight up, causing a lot of yelps and groans from the paratroopers in back. They reached 10,000 feet—and saw the two fighters pass right under them, at around 4,000 feet. Bing held this altitude until he saw the fighters start to climb—that's when he put the C-17 into a screaming, banking dive. Again, a chorus of misery sounded from the back, but all Bing could do was yell back to them, "Hang on!"

Bing used all his strength to pull the big plane out of this forced descent, somehow getting it to level off at 500 feet. In the brightening sky, they could see the navigation lights of the two fighters, now flying up around ten angels.

Bing then got proactive and started zigzagging. First he went right, then left, then right again. He was carving huge S-patterns just a hundred feet above the warm waters of the Gulf. More fishing boats were in evidence now, but the C-17 was moving so fast that Bing imagined that they appeared as nothing more than a blur to anyone below.

After ten minutes of this, they saw the two fighters finally fall off the radarscope. Baffled or just low on fuel, their pilots had turned in the other direction and eventually disappeared.

Bing reached up to flick a bit of sweat from his forehead and discovered an ocean of perspiration was raining down on his brow. He looked over at Jackson, who was just as soaked. But then the copilot pointed out the front cockpit window.

Bing looked in that direction and saw, in the early-morning sunlight, the hazy shoreline of Dubai coming quickly into view.

Dubai

The filming company had arrived on el-Qeezi Boulevard thirty minutes before dawn. They were a Saudi outfit specializing in TV commercials for high-priced clients.

The client today was, oddly enough, a TV station: Al-Zareesh, the upstart media giant that was fast becoming famous as the CNN of the Muslim world.

Al-Zareesh was starting its own worldwide media blitz hoping to attract more Muslim viewers in Southeast Asia, Africa, and even South America. They were expert at getting scoops craved by Muslim viewers, like unedited bomb damage footage from Iraq, the Americans' accidental bombing of civilians in Afghanistan, and hostages being executed in Pakistan. It was a mystery to most just how Al-Zareesh was able to get this footage first and exclusively, but it was how they'd made their mark in the Persian Gulf, and now they were taking their message to other parts of the world.

That's why the Saudi company was here today. To get establishing shots of Al-Zareesh's vast and grand headquarters, both on the outside and within. They would be included in an elaborate five-minute commercial already booked on dozens of channels throughout the Muslin world.

As the exterior shots would come first, the director wanted to catch the early-morning light to give the commercial an almost religious glow. To this end, the film crew had set up in a parking lot about 500 feet from the station's enormous antenna tower. The director's plan was to get the first rays of the sun bouncing off the station's faux lighthouse—it would be the opening shot of the commercial, so it was important that he get it just right.

He had his ten-man crew set up all their equipment, take light readings, and do focus tests. Then they sat back to wait.

The sun began peeking over the water just a few minutes later. The director called his crew to attention. A few offset lights were turned on. The camera was refocused again. The camera's lens gate was checked. Everything was ready to go.

Then suddenly, the ground beneath their feet started shaking. Then it seemed like the air itself began vibrating. Then a great rush of wind hit them like a mini-hurricane.

The camera was rolling and it caught in full color what happened next.

A huge aircraft appeared right out of the sun. It seemed to be glowing just like the morning light, as if it were made of the same thing. It came upon them so quickly there was no noise. It seemed like something from a dream. It was flying so low they could see it was disturbing the water underneath it.

The plane turned sharply about a quarter mile offshore. Only then could the film crew see its size. It was as big as an airliner, but its fuselage seemed to be changing colors and shape as they watched.

It kept turning very sharply, until it flew right over the film crew. As it raced by, they could see the plane's rear cargo ramp was open. They could even see people inside the rear of the airplane. As they watched, these people pushed a barrel-sized object out of the back of the aircraft.

This object landed directly on top of Al-Zareesh HQ's roof, hitting with a loud *thump!*

The film crew stood transfixed, wondering what had happened.

Then the explosion came . . .

First, it was just a bright white light. Then the noise—tremendous and intense. Then the flames erupted and a whirlpool of smoke and debris enveloped them—all this happened in less than a second.

The shock wave hit the film crew a moment later. It knocked them all backward twenty feet or more. Luckily for the crew members, they landed in the shallow water of the beach nearby, causing cuts and some broken bones, but nothing serious.

They were all in shock, though. When the smoke and flames cleared and the ground stopped shaking, they were finally able to see again.

It was only then that they realized the Al-Zareesh TV studio, including the 200-foot transmission tower, was simply gone.

Those crew members that could, got to their feet, stunned and wet. As they dragged themselves to the shore, someone looked up and saw the mysterious plane was returning, heading back in their direction. Now a great panic set in as the film crew was sure the people flying the airplane were coming back to bomb them as well.

But before they could even react, the plane was over them again. It did not drop a bomb this time, though. Instead, it reduced its speed even further, so much so the film crew could clearly see the people standing in the open cargo bay again.

This time, these people were holding up two things they obviously wanted the film crew to see.

One was a large American flag.

The other was a crude, handwritten sign that read *Don't Fuck with the USA.*

Iran

Moon was crazy—Gunn knew that for sure now.

The diminutive intelligence agent was standing at the rear cargo door of Gunn's AC-17, a borrowed parachute on his back, and little more than a laser designator and a sat-phone in hand, waiting to jump into a gigantic storm cloud.

Gunn was certain Moon would be killed, either by the jet blast or by tumbling directly into a thunder and lightning storm. But even if he made it, he would be parachuting into *very* hostile territory as what lay below them at the moment was the *very* hostile country of Iran.

Gunn wasn't sure how Moon had talked him into this. The Syrian guy Moon had interrogated back in Pakistan had told him the plan was for the Bien Cache Guerriers and their suit-case bomb to pass through Iran on their way to the United States. This didn't sound right to Gunn at first. Al-Qaeda was a Sunni terrorist organization, and Iran was a largely Shiite state. The two separate sects of Islam detested one another and, to prove it, killed each other on a regular basis. However, Moon said the bald, misshapen Syrian had told him, "They have just one thing in common: They hate the U.S. more than they hate each other."

This was why the Iranians were giving aid and comfort to the Bien Cache Guerriers.

The Syrian had further told Moon the Bien Cache Guerriers would be in Tehran for one day before continuing their long-winding, five-day journey to the U.S. The trouble was the Syrian had never been told exactly where the secret warriors would be housed, only that if past history were any indication, it would be in one of Tehran's very few luxury hotels.

Which had brought Gunn and the others to this point, flying over Iran, in the dark. And as if that wasn't frightening enough, they'd been following a huge thunderstorm since leaving Pakistan around four in the morning. Their objective, code-named Second Base, was to try to get Moon on the ground in the Persian capital, so he could find out where Bien Cache Guerriers were being stashed. Or die trying.

That the Ghost plane's deception systems were working well so far was a huge relief to Gunn and his crew. However, if Iranian Air Force fighters suddenly appeared, the Ghost plane would probably be a dead duck. But it was paramount that these "white terrorists" and their abettors be stopped as quickly as possible. Gunn and everyone on board Ghost Plane 1 agreed on that, thus their ultra-risky mission.

They'd crossed the border into Iran around its desolate southeast corner, where they knew Iranian military stations were at a minimum. Gunn had maintained a constant 500-foot altitude, staying within the fast-moving storm, riding it northwest as it swept off the Gulf and headed directly for Tehran. It had been a bumpy ride for those concerned, but again, problem-free so far.

But now that they were approaching Tehran itself, the plan suddenly seemed absolutely nuts. Flying right over the Persian capital? In a storm? Yet Moon was demanding to go—and there was nothing Gunn could say to him to change his mind.

"Here!" Moon started yelling now. "I'm going—keep your phone line free and your eyes open!"

With that, the intelligence agent went out the door.

Gunn banked the plane slightly to the right hoping to redirect the jet blast and also hoping to spot Moon's open chute. But all he saw was even thicker storm clouds. He continued turning the big airplane, but still detected no sign of Moon. Finally he just laid back on the throttles. All they had to do now was keep circling until they heard from Moon or were shot down.

Whichever came first.

IT was raining so hard when Moon hit the ground, he could barely see his hand in front of him. This was good for him, though. Uncomfortable, but good.

It was still an hour before dawn and Tehran was about thirty minutes away from waking up. He'd come to earth on the southern outskirts of the city, near the slums of Qah, an urban sprawl so dilapidated and chaotic it gave him perfect cover to move into Tehran proper itself.

The slum's streets were full of litter and flooding from the heavy rain. Moon moved along, unimpeded, passing by the occasional military checkpoint with no problems; he looked like another drugged-out, hungover slum-dweller, stumbling home after a night of imbibing. No one paid any attention to him.

He eventually found Revolutionary Boulevard, a main thoroughfare in downtown Tehran. It was just a block over from Embassy Row, the place were those few countries still friendly with Iran kept their diplomatic quarters.

This location was convenient for quick access by foreigners and home diplomats alike. From what Moon knew about the Iranians, he guessed the Bien Cache Guerriers were sleeping somewhere close by.

He bought a cup of tea from a street vendor who was just setting up his huge umbrella for the day. Moon used a U.S. five-dollar bill and tipped the man two dollars, at the same time trying to ask him the Farsi equivalent of "Where do the strangers stay?" But the man seemed to be partially deaf and mute and he did not understand. So Moon continued down Revolutionary Boulevard, hoping the rain would keep up and continue to hide him.

He reached the corner of Revolutionary and Ghazi Street and that's when he caught a break. He spotted six blonde women under one umbrella, standing on the curb, looking for a taxi.

Prostitutes . . .

Moon hurried up to them, two hundred-dollar bills crumpled in his hand. The women ignored him at first. But when he flashed the first hundred and asked if any of them spoke German, this got their attention.

One replied: "Not German, Russian . . ."

Moon asked her in Russian: "Where are they?"

"Who?"

"The mullahs' special guests," he replied. "That is what you are doing here this early morning, right?"

"Why does a wet little man have so much money?" the woman asked him.

Moon displayed the second hundred-dollar bill. "Why do you ask and not answer questions?"

The woman pointed to the hotel over her shoulder. "German pigs," was all she said.

Moon gave her the $200 just as a taxi pulled up. He put his finger to his lips as a way of asking for their silence. The woman who'd spoke said to him, "Our pleasure. We owe them no favors."

Then the women climbed into the cab and roared away.

Moon hurried to the rear of the hotel, which was named the Bazadi Grand Hotel. He noted that a police car was conspicuously parked out front. The hotel looked no more special than any ten-story Ramada found in the United States. But for Tehran that equaled exclusive lodging.

He checked the Dumpsters in the rear of the place, scattering a pack of rats looking for an early-morning meal. It started to rain even harder; the clouds were so thick, it was almost like the middle of night and not just a few minutes before dawn. All these atmospherics were good for Moon, though.

There was little refuse in the Dumpster, a clue that not many people were staying in the hotel. What trash there was consisted mostly of cognac bottles and cigarette butts. Moon scooped up a handful of the expended cigarettes. They were Heilskriegs—a German brand. More good news.

A delivery truck was making its way down the alley. It was carrying yogurt, tea, and paper products. Moon was hoping that it wouldn't stop at the backdoor delivery entrance of the hotel, and it didn't. This told him what he wanted to know: The Bien Cache Guerriers were inside this place. The police car out front was their security, the hookers and booze were their comfort, and just to make sure they weren't further detected, most of the staff and all other guests had left the hotel.

In other words, Moon had his target.

Or so he hoped . . .

He started dialing his sat-phone.

THE sky was still dark and stormy when the huge airplane arrived over Revolutionary Boulevard. To those few who saw it—sidewalk vendors and prostitutes hurrying home before the religious police took to the morning streets—it seemed to be moving impossibly slow for such a large airplane. It also seemed to be searching for something while cutting through the rain and fog. The Tehran airport was nearby and again witnesses thought perhaps the plane was lost and looking for the airport—as unlikely as that was in this day and age. It *was* about the size of a large airliner, though. Yet, it wasn't making any noise, and it seemed to be able to reflect the color of the rain clouds at will. And it kept circling and circling.

Those witnesses on Revolutionary Boulevard itself then saw a bright red beam of light cut through the rain and mist. It crossed the street from an alley opposite the Bazadi Grand Hotel and seemed to be moving all over the western face of the building.

It might have seemed like a coincidence at the time, but the huge circling airplane came back into view shortly after the red beam was spotted.

Then, suddenly, everything exploded.

It came as sixteen long streams of fire and light burst out of the sky and crashed into the hotel. Then the noise arrived—it was ear-splitting, deafening. Ungodly. It was so loud, it broke windows all along Revolutionary Boulevard. Then came a huge explosion of fire and smoke, the intensity so extreme it cracked the asphalt up and down the thoroughfare like an earthquake.

The airplane seemed frozen in the air; hovering like a large bird, spitting out all this destruction. The area around the Bazadi Grand erupted in flames; even the police car disappeared in a flash. It was impossible to say just how long the display lasted. Certainly no more than fifteen seconds. But when the streaks of fire coming from the airplane finally stopped, the Bazadi Grand Hotel was gone. Vanished.

Vaporized . . .

GUNN'S headphones suddenly exploded to life.

"We might have a visitor," his copilot was telling him. "Looks like an F-14 has just taken off and is turning this way."

The radar report was not a surprise. The AC-17 had been flying over the center of Tehran for about ten minutes, unimpeded up until now, apparently undetected. Cloaked or not, though, such activity could not go on very long without someone noticing it.

The fact that Tehran Airport was hampered by the bad weather and that there were a number of airliners circling the city waiting to land had also helped shield the Ghost plane from Iranian eyes. But now after laying waste to the hotel holding the Bien Cache Guerriers, they'd caused a commotion and finally the Iranians were waking up.

Iran was the only military left these days flying the venerable F-14 Tomcat—a sale of a number of the U.S.-built F-14s had been made to prerevolution Iran and, though chronically short of spare parts, the mullahs had somehow been able to keep the old warhorses flying.

No doubt this F-14 was being sent aloft to find the mystery aircraft reportedly flying low over the city amidst the rain and fog. To add to the confusion, though, Gunn's copilot had inserted an MP3 previously prepared by Moon into their communications set. It sent out a message over many of Tehran's radio frequencies mimicking a call to Tehran Airport that said an airliner had crashed into the center of the city and that the smoke and flames were tremendous. Judging by the barrage of radio traffic that followed this bogus transmission, Gunn was certain the deception worked at least to some degree.

But again, he knew that once detected, there was no way they could outrun a jet fighter. They needed their masking technology to work just one more time.

Their mission was almost over. All the Bien Cache Guerriers were most likely dead, victims of the AC-17's murderous fusillade, helped by Moon illuminating the target with his laser designator. And the authorities, or at least people at Tehran Airport, were under the assumption that a huge plane had crashed into the Bazadi Grand Hotel.

This meant Gunn and his crew had just one more thing to do before they could make their dash out of Iranian airspace.

They had to pick up Lieutenant Moon.

GUNN thought Revolutionary Boulevard was as good a place as any to attempt a landing.

It was a long stretch of asphalt, no overhead wires, no trees, and very few cars, parked or otherwise. While the road was not as flat as Gunn hoped, he couldn't worry about that now. It would be just a matter of time before the Iranians figured out that the Bazadi Grand Hotel had been blown to kingdom come and not the victim of an airplane crash. Then the hunt for the mystery plane would be on for real.

Yet this was the only way Moon would be able to be retrieved from the hostile capital—landing on its most famous street. So that's what they were going to do.

They did a tight circle around the boulevard. About halfway through it, Gunn's copilot saw the faint image of a man running down the roadway.

"There he is," the copilot said. "Right where he needs to be."

Gunn saw him, too, and yanked back on the throttles so hard it was like jamming on the brakes. Everything in the plane shuddered as their airspeed went down to barely 100 knots.

Gunn keyed his chin mic. "Open rear ramp . . ."

Two of the gun crew in back strapped themselves to long safety harnesses, then lowered the massive rear cargo door. A great swirl of smoke and exhaust invaded the plane's cargo hold, nearly asphyxiating the gun crew. They grabbed their emergency air masks and strapped them on. Then they signaled A-OK back up to the flight deck.

Gunn pulled back on the throttles even more. Moon was now about a half mile away. He watched his speed drain off to below 90 knots—very close to a stall.

At that moment, his copilot reported some chilling news. "Our visitor has spotted us and is heading our way."

This is just what Gunn did not want to hear: The Iranian F-14 was coming toward them.

Gunn pushed the big plane back up to 500 feet and flew right over Moon's position. Incredibly, he saw the intelligence agent gesturing madly from below. He was not waving *at* them as much as telling them to get away, fly away. Leave him here. Save yourselves.

Five words came into Gunn's head: "Not in a million years."

He looked over at his copilot and said, "Let's go around again and prepare for landing."

No sooner were the words out of his mouth than the radar started barking again. The Iranian Tomcat was just a mile away and getting closer.

The rain became worse; the clouds above them getting darker and thicker. But these alone would not mask them from an F-14 up close. They would need extraordinary help for that. To this end, Moon had left them a CD of computer programs that he said were other ways to use the Star Skin to disguise the aircraft. He'd labeled the CD "Program 99." Gunn asked the copilot to quickly go through it and look for a miracle.

Then he turned, lowered the landing gear, and started dropping again.

MOON was frantic.

Police cars were approaching, their sirens wailing, and what sounded like a jet fighter was getting close overhead. He knew now he was as good as dead. With the hotel engulfed in a massive blaze, it was just a matter of time before the police found out what had happened and started looking for people in the city who didn't belong there. He'd be caught and executed by the Iranians. Such was his fate . . .

But he didn't want to take down the crew of the AC-17 with him.

Yet, now he could see Gunn was going into an obvious landing profile, attempting to set down in the middle of Revolutionary Boulevard, basically a suicidal act. Moon was a spy—being caught and killed was always part of the job description.

The trouble was, Gunn hadn't read the book.

As he watched the AC-17 approaching, an F-14 suddenly burst out of the clouds. Moon's heart went into his throat. He dialed his sat-phone and just started screaming: "Program 99! Program 99!" But he had no idea whether Gunn and the Ghost plane crew could hear him or not.

The F-14 swooped down out of the black sky. It wasn't attacking the big cargo plane—not yet anyway. Instead it was suddenly riding parallel to it.

Moon saw the AC-17 level off, and for a few very weird moments the two aircraft rode side-by-side with each other, the F-14 pilot looking at the big plane off to his right.

Moon was transfixed. He was certain the game was up and the Tomcat would shoot down the big cargo plane at any moment; it was so obvious that this was an American military aircraft. Had the gunship's crew heard his desperate sat-phone call?

He had his answer just as the two planes flew right over his head, no more than 250-feet high. That's when he saw the emblems the Star Skin was displaying on the gunship's fuselage and wings.

Not the Iranian national insignia; the Persian pilot certainly would not have fallen for that. Instead, the image on the plane's fuselage and wings was the red star and straight lines of the Chinese Air Force.

Program 99 . . . Something that might have helped them during their dash across China, but put to better use here.

Seeing the Chinese markings startled the Tomcat pilot long enough for the AC-17 gun crew to open one of their panels and fire off a long burst from their twin miniguns.

The F-14 simply disappeared in a cloud of fire and dust.

Moon was astonished. He had to dodge some of the small pieces of wreckage that were blown back toward him. Then he saw the big AC-17 turn once more and start its landing approach yet again.

This time he was ready—if Gunn and his crew were so determined to save his life, then he was not going to argue with them.

The big plane touched down and rolled right at him. He realized that it was not going to stop, so he started running parallel to its approach. When the plane's wings went over his head, he started running sideways. He got as close as he could to it, but now human endurance was getting to him. He started failing, his legs suddenly wobbling.

That's when a pair of hands reached out of the open door and grabbed him around the shoulders. The next thing he knew, he hit his head hard on the cargo compartment's floor. It knocked him loopy for a moment. But then he found himself looking up at three of the AC-17's gun crew as they were looking down at him.

Still dopey, Moon somehow managed a smile.

"Dong chow!" he whispered urgently in Chinese.

Roughly translated, it meant, "Let's get out of here!"

CHAPTER 22

Over the Mediterranean

Amanda Faith had never flown so high, for so long, with so little result.

She was behind the controls of Ghost Plane 3, the aircraft carrying the two M1A1 tanks. But this flight had nothing to do with Marine Armor, at least not yet.

Right now, the most important piece of equipment aboard the airplane was duct-taped to her communications suite. It was a jimmy-rigged contraption conjured up by Lieutenant Moon in his mad scientist workshop before the three planes left Pakistan. He'd called it "HAE-1." To work, it would have to tap into the NSA's most classified eavesdropping network.

Moon had received a lot of valuable intelligence from his Syrian prisoner. One nugget was the identity of the person who'd made arrangements to buy the execution tapes from the PKD. His name was Amad Amad. He was an oil prince, an arms dealer, and the owner of Al-Zareesh TV. He'd been secretly funding the mountain terrorists, as well as the Bien Cache Guerriers, for his own financial gain.

The Syrian told Moon that Amad had just purchased a

new airliner for his own personal use. He also knew its call sign—"Allah Is Peace."

Moon had been able to use his NSA resources to determine that Amad was leaving on his private jet that morning for a trip that would take him out of the Middle East, across the Mediterranean, to Monte Carlo for a layover and eventually to the United States. Here, he was to be given an award by a congressional political action group as recognition for aiding U.S. companies to sell their wares in the Persian Gulf region.

It all sounded well and nice until one peeled back the onion layers to find that the award was actually a recognition for the many arms deals the prince had overseen—to U.S. allies, and through intermediaries to some U.S. enemies as well—that had resulted in hundreds of billions of dollars of weapons flooding into the most volatile region on Earth, at the worst possible moment in history.

When combined with his support of the terrorists and his willingness to sell the videotapes of the USAID hostages as well as the Bien Cache Guerriers' actions, Prince Amad seemed at the center of this unseemly universe.

That's why, at the very least, the 201st had to find him and keep track of him, in anticipation of stopping him, somehow, someway.

This was Amanda's mission, known as Third Base: The rigged-up HAE-1 could locate, at least in theory, the frequency used by the prince's private jet. Once the radio signal was intercepted, she would try to find and then follow the private jet, keep it in sight until it was determined if the other two C-17s had completed their missions. Then the prince could be dealt with.

To do this, Amanda's airplane was acting as a kind of AWACS plane at the moment, circling very high above the Persian Gulf, invisible to radar, using the last of the dark hours to hide herself, working the HAE-1 and trying to find the modern-day Dark Prince.

The endless circling had given her time to think, though—too much time, as it turned out, because she found herself allowing discouraging thoughts to leak in.

She'd been running purely on adrenaline since the whole overseas adventure began—but now, orbiting at 60,000 feet, looking up at the stars, she was wondering about the futility of it all.

They'd done more in the past thirty-six hours than some special ops teams did in their entire service life—yet they'd not been authorized to do any of it. They had tried their best to rescue the USAID hostages, and return Newman's daughter to him—and failed. Lieutenant Bing had left on what amounted to a sneak-attack bombing run—and attempts to contact him on the sat-phone had also failed.

Gunn had also gone on what amounted to a suicide mission—and she had not been in contact with his plane either . . .

So, was it all worth it?

What did it say about the state of affairs in the U.S.—in the world—when a virtually assured catastrophe could only be prevented by a 100 or so people flying around in unauthorized planes, doing very unauthorized things?

Where were the great armies of the American might? What ever happened to the war on terrorism? From this height, nearly directly over the center of the Persian Gulf, Amanda could see the bare outline of Iraq to the north. The lives, the money, the prestige wasted up there? Hadn't it led almost directly to the problem they now faced here? How could the power of the U.S. be made so useless by religious fanatics holed up in far-off caves?

No, her dreams had started in the stars, and now she was realizing why. Because the things going on down here were vile, frustrating, corrupt, and rife with ego.

What was the point? It was like rolling a pebble up a hill, only to have a boulder roll back down in return for your efforts.

If only . . .

Suddenly her copilot, Lieutenant Stanley, let out a yelp.

"I think we've got him!" he reported anxiously.

Amanda couldn't help herself, "You mean, you've reached Major Gunn?"

"No," came the reply. "I think we've found the prince's private plane."

* * *

NOW came the hard part.

Using the HAE-1's ability to tap in to the NSA's all-encompassing tracking system, they had indeed found Prince Amad's airplane. It had taken off from a secret base in Saudi Arabia and was heading northwest as predicted. It was currently over Syria, heading for the Med.

But even better, the second part of Moon's contraption gave them the ability to not only listen in on the chatter inside the cockpit of the prince's plane as it made its way northwest, they could also listen in on conversations taking place inside the airplane. The passenger cabin, the bathrooms, *anywhere*. This just confirmed to Amanda that the NSA was a very scary outfit.

It took only five minutes of listening in to convince them that the prince was all about chasing money, power, and ego, yes—arming all sides with the expensive weapons of war, just to add more misery to the world.

But they also heard something else—and suddenly it all seemed to make a little more sense.

Because within the conversations going on inside the prince's luxury aircraft, they heard one particularly familiar voice.

Congressman Adamis Toole . . .

Talking, laughing, drinking . . .

On board the plane.

With the Dark Prince.

AMANDA called the Marine commander, Captain Cardillo, forward and let him listen to the amazing eavesdropping device.

It took only a few minutes for them to realize they had to do more than just follow the prince's airplane. They had no idea what had happened to the other C-17s. They had to go on the assumption that Ghost Plane 3 was the only one left of the 201st. But after discovering this unholy marriage of Toole and the Dark Prince, they knew it was up to them to do something.

But what?

"Go after them!" Lieutenant Stanley said. Captain Cardillo agreed.

"Get on his tail," the Marine officer told her. "Then we'll figure out what to do next . . ."

Amanda checked their position against that of the prince's airplane and did some quick calculations. The private jet was flying at 300 knots. The C-17 could max out at 480 knots. The private jet was about an hour west of them. She could make up the time in about thirty minutes, and still stay in the nighttime.

With that, she turned the big plane west and laid on the throttles.

"Fasten your seat belts," she said over the intercom, "we're in for a bumpy ride."

THE next half hour was spent catching up to Prince Amad's airplane and listening in on what they could pick up from the NSA eavesdropping device.

It was mostly business talk mixed with crude jokes and insider gossip about Washington figures and celebrities.

But one conversation was particularly revealing. At one point, the prince explained that while he had many friends in Washington, as well as in the U.S. oil industry, he worried that "indiscretions" could waylay him someday, and he was loathe to get caught up in the U.S. judicial system.

Congressman Toole immediately put his fears to rest. He told the prince that he would not only suggest to the White House that he be given a retroactive pardon for all "indiscretions" now and in the future, but that he would personally bury a measure in the next appropriations bill that would confer onto the prince full diplomatic immunity.

Problem solved.

From that moment on, whatever Prince Amad got caught for, he would not have to fear the law.

AMANDA did some of the best flying of her career and caught up to the private jet just off the coast of Cyprus.

The more they listened in, the more they realized the prince and his cohorts were bent on sowing destruction and confusion around the world—all for monetary gain. Terrorist acts inside and outside the U.S. War between Israel and its neighbors. Even a nuclear war with Iran would profit all of them immeasurably.

It was becoming increasingly clear to Amanda that somehow the prince had to be stopped before his plane set down in Monte Carlo. At that point her aircraft would finally be out of gas and there would be no way for them to continue the pursuit.

She wished she were in her fighter plane. She would have had no problem at all shooting down the private jet—if just a fraction of what the passengers were talking about came true, the world would be reeling for years, and thousands, maybe hundreds of thousands would die. But what could she do? Ghost Plane 3 had no weapons she could use.

Or did it?

They were now about a mile behind the private jet and about a quarter mile above it, riding their wake, ever on the lookout for other planes in the area. Amanda called Cardillo to the flight deck and told him her idea to stop the prince. Cardillo was stunned. He told her it could result in the deaths of them all if it didn't work. But again, they all knew it was a sacrifice they might have to make if it meant derailing the Dark Prince. Amanda asked everyone on board to vote. Action or no action?

The vote was unanimous.

Cardillo and his men went to work. When all was in readiness, Amanda moved the big C-17 ahead and above the private jet.

Then, ever so slowly, she lowered herself in altitude until she was flying in front of the private jet.

Then she ordered the C-17's cargo ramp opened.

It was about this time that the pilots of the private jet realized the stealth plane was flying directly in front of them, not 500 feet away.

They sat frozen for a few moments, wondering how this huge plane had suddenly stolen up on them.

That hesitation cost them. Because before they could act,

they saw a tank was tied down in the back of the plane. They could also see a man in the tank's turret.

They could almost hear him yell, "Fire!"

The shell shot out of the tank's 122mm gun and impacted directly on the nose of the private jet.

The explosion was so great it disrupted the air behind the C-17, blowing it back, and nearly knocking the plane out of its flight envelope.

Amanda held on tight and rode out the wave of turbulence. Once it subsided, she looked over her shoulder and saw the remains of the private jet, on fire and falling slowly into the Mediterranean.

"Look out below," she whispered.

CHAPTER 23

Persian Gulf

Moon finally got ahold of Colonel Newman.

Ghost Plane 1 was over the Persian Gulf when it happened, having successfully escaped from Iranian airspace. They found themselves dodging U.S. aircraft all the way down the Gulf waterway, but the last bit of darkness and their stealth technology kept them hidden from any curious eyes.

Using one of the confiscated sat-phones, Moon had tracked down Newman to the base hospital at Nellis AFB, near Las Vegas. He was being held there in protective custody, this after it was discovered that three of his C-17s training inside Area 153 had disappeared.

Sleep-deprived and severely depressed, Newman—with the help of his friends in Area 153—had managed to get himself hospitalized instead of thrown into a military jail. He'd been interrogated extensively, though, but had vowed to say nothing until he heard the fate of his daughter.

Moon had finally gotten through to him by working his contacts at Nellis to get a cell phone into Newman's room. That's how he delivered the difficult news about his daughter to him. After a long silence, Newman replied, "At least they can't hurt her anymore."

The sad thing was, Newman told Moon the U.S. media was just now reporting that five USAID hostages had been taken in Pakistan and that the U.S. government was consulting with the Pakistani government about how to obtain their early release.

Then Moon got to the matter at hand. The Ghost planes were now fugitives from the U.S. military. They needed somewhere to go and they needed it quick.

But Newman was prepared for this. Ironically, he gave Moon a coordinate: 6 degrees latitude by 12 degrees longitude.

"Go there," he said. "You'll be safe until we make contact again."

Then Newman abruptly ended the conversation.

MOON gave the information to Gunn, and then went about contacting the other two Ghost planes. It took him a while to find compatible sat-phones, but finally he had conversations with Bing and Amanda. Both were over the Med, safe but desperate to find out what came next. Moon gave them Newman's coordinates and said he hoped they'd all meet again soon.

Meanwhile Gunn had punched the coordinate into their GPS system and it came back as a pinhole of a place in the African country of Cameroon called Wum Bakim.

Gunn did a quick estimate and determined that they would run out of gas about thirty minutes before getting anywhere near the place.

But then Moon said, "Not if you shut down two of the engines."

Gunn just looked at him, and for the first time actually did smile.

"When we get back, Lieutenant Moon," he said, "I'm recommending you be promoted to captain."

*   *   *

Toward Cameroon

They flew on, again racing against the sunrise.

They crossed over some notorious places like Saudi Arabia, Yemen, and the Darfur section of Sudan.

The plane had electrical problems the whole way, due in part to shutting down two of the four engines. This meant the Star Skin was not working up to capacity. But by this time, everyone aboard Ghost Plane 1 was so tired and miserable, getting shot down would have been a pleasant diversion.

Somehow, someway, they crossed over the border of Chad into Cameroon just as the sun was coming up. Very close to the tiny settlement of Wum Bakim was an air base, sitting in the middle of the jungle. They saw it only because Gunn was wearing his RIFs. Incredibly, its hangars and support buildings were hidden by the same exotic camouflage netting as had been used at the 201 base back in Area 153.

"I should have bought stock in this stuff," Gunn said, looking down at the camo covering the hidden base. "Who knew it had gone so global."

He brought the big plane down on the base's single runway. The moment the wheels touched the ground, the last of his fuel ran out. The engines stalled just as he threw them into reverse thrust. It took a while of rolling, but finally the big plane slowed down and came to a stop.

In a weirdly familiar moment, nothing happened right away. Gunn looked around and saw the other two C-17s had already arrived and were sitting in two of the hangers. This was a great relief. It meant Amanda was safe.

Finally an ancient army truck pulled out onto the runway and drove over to them.

Gunn, Moon, and the others climbed out of the plane to see Amanda and Bing getting out of the truck. And this time she did give Gunn a hug. A small one, but a hug nevertheless. He reached in his pocket and came out with the squirt gun. He handed it to her, which made her laugh.

"We'll talk about his later," she told him.

A very tall man then got out of the truck. He was close to

seven feet, coal black, and wearing an elaborate military uniform.

Amanda handled the introductions.

"Major Gunn, Lieutenant Moon, this is Colonel Mdosi . . ."

The African officer broke into a wide smile and shook hands with both of them.

"Welcome to you all," he said in perfect Queen's English.

Gunn told him, "We appreciate you taking us in like this. We hope it doesn't cause you any problems."

Colonel Mdosi just laughed. "Problems or not, you are welcome here," he said, adding, "you see, I'm a friend of Colonel Newman, too . . ."

Don't miss the page-turning suspense, intriguing characters, and unstoppable action that keep readers coming back for more from these bestselling authors...

Tom Clancy
Robin Cook
Patricia Cornwell
Clive Cussler
Dean Koontz
J.D. Robb
John Sandford

Your favorite thrillers and suspense novels come from Berkley.

penguin.com